Tara Pammi can't remember a moment when she wasn't lost in a book—especially a romance, which was much more exciting than a mathematics textbook at school. Years later, Tara's wild imagination and love for the written word revealed what she really wanted to do. Now she pairs alpha males who think they know everything with strong women who knock that theory *and* them off their feet!

Lucy Ellis creates over-the-top couples who spar and canoodle in glamorous places. If it doesn't read like a cross between a dozen old fairy tales you half-know and a 1930s romantic comedy, it's not a Lucy Ellis story. Come and read rambling exposition on her books at lucy-ellis.com and drop her a line.

Discover more at millsandboon.co.uk

BOUGHT WITH THE ITALIAN'S RING

BY
TARA PAMMI

REDEMPTION OF A RUTHLESS BILLIONAIRE

BY
LUCY ELLIS

MILLS & BOON

First Published in Great Britain 2018
by Mills & Boon, an imprint of HarperCollins*Publishers*
1 London Bridge Street, London, SE1 9GF

Bought with the Italian's Ring © 2018 by Tara Pammi

Redemption of a Ruthless Billionaire © 2018 by Lucy Ellis

ISBN: 978-0-263-93521-9

MIX
Paper from
responsible sources
FSC® C007454

This book is produced from independently certified FSC™ paper
to ensure responsible forest management.
For more information visit www.harpercollins.co.uk/green.

Printed and bound in Spain
by CPI, Barcelona

BOUGHT
WITH THE
ITALIAN'S RING

CHAPTER ONE

HER SKIN PRICKLED. Her body, even though overheated from two hours of dancing, suddenly tingled.

Pia Vito could almost pinpoint the moment the piercing awareness claimed her, the moment a sudden chill replaced the warm breeze coming in through the wide doors of the vast ballroom on her grandfather's estate.

It was the moment *he* walked in.

Raphael Mastrantino.

Her grandfather Giovanni's godson and protégé.

CEO of Vito Automobiles.

The man Milanese society seems to be in awe of.

The women around her went into a quiet frenzy, sending longing looks his way, detailing his finer points to each other.

From the moment she had discovered her long-lost grandfather Gio, and he had accepted her as his granddaughter at the beginning of the summer, all Pia had heard from him was stories about Raphael Mastrantino.

And her drama-prone grandfather hadn't exaggerated for once.

No other man could have prowled inside the ballroom with such arrogant confidence, as if he owned the estate and all the people in it.

No other man would look that striking in a plain white shirt while making the rest of the tuxedo-clad men look overdressed.

No other man could have commanded the attention of an entire ballroom by his mere presence.

Piercing eyes met hers across the ballroom, held hers, as if determined to see through to her soul.

It was as if an electric arc had built up between them—the very concept she'd been explaining to her fifth grade students back home.

No adjective she knew could describe the sheer masculinity of him. Broad shoulders tapered to a lean waist, long legs. The ruthless planes of his face, the stark angles were those one only saw in sculptures.

It took every ounce of energy she possessed to keep her smile in place.

Not even a facsimile of a greeting appeared in his hard face. With his cynical and appraising expression, even from a distance Pia felt his derision to the tips of her toes.

Any warmth she'd felt amidst the dancing crowd dissipated as realization struck.

Her grandfather's godson didn't *approve* of her? Why?

Which was why she had felt his gaze on her back like a concentrated laser beam.

Ignoring his presence—which was like the earth trying to ignore the sun—her movements awkward and stilted, she adjusted her path exiting the dance floor and kept moving, head down.

She ran straight into something so solidly male her breath jumped into her throat. Cursing herself, she looked up. And was caught in the darkest eyes she had ever seen, draped by the lushest lashes no mascara could ever reproduce.

When had he moved so close?

His fingers had landed on the patch of bare skin that her dress and gloves left on her arms. The pads of his fingers pressed into her flesh, not quite hard but not gently either. As if he knew of her intention to escape him.

The scent of him, warmed by his skin, drifted up toward her nostrils and she breathed in deeply. A furious flush began to work its way from her chest to her neck and upward at his continued scrutiny.

She had never been comfortable with men, had no idea of that subtle, sophisticated flirting language all her fellow teachers, at least the young ones, seemed to know. Even with Frank, it had taken her two months to put a sentence together.

But this felt as if she were naked, as if her worst fears—her loneliness after her grandmother's death, her overwhelming need to belong somewhere, anywhere—as if it were all on display for his eyes.

"You are not running away from me, are you, *cara mia*?" came a taunt in the deep, silky voice that let loose butterflies in her stomach.

When she'd banged into him, she had braced herself with her hands and there they rested now. On him. His abdomen, to be precise. He was a granite wall under her hands. She fluttered her fingers over him, curious to see if there would be softness, if she could find more give...

The pressure of his fingers increased over her wrists, arresting her explorations. "Do you not speak then?" This time, he sounded coldly angry. "You communicate instead by touching men?"

Pia pulled back as if burned.

This was ridiculous. She managed twenty eleven-year-olds every day in the classroom! How dare he give voice to something so embarrassing, something she'd only done as a reaction to stress?

"My head hurts," she somehow managed to say and it was partly true. "I'm not used to so much jewelry. The designer heels I'm wearing are killing my feet. Please excuse me."

"How charmingly you lie, Ms. Vito."

He delivered the insult in such a smooth voice that it took her a few seconds to realize it.

"Next, you will tell me you hate these kinds of parties and you were just putting on a good show for Gio's sake. That the jewelry and dress and shoes—the ones that incidentally proclaim you as a walking fortune—are not really *your thing*." He twisted the last two words into a mocking American twang. "That you didn't really enjoy dancing with every man who asked you with that innocent invitation in your eyes. That this whole evening is an elaborate charade you're suffering through like a good sacrificial lamb."

That was exactly what she had been doing.

The dress, the shoes, the jewelry, even the complicated updo her hair was twisted into, none of it was her. But she had kept quiet.

Because she'd wanted Giovanni to be proud of her.

Because she'd wanted to be someone else, even for one night. Sophisticated and charming and polished—not a woman who fell for lies and found herself in crushing debt.

Yet this arrogant man made it sound as if the idea of Pia not wanting the attention, not liking being on display were impossible.

"You've already drawn your conclusions, Mr. Mastrantino."

"How do you know who I am?"

"Gio told me you'd be the most handsome, the most powerful and the most arrogant man I've ever met. He was right." Heat climbed up her chest as he raised a brow.

She looked around the ballroom and every pair of eyes was trained on them. Locating her grandfather's silver hair, she sent him a *please-rescue-me* look.

As if he hadn't even seen her, Gio carried on his conversation.

A pulse of panic drummed through her. It was as if Mr.

Mastrantino, Gio and even the guests were playing a game, but no one had told Pia the rules.

"Then you have the advantage, for he told me nothing about you. Until I saw the invitation, I didn't even know you existed. A ball in honor of Pia Alessandra Vito." He was a few inches taller than even her uncommon height and for the first time in her life, Pia felt dainty, even fragile. "Giovanni's long-lost granddaughter, finally returned to the bosom of her loving family, his legacy displayed like a crowning jewel to society."

Why was he so *ticked off* with her?

But his possessive touch stilled everything within her. Her breath hitched, and her insides seemed intent upon some kind of rearrangement. Like molecules under heat.

"The Cinderella story of the year," he continued, a hardness in the curve of his sensual mouth. "I assume Gio has already also *bought* a prince for you to dance with before the stroke of midnight too, *si*?"

Bought a prince for her?

As if a man had to be paid to be with her! Pia could feel the color leaching from her face.

Raphael had no idea how deep his thoughtless comment dug into her. How much it hurt.

"Gio knows I don't want a…" The words stilled as she tallied all the men that had been hounding her tonight.

Why had Gio invited so many young, eligible men? Why had each and every one of them made a beeline for her? True, she was the guest of honor, but still. There were other women at the ball.

A shiver curled around her spine.

"Non?" Raphael inflected it enough to tell her he didn't believe her. "Why do you think all these men have been falling over themselves to dance with you? Your great beauty?" His gaze raked her, and then dismissed her. "Your charming conversation? Your magnetic presence?"

With each derogatory question out of his mouth, Pia knew he had it right. But she was damned if she would stand there another moment and let him mock her.

She turned and stumbled. A pained gasp fell from her mouth.

Strong arms wound around her waist from behind before her bottom kissed the black-and-white marble floor. His muscular forearms brushed the undersides of her breasts, pushing them up. A burst of heat filled her lower belly.

Pia clung to him, her breath in disarray. It was too much sensation, too raw.

Slowly, gently, as if she were a newborn calf, he turned her around. In a movement that was as fluid as it was economic, he knelt in front of her.

Her heart pounded.

A pin could have dropped in the ballroom and it would have been an explosion.

His trousers stretched tight over his thighs, his austere face raised to her, he cradled her foot in a tender clasp. A lock of his thick black hair fell forward on his forehead. Those dark eyes moved over her face, down her throat, where her pulse pounded violently, to the sight of the upper curves of her meager breasts plumped into fullness by the bodice.

A tightness emerged in his face.

Tilting his head down, he placed her right foot on his left thigh. The tips of her fingers rested on his shoulders and she felt the muscles there shift and clench.

With uncharacteristic malice, she hoped the pointed heel would bruise his rock-hard flesh.

His fingers unbuckled the small belt of her sandal with a nimble touch. He plucked the heel off her foot, and fingers wrapped around her bare flesh.

Pia flinched as pain and awareness mingled, spreading up from her ankle.

His nostrils flared, his mouth pinching into a stiff line. Long fingers rubbed the small ridge the strap had dug into her skin. Back and forth, softly, slowly, until a soft moan—a raw, unrestrained sound—fell from her mouth.

Holding her gaze, he touched her more boldly, more purposefully.

A strange, forbidden craving released in her lower belly, warmth pooling there. Her heart beat in rhythm to those fingers. When he moved one finger upward, almost reaching her knee, Pia jerked her foot back.

And then, because of the uneven balance, toppled onto him.

With a curse, he caught her. But he was still so tall that when she fell, his face was buried scandalously against her belly. The warmth of his breath against her soft muscles set off such a deep clench in her sex that Pia whimpered.

His hands on her waist, he gave her a gentle nudge. Her entire body was a shivering, needy pulse. Pia looked down at his hands. "Let me go."

He shrugged those broad shoulders, an innocent look in his eyes. "You will fall if I let you go."

This man was dangerous. What he so easily made her feel—this hitch of her breath, this nervous knot in her belly, the warmth unspooling in every muscle—every forbidden sensation was dangerous.

This time, instead of putting her foot on his thigh, she put her hand on his shoulder, balanced herself and shed her other sandal. Then she picked them up with her left hand, muttered a rushed *thanks* at his shoulder and straightened.

She moved no more than a couple of steps when he stood in front of her again. "It is not the stroke of midnight yet, so surely it is not time for you to disappear, is it?"

Pia faced him, still shuddering after that intimate slide against him. Hard and lean and unforgiving, his body had left an imprint on hers. "You're no prince. More like the devil."

A white smile flashed in his dark face.

Pia sighed. The man's will was unbending. Her feet hurt, her head was throbbing, she really was tired. But of course, her grandfather's godson had come to the ball with an agenda.

He turned her around with his hands on her shoulders and gently pushed her to the center of the dance floor. One arrogant nod of his head and the orchestra began playing a classical waltz.

One large hand spanned her waist while the other clasped her fingers. Her body stretched tight and stiff to resist gliding against his. For a few minutes, they moved around the floor seamlessly, yet she couldn't relax, couldn't muster a single calm breath. His scent weaved around her. He was hard and lean everywhere she touched him.

"My ego would suffer if I didn't already know that you are just as stiff and awkward with other men," he whispered against her ear while his arm rested around her waist.

Pia found herself sinking into the depths of those black eyes. She was plain and awkward, yes, but no coward. "I'm sure I could hardly dent that humongous ego."

His laughter, a deep, husky sound startled the life out of her.

Of course, graceful dancer that he was, he didn't let his own steps falter.

Long fingers fluttered near the underside of her breast making Pia aware of every inch of her skin. "Tell me about yourself." For all her supposed resistance, he had somehow pulled her closer. On a side step, her hip rubbed against his thigh. Pia shivered. "About your dreams and aspirations," he continued, as if he felt nothing of the torture he put her through. As if he felt nothing *period*. "Maybe your favorite ice cream or your favorite Italian designer. Or what you're planning to ask Gio to give you for your birthday present."

"Birthday present?"

"You know, to make up for all the years he missed. A yacht? Are you fond of sailing? A condo in Venice?"

"I've no idea—"

Another turn around the hall, but this time with the sensation of his palm covering her upper back. She couldn't take much more of this heightened awareness. "How old are you?"

"Twenty-three."

"Quite an accomplishment for one so young."

Her body was so aware of him that her mind couldn't grapple with the intent in his words. "Please, stop. Just stop. I'm not...good at this."

His thumb traced the veins over the back of her hand almost absently. "What is the *this* that you're not good at?"

"Dealing with men like you. Playing ridiculous games. I'm not like other women you probably know. I'm nothing like the women I know."

His gaze swept over the tiara in her hair, the diamonds at her throat. "I would say you're doing just fine. From everything I see, you have Giovanni wrapped around your finger."

"I don't know how to decipher your words. I don't understand why you're determined to make a spectacle of me in this crowd. I don't know why you're—"

Her attraction to Gio's godson was the last thing she needed. Especially when, clearly, he bore no goodwill toward her.

A finger under her chin, he tilted her face up to look at him. The stark beauty of him hit her hard again. "Why I'm what?"

"Why you're even touching me like this... I don't know

why I'm reacting to you like this. Why my heart is beating so hard I feel like it might rip out of my chest. Why there's this…" His eyes flared and Pia caught the words that were bent on pouring out of her mouth. "And why you're so intent on proving that you affect me like that even as your eyes are full of contempt."

His mouth lost that cynical curve; his eyes became searching, intent. It seemed she had finally shocked him.

His hold gentled and Pia slipped away. The marble floor was cold against her bare feet reminding her she had left her heels behind.

But she was no more Cinderella than Raphael Mastrantino was a prince.

Raphael ran a finger along his collar, his body humming with awareness, with unspent energy as if he were a randy youth.

His attraction to Pia—instant and all consuming—defied logic. She was not beautiful, not in the conventional sense, not sophisticated for all her dress and jewelry—and yet there was something irresistibly alluring about her.

Which woman among the society he lived in would so openly admit what she felt for him? And with that artless dismay that she was attracted to him?

No, first there were games, games that every woman played. Even his mother played them when Raphael refused to buy her the latest model of the Vito Viva. Either she cooked his favorite food every night or she shed phony tears over his father's death—an entire episode meant to guilt him and remind him that he should be a good son who granted each and every one of his expensive wishes.

Even his four sisters played games, with Raphael, and with their boyfriends who had inevitably turned into husbands.

No one admitted in that raw, unsophisticated way what

a man made her feel. No one moaned like that—as if she were sinking into a whirlpool of pleasure when a man touched her ankle. No woman that he knew stared at a man with those big, luminous eyes as if he was the answer to her every fantasy.

Coy looks, innuendoes laced with sexual tension, teases, throwing herself at other men to make him jealous—the list of things his ex-wife, Allegra, had tried on him a few years ago were innumerable.

I'm not good at playing games.

There had been a genuine quality to her distress, to her confusion. As if her body was betraying her and she didn't know what to do.

Either she was truly naive—an anachronism with her faint blushes and her trembling mouth—or she knew just how to appeal to a man as jaded and cynical as he was. Perhaps she had decided that the right way to court his attention would be to cater to that traditional man in him, the Neanderthal that Allegra had called him so many times.

Was that it? Had she thought to counter his distrust by catering precisely to his tastes?

A chill ran down the length of his spine as he made his usual rounds through the mansion as he usually did when visiting.

He had no doubt about how much Gio would have talked about him over the last month. As his godson and his protégé, he was Giovanni's pride and joy. Raphael had turned the small spare automobile parts company that Gio had handed him into Vito Automobiles, a leading manufacturing company.

Giovanni had been his lifeline when he'd been sinking as a seventeen-year-old. He'd been a light in a long, dark tunnel that Raphael's weak father had plunged them all into.

Not that it stopped Giovanni from also being manipulative as hell. Throughout the evening, he had stood on the periphery of the crowd, watching, with a satisfied smile on his face. Like a puppeteer intensely delighted with the results of his string pulling.

Whatever the old man was up to, it would eventually fall to Raphael to clean it up. Just as he kept Giovanni's hounding relatives at bay. Just as he ensured that the leftovers from Gio's time on the board—men who would stab Raphael in the back before he could blink—didn't leach away the gains he had made.

Just as he took care of the various and sundry branches of Mastrantino families without any expectations in return.

And yet, as he questioned one of the staff members about Pia, Raphael was suddenly aware that this was unlike any other responsibility he shouldered.

For no bickering ex-wife of Gio's or grasping cousin of his mother had ever caused his blood to pound like this.

No woman had ever called to his baser instincts like this supposedly innocent granddaughter of his godfather.

CHAPTER TWO

COOL WATER SLUICED off her back and limbs as Pia swam lap after lap in the indoor pool on Gio's estate as if the very devil were after her.

Raphael Mastrantino was very much the devil.

The man's arrogance!

She worked off her fury in the water.

Of all the men to be attracted to.

She groaned and dunked her head in the water. He'd been so warm and solid around her. She could still feel the languorous weight of his hands on her waist. The length of his hard thigh rubbing against hers...

The only satisfaction left to her was that she'd surprised him even as he had mocked and taunted her.

She and Raphael Mastrantino lived in different orbits of life. He wouldn't have even looked at her, much less danced with her, if she hadn't been dressed up to the nines *and* if she wasn't Gio's granddaughter. What she didn't understand though was why. Why had he pounced on her like that?

Her arms lagged on her strokes as her thoughts whirled. Just as she decided to get out of the pool, she saw Raphael standing at the edge.

The floodlights cast an outline along his broad frame.

His white shirt was unbuttoned to the middle of his chest giving a glimpse of ridges of tight muscle with sparse black hair. Her belly swooped. The raven's wing of his hair had a distinctly rumpled look.

What would it take to shatter that arrogant cynicism, to bring a man like Raphael to his knees?

She shivered at the direction of her thoughts.

A bottle of Pinot Grigio and two wine flutes hung from his fingers. "I had to bribe one of the staff members for your location."

"I don't like you, Mr. Mastrantino."

"I think you like me a little too much. Which is why you're hiding."

The gall of the man! Pia had never met a more annoying man in her life. "Just because my body thinks you're a prime male specimen and is attracted to you—which, by the way, is based on millions of years of evolution and a chemical reaction that drives a woman to choose the strongest man as her mate—it doesn't mean my mind agrees."

His black eyes gleamed. The thin line of his lower lip curved with mocking amusement. "So you've dropped the act of trembling mouth and soft gasps then?"

He almost sounded disappointed. Pia sighed. "Distance helped me remember the hormones part of it. It's when you're close that I…" She shrugged, trying to go for casual, which her stutter totally ruined. "That I'm unable to handle my reaction."

Just looking at the darkly sensual face stretched her skin tight over her body. And other parts. Parts that had never clenched and tightened with such wanton awareness.

"You should call me Raphael."

"Not necessary."

He placed the bottle and glasses on a table then settled on a lounger, propped his elbows on his knees and returned to his intense scrutiny of her. "Because you'll run away every time I'm around?"

"I've been suitably and repeatedly impressed with what an important, powerful and wealthy man you are. You run a multinational automobile company in the city, apparently control and manage not only Gio's finances but your mother's family' finances and your father's and all the numerous cousins thereof.

I, on the other hand, mean to spend the summer getting to know Gio. I let him railroad me into this ball because it meant a lot to him. So the chance of you and me spending time in each other's company is pretty low."

"When the summer is over?" he shot back instantly, picking the one thing Pia didn't want to discuss.

"This summer is just holiday. I wasn't even sure if Gio would believe me. But I do have a life elsewhere." A life without her grandmother, a life without any close friends. A life where no one really cared about her.

Which was why she'd been such an easy mark for Frank.

"Is Gio aware of your supposed intentions?"

"No, and they're not supposed," she said, losing her temper. Would nothing please the man?

The water lapped around her silently. "You're staring," she said softly.

"You look like a different woman."

"I was terrified all evening that I'd spill something on that gorgeous, expensive gown. I have a habit of getting into worse messes than my students. I'm not used to wearing contacts. Now there is no war paint on my face. And my hair is back in its natural, uncontrollable state." She pulled a coiled curl that was already dry.

He followed the action as if he was transfixed. "Your students?"

"I teach Science to fifth graders."

Surprise dawned in his gaze. It tracked her wet face, lingering far too long than was proper over her mouth, and then the slope of her shoulders, visible over the water's surface. A shiver snaked down her spine.

"An elementary teacher? I find I'm overwhelmed by curiosity about you. A rare occurrence."

Pia stared, wishing she'd misheard him. But the world was quiet around them. Only a slight breeze and the whispers of the trees all around the pool. It wasn't just curiosity that made his voice deepen, that made his mouth tighten.

"What do you have against me?"

Moonlight caressed the dark column of his throat, the smooth velvety skin pulled taut over a lean chest. He tilted his head down, a devilish twist to his mouth. "Other than the fact that you're manipulating an old man's misguided affection for you?"

His words shocked Pia so much that she dropped her hold on the tiles, sank in, and then came up sputtering water out of her nose and mouth.

He thought she was after Gio's fortune?

He frowned at her chattering teeth. "Get out of there before you freeze."

"No," Pia said stubbornly, a rush of anger heating up her still muscles. "*You* leave."

His hands went to the buttons on his shirt. Taut skin stretched over lean muscles appeared as he unbuttoned. "Either you come out or..."

Glaring at him, Pia walked up the steps.

The moment she was out, he wrapped the huge towel around her. Heart thundering in her chest, Pia pushed her wet hair off her face with trembling hands.

As if she were a child, he gave her a brisk rubdown, up and down her arms. Throat dry, Pia stared at his chest. Her cheeks burned when he repeated the movements over her chest, hips and back. Those large hands didn't linger anywhere and yet warmth began to pool in her belly.

"You stayed too long in there." His voice had gone husky, deep.

She shivered again.

"Sit," he commanded, and Pia obediently sat on the lounger. He handed her a glass of wine and it was exactly what she wanted.

Silently, she took a sip.

For a few minutes, they sat like that, side by side on loungers, not talking. Not even looking at each other. But that awareness that had consumed her in the ballroom thickened the air around them. His touch, impersonal, still lingered.

Her attraction to him was natural.

He *was* the most strikingly handsome man she'd ever met.

She refused to be ashamed by it. But neither did she want to keep confronting it, to keep thinking that she was somehow less than him because she wasn't sophisticated or beautiful or polished enough. She'd had enough of Frank manipulating her insecurities. "All I want is to spend the summer with my grandfather. I really don't see why that should be any of your business," she said softly.

"I am Giovanni's friend. I am more friend than all of his useless, bickering, social climbing family put together. I would do anything to protect Giovanni and his interests. It is my business if you put one step wrong with him."

"What have I done that offends you so much?"

"You seem to have no scruples about cheating an old man who has done nothing but welcome you into his life with open arms without even checking if you truly are who you claim to be."

"So now I'm not only a gold digger of the worst kind but also an impostor?"

"All evidence points to it, *si*."

Pia fisted her hands, the urge to strike that smug condescension from his face burning through her. "Gio's lover, Lucia, was my *nonna*. She left him after they had a huge row and settled in the States. My parents died when I was three and she raised me." She stood up, her pulse skittering all over. "I found Lucia's letters to him after she died and called him. That's the truth."

"It's also true that he's given you thousands of dollars in the one month you've been here."

If only the ground could open up and swallow her whole! Mortification filled her cheeks.

She couldn't even be mad at Raphael, because from his point of view it looked like she was a grasping, greedy woman. But to be so cynical as to question her whole motive for visiting Italy...? "Gio wouldn't have told you," she mumbled half to herself.

"I keep an eye over Gio's finances. His three ex-wives learned it was better to live with what he provides them than to take me on."

She forced herself to meet his eyes. "You're making assumptions based on one transaction and out of context."

"I assume based on facts and not feelings. I learned to do so a long time ago."

The towel slipped from her shoulders so her hair was dripping onto her back. And the one-piece she wore was not the most convenient costume when wet. But Pia was determined to make him see. Even if it meant admitting the most humiliatingly painful episode of her life. Even if it meant giving voice to her foolishness. "Giovanni gave me that money to pay off...credit card debt."

"So you did your research before you contacted him," he said in a silky, almost bored voice.

Her grip far too tight on the stem of the wineglass Pia stared at him. "This is pointless if you won't even give me a chance.

"You have to protect Giovanni, true, but one would think you'd at least give me a chance when his happiness is involved." She wouldn't beg him to believe her. Shaking with hurt and humiliation, she stood up.

He reached out and caught her wrist. A jolt of fiery sensation raced from her wrist to her breasts, to the spot between her thighs. Pia jerked her hand away, breath coming in hard and fast.

"Stay." Tension radiated from him, confusing her. "I will listen, *si*? Whether I will believe…"

She sat down and looked at her hands. Words came and fell away again. Taking a deep breath, she blurted it out. "I racked up that debt because I was foolish enough to fall for a con man."

His expression instantly turned thunderous. "Fall for a con man? What do you mean?"

"I believed a colleague when he said he loved me. I went back to work after nursing Nonni for two years and he was the new gym teacher at the school where I worked. He… cultivated a friendship with me for weeks, then asked me out. After a few months, he…told me he'd fallen in love with me.

'I trusted him and loaned him money when he said he was in trouble. Again and again. I gave him the little Nonni had left me, and then when that was done, I…" The words stuck like glass in her throat. "I emptied my savings, and took a loan on my card when he said he desperately needed money to avoid a loan shark."

His expletive punctured the silence around them. Did that mean he believed her? Pia found she didn't give a damn. Frank had deceived her in the worst possible way. Nothing Raphael said or believed could be any worse.

There was a strange strength in the fact that she'd already been through the worst.

"So you're as naive and meek as you look? How could you trust any man so much that you risk everything you have?"

She flinched as if he'd slapped her. Tight lines emerged around her mouth and she blinked rapidly. Moonlight flickered on her delicate jawline that was clenched taut.

Raphael killed the thread of regret that hit him. He wasn't going to coddle her.

She looked down at her hands and then around her. When she spoke, her voice had lost that husky timbre. It was as if she was forcing herself to say the words. Just for his benefit.

"I was lost, lonely after Nonni passed away. I hardly had any friends after being her full-time caregiver for two years. He was charming, attractive. He singled me out almost immediately after I went back to work. He even did me the favor of explaining to me that he had done his research and picked me as the prime target. The other teachers had unwittingly given him enough ammunition."

Even as he'd cruelly called her weak, she was anything but in that moment. He knew that it took guts to pull yourself up when everything was lost. And yet, she'd not only done it, but she was facing him down too. "How?"

"They told him that I was…shy, and inexperienced. That they thought I needed to start living now that Nonni had passed away. They told him I'd never had a boyfriend and would probably be grateful for his attention." When he growled, she hurried on. "I think they meant well. They couldn't have known he would prey on all my insecurities."

"This man? Is he following you here?"

"No." Conviction resonated in her tone. "When he realized I didn't have any more money, he couldn't dump me fast enough. Making it very clear that the only reason he'd been with me was because I was such a pushover."

"So you didn't tell him about how your new grandfather was wealthy beyond imagination? No surprise visit from this lover of yours to play upon Gio's heartstrings a little more? Have you already figured out that Gio's an old fool who would love to see a little romance?"

"Stop, please. He's not coming here. Frank's out of my life," Pia replied, a sick feeling in her stomach. She could see what Raphael was getting at. And that his suspicions had basis only increased her shame. "For one thing, I didn't know until I got here that Gio was wealthy. I don't care whether you believe that or not," she pushed on, when she sensed he would interrupt again. *Blasted man!* "I was just happy to know that I had family. That I wasn't alone…"

How could she make him understand how lonely she had been after Nonni's death? How much Frank had played on that loneliness?

Or what Gio's affection, his kindness meant to her. "And, yes, I'll even admit that if Frank had learned that Giovanni Vito *is* Vito Automobiles, he probably would've—" she forced herself to say the horrible words "—married me and sealed off the deal so that he could suck the blood and marrow out of Gio."

She shivered violently. Raphael silently draped another plush towel around her shoulders.

Pia thanked him, the words tasting like ash in her mouth. She didn't want his kindness. She didn't want anything from this man.

"I need details about this Frank person."

She nodded. "Will you leave me alone then?"

"What Giovanni did—"

"The money he gave me, it's a loan. I didn't take a dollar more than the debt. And I intend to pay off every single cent." She pulled her towel snug around her chest. "Your relationship with Gio, his affection for you, that's the only reason I told you. You and I have nothing to do with each other, Mr. Mastrantino."

* * *

She was wrong.

Whether she was Gio's granddaughter or not, whether she was disconcertingly naive or a cunning con woman, Pia was going to be his problem.

Lashes spiked with small water drops, her damp hair curling wispily against her face, she looked incredibly young. And even with her declaration that she'd learned her lesson, there was still something very naive about her.

It was disconcerting how much he wanted to believe her.

There was grief in those big luminous eyes of hers, an earnestness that beguiled him.

But more than that, he wanted to taste that trembling mouth. He wanted to wrap her tiny waist with his hands and bring her closer until he was wet along with her; until her soft curves brushed up against him.

Until he could kiss away the trouble caused by another man.

He wanted to wrap her in some sort of protective co-coon so that nothing deceitful could touch her.

Dio mio, he had met her five hours ago and even he was already lured in by that innocence. Giovanni would do anything for this creature.

But the fact that she could be telling the truth only made the problem worse.

Not only had Gio had her decked up in diamonds and couture, he had released her into a hungry horde of Milanese social climbers.

At least if she'd been a con woman, she would have been able to handle herself.

He reached for her when she walked by him to leave. Feeling the calluses in her palm, he pulled up her hand.

Her fingers were long and bare, with calluses at the tips of most. He had a sudden flash of Allegra's perfectly manicured nails with baby-soft skin.

"Why do you have calluses?" All this was just to know her, he reminded himself. To create a picture of her life for himself. To see if there were any holes in it. To see if a lie would crack through her elaborate pretense.

Or it's because, for the first time in years, you can't stop yourself from touching a woman. Because the need to touch her, to taste her, is pounding in your blood.

Fingers tracing his palm, sending pulses of heat through him, she frowned. He felt as if he had been earthed. "I could ask you the same. I thought CEOs had pampered, manicured hands and wore tacky, gold bracelets."

A strange, masculine satisfaction whirled through him.

"I'm an automobile engineer first, a CEO second. I restore vintage cars when I find time." He was already stretched superthin as it is and now this—*her.* "Which is very little. Now tell me, why do *you* have calluses?"

"I carve wooden toys in my free time. A hobby really. Frank—" a stiffness thinned her mouth "—set up an on-line shop for me. The cash always came in handy and my students' parents provided good word of mouth."

The man's name on her lips pulled Raphael back to the matter.

She blinked owlishly, as if trying to keep him in focus. He clenched his jaw tight. More pieces were falling into place.

If she was conning all of them, he would see her in jail. But Raphael was forced to rethink his misgivings, to consider Gio's trust might not be misplaced. She knew things about Lucia and Gio that no one did, at least, that was what Gio had told him.

Also, he was a good judge of character.

He'd been forced to be after his father's suicide. He'd had to learn on his feet which creditor could be counted on to wait, which creditor was loyal to his father's tarnished memory and which one would revel in humiliating his mother and sisters if Raphael came up short.

If she was innocent… He could hardly bear thinking about the hordes of hungry, young, single Milanese men that would descend on her… Just tonight, it had taken every ounce of the force of his ruthless reputation to beat off the men who had wanted to follow her.

Men who'd have stood in his place right now and watched moonlight sparkle in her eyes, seen the wet swimsuit cling to her toned, lithe body, seen the artless display of grief and joy that came into her eyes when she spoke of Lucia and Giovanni.

"If I have to carve a million toys to pay Giovanni back, I will," she said with a fierce pride shining in her eyes.

He hardened his tone. "Even if you're telling the truth, I can't just let you walk away without making sure that you've not crushed his heart," he added for good measure.

Her soft sigh pinged over his nerves. Did she know how arousing that was? Did she even realize that the sight of her big, searching gaze, the way she stared at a man as if she meant to see through to his soul, could do things to a man she might not want?

"Why do you think I agreed to that—" she pointed to the house now cloaked in dark shadows "—ridiculous show? Telling Gio about Frank probably wasn't a good idea. All those men he invited, the way they were crowding around me… I didn't realize his intentions until you pointed out how much attention I was getting. Clearly, he thinks I can't take care of myself."

He'd been cruel to taunt her like that. Not that he was off the mark. But there was also an attraction to her that was rare. It was disturbing to think of her coming up against the men who only saw her as a ticket to their life's fortune. "Can you?"

"Even if I can't, the last thing I want is help from a man like you," she bit out, stepping back from him.

He raised a brow. *"A man like me?"*

"My experience with Frank taught me a valuable lesson. My so-called boyfriend that couldn't dump me fast enough when the money dried up. You're just like him—gorgeous, confident, arrogant—except a million times more. The women—they couldn't get enough of you even when you barely glanced in their direction. And the men were so eager to please you, wanting to be like you.

"You...exert your power or charm, or whatever the hell it is, over everyone you meet. You wield it to bend people to your will. Someone like me, you'll use my attraction to you to put me in my place, to prove that you're right no matter what the truth is. To prove that I'm somehow less because I'm not everything you are. Accusations that have no basis in truth, I can handle. But you mock who I am and that I won't forgive."

He felt as if she'd punched him, because it was exactly what he had thought of her. *"Someone like you?"* He repeated her words to hide his reaction.

Pain streaked through her eyes. The depth of her emotions, the sheer transparency of them was like nothing he'd ever seen before.

"A shy, plain, boring elementary teacher who knows nothing about men." She repeated the words as if by rote, and suddenly he knew in his bones who had said them to her. "First you'll use it to dig into me to figure out if I'm telling the truth.

"Then you'll use my lack of sophistication to persuade Gio that he's right and that I need to be wrapped up in bubble wrap because I'm too naive, too foolish. That I'll somehow bring someone like Frank into this...kingdom of yours.

"I don't care whether you believe me or not. Just stay

away from me. We don't have to see each other for you to make sure that I'm not fleecing Gio, do we?"

Her slender shoulders straight, the line of her spine a graceful curve, she looked like a water nymph. Leaving Raphael spellbound in more than one way.

If she was a con woman, he'd see her in jail. But if she was indeed Gio's granddaughter, she was absolutely forbidden to him.

Even if it was the most real conversation he'd had with a woman. Ever.

CHAPTER THREE

STAY AWAY FROM ME.

Pia's words followed him as Raphael walked around the estate and made sure the staff put every last inebriated or otherwise high-flying guest into their vehicles. He bid the tired staff to their beds after they put the ballroom to rights.

He didn't know if Gio thought the ball successful but Raphael thought it had been sensational.

Whoever Pia was, she'd meant those words. His accusations had hurt her, but it was the other thing she'd said that pricked him even now.

You mock who I am.

Had he mocked her because with her naive views and long sighs she'd seemed like an impossibility? Or had he mocked her because he resented that innocence, those stars in her eyes?

Because he'd never had a chance to be like that.

He was about to call it a night and settle into one of the spare bedrooms, as he sometimes did, when he spied the master of puppets.

Scowling, he followed Giovanni into his study and closed the door behind him with a loud thud.

Giovanni handed Raphael a glass of red. As if he'd known that his godson wouldn't leave without this talk.

"Shouldn't you be in bed?" Raphael said as Giovanni plopped down onto the sofa with a long sigh. Because of his agile mind and his penchant for playing games, Raphael sometimes forgot that Gio was old. His wrinkled hands shook as he lifted the glass to his mouth.

"You're far too excited, Giovanni. This is not good—"

"What do you think of my new granddaughter?"

Knowing that he wouldn't get a word in until they talked about Pia, Raphael shrugged. "I wouldn't be surprised if you'd custom ordered her at a store."

The old man frowned. "What? Why?"

Raphael stared into his drink. But it was the long fluid line of Pia's back, the drop of water that had run down her damp skin that he saw. The outrage in her eyes when he'd accused her. The hurt when he'd called her naive and meek.

"Raphael?" Gio prodded.

"She fits your requirements for a granddaughter a little too perfectly, don't you think?"

A sneaky smile twitched around Gio's lips. "So you admit that she is perfect."

Raphael raked his fingers through his hair, frustration and something else—no, not something else. It was lust pounding at him. Lust that had never seemed so complicated or so fierce before. And the last thing he needed was for Gio to scent how attracted he was to Pia.

"I don't mean it that way. An innocent, shy, clearly out of her depth orphan who travels across the world searching for her legacy, searching for her grandmother's lover… Damn it, Gio, you've always been desperate for a child, for someone to love. She's the perfect lure to tug at your heartstrings."

"She's nothing like my fiery Lucia—"

"Or her manipulative grandfather, if you're truly that," he added.

"*Si.* She's young and sweet. I feel as if the burden of looking after Lucia was too much for her. No wonder that man preyed on her."

Raphael scowled. "Did you even check the legitimacy of her claim before you advertised her to all of Milan with her inheritance hung around her neck like a sign?"

Gio frowned as the meaning sank in. "I have no doubt that she's Lucia's and my granddaughter."

"Excuse me if I save my teary-eyed approval for later."

"You have become a hardened ass, Raphael. Mistrustful of your own shadow."

"I'm realistic. After three marriages, one would think you would be too. One would think you'd see beneath the wide-eyed innocence and the fragile naïveté."

Silence met Raphael's outburst. A pounding was beginning behind his eyes. Something was very wrong with this talk and yet he couldn't place it.

Giovanni studied him over the rim of his wineglass. "I watched you watch her tonight. I heard some of the things you said to her. You were exceptionally cruel."

Raphael blanched at the matter-of-fact words. He had been, and that was not counting the stuff he'd said later, at the pool. He didn't like losing control of situations around him. He loathed losing control of himself. Thanks to her, both had happened tonight. And it had erased the little charm he usually had.

He'd aimed where it would hurt most and shot. He prided himself on his reputation for ruthlessness, and yet tonight it sat like acid in his mouth.

"And you didn't come to her rescue, knowing what I would do. What the hell are you playing at, Gio?"

"I knew you would grill her, that you would try to poke holes in her story. I didn't know you would dance with her, or hound her until she ran away from you. I didn't know you would lose your legendary control." He said it as if he was calculating a complex puzzle. "What did she say when you cornered her by the pool?"

A chill climbed up Raphael's spine. He'd been so close

to kissing her. If Gio had heard of it… "*Christo*, did you have the staff spying on us?"

Suddenly, the frown cleared. His eyes twinkled, in that satisfactory way that raised every hackle Raphael had. "You were more ruthless than usual. You are attracted to her…" His gruff voice deepened. "You want her." Raucous laughter burst out of him, and he slapped his thigh hard.

Raphael scowled. He had a feeling this was what Giovanni had waited and watched for. "I'd like to remind you that the woman you're talking about is your grand-daughter."

"She got behind your…defenses, isn't that what they say? And you don't like it. Tell me, Raphael, are you interested in Pia?"

Raphael sat back, something about that question sending a chill wave through him. "You talk as if she were cattle you're trying to sell," he evaded.

All he wanted to do was walk away. From this discussion and from that woman.

Of all the people in his life, Giovanni was the one person who could see through his ruthlessness, who'd known Raphael before he'd become hard and cynical. Who knew that Raphael didn't like even a bit of weakness, any trace of vulnerability. And being attracted to a woman in a way he didn't understand was a weakness.

But he couldn't leave. Not until he knew what Giovanni was up to.

"Answer the question."

"I'm rarely interested in any woman for more than one night." He made his voice harsh. "And definitely not in a woman who flees if I so much as touch her hand."

Finally, he saw a flash of his godfather's infamous temper in his eyes. His mouth lost that arrogant twist that always meant Gio was up to no good. Since he usually reserved that for his parasitic relatives or money-hungry exes, Raphael didn't much care.

"Do not cheapen her."

"I'm the one cheapening her?" He took a deep breath, modulated his tone. "Tell me, Giovanni. What does it mean if she's your granddaughter?"

"It means she already owns a piece of my heart and I will do everything in my power to do right by her. It means she inherits everything I own. Including my stock in VA."

Dio, he was going to give her the stock in VA?

The stock that Raphael wanted. He could have bought Gio out ten times over in the last few years. Could have established his exclusive ownership of the company.

For reasons he refused to share, Gio had always denied Raphael's request. Even though Raphael was the only one with executive and operational powers at Vito Automobiles, Gio refused to leave the board. In short, the old man had always loved playing games.

"So now all that stock will rest in the hands of a woman who, by her own admission, was so desperate to be loved, to be wanted, that she fell for the sweet words of a lowlife? Who not only signed away the little money she had but actually racked up a credit card debt because she couldn't bear to lose him?

"That is the woman who'll inherit your wealth? Do you know what the jackals will do to her?"

"Which is why I want to ensure her well-being. If I died tomorrow, Pia would be all alone in the world."

"And so you have advertised her to all of Milan with the size of her inheritance hanging around her neck like a bloody flashing neon sign.

By tomorrow morning, the vultures will be circling, determined to get their hands on Pia."

"I didn't advertise her, Raphael." A shadow of pain crossed Gio's usually animated features. "I celebrated her presence in my life. After years of wondering about Lucia, I finally have someone to call my own. I want to give her everything she could ever want. I want to cherish her, pamper her, protect her.

"That child is… Her innocence, there's something so fragile about her.

"Would you deny me the chance to right my wrongs? Would you deny me the pleasure of showing off my grand-daughter to the world? The chance to find a man worthy of her among the vultures?"

By sheer dint of his will, Raphael kept his shock to himself. He'd been right. Giovanni intended to buy a prince for Pia. And hand her over lock, stock and barrel. Along with his shares.

He couldn't care. He didn't.

"That's up to you. Just…don't give her any more money. Not until I confirm her claim."

"You do what you have to do, Raphael. Who knows, maybe she'll take my seat on the board?"

He wouldn't, however, watch years of his hard work being thrown away. "She's an elementary school science teacher and you want to throw her into the shark-infested pool that is the VA board? They'll pick the meat off her bones."

"She will have you to advise her and guide her."

He stood up, and put away his wineglass. "I have neither the time nor the patience to teach that woman anything. I have enough on my plate with Alyssa, with the company, and now I find out that—" he bit off the last part. Giovanni had always had a soft spot for his stepdaughter, who happened to be Raphael's ex-wife and Alyssa's mother. He didn't want Gio sticking his head in Raphael's business just as he wanted nothing to do with Pia.

"As long as you keep her away from VA, I don't care if you sign away your entire fortune to her."

Giovanni watched as his godson walked out. His breath left on a sigh of satisfaction.

By the time he was through, neither Raphael nor Pia would like him very much. But he didn't care. There was only one man to whom he would trust his granddaughter's well-being. Just as he had trusted only one man with his precious company.

CHAPTER FOUR

PIA STOOD OUTSIDE Raphael's imposing set of offices on the tenth floor of Vito Automobiles in front of his assistants' desks—apparently Raphael required two assistants—and fought the urge to turn tail and run.

She would have to run a long way though, for the stretch between the bank of elevators to the wide swath of those desks was an ocean of gleaming marble.

Stay away from me.

She cringed at the words she'd thrown at him a mere ten days ago. If only she could somehow manage a semblance of sophistication in his presence. If only her insides didn't turn to jelly the moment he was near.

But she'd never experienced anything like her attraction to him, and she didn't know how to control it.

She was still debating whether she should just cut her losses when the door to his office opened and he stepped out.

His suit jacket was gone, and he seemed to have carelessly pushed the sleeves of his white dress shirt back, revealing hair-roughened forearms and a gleaming Rolex. His hair needed a trim, and there were dark shadows under his eyes.

He was so painfully gorgeous that he took her breath away.

"Pia? How long have you been waiting?"

His frown cut through the light-headedness.

The two assistants' gazes swung to her. They shot to their feet, a torrent of Italian volleying out of their mouths.

Pia forced herself to move toward him. "I just arrived and I... I hadn't even had the chance to inquire if you were around."

He scrutinized her, from her wild hair to her summery blouse and her denim shorts—which suddenly seemed far too short—even down to her wedges, cataloging, it seemed to her, every detail before returning to meet her eyes.

There was that intensity again, that displeasure—as if there was something about her he didn't like. "Come in."

She clutched the strap of her purse tight. "It's nothing... important. Relevant even." Her idea was ridiculous. Outrageous. "I'll talk to you when you see Gio...whenever."

She hardly turned on her heel before he was there, next to her. The warm, male scent of him buckling her knees. His fingers wrapped around her bare arm sending a shocking pulse of awareness through her.

He didn't really pull her, yet Pia found herself drifting alongside him. "No interruptions," he warned the gaping assistants before closing the door.

Pia looked around his huge office, more to avoid looking at him than with real interest. A dark mahogany desk took center stage with a sitting area to one side, and a walk-through to a bedroom and walk-in shower.

She retreated to the other side of the desk while he leaned against the closed door, all casual elegance. "You should not roam by yourself in a strange country."

Some heretofore-unknown imp goaded her. "Worried about my safety?"

He rolled his eyes, which in turn made her smile. "Giovanni Vito's American granddaughter is quite the sensation right now." His gaze skimmed her face for an infinitesimally breathtaking moment. "You're a shiny target for any number of men."

He called her the vilest of things, took offense to her presence in Gio's life and yet, something in his expression made her wonder if he actually *was* worried about her.

Or maybe she was beginning to delude herself.

She sighed, helpless against the longing that, for one moment, he would see *her*. Pia. Not Giovanni's scheming granddaughter. But then, if she weren't, he'd probably not even look at her at all.

"I begged Emilio to give me a ride since he was coming into the city anyway. Gio is visiting his sister."

His gaze lingered on her mouth. Just for a fraction of a second, but there. Luckily, the desk hid her trembling legs. "Which one?"

"That mean old dragon Maria."

One brow shot up.

She colored. "She's the one who created the rift between my grandmother and Giovanni. Filled both their heads with lies. Turned their young love bitter."

He scoffed. "Don't you think *their love* should have stood against Maria's meddling? It shouldn't have sent Lucia running across the ocean and Gio to marry three different women just to mend his broken heart."

"I know what my Nonni felt each and every day of her life. And I'll… I'll thump you before I let you poison the memory of their love."

He pushed off from the door with a feline grace that sent her pulse speeding. "And Giovanni keeps assuring me that you are a sweet, too-good-to-be-true young woman who likes everyone in the world." He spoke as if her very existence was an impossibility.

Tracing the edge of the desk with her fingertip, she walked around it before he could reach her. "I usually don't hold grudges."

"Is that a warning, Pia?" he said softly behind her. She hadn't realized how close he was. "You will only let me accuse you of so many things before I become unforgivable?"

She shrugged. "My *nonna* meant everything to me. I can't forgive someone who caused her considerable harm. Which is why, while I resent your accusations, I try my best to understand your reasons for behaving as you do." She looked up and met his gaze. "You care about Gio."

Shadows filled his eyes before he nodded. "He means everything to me," he said, using her own words. "He's the one person who always believed in me. Who never asked anything of me."

The stark emotion in his voice, the honesty in his eyes—Pia shivered. This was the true Raphael. A man whom no one saw. A man, she was becoming sure, who didn't appear much. A man she respected and even liked. She cleared her throat, wishing she could shrug off the increasing connection she felt with him. "Now that we've established a common goal—"

His arm shot out to capture hers when she would have sidled away again. "If you don't stop being so nervous around me, I'll give you a real reason."

"Like what?" she goaded, pushed by his nearness.

"Are you sure you want to know?"

No, she didn't. This was dangerous. She had no business playing games with Raphael. So she sat down.

To her immense relief, he took the opposite seat. His long legs folded along the length of her own without touching. "You've been avoiding me."

"I've been avoiding the entire male population of Milan. Unsuccessfully."

His frown deepened, while his long fingers played with a paperweight. "So Gio is still determined to find a prince for his perfect princess. Tell me, is it because you've been thwarted in love that you've decided to let Gio buy you a nice, convenient husband instead?"

She stood up so fast her head whirled. "If all you're going to do is mock me, I've—"

His arm shot out and caught hers, stalling her. *"Mi dispiace, si?"*

"You can't say things with every intention of cutting me, and then expect to be let off by saying sorry. The last thing I want is to involve you. I came because I've no choice. And because, believe it or not, I trust you."

His gaze flared, caught hers, compelling and dominant. But it was she who held it, letting him know she might quiver at his touch but it didn't make her weak.

A muscle flicking under his jaw, he looked away first.

Pia felt as if she had won a minor battle. She took a drink of water and watched him over the rim of her glass.

Whatever had passed between them, it was gone. Smoothed away beneath his perfect featured mask. "Tell me why you're here."

"You were right. Giovanni hosted that ball with the intention of introducing me to eligible men. *Introducing* being a euphemism.

"I haven't had a day to myself since that blasted night. He's dragging me to party after party, brunch after brunch as if I were…a mule he's determined to be rid of." Raphael's mouth—that sensuous mouth, twitched, and Pia glared at him. "It's not funny.

"I can't turn around before there's a grandson or a son or a twice removed cousin of one of Gio's friends visiting. There's so many of them I can't even keep their names straight. If I refuse to go on an outing, Gio encourages my *escort* to walk around the estate with me. If I refuse to accompany one of them to a party, Gio takes me there anyway and then abandons me with them.

"I know and you know and the whole damned world knows that it's not my infinite charms or my breathtaking personality that brings them to me in droves. But Gio refuses to acknowledge it. Pretends as if he can't hear me when I say half of them are just plain…"

"Idiots?" Raphael offered unhelpfully.

"I've had enough of the false attention, the warm looks, the overdone praise of my nonexistent beauty. I've taken to packing a picnic lunch first thing in the morning, and escaping to remote corners of the estate to avoid them."

"No one can stop Gio when he gets an idea into his head. Why do you think he's estranged from not only three ex-wives but also his brothers and sisters?"

"He'll listen to you. He thinks you walk on water."

Raphael shook his head. "I already warned him this would happen. But he's determined to find you a…" He raised his hands palms up. The defeated gesture didn't suit him at all. "Don't shoot the messenger.

Why don't you tell him to back off?"

"Every time I bring it up, he gets all teary and sentimental, starts rambling about the mistakes he made with Nonni and about leaving me to face men like Frank alone. He works himself into quite a temper.

"He raves about going to his grave knowing that you and I are all alone in the world. He feels responsible for you too, you know."

Raphael snorted. "You do realize that your grandfather is a manipulative bastard, *si*?"

"That's a horrible thing to say."

"Doesn't make it any less true. Giovanni will manipulate you until you agree the sun revolves around the earth."

She rubbed her forehead, something clicking. "Wait… so you don't think I'm an impostor anymore?"

"My PI informed me that you're indeed Lucia's granddaughter. And Giovanni's."

Which was why Raphael hadn't visited Gio. But four days and a million thoughts hadn't been enough for him to figure out how to handle the fact that Pia *was* Gio's granddaughter. Or to convince himself not to *handle her,* in any way.

There were a hundred more beautiful, more sophisticated women among his acquaintants. Women who would suit him for any kind of arrangement he wanted. Women who didn't look at him with barely hidden longing.

Women who were not his complicated godfather's innocent granddaughters.

He'd been waiting it out. Telling himself that she was just a novelty with her honest admissions and her innocent looks.

That he'd always preferred experienced women—both in bed and when dealing out of it.

And yet, from the moment he'd seen her standing outside his office, awareness had hummed in his blood.

Today, she looked the part of an elementary teacher with her black-framed geeky glasses, her brown hair in a messy knot precariously held together with a wooden stick, he realized with a grin, and a frilly, floral blouse and worn-out denim shorts that clung to her nicely rounded buttocks and displayed her mile-long legs.

With no makeup on, she should have looked ordinary. But he'd already looked past the surface. Knew that beneath the plain facade was a woman who felt everything keenly. Knew that if he touched her, she would be as responsive and ravenous as he was.

The summery blouse made her look more fragile than usual. He wanted to trace the jut of her collarbone with his fingers. And then maybe his tongue. He wanted to pull that stick in her knot so that her hair tumbled down. He wanted to slowly peel those shorts down until he found the silky skin of her thighs so that he could…

Fingers at his temple, he forced the far too vivid, half-naked image of her from his eyes. Christ, even as a hormonal teenager he hadn't indulged like that. For one thing, he'd never had a spare minute.

"You had a PI dig into my background?"

He shrugged, glad that he was sitting. "Gio has been hoodwinked by three ex-wives into not only marrying them but settling fat alimonies on them."

She got up, walked around the coffee table that separated them and sat down at the other end of the sofa he was sitting on. Tilting her chin up, she gave him a haughty look. "I'm waiting, Raphael."

He grinned. "For what?"

"An apology. What do you think?"

"Didn't you just tell me you don't want apologies for things I'm not really sorry about?"

"You're the most arrogant, annoying man I've ever met."

"Tell me what brought you here, despite that."

"Last night we had a really bad argument. He was pushing me into a corner and I… I said something really awful." Big fat tears filled up her eyes. And just like that Raphael went from mild irritation to a strange tenderness in his chest.

Raphael leaned forward and took her tightly clasped hands in his. Even as he fought it, awareness seeped through him from her hands. The rough calluses on her hands, the slender wrists, the blunt nails—everything about her enthralled him.

He looked up and his gaze snagged on her wide mouth, pinched in sadness. "What happened?"

She tugged at her hands and he let go with the utmost reluctance. "Of all the men who have been…*pursuing* me, for lack of a better word, I like Enzo the best and it was easier to spend time with him than run around trying to avoid the rest of them. I enjoy his company and we've been pretty inseparable the last two weeks. He's kind, genuine and he told me the first moment that—"

"Enzo Castillaghi?" Raphael snapped. Everything inside him came alert.

"He's gay and he told me within two minutes of meeting me. He said his family would lose it if they knew. Both Giovanni and his father, Stefano, are pushing really hard for this to go through."

Raphael jerked up straight, his blood curdling. "Stefano? He was there?"

Pia nodded, her gaze searching his. "I didn't realize Gio knew so much about my thing with Enzo. Anyway, yesterday afternoon out of the blue Enzo and Stefano arrived for lunch. After lunch, we… Enzo…proposed to me in the garden while they watched from the terrace. He said he liked me, and we could marry as a convenience for now. It would get his parents off his back and I… Gio and the unwanted attention.

Just as a stopgap measure."

Raphael cursed hard and long.

For Gio to make a deal with Enzo's father, Stefano Castillaghi, when he knew how much Raphael loathed Stefano, and with good reason… Something wasn't right. The thought of Pia married to Enzo while Stefano pulled his strings from behind, while Stefano got his hand into Vito Automobiles… His blood boiled.

What the hell kind of a game was Giovanni playing?

"Raphael, you look downright scary. Is the Castillaghi family that bad?"

Somehow, he managed to swallow the poison that swirled within. "Enzo is harmless but completely under his father's thumb. Stefano, on the other hand…"

"What about him?"

Raphael wondered if she realized she was touching him. That all he'd have to do was tilt his head and his mouth would touch hers. A thread of her scent warmed by her skin teased his nostrils. Damn Giovanni!

"What about Stefano, Raphael?"

He ran a hand through his hair. This day was going from bad to worse. "Stefano was my father's business partner for twenty years. Even as families, we were very close. As a business, my father, Stefano and the third partner made some unwise, risky investments. When the investments failed to pan out and the business went under, we found that Stefano and the other partner had cleverly claused themselves out of the debt.

My father was the only one responsible. We lost everything—our house, the business, the cars—overnight because he was determined to pay everyone back. But it wasn't enough."

"Couldn't Stefano and the other guy be held responsible by law?"

He hated talking about that time. Talking about the man he'd once hero-worshipped. Being reminded that the void his father had left had only hardened with bitterness. "No."

"You're not telling me something." Distress rang in her voice. "Your father...what happened to him?"

How could she know what he had left out? "He killed himself."

Her hands clasped his tightly, her silence saying more than words ever could. He didn't know why he held on to her fingers as if she were a lifeline. He didn't know what magic she wove but something shifted in his chest.

"Was he a good man, Raphael?" she asked in a soft voice. It was a question no one had ever asked, and it burrowed through his flesh and blood like an arrow, lodging deeply and painfully.

"He was a coward," he said harshly. And flinched, for his own words hurt him. Still. After all these years.

"You...how old were you?"

"Seventeen."

"Raphael, you don't think—"

He pushed away from her, loath to discuss his father and the past any longer. "I owe Giovanni everything but I'll be damned if I let Stefano's shadow touch Vito Automobiles. What was your answer to Enzo?"

Her gaze turned searching, and then she sighed. "I refused him. Enzo is sweet. And this offer…it will get everyone off my back, and maybe provide a measure of relief to Gio too. But marriage is sacred."

He snorted. She glared at him. "It is for me. I could no more marry Enzo as a convenience than I could marry… *you* to make Gio happy."

"There's one point in my favor over Enzo, *si*?" That she distracted him enough to joke less than a minute after thinking of Stefano Castillaghi said something about his attraction to her.

"Fat good that does me," she mumbled.

"What does that mean?" he asked, genuinely curious now. *Dio*, no woman sent him on a roller coaster as she did.

Color stole up her cheeks. "Can I finish telling you what happened?" she said tartly.

He grinned, liking her all riled up like this. *"Si."*

"After they left, Gio told me I should accept Enzo, that he would be a kind husband. When I said I had no intention of marrying in the near future, he got…agitated. I told him I'd had enough of him manipulating me. He said it was his right to select a husband for me, to make sure another man didn't cheat me like Frank did.

"We yelled at each other some more and I said if he kept pushing me like that, if he… I'd leave and never return, like Nonni had done." She rubbed a hand over her eyes, but the tears fell anyway. "His face went white…he couldn't speak. One of the staff called his physician.

"This was not like one of his usual temper tantrums, Raphael. The doctor took *ages* to get there and I thought—

God!" Her tears turned into soundless sobs and Raphael pulled her into his arms.

She came to him as if she had no strength left. Arms vined around his neck, she buried her face in his chest.

A strange sort of weight seemed to lodge in his own throat. He wasn't worried about Gio. The mean old bastard would live to a hundred and torture Raphael and Pia in the process.

No, it was the sound of Pia's wretched grief that shook him.

He had never seen anyone grieve like that. With everything of themselves poured into it. His belief that all she wanted was easy money from this trip—suddenly, his cynicism, his hard shell, felt dirty near her.

Her back was slender against his broad palm; even now he was unable to stem the awareness of her soft body against his. "Pia, nothing will happen to Gio."

"We don't know that. I can't lose him. Not when I've only just found him. To see him lying on the bed, helpless like that... All I could think of was my Nonni. I can't... I couldn't forgive myself if anything happened to him. I can't let him go on worrying about me."

"You can't marry a gay man however decent you think he is," he added softly, just to make sure they were on the same page. Right now, he couldn't even try to fathom the underpinnings of his godfather's Machiavellian mind.

She sniffled elegantly and wiped her cheeks. "No, I can't. I couldn't sleep. I was working on a toy and finally I hit on the perfect solution."

Raphael pulled her hands away from his neck because the graze of her breasts against his chest was more than he could take in his current mood.

And because, while she was obliviously dwelling on her worries over Gio, his attention had wandered from her grief, from Stefano, to the pressing weight of her thighs

against his. To the span of her tiny waist and the flare of
her hips in his hands. To how soft and sweet she smelled.

To the semi hard-on that was fast swelling into something else.

He only meant to create some distance between them.

But the moment she realized what he'd done, her eyes
widened. Furious color rushed up her neck and she sidled
off his lap as if she were on fire. Or maybe it was he who
was on fire.

"I'm sorry. I didn't mean to… I just…"

Pretending a calm he didn't feel, Raphael poured a glass
of water and handed it to her.

Did the woman still not realize how close he had been
to kissing her again? Was she really that naive? Did she
not realize her appeal, as unconventional as it was? Had
the lowlife she'd mentioned shattered her confidence completely?

It was still nowhere near what Enzo with his kindness
and Stefano with his schemes would do to her.

The thought shattered his desire. He couldn't let Stefano get his dirty hands on the company he had made into
a global leader. But he was also running out of options.

Options that didn't involve Pia. And getting involved
with Pia, his gut told him, was not a path from which he
could turn back. Even if he wanted to.

He felt as if there was an invisible noose tightening
around his neck.

It made his voice harsh when he said, "What is your
solution, Pia?"

"You should pretend… I mean *we* should pretend to be
interested in each other." When his frown morphed into
a scowl, Pia hurried on. "As if we were dating each other.
As if we were…violently attracted to each other and nothing else, no one else would do. It's the perfect solution,"
she added when he just stared at her.

"How?"

She folded her hands, realized how defensive she looked and dropped them. Did the man have to look so displeased just by the notion of them dating? "Gio thinks the world of you. If you weren't so utterly out of my league, I think he would have pushed you and me toward each other."

"What?"

"Do you need me to spell it out? It's all I've been hearing from Gio, from everyone's mouths since I arrived in Milan. About the kind of women you go for. Even Gio isn't foolish or stubborn enough to wish for something between us. Which, perversely, makes it the perfect solution."

"I have to admit your scheming does prove you have Vito blood."

"Most of the men I've met over the last few weeks, Enzo included, wouldn't dream of coming near me if you made it clear that I belonged to you. They are all in awe of the force that is Raphael Mastrantino," she added caustically.

His lips twitched. "Are you mocking my reputation?"

Pia smiled. His eyes lit up; he looked incredibly gorgeous. "I wouldn't dare."

"And you would be okay *belonging to me*?"

She shuddered. "It's archaic, but nothing else, I fear, would keep them away. This way, you can rest easy that I won't get my hands on Gio's fortune. Gio would be thrilled that I have somehow enthralled you and I… I can make plans. As much as I'm making a deal with the devil."

"I am the diablo?" he said in a soft croon that sent shivers down her spine.

"*Si*," she replied.

But Raphael was no devil. Nor Prince Charming either. He was more like the big bad wolf. But sometimes it was the wolf that provided the most protection. It was the wolf you could trust to keep others at bay.

How she would survive a fake relationship when she

couldn't even look at him without melting on the inside she didn't know. But this was the only way.

For Gio and for her own peace of mind.

He reached out to her and tilted her chin up. "What plans would those be?"

"Plans that don't concern you."

"If we start this charade, I will know everything about you, Pia."

Why did that sound like a declaration of possession? "What does it matter when you can keep me away from the till?"

Just silence. And those intense black eyes. Pia squirmed like a fish on a line.

"I... I've been thinking about staying beyond summer. Last night, seeing Gio's reaction... I realized I was just fooling myself about returning. There's nothing there for me. Not anymore.

"At the risk of confirming your worst suspicions, I want to stay here and take care of him. The thought of leaving him alone, with all his relatives who really don't care about him, leaving him with hired help, it twists my stomach."

A tightness emerged around his mouth. "Taking care of Gio, or any old man, is a full-time job, Pia."

"I know that. When Nonni was ill, it was just me and her. I took a long leave of absence and I looked after her for two years. I can—"

"How old were you?"

"Twenty. I had been working only for a few months."

"Didn't you miss having a life? The excitement of your job and friends?" His disbelief was apparent in his voice. As if he had personal experience to negate her claim.

"All we had was each other. I know Gio has you but you're always so busy."

"I see the logic in your plan. It serves both our purposes, *si*? But whether it will work, whether Gio and the world will believe that I would be *violently attracted* to such a—" he let his gaze roam over her with a thoroughness that both excited and embarrassed her "—what did you say? *Shy, plain, boring elementary science teacher,* that I'm not sure about."

In the process of tugging her bag over her shoulder, Pia stilled. Smoke should've been coming out of her ears. The gall of the man! She turned to face him, and his warm, wicked smile carving deep grooves in his cheeks, stole her indignation.

It changed him, that smile. The way he had held her when she'd cried—that was a Raphael she could like. "Just as it'll be hard for me to act as if you're God's gift to women," she said with a put-upon sigh. "But I'll do anything for Gio."

He took her hands in his and tugged, a devilish twist to his smile. "Simply liking will not be enough, *cara mia.* First, you have to stop being so nervous and jumpy around me. Then you have to act as if you adore me."

He dipped his head while locking Pia against the door with his arms on either side of her, "And then—" his breath stroked her neck while the scent of him enveloped her "—as if you can't keep your hands off me."

"No," she whispered, her entire body languorous as if someone had replaced the blood in her veins with warm honey.

A feral smile curved his mouth. "*Si.* Didn't the gossip mill tell you the last bit about me?"

Pia couldn't move her gaze from his mouth. The defined upper lip and the lush lower lip. No man should have lips like that. The need to taste that sensual mouth, the need to press her body against those hard muscles was like a physical ache. How could she feel an attraction this strongly when it was one-sided?

"That you never have a girlfriend, only lovers," she

forced herself to say, remembering the tidbit. And yet, apparently, it didn't put off most of the women.

"If we have to make the entirety of Milan believe that we're together, I can't be seeing other women on the side, *si*? So it'll be up to you to keep me in—"

Pia slapped her palm over his mouth, a thrill running through her.

If she wanted to live in Italy, if she wanted to be a part of Gio's life, it meant Raphael would forever be a part of it too, in some way.

Was she forever going to spend it shying away from him? Twisting inside out because of her attraction to him? Letting him mock her like this?

Something within her rebelled, made her say, "Maybe it won't be so bad pretending to be your girlfriend."

His eyes widened. "I realized something about Frank and me in the last few days. He singled me out for his attentions for a reason. I… I wouldn't have been taken in by his sweet words if I'd had more experience with men, *si*? Both emotionally and…sexually." It was one thing to want to take down his arrogance a notch, and completely another to do it with his mouth against her palm, his stubble scraping her fingers.

He wrapped his fingers around her wrist and tugged it back, his face so close to hers now that she could see the slight widening of his pupils, the flare of his nostrils. He wasn't just playing with her, something whispered at the back of her mind.

"Even I didn't realize how perfect we are for this pretense. It's clear that I'm not the type of woman who could interest you in a million years." The sound of his choking laugh made her glare at him "And… I could never have a relationship with a man like you."

"Non?"

"No. You're arrogant, cynical and…far too gorgeous for

me. I'd have to beat off women for the rest of my life. I'd be reminded every day how fortunate I was to have you. Things would always be unequal between us. Love or not, I'm determined not to be with a man who looks down on me, who thinks he's doing me a favor by being with me."

A faint flush appeared under his cheekbones. "Pia, whatever that lowlife said—"

"Let's not forget the whole you despising marriage thing," Pia cut in, refusing to let him finish. The last thing she needed was Raphael's pity.

"You still want to marry?"

"Of course I do. I refuse to let Frank break my beliefs that've been a part of me much longer." Though he had come pretty close. "My parents, from what I remember of them, were devoted to each other. I want a man who'll respect our relationship, a man who'll trust me, a man who wants to spend his life with me. And in the meantime, I can hone myself on you, can't I?"

"What would this…*honing yourself on me* entail exactly?" He made the words sound so utterly debauched, so wickedly filthy that Pia could feel heat burning up her neck.

Turning the handle behind her, she slipped out without answering. But his laughter, a deep, sexy sound, a sound that rendered his assistants awestruck, a sound that sent tingles up her spine, stayed with her all the way through the ride home.

Making her wonder what she'd signed up for.

CHAPTER FIVE

Dress for me tonight.

RAPHAEL'S TEXT THAT very evening, just as she had been getting ready to leave with Gio, mere hours after they'd made their deal, stopped Pia in her tracks.

Dinner at his sister's house. It was the perfect occasion to advertise their new relationship. She could just imagine the arrogant gleam in his eyes, the roguish curve of his mouth as if he were standing in front of her.

That's how Gio caught her, standing in the hallway, looking at her phone, first baffled, then furious and then with a goofy smile on her face. Because the arrogant Italian would've known how much it would rile her to get that command from him.

And he couldn't have orchestrated it any better if he had stood there and kissed her.

When Gio had inquired who had made her smile, Pia had instinctively ducked the phone behind her. Realizing Gio was exactly why she'd begun this, she'd reluctantly shown him the phone.

Her grandfather had stared at the phone for a long while. Which had caused her to wonder if she'd made a horrible mistake. When he had finally looked at her, Pia had expected a hundred questions, meddling, plans. Gio, she'd begun to realize, could be like a little boy sometimes—temperamental, impulsive.

But Gio had said nothing. Asked nothing.

She'd have thought he didn't approve if he hadn't uttered, "He is a good man, but hard. Do not let him break you like I broke Lucia, *si*?"

He'd been worried at her revelation, but on the drive to Raphael's sister's house, Pia had sensed Gio's relief too. Almost as if he had known this would happen.

As if it was what he'd wanted.

The growing unease that she'd started something that had no exit strategy only deepened as Pia smiled at, shook hands with and exchanged air-kisses with a crowd of curious, but mostly friendly faces as soon as they arrived at his sister Teresa's house—a posh Mediterranean-style villa with colorful ivy climbing decoratively up its white walls.

Golden sunlight washed over the villa. The early dinner was al fresco with people spread all over the house and the immense backyard with white tables spread around. A festive atmosphere reigned with kids chasing each other and people talking in groups. But the moment Gio and she had walked in, a hush fell over the smiling faces.

She tried not to cringe as attention focused on her. More than a few faces were familiar, even a couple of men who had attended her ball. Suddenly, her plan sounded ridiculous, even stupid.

She was going to pretend to be familiar with Raphael in front of all these people? Pretend like just the thought of being romantically involved with him didn't make her feel plain and dull? Didn't make her want to hide and do something wildly exciting at the same time?

And where was the dratted man anyway?

Pia met Raphael's four sisters and their husbands, scores of his nieces and nephews—they were a fertile bunch, apparently—a host of his cousins and their spouses, two aunts, one uncle and finally his mother Portia Mastrantino.

That same distrust she'd seen in Raphael's eyes showed in his mother's eyes.

Noting the white shorts and skirts paired with spaghetti tops and the humidity that was making her hair wild, she was glad that she'd dressed in a plain cotton navy blue top and printed shorts with her favorite Toms wedges, whatever Raphael's imperious command.

After more than an hour of blank smiling, Pia sneaked into the house, needing quiet.

Sitting on a chaise longue in cargo shorts and a navy blue T-shirt that exposed corded arms and hair-sprinkled wrists, Raphael looked utterly different and yet just as magnetic. Floor-to-ceiling glass dipped him in sunlight. His olive skin looked darker, his shoulders broader with the fabric stretched over his lean chest.

He was bouncing the most adorable little girl on his knee.

The little girl screamed and laughed as Raphael pretended to lose his grip on her while she slid down his long legs to the floor. Every time he caught her at the last second, she squealed, shuddered, scampered over to his knee, climbed over his chest and wrapped chubby arms around his neck and slobbered a wet kiss over his cheek.

Again and again, he pretended to lose her, she did it all over, planting another wet kiss over his other cheek. His dark eyes roared with laughter, love, eagerly awaiting the moment when she would kiss him.

A pulse of longing reverberated through Pia at the sight. Such cynicism when he addressed Pia and now for this girl, such affection.

Was she a niece? A cousin's daughter?

Suddenly, the little girl hiccuped. Her chubby face scrunched tight. Holding her as if she were the most precious thing to him, Raphael asked for a glass of water. Three dark-haired voluptuous women rushed to his aid, all of them dressed in the latest designer clothes—thanks to Gio, Pia now had a useless font of information about couture.

The women hovered over Raphael anxiously, ready to do his bidding. To his credit, Raphael had eyes only for the little girl. He didn't notice the adoring glances or how each woman found a way to sidle closer to him or touch him in some way.

Hot embarrassment poured through Pia. Followed by a thread of sheer possessiveness that rocked her.

Was that how she watched him too? With that barely hidden longing and her attraction plastered all over her face?

Worst of all was the sinking awareness that she was nowhere near the league of the women that hovered around him like bees around honey.

Something about Raphael, even as she disliked his cynicism, made her body sing, made her mind weave impossible fantasies.

She couldn't forget that Raphael had agreed to their pretense for his own benefit. And not because he saw her as a woman worth his interest.

Feeling something prickling at the back of his neck, Raphael looked up amidst Alyssa's slobbering kiss on his cheek.

Pia stood at the center of the room, her eyes wide behind a pair of black-framed spectacles. Sunlight drew an outline of her lithe body in a simple T-shirt and shorts that bared her long, tanned legs. She'd braided her hair but was losing the fight against it. It fell in unruly curls around her face.

Among the women dressed in casual couture with designer handbags and diamonds dripping at their ears and wrists, she stood out like a wildflower amidst pricey, carefully cultivated crossbred prize orchids.

No makeup, no artifice.

Emotions chased across her face, the naked vulnerability in it rousing desire and a fierce protectiveness within him.

Pretending a liaison with her, however harmless she thought it, wouldn't be without consequences. His conversation with her at his office, Gio's Machiavellian maneuvering of them both toward what he deemed inevitable, every instinct Raphael possessed told him that it was a bad idea, screamed at him to keep his distance from her.

And yet, how could he leave her to the jackals Giovanni had unleashed on her? To Gio's ridiculous schemes? The thought of any man, even Enzo, touching her, the thought of her bestowing her friendship, her loyalty, her affection on any other man—it was becoming unbearable.

Was she going to fare any better with him? The question had been haunting him since he'd agreed to her scheme.

"Pia?" he whispered softly.

She lifted those luminous eyes to his. A jolt of sensation hit his muscles at the artless want in her eyes. Her open desire for him made every male instinct in him rise to the surface.

Color washed up her cheeks and she blinked. "I was looking for you," she finally said, pushing the glasses up on the bridge of her nose. "I don't think we should—"

He could see Giovanni and his mother and a couple of other people walking into the huge room. "Come and meet my daughter, Alyssa." He cut her off abruptly.

"Your daughter?" She looked like a deer caught in headlights, ready to flee any moment. "You have a daughter?"

His daughter slid off his legs, sauntered over to Pia, wrapped herself around Pia's bare leg like a vine and looked up. The thought of Pia's dislike for him translating itself to Alyssa made him cover the distance between them.

All her distress forgotten, Pia picked up Alyssa with a soft laugh. Raphael watched transfixed as she buried her face in Alyssa's tummy with a sigh.

He could hear Gio in the background saying what a pretty picture the three of them made, the manipulative bastard! Could imagine his mother's shock; could practically hear the wheels turning in her head; could hear the soft whispers spreading from mouth to mouth.

Raphael had never believed in fate or higher power. None of them had ever come to his aid. Always it had been his own decisions and actions that had made his path. Even after Giovanni had taken him under his wing, it was Raphael who'd pushed himself to set new goals, to reach new heights in his business.

And yet, as Alyssa twisted one of Pia's curls around her chubby finger and tugged hard, sending a gush of pained tears to Pia's eyes and laughter spilling from her mouth, it felt as if he was taking a step that couldn't be undone.

He laughed at the way Pia cooed at the three-year-old in fractured Italian, begging her to let go of her hair; at the way she instantly dropped to her knees when Alyssa demanded to be set down and tugged Pia in that boisterous way of hers.

Amused, he watched as his daughter and Pia charmed each other for the next hour. He watched his daughter, who barely tolerated strangers, instinctively trust Pia, and he watched as Pia, who'd been so uncomfortable with the sophisticated crowd, fell for his girl.

Slowly, Alyssa began to sway where she stood. Pia gathered Alyssa—who didn't let anyone except him or his mother put her to sleep—and she neatly cuddled into Pia's chest, sucked her thumb into her mouth and promptly fell asleep.

"Don't wake her up," Pia hissed at him when he tried to untangle her hair from his daughter's fist.

Only this woman could make him laugh just as much as she could turn him on with one look. "Unless you want her to rip out your—" his gaze fell to the thick honey-brown strands that were like rough silk between his fingers "—lovely hair, which would be a shame, I have to do this." Firmly, he uncurled Alyssa's fingers until Pia's hair was free. "Believe me, she has ripped out my hair from the roots far too many times."

"You don't look like you've lost any," she threw back, and then blushed when he grinned. He took Alyssa from her, gave her to his sister, who left with a wide-eyed glance at the both of them.

Having lost their buffer, Pia stepped back from him hurriedly. She frowned as she noted Gio and his mother in deep discussion outside the French windows. "You didn't tell me you have a daughter."

"Alyssa is no one's business but mine," he said before he could modulate his tone.

Hurt flashed in her eyes before she lifted her chin in defiance. "Is your ex-wife here too? I'm not really comfortable stepping in between—"

"Allegra is not a part of our lives anymore. She lost all her rights to Alyssa."

"I wouldn't have suggested this ridiculous charade if I'd known you had a daughter. I won't be a part of anything that could harm that little girl. Maybe she's too young to understand which woman her father is…has…"

He raised a brow.

She was the first woman who hadn't immediately thought to use Alyssa like a ladder toward him. The first woman in his sphere who had considered his child's interests before her own.

She was the first woman he'd ever met who *always*

put someone else before her own needs—first her Nonni, Gio and now a little girl. Even his mother, who adored her grandchildren, sometimes used Alyssa to try to manipulate him.

But Pia… Could Pia be truly different in this too?

"Do you always stammer when you talk about what men and women do?" he goaded.

"It can't be good for her to know you and I…you and me…"

"My mother and my sister Teresa are the only ones who're allowed to look after Alyssa," he offered. He'd never explained his actions to anyone and yet the words fell from his mouth. "I need a woman for only one thing and I do that when I'm out of town."

"You need a woman for only…" Her words trailed off, a flush dusting her cheeks. "That's horrible and so…clinical. Are you saying you'll never need a woman, even in the future, for anything else?"

"I'm saying exactly that. I don't intend to marry ever again."

"What about affection, companionship, y'know…"

"I've never met a woman who made me feel or want those things. Alyssa has me, and my mother and sisters for a woman's influence." He took a step toward her, more turned on by this ridiculous conversation than made sense. The infuriating woman took another step back. "My mother will understand that our relationship is not something I want discussed in front of Alyssa. She wasn't even supposed to bring Alyssa today. But I bet she couldn't pass up the chance to meet you."

"When I met her…she…" Pia hesitated. When he just stared back at her, she finally said, "I could be wrong, but I think she…doesn't like me."

"She doesn't."

"Why? She doesn't even know me."

"You're the prime contender for Gio's fortune."

"That's a horrible thing to say," Pia said laughingly. But the seriousness in Raphael's gaze sobered her up. "How do I know you don't feel the same? Do you see your piece of the pie getting smaller? Maybe *you're* the one manipulating *me*?"

He laughed, as if the very idea was ridiculous.

The confidence he wore like a second skin—that didn't come without bending life to one's will. Giovanni had told her how Raphael had taken VA public, made gains they hadn't seen in the last decade. He'd been ruthless about the changes he'd enforced, wasn't the least bit sentimental about what needed to be done, but his execution was always effective, she'd been told by her grandfather, curiously with something like regret in his eyes.

More profits. Better stock prices. He had no friends he trusted, no one was indispensable to him. No weakness was allowed in himself or tolerated in others.

The shadow of his father's suicide, Pia realized now, would forever cast a black shadow on Raphael's life, and would never let him be anything but a man who loathed weakness.

"If you're wealthy, then why would your mother worry?" she countered.

He shrugged, but Pia could see it bothered him by the tightness of his mouth. "She grew up in a very wealthy family and my father kept her in the same style. When we lost the house and our lifestyle, a lot of her friends and connections turned their backs on her. She took it very hard—wouldn't leave her bedroom, refused to eat. She became a ghost."

"It couldn't have been harder on her than it had been on your father, could it?" Pia was unable to keep the sarcasm out of her voice.

She waited for a cutting comeback. He simply frowned.

"I'm sorry, that was unkind. It's just that…your father was betrayed by people he trusted. People with whom he shared his fears and dreams and hopes. Your mother still had him and you and your sisters. What's a fortune when you have family and friends who love you?"

"You really believe that, don't you?"

Pia shrugged, uncomfortable with his scrutiny. "I just… I can imagine what your father must have felt. What Frank did to me is minuscule by comparison, and yet I have days where I can't trust my own judgment. Days when I can't believe that everything he did was with a motive—pulling me from the dark cloud of Nonni's death, persuading me to step out of the house for an evening.

"Gio didn't help by doing what he did either. I can't trust anyone—man or woman—when they say something nice to me. I can't help but search for deeper motives. Perversely, it's what makes me trust you."

His frown only deepened. "What about me?"

"Your animosity, your suspicions. I can count on you to be brutally honest, even if I don't like your assumptions. The reason why I…" *like you.* She cut herself off at the flare in his eyes. Words solidified the feeling in her chest. The last thing he needed was to learn that he was beginning to grow on her. "I don't understand why your mother doesn't like me still."

"She lives in a permanently terrified state that I will take the same risks with my money that my father did and doom them all. She made sure I allocated lifelong separate funds for my sisters, for Alyssa and her."

"Funds you cannot invest in your business?" Pia asked, shocked by the implications. It not only showed a distinct lack of faith in Raphael's abilities as a businessman but also a callous obsession with wealth over her son's feelings.

"*Si.* Over the last few years, she got used to hearing Gio's continual claims that he will leave everything to me—which he did to annoy his ex-wives and their constant bickering for more settlements. It has turned into her insurance against my possible failure and downfall. Now you are a threat to that insurance."

Was it any wonder he assumed she was out to fleece Gio with the mindset he already had?

To believe that one's own mother saw one as nothing but a source of her income… Could Raphael see himself as anything but a provider? Had he even been allowed to grieve for his father before he'd had to take on the mantle of his family?

Because, despite everything, it was clear he cared about his family. She had called him ruthless, but not enough to stop shouldering the responsibility of his sisters and their families.

And he adored his daughter.

Suddenly, Pia saw Raphael more clearly than she ever wanted to. She didn't want to see any depth to his hardness, any soft edges beyond his cynicism. She didn't want to see Raphael as anything but an impossible fantasy and a reluctant ally.

She didn't, couldn't afford to see him as a man worth knowing.

CHAPTER SIX

WIDE EYES DRESSED with the longest lashes searched and studied his face unblinkingly as Raphael waited. Dappled in the sunlight, she looked exquisitely innocent. Desire was a permanent drumbeat in his blood anytime he was near Pia. But it wasn't just that anymore.

She had a way of looking at him that made him feel bare. Of making him speak of things he'd never mentioned to anyone. Of looking deep beneath his words and showing him a side of himself he'd never seen before.

The shame of his father's suicide was a wound that had festered for too long. And yet, beneath it, he recognized the pain of betrayal he hadn't seen until now.

He had worshipped his father and overnight, his hero had both abandoned and betrayed him. But in memory, his father had lingered on in what he had felt then was the epitome of weakness.

"Take care, Pia," he whispered. Until now, he'd let Gio coerce him. But the feeling of losing control made him snarly. "Is it any wonder Giovanni wants you tied up to some man as protection? You stare at me as if you mean to gobble me up."

"Not any man, just you," she replied, and then blushed furiously. "It's good to know that you care about your daughter."

Instead of mollifying him, her apparent approval riled

him. Damn it, the woman turned him inside out. "Because you assume I'm an uncaring monster?"

Another step forward by him and another backward by her. "All indications said so."

"Stop backing away." The comment hissed out of him in a low growl.

"Stop crowding me. Stop…" A panicked gasp fell from her mouth. "This is a bad idea on so many levels."

Every time he came near, he could see the pulse fluttering madly in her neck. See her breaths hitch in and out. Feel warmth arc between them.

But despite the attraction, he was beginning to believe she wanted nothing to do with him. The thought rankled.

He'd never been vain, but no woman had ever *resented* his attentions. Not since he had become taller and broader than any boy he had known in his teens. Not since he had remade his family's fortune ten times over. Not since he'd become one of the most powerful men in Milan. "What is a bad idea?" he asked, closing the distance between them once again.

"Why would Gio involve Enzo and Stefano even indirectly if he knew how much you loathed him? You were right, he…"

"Manipulated us, *si*," Raphael finished for her.

It burned Raphael that Gio would use Stefano to rope him in, but Pia was right. Unless Raphael did something to calm Gio down, his schemes would only get wilder. No measure would be unacceptable if Gio thought he was doing it for their good.

If he thought it would push Raphael into taking Pia off his hands.

"Then you know why we can't—"

"Let Gio think he's been successful. Let the whole world think you've beguiled me," said Raphael.

"How do you think I feel knowing that he went through

this elaborate charade to…*coerce* you into this with me? As if I were useless inventory he wanted to move? As if I were a pawn to entice the mighty King?"

"He's manipulative, *si*, but it doesn't mean he's not worried."

Shaking her head, she backed away. "But I don't like—"

Before she could utter another word, Raphael caught her upper arms, tugged her toward him. "I told you what I would do if you did that," he said with a growl before he touched his lips to hers in a soft buss.

He only meant to shock her, he told himself. To show her that being attracted to him wasn't the end of the world. That her idea was indeed the perfect solution for now.

Except all his reasons flew away the minute her mouth stilled under his.

Her hands caught on his chest. The long lashes cast crescent shadows on her cheeks. But it was her wide eyes that snagged Raphael. The slumberous desire in them. The soft mewl of pleasure that fell from her mouth as her palms moved and settled over his chest. His heart thundered like a wild beast under her palms, her body's warmth slowly infiltrating his.

One kiss… All he wanted was one kiss.

One taste of the tantalizing lushness of her mouth. One taste to see if she was as sweet as she sounded.

One moment with the woman who stared at him like no other did. As if he were her deepest fantasy.

"Raphael…" Her entreaty incensed him. How dare she walk into his domain and turn him upside down?

Fingers curled around her nape, he tilted her face and slid his tongue over her trembling lower lip.

She moaned into his mouth—a tremulous whimper that heated his blood. And shuddered. Her body softened and his hardened. Fitting his mouth flush against hers, he moved it this way and that. Heat stirred from that soft friction and her fingers became stiff against his chest. Digging and pressing. Grasping.

He kissed her mouth again and again, a soft slide, a hard press, teasing and taunting, somehow controlling the feral hunger blooming in his blood. "Open your mouth, *tesoro*," he pleaded, every muscle curling in heated anticipation.

Her body arched into his touch even as she said, "They're watching…please…"

And yet, she pressed closer, until her small breasts were plastered against his chest. Until her thigh was encased between his own. He stroked his hands up and down her back, soothing those infinite tremors, willing her to take the leap. Mindless hunger consumed him. "Give in, *bella*. Kiss me."

And merciful God above, she did.

Slowly. Softly.

Like a whisper of a butterfly's wing, she pressed a tentative kiss at the corner of his mouth, flicked his lower lip with the tip of her tongue. From one corner of his mouth to the other, she kept kissing him until it felt like there was a hot poker inside of his own body. Until the control he was exercising spewed hot shivers all through him.

Again and again, standing on her toes, sinking her hands into his hair, pulling him down… All he'd done was touch a spark to dry tinder and she'd exploded. His body's hunger deepened. His need deepened.

With a growl, Raphael stopped her explorations. Holding her still, he plunged his tongue into her mouth, again and again, the kiss turning instantly carnal. He licked the warm cavern of her mouth, curled the tip of his tongue against hers, begging her with his caresses.

He was pleading her for surrender, for he instinctively knew only sweet entreaty would do with Pia. She wasn't delicate inside, only outwardly. That sweet innocence of her spirit, he would do anything to keep it intact.

Shuddering, she returned the pressure, her tongue touching his in tentative strokes. His moan imploded, reverberated through his own body as the kiss grew urgent. He kissed her hard and fast, his need only increasing the more he took. Sweet and hot, she was like a drug he'd never known.

Christo, she was responsive, ravenous as he was.

He dug his teeth into her lower lip and tugged. She whimpered. The sound was so soft, so much of submission and surrender.

His erection, already incredibly hard, lengthened against the cushion of her soft thigh. Flipping them, he held her against the wall, pulled her leg up until it was wrapped around his hip. Groaning at the indescribable sensation, he cupped her behind with his hands and pressed her against him tighter. Rocked himself into her groin gently.

Pleasure balled at the base of his spine, warmth seeping through her clothes to touch his skin. God, he wanted to be inside her before he took another breath; he wanted to move inside her while she stared at him with those wide eyes...

There was the sound of a cough, a whispered snarl from Gio. Raphael backed away as if burned. A curse flew from his mouth. His breath burned in his lungs, his body raging to finish what they'd started.

Dio mio, when had he been so aroused from just a kiss? With his daughter in the other room, with his mother and sisters and half of bloody Milan watching? When had his hunger ever betrayed him like that?

Breathing hard, he counted to ten, his erection no less painful at the end.

Eyes big in her gamine face, Pia remained flat against the wall where he'd pinned her with his body. Hair wild from his fingers, mouth bruised from his kisses, eyes wide.

A fierce satisfaction filled him to see the marks of his passion on her. To see her— He cursed again.

Damn it, this wasn't one of his sophisticated lovers who knew the rules. This wasn't a woman who wanted Raphael for one quick screw or even a short affair. By her own admission, she didn't even know her own sexuality, as explosive as it was.

She looked so bewildered and so innocently seductive that it doused the heat running through his veins and replaced it with a strange unsettling feeling. As if he'd opened a door to something much more complex than a kiss.

"Pia?"

She ran a tentative finger over her lower lip and a groan vibrated in his chest. "I feel…as if…" She wrapped a trembling hand around her nape, moved it forward over her neck, placed her palm over her heart. "My heart is thundering. Frank never kissed me like that. No, he tried. It just never felt like that. As if I were sinking and flying at the same time."

He fisted his hands, her words balling into pleasure at the base of his spine.

"Why did you stop?"

Christo! That was the question she asked? "Because I was this close to taking you against the wall. And I heard Gio—"

"Taking me…" Her gaze took in his balled fists, the muscle jumping under his jaw, moved to his groin and noted the evidence… "Oh." Liquid longing peered out of her gaze.

He closed the door with a slam on prying ears, his temper getting the better of him. "Don't look at me like that."

"Look at you like what?" Slowly she pushed up from the wall, a faint tremble to her movements. The passion cleared from her face, her jaw lifting in that stubborn way.

"Why are you looking at me *like that*? As if I've done something wrong?"

"It was just a kiss, Pia." It hadn't been just a kiss. In thirty-four years, he had never lost his mind like that. He'd never wanted to take a woman against a wall, propriety be damned. He'd never been so desperate to protect and possess someone as if his breath depended on it.

"Was it? Because it feels—"

"*Si*, it was just a kiss." He bit out the words so forcefully she flinched. "A show for Gio and my mother and all of Milan." Ignoring her pale face, he continued on, the ruthless bastard that he was. "I have kissed a hundred women just like that and done a lot more besides. It's lust, nothing more, nothing to be upset about. Nothing to weave dreams about.

"Just because you react like dynamite to a spark when I touch you, it doesn't mean we would suit," he added for good measure.

Color fled her cheeks and he fisted his hands. *Could he do or say nothing right with this woman?*

Christo, this was Gio's precious granddaughter. Touching her when he had no intention of going any further, kissing her when he knew she was innocent, but even more than that, there was something about Pia that got under his skin, that lingered long after she was gone.

There was something about her that made Raphael want, something in her gaze when she looked at him—as if she could see more than what he was: a ruthless, hardened cynic.

How dare he kiss her, then act affronted because she liked it? Dear God, she could still feel the sharp pulses between her legs. Could feel his warm breath on her cheek, his fingers on her buttocks.

That kiss had been such pure pleasure that she couldn't

feel the ground now. And yet, Raphael seemed determined to flatten her with reality.

A show? Who was he kidding?

"We're both responsible for that kiss turning into something else," she said, her voice vibrating with hurt and anger.

"*Si.*"

"Then you're unhappy because I enjoyed it more than you think I should?"

"I lost control. And it won't happen again."

"The kiss or losing control?" Pia demanded, her heart already taking a beating. How could she forget the impression of the hard column of flesh that he'd pressed against her belly? Had that been part of the pretense too? When he opened his mouth, she held him off. "Stop talking before you say something I can't forgive."

Eyes flaring, he looked away. In profile, his face was tight with control. His impressive chest rose and fell.

"Are you all right?"

"No. I'm not all right." She wished she could lie, but what was the point? Just as she couldn't become beautiful or sophisticated, she couldn't play games either.

Oh, why had she involved him in this farce in the first place? She'd thought she'd somehow resist her attraction to him, but she hadn't counted on finding such a complicated man beneath. He was tying her up in knots—and that was when he wasn't kissing her. "I don't kiss a man as if my life depends on it, and then coolly wipe it from my mind."

When he reached for her hands, Pia shied them away. A tic beat violently under his jaw.

He didn't want to have kissed her, yet he didn't like it if she turned away from his touch. What did he want from her?

"You have to. I won't let it spiral like that, but if we have to keep this pretense up some intimacy will be required."

Understanding dampened the scorching trails his body had left across hers. This was how he usually had his affairs. Except she hadn't followed the script. "I can't just separate it like you do. I can't turn it off when it's inconvenient."

His eyes flared. "Convenient? Nothing about my life has been convenient since you decided to storm into it. First, he had all of Milan tripping over themselves to get to you. Then, he puts you in my way by involving the damned Castillaghis in this whole thing. Do I worry about the threats my ex is making about Alyssa or do I worry about which man's trap you'll fall into next? My whole life has been turned upside down because of your presence. Damn Gio and damn…"

Pia flinched at the vehemence in his words. Did he really resent her presence in his life so much? Tears prickled at the back of her eyes and she shut them away.

Perhaps sensing how she'd retreated from him, he took a deep breath, ran a hand over his eyes. Whatever he claimed, it was clear that the kiss hadn't left him unaffected.

He reached her and traced a finger against her jawline. The tenderness in the gesture stole her breath just as much as the kiss had done. Made her long for something that he clearly wasn't going to give. "You kiss me like you can't stop, you snarl at me for turning your life upside down, and then you touch me as if I'm precious. I don't understand you, Raphael."

"How is it that a smart science teacher can't figure out cause and effect?"

"Cause and effect?" she repeated stupidly, blinking up at him.

"No good can come of this. I will never marry again, much less love again. And you, even after what that man did, you still have stars in your eyes. I kiss you because I can't help it." A ragged growl punctured his words. "I kiss you because everything about you drives me crazy. All I can think of when I wake up or go to bed or when I take myself in hand is how good it would be to move inside you. How good it feels when you come alive in my arms. But all I want from a woman is one night, a short, torrid affair at best. You're not offering that, are you?"

She shook her head automatically, and he snorted. "I didn't think so."

With one searing glance at her mouth, he walked away, leaving Pia quaking as if she'd been through an earthquake.

An affair with Raphael—even one night with him—letting his strong body cover hers, welcoming that hardness into her body, letting him see her at her most vulnerable… Heat flushed from every pore. Her body trembled just at the images, hungered for what she knew would be unbearable pleasure.

But it was her heart, drumming even now, that she was afraid of.

Frank had only chipped it. Raphael, given a chance, would crush it.

CHAPTER SEVEN

ANY DOUBTS PIA had about Raphael's promise were proved unnecessary over the next few weeks. Any momentary, crazy belief she might have had in his matter-of-fact statement that he wanted her despite his legendary will, shredded in the freezingly polite way he treated her.

Forget kissing. He didn't even touch her unless it was for an audience. Even then, he barely held her arm with the tips of his fingers as if she would contaminate him. Even his accusations had felt more personal than this.

The news that Raphael Mastrantino was dating Giovanni Vito's granddaughter swept through society faster than the heat wave that had descended on Milan.

If Pia had thought she'd garnered too much attention as Gio's American granddaughter, it was nothing compared to the glances and whispers thrown her way as the woman who'd caught Raphael's interest. His public possessiveness had fended off any other man's interest, exactly as she'd intended.

Giovanni, while he said he was delighted with this turn of events, was strangely toned down.

Pia, however, hadn't foreseen how torturous their little facade would be to her. Or that the more she saw of Raphael, the more she found a man worth admiring.

He was the perfect son, the perfect brother, the perfect boss, although a little distant, if all the things Pia had heard at an office party were to be believed. From Gio, she knew he was the perfect godson. As one woman had explained in lurid detail at another party, unaware that Pia stood behind her, he was a perfect lover.

No, scratch that, the woman had been aware that Pia was there and had taken a petty satisfaction in making sure Pia overheard.

In front of Milan and Gio and his family, he was the attentive boyfriend or lover or whatever the hell it was that they were pretending to be. Every day, he sent her flowers or candy or some other treat. When she'd asked if he'd bought her a subscription for a gift club for the next few years, he'd snarled something in Italian.

She'd had her answer, which festered. She was nothing but a painful chore for him, an item on his damned to-do list.

Between a huge deal VA was cooking with a manufacturing company in Japan and his time with Alyssa, he was hardly available anyway. Their pretense was barely a blip in his life. Whereas for Pia, every carefully orchestrated touch was torture. Every moment she spent in his company, she was caught between wanting to run away and desperately wanting more.

As if that wasn't enough, Raphael came to see Gio most evenings. Sometimes, it was a quick chat under Gio's watchful eye.

Sometimes, they dined outside with the spectacular view of the setting sun drawing pink and orange mirages on the lake. If there was enough light or if Gio petulantly demanded that he hadn't seen enough of them together that week, Pia joined them. She brought out a piece of wood and worked on it quietly while listening to Raphael relay the news and politics of Vito Automobiles.

He spoke with a deep, confident voice, his Italian soothing to her ears. Even though she only understood a few phrases, Pia heard his passion for his work, his affection for Gio in the way he relayed tidbits about people they both knew.

She could just sit there and listen to his voice endlessly.

Pretending that all the hours she spent in his company gave her rights over him, while pretty much every woman snidely commented that it was the Vito Heiress that had snared him, grated like salt on a wound. As if she didn't know that Raphael wouldn't have looked at her twice if not for the fact that she was Gio's granddaughter.

On one such scheduled outing, she'd persuaded Raphael to bring Alyssa along. She adored that little girl, and to her shame, Pia desperately needed a buffer—there was only so much one-on-one she could take with Raphael before she did something crazy.

Raphael had returned after a week-long trip and any hopes she'd had that she would be over him were dashed to tiny bits when she saw him striding up the pathway with a squirming Alyssa on his shoulder and his mouth stretched in carefree laughter.

They spent the next two hours with Alyssa at a *gelateria* in Menaggio, another one of the picturesque villages lining up Lake Como. Pia held a chubby, sticky and sleepy Alyssa in her arms while Raphael parked the car in front of his mother's house.

When he asked to take her back, Pia shook her head, loving the feel and weight of the little girl. Despite her mother's absence in her life, Alyssa was such a darling little girl that Pia couldn't help but fall in love with her.

And every time she was with Raphael and Alyssa, Pia couldn't fight the rightness of it. Couldn't fight the longing that drowned her. As if she were the piece of the puzzle that he and the little girl were missing.

But it was ridiculous. Even if he asked her, she didn't want to be with a man like Raphael, did she? Ruthless, rigid…

Raphael leveled the strangest look back at her.

"Show me the way," Pia said in a husky voice. Only when she followed him down a quiet corridor did she realize that the house was empty and her only buffer was snoring slightly.

"I'll get her into her pj's," she said to Raphael.

Again, that intense, almost searing look.

"You can trust me with her, Raphael," she burst out, a tight knot in her throat. "I adore her."

His mouth tightened, as if she'd threatened his very safety. "My mother should have been here. She knew I had plans tonight."

"You don't want me in Alyssa's life," she said, busying herself by looking through the drawers for clean pj's. It wasn't personal, she told herself. But it was a lie.

She wanted things personal between them. She wanted him to tell her private things, things he never confided in anyone. She wanted him to tell her what his ex had done that he didn't trust any woman anymore.

She wanted their facade to be true. She wanted to be the woman that Raphael forsook any other woman for, that Raphael broke all his rules for.

"I get that. Believe me, I do. I think you're a wonderful father. She won't wake up. And you can go call your mom while I settle her down."

Instead of reassuring him, her words made him look even more forbidding. With a short stiff nod, he walked out of the room.

By the time, Pia had cleaned up and changed Alyssa, the sun was beginning to set. Making a face, she pulled her damp T-shirt off her chest.

The moment she walked into the outer lounge, Raphael stood up. His gaze took in her wet T-shirt. He scowled. "You should have called me when she woke up."

"She didn't. I had some trouble working those monstrous taps at the tub and splashed myself." It was the first time they had been alone since that episode at his sister's house. Pia wiped her damp hands on her jeans, butterflies partying in her stomach. "Didn't you have an engagement to get to? I can stay until your mother comes back."

"Teresa will be here any minute. Then I will drop you off and continue to my engagement."

Pia nodded, unease climbing up her spine. It was the way he said it. It was the way he wouldn't meet her eyes.

"Who are you meeting?" she asked. She tried for nonchalance but wasn't successful.

"It's an old friend who's in town. We have a standing engagement when she's here. I completely forgot about it. But since she's here—"

Pia's heart sank to her toes. "She? It's a woman?"

"Si."

"Is she single?"

"Si."

It was like getting blood out of stone.

"So this engagement is sort of a date?"

His silence told Pia everything she needed to know.

Walk away, a part of her screamed. *Turn your back on this, on him*, came another warning.

But dear God, she'd make herself crazy imagining all kinds of scenarios. "If it's a date, won't she talk about it later? You know, to someone who knows Gio? Wait, doesn't she know that you…you're supposed to be engaged?"

"I'm sure she's heard the gossip now."

"And yet, she called you?"

He pushed his hand through his hair roughly, his gaze never leaving hers. A sense of dread curled up in Pia's stomach. What was he saying that she wasn't understanding? God, how she loathed her lack of sophistication.

Instead of answering her, he dialed Emilio on his cell

phone, ordered him to pick up Pia, and then hung up. "It's getting late. You should be getting home."

"I don't get it. How can she want to go on a date if you're in a relationship?"

With me, she left out the pathetic lie that she was beginning to wish was true.

"It's not that kind of a date. Ava and I know each other from university. We're friends and—"

"Lovers?" She had no idea how she'd been able to say it without choking.

Their gazes collided and held, a hundred unsaid words flying in between. Finally, he nodded.

Everything fell into place. "So you're going there to just…" Heat climbed up her face. "You're going there to have sex with her?" she forced herself to say, images of him kissing some faceless woman bombarding her.

"Ava and I go way back and I just… I need to be anything but your lover right now."

Anger came to her rescue. The thought of Raphael with another woman made bile rise to her throat. "Are you that heartless?"

"Heartless?" A tightness crawled up his face, making him that arrogant stranger from the ball. "You've begun to believe your own lie, *cara mia*. I don't remember promising you anything, much less my fidelity. You mean nothing to me, Pia. You need to remember that you and I wouldn't have crossed paths if not for the fact that you're his granddaughter. *His precious princess.* And the cost of touching you is…far too high for me."

Each calculated word landed like a poisoned arrow. God, how could he hurt her like this? Why was she letting him?

She had had enough of this pathetic spectacle she was making of herself. Enough of wondering if he would ever look at her with something other than polite courtesy.

"Brutally honest, as ever. At least you're reliable. But you know what? I can't do this anymore. I—"

"You can't do what?"

"I can't pretend to be your bloody girlfriend. Frank was right. I'm not sophisticated enough for these kinds of... Find a way to call this thing off. Find a way to protect your bloody company from Giovanni's meddling. But I'm done with this, with you."

She turned and angrily swiped at her cheeks. Damn it, she refused to cry in front of him. His pity would kill her.

But she got no more than a few steps before he slammed his palm on the door. She couldn't turn. She couldn't bear to look at him anymore. "I don't understand you at all. Foolishly, I thought I was beginning to. That you were more than the ruthless, ambitious businessman that everybody calls you. What you're thinking, it's horrible, clinical."

The warmth of his body, the scent of him seeped into her back. One more step and she would be in his embrace. Oh, how she wanted to take that step, how she wanted to lose herself in him...

"You, this pretense, it's driving me crazy, don't you get it? I'm wound up so tight I can't sleep. I can't work. You're—" But she cut him off before he could say the horrid words.

"I'm ruining your life—yes, I know," she said loudly, tears knotting in her throat. "You think it's easy for me? The whispers I hear, the snide innuendoes, that the only reason you're with me is because of what Gio has. That Gio's wealth compensates for what I lack.

"It's like reliving the episode with Frank. Only, this time, I know the truth beforehand."

"Damn it, I'll knock the bastard's teeth down if I see him ever."

"Just tell me one thing. Were you lying the other day

at your sister's house? Were you just protecting me and my tender feelings? Was it the fact that you haven't been with anyone recently that made you lose control? Tell me that being with another woman while you want me doesn't bother you, and my rose-tinted glasses will come off."

Raphael couldn't answer her. He couldn't say no. It didn't matter that even the very idea of touching Ava felt like a betrayal of his own self.

Damn it, even his overnight trip to Venice, his meeting with an old friend, which should have progressed from the restaurant to her hotel room, it had taken all his wits just to get through the dinner.

All he could see in the woman who'd been a friend for years was the brittleness her two divorces had given her, the false warmth of her smile as she'd played footsie with Raphael's leg under the table, the utter lack of connection between them.

Because of the infuriating woman and her outdated ideas about affection and companionship and respect, all his old connections began to look cheap and tawdry.

She was turning his life upside down.

He owed her nothing. He needed her to see the true him. He needed her to realize that he was no hero and definitely not hers.

And yet, the words wouldn't rise to his lips.

All he could see were her big eyes that saw too much. Her lush lips. Her chest falling and rising. The raw honesty of her emotions was written across her face. So was the desire that she couldn't hide every time she looked at him. And the ease with which she was fitting into his very life. Her adoration of his child...

The remembered taste of her was a siren's call he couldn't resist. Without warning, he suddenly kissed her. Hard and hungry with not a bit of his usual finesse. He devoured her mouth with bites and licks and nips until she was moaning and arching into his touch.

"This is what you want, Pia?" he said, pulling her skirt up. Sending his hand on a foray for silky skin, even as he plunged his tongue into her sweet mouth and swallowed her yes.

How he wanted her now, here. He wanted to thrust into her wet warmth and get rid of this madness.

What magic had she woven around him?

He cupped a barely covered buttock with one hand while his other met the soft, sensitive skin of her inner thighs. Mouths tangled, he pushed aside the silky thong she wore until he could find her core.

Sweat dampened his brow. A current of electric desire pooled in his groin as he found her soft folds.

Dio mio, she was ready for him. Silky and slick against his fingers.

He swallowed her soft gasp, pressed her against the door. Pulled her leg up until she was wide-open for him.

Without giving her a moment to breathe, he set a fast rhythm with his fingers. She sobbed, she moaned, she was like a spark plug touched by the fire.

Madness filling his blood, Raphael snaked his tongue around hers and increased the pressure of his strokes.

The moment he rubbed her swollen clit in concentric circles, she broke apart. Her spasms against his fingers sent his own blood rushing south. Her soft cries pelted against his skin.

He wanted to push her hair from her damp forehead. He wanted to take her in a soft kiss. He wanted to tell her she was incredibly beautiful, that her passion would bring any man to his knees.

He did nothing of the sort.

If anything, tonight only proved how wrong they were

for each other. How dangerous she was to his control. How easily he could break her spirit.

He pushed away from her. Like the ruthless bastard that he was, he didn't even try to hold her up when her knees shook beneath her. Her eyes were closed; her face was turned away.

But he didn't miss the lone tear that tracked a path down her cheek.

"That is all I can give you, Pia. That is all I give any woman."

He walked out of that room and the house and went outside to wait for Emilio.

CHAPTER EIGHT

"HOW DARE YOU go behind my back after everything I've done for you?"

Raphael refused to look up before he finished perusing the design document as Giovanni walked into his office with all the force of a stomping elephant. The rush of affection welling up in his chest was a soothing balm against the guilt festering for the actions he'd taken.

Giovanni meant the world to him.

He had taught Raphael to aspire to bigger dreams, had spotted Raphael's unusual talent for fixing cars of any kind, believed in his talent and hard work when even his mother hadn't.

He'd been expecting this siege for a week now. From the minute he'd set about buying more and more stock in the company. Getting the members to oust Gio from the board—whose proxy had rested with Raphael all this time anyway.

If he succeeded, Gio wouldn't ever be able to bring someone like Stefano onto the board. He'd never be able to manipulate Raphael again. He'd never put Raphael in a situation where he had to face Pia again.

But of course Gio had his spies in the company just as Raphael had his at Gio's house.

Once he finished, he closed down the design software and leaned back in his seat.

"Good afternoon to you too, Giovanni," he said casually, and only then looked up to meet his gaze.

A thread of unease wrapped itself around his chest, tugging hard.

His eighty-four-year-old godfather had the stubbornness of a mule and the constitution of a boxer. And yet, his pallor was visible under the olive of his skin. Concern pushed Raphael out of his chair as Gio huffed into his office with short breaths and irately dismissed his chauffeur Emilio.

Who cast a worried glance at Raphael.

"You look like hell, Giovanni." Try as he might, he couldn't stop the concern seeping through. Emotion was a weakness that Gio would lap up.

Giovanni walked into the sitting area, his body vibrating with his famous temper. "I look like hell because my godson—the boy I taught everything—is a backstabbing cheat." A string of Italian fell from his mouth as Gio detailed all the *backstabbing* Raphael had done.

However pale he might look, Raphael didn't intend to go on the defensive. "Have you no explanation for why you are trying to push me out of my own company?"

"I'm cleaning house. I should've done it years ago."

"You're the bloody CEO, Raphael. What more could you want?"

"You and I are both aware that a quarter of the board members are always looking for ways to go behind my back. I'll not tolerate any dissent. This is my company now, Gio."

"No one would dare question your command. They know it's you who drives the stock prices higher. Your reputation is fierce. And if they crawl back to me, it's because they know you loathe them."

"I loathe them because they're not worthy of anything." Half of them had turned his father away during the hour of his need. "I'll not allow any vipers on the board."

He was deceived by the very people he trusted.

Pia's words wouldn't leave Raphael alone. In eighteen years, he'd not once looked at it that way. He'd only seen his father's actions from the perspective of a seventeen-year-old boy. But never as a man who'd been betrayed, as a man who'd been honorable until his last breath.

"Your work consumes you." He sighed. "I think at the cost of everything else. This compulsion you have to reach even higher goals…"

"It is what keeps my family in the style they're used to."

"*Si*, exactly. This wealth, retrieving your family's social standing, it's an obsession. Marco wouldn't have wanted you to sacrifice your personal happiness."

Hands clenching into fists, Raphael turned away. "I'm nothing like my father."

Gio's head jerked toward him as if Raphael had committed blasphemy. "Businesses fail, Raphael. Men make unwise investments, bad choices."

His throat raw, Raphael gave voice to the pain he had bottled for years, the complaint he hadn't let himself make even in the darkest of his nights. "He took the coward's way out. He should have been a stronger man." *For me.* Shame choked those two words.

"He adored your mother—did you know that? He spent years building his little business, trying to win her hand. But at the first sign of calamity, Portia fell apart. She blamed him. Your mother's inability to cope with the loss, the weight of your sisters' disappointments, the large unit of leeches that constitute your various uncles and aunts and cousins, and their taunts—that was what sent him to that early grave. No one believed in him anymore, Raphael, not even the woman he loved."

Raphael felt winded as if he'd been dealt a hard blow. He'd thought of his father as a coward. Instead, had his heart simply been broken? Had he given up on them because they had given up on him? Because he couldn't bear to be diminished in the eyes of the woman he loved?

His father had been a man who'd cared deeply, a man who'd loved his wife, his family from the bottom of his heart.

His vulnerability had only brought him ruin and a broken heart. "You backed me into a corner. And I fought back."

A shrewd light entered his grandfather's eyes. "How?"

"You'd hear it from my own mouth? About Pia?"

He shrugged and examined his nails. "What does my granddaughter have to do with you buying up stock?"

"*Basta!* Stefano Castillaghi, Gio? You think I'd let that bastard touch VA? Did you think I'd ever give you the chance to pull something like this again?"

"So you claimed Pia." A cat wouldn't have looked as satisfied as Gio did. That his hunch had been right made Raphael's blood boil.

"I didn't claim Pia as much as I agreed to her scheme about pretending that I did. You terrified her with your demands and your ill health. She came to me as a last resort."

Silence thundered in the air instead of the outrage he'd expected. Damn it, had Gio known that it was a pretense too?

"No one will come near her again. At least no one that cares about her and not her wealth. In the last month, all of Milan has seen how possessive you are of her. Do not think I have not seen you look at her like a starved dog stares at meat."

"*Christo*, Giovanni. Do not be crude. That is your granddaughter you speak of."

"See how protective you get of her? You might as well see the pretense through and marry her, Raphael. You want the company? It's yours. You want my share of stock that would rightfully be hers? It's yours. All I ask is that you take care of her. You watch over her when I'm gone. Marry her, Raphael."

All his bluster had been leading to this. Every move he'd made since the night of the ball had been toward this. "You know I'll never marry again."

"Pia is different from Allegra, from any other woman you've known."

"She's not my type," he said, even as the idea took root, digging into him and settling down. He forced a harshness into his voice. "She's neither beautiful nor sophisticated. She wears her heart on her sleeve. She sees too much where there's nothing."

He hadn't thought of her as anything less than intoxicating for so long. He was always on edge because his only satisfaction came from his imagination and his hand, while seeing Pia every day. While touching Pia. While her subtle perfume and body heat sneaked into his bloodstream.

Worse was the bruised look in her eyes after what he'd done at his mother's house. She barely even met his eyes anymore.

Gone was the laughter, the teasing wit, the endless questions about his past, his mother and sisters, and even Alyssa.

With one ruthless move, he'd shattered her rose-tinted glasses but he hadn't realized how much it would disturb him that he'd become less in her eyes too. He'd thought it was better to alienate her but it had backfired. And he hated himself for what he'd done to her.

"A girl with more substance than glitter is not your type, *si*." Giovanni snorted with that proud wisdom that the old thought they had over the young.

Raphael could not say it was not justified. This one time.

He had gone for the glitter once before, had come away burned. Allegra was all polished veneer with no strength beneath. His mother had once been called the beauty of Milan. She was not cruel or fickle like his Allegra had been. She even loved him and his sisters, in her own way. But Gio was right, she possessed nothing of substance. She had had nothing to offer his father when he'd needed her the most.

And Pia was as different from his mother or Allegra as he himself was from his father. He would never trust anyone like his father had done. He would never need a woman's strength like Marco had done. He just didn't have that kind of vulnerability.

Would it be so bad though?

Giovanni, sensing victory, went in for the kill shot. "You're a fool if you don't see that I offer everything you want, Raphael." He stood up, and again, Raphael was hit with how old and frail—no, how ill Gio looked. "But I'll not have you chasing her away."

Shock hounded away concern. Damn it, his priorities were all skewed. "What are you talking about?"

"She's talking of returning to the States for a short trip. That she…whatever it is, it's because of you. You owe me this, Raphael. You owe me the peace I would get knowing that Pia is safe in your hands. Before—"

Raphael never got a chance to reply, for Giovanni collapsed midway through the sentence. Heart jumping into his throat, Raphael barely caught him before Gio hit the ground.

And while he watched the paramedics carry Gio out, Raphael knew everything had changed. With his attraction to Pia getting out of hand every single day, with Giovanni's mad schemes spilling over into his health, with the sharks that would forever circle Pia whatever measure he took, there was only one solution.

His fate was sealed and so was Pia's and he would be the one to make the stars fall from her eyes.

Because he could never give her what she wanted, and now he would be preventing her from finding it with anyone else.

CHAPTER NINE

RAPHAEL'S APARTMENT WAS located in a trendy, upscale area of Milan's fashion district. The lights and fanfare of the canal district were visible from the tenth-floor apartment. Yet there was utter privacy too.

After the harrowing week at the hospital with Gio, the quiet and the ultraluxury didn't sit well with Pia. Both of them had spent the whole week in the hospital, keeping a silent vigil by the side of the man they adored.

She hadn't argued when he had commanded that she would rest at his apartment for the night.

They both knew she needed the break. At least they'd learned that the heart attack had been a mild one, and that Gio's diet was the primary culprit.

She poured herself a glass of Chianti from the wine rack and walked through the open, contemporary plan. She wished Raphael had stayed but he'd barely showed her to a room before he'd made his escape.

Maybe he was afraid she'd pounce on him again.

A harsh laugh escaped her as she remembered asking him if he was also afraid that she was stealing his share from Gio's wealth. Clearly, Raphael had his own fortune to manage and didn't need Gio's. She explored the steel and chrome kitchen, the state-of-the-art gym, two balconies, a humongous study with a dark mahogany table in the center with a picture of Alyssa and floor-to-ceiling bookshelves with mostly books on automobiles and engineering, a sitting room and two guest bedrooms.

She took a long shower in the attached bathroom of the guest room, only realizing then that she didn't have any fresh clothes. Delving into the closet provided a white dress shirt, pressed and folded and a couple of packages of women's new underwear. The bra was two sizes two big. Trying hard to rein in her riotous curiosity, Pia donned the underwear and the shirt which fell to her thighs. And knew it was Raphael's.

Instant comfort surrounded her at the faint scent of him. But it was unbearable too. Because nothing had changed.

She still wanted him. And not just for a quick screw, as he had called it. Even with things awkward between them, she couldn't help but soak in the warmth and strength of his presence over the last week.

Efficient and ruthless as ever, he'd chased away the hordes of Gio's relatives that had descended on the hospital with one look. When one had called him a backstabber, Raphael had simply shrugged it away.

He'd been fierce, as if he could hold Gio to this earth by the sheer force of his will. He had let her borrow his strength, his conviction. He'd even made her smile when he'd snarled that the old goat was far from done manipulating the pair of them.

But Pia knew him now. She saw what no one else did under that ruthless exterior. Gio's attack had shaken him. She could feel something eating away at him, not that he would talk about it. And least of all with her.

He'd made it perfectly clear he wanted nothing to do with her.

As she sank into a deep slumber, Pia could think of no other man she'd want by her side protecting her.

No man she wanted to know more. No man she wanted to risk her heart with.

* * *

Raphael had just finished his quickly put together 2:00 a.m. dinner, and poured himself a glass of red wine when he heard soft steps behind him.

Dannazione, he had tried not to wake her…

Closing his eyes, he stayed where he was, with his back to her. But he could see her reflected in the glass panes in front of him.

Clad in his white shirt, which fell tantalizingly to her thighs, she was rubbing sleep-mussed eyes behind him. He should have trusted his instincts and stayed at the hospital.

But he'd given his answer to Gio tonight and the knowledge of it was like the continual strike of a spark plug to fuel.

"Raphael?" Her husky voice floated toward him across the kitchen.

Swallowing the last of his wine as if it were water, he turned.

Her hair created a vaguely golden halo around her face, her long, long legs—toned and nicely tanned, bare from her thighs down—hit him hard. All these days, he had watched her, wanted her, with a desire that grew stronger by the minute. He'd held off because he had no intention of taking her when he didn't want a relationship. No intention of being roped into anything he didn't want.

Now there was nothing to hold him back. Nothing to stop him from possessing her.

"Sorry I disturbed you. Go back to sleep," he said, not quite meeting her eyes.

She shook her head and a mass of hair fell forward. It was an utterly feminine gesture he was sure she didn't even realize she'd made. He kept the marble island between them, as if physical distance could somehow negate the hot pounding of blood in his veins.

"I had already woken up. For a few minutes, I couldn't

remember where and why." She rubbed her eyes with the back of her hand.

That she felt so comfortable with him to stand in his apartment in the middle of the night, half-dressed, when she'd always been like a skittish horse around him, it denoted a level of trust he'd never wanted. "And then I had this sick, twisted feeling in my tummy. I thought I had lost Gio and you were… Then it all came crashing down and I jerked awake."

She leaned back against the wall, which made the shirt pull up. Another inch of toned thigh was displayed and his body tightened another notch. Her pose made those small high breasts of hers jut forward.

Alluring and sexy and like a gift for him to unwrap. He swallowed hard.

He needed to go to bed and so did she. Separately. And yet he couldn't help asking, "I did what in your ghastly nightmare, Pia? What could be so much worse than walking away when you were trembling from the orgasm I gave you?"

"You were screaming at me that it was all my fault. That I… I killed Gio."

Reaching her, careful not to touch her, he said, "You've had a strenuous week."

She dragged her fingers over her face, leaving impressions, "Oh, God, what are we going to do?"

"We're just going to sleep for about forty-eight hours." The image of sleeping with her—their limbs tangled, her lithe body pressed against hers—hit him with a fierce longing.

"I couldn't sleep with all these thoughts swirling in my head. Would you tell me the truth if I asked you, Raphael?"

He instantly became wary. "If I can," he said reluctantly.

He'd always been the protective type with his sisters and even with Allegra. After everything she'd done, it was he who had finally dragged her to the rehabilitation program. Whether he believed she'd get through it was a different matter.

But with Pia, he was aware of all of his shortcomings. It was as if she constantly held up a mirror for him and he couldn't bear to see what it would show. He didn't want to hurt her. He didn't want to do anything that would break her pure spirit.

He couldn't stay away from her either. Not anymore. Suddenly, he felt as if he could breathe again.

"Did I cause Gio's attack?"

"Pia—"

"No, please. You don't know. But I…a few hours before the attack, I told him I wanted to…to take a trip."

He stayed silent, not trusting himself to pour out the whole terrible argument he'd had with Gio.

He had been pushed and shoved to this step by Gio, by circumstance, even unknowingly by Pia, but he wasn't going to doom their relationship from the beginning.

Pia, he knew, didn't give two hoots about VA or the stock or Gio's fortune. The last thing she needed was to know what Gio had offered Raphael.

"I wanted to get away for a while. I thought I could go back to the States and tie up some loose ends. I told him it was just temporary—"

"Because you wanted to avoid me after what I did?" This more than anything angered him. "Did you think of how Gio felt at that? Do you always run away if it gets hard, Pia? Isn't that what you did when that man cheated you?"

She paled as if he'd struck below the belt. She tilted her chin in that stubborn way of hers. "I wasn't running away. I needed a break. It was hard to be around you knowing that every minute you spent with me was under sufferance."

"That's—"

"Please, no lies. The one thing I know I'll always have from you is honesty. Don't take that away from me now. You can barely stand to look at me when we're together." Pain flashed through her eyes, the raw intensity of it skewering Raphael where he stood. "You… I forced you to give me what you didn't want to. I clearly can't take a message."

"*Dio mio!* Is that what you think? When will you understand that—?"

"You've made it clear that I'm nothing but another millstone of responsibility around your neck. Another person who's dependent on you, another duty you perform even though you resent the hell out of it.

"I'm not angry with you. I see all the responsibilities you shoulder, how seriously you take them. I just can't bear to be one of them. I don't know how to make Gio believe that I can look after myself."

He reached her and ran a finger over her jaw. She had such soft skin and he wondered if she was like that all over. "And what if saying no to you was the hardest thing I ever did. That even if you hadn't waylaid me, I wouldn't have been able to go through with it with… Ava. That every time I close my eyes, I feel that velvety, swollen center of yours between my fingers. That every time I hear your voice, it reminds me of your soft moans and throaty cries. That every morning, I wake up with an erection and that I get myself off like an uncouth teenager by picturing you bare and writhing beneath me, begging me to take you." She stared at him with such wide eyes, such naked lust that Raphael was tempted to take her right there.

He brought her hand to his abdomen and then down below where his hard-on was throbbing painfully. "I can't breathe your scent without getting hard like this. Do you believe me now, *tesoro*?"

Liquid longing filled her eyes. She bent her forehead to his shoulder and breathed hard while her hand shaped him.

Raphael buried his face in her hair, something more than lust driving him. Tenderness, he realized. He wanted this. He wanted her. And not just for one night or for a short affair, as he'd thrown at her cheaply. The thought of Pia ever sharing this intimacy with any other man drove him out of his mind.

She was his, whether she knew it right now or not. "For the first time in my life, I want to be selfish. I want to take you for myself and damn the consequences. You don't know how many times I had to remind myself that you're my godfather's granddaughter."

Pia stepped back, heart pounding a hundred times a second. She could still feel the shape of him in her palm, could feel the tension radiate from him. Stark and etched with want of her, only for her, he was the most beautiful man she'd ever known. "But I'm not just his granddaughter. I'm *Pia*, Raphael. And I wish—"

He covered her mouth with his palm and pulled her to him. "Pia, look at me. Listen to me, *cara mia*." Roughly, he pushed his hand through his hair. "Sophistication or beauty or whatever you think you lack—none of the women I know could hold a candle to you." A frustrated hiss left his mouth. "It is exactly why it's hard to take you."

The words came so simply, so easily then. "But you're not taking, Raphael. I'm giving myself. Isn't that my decision?"

A hard curse fell from his mouth, harsh in the silence. Clasping her cheeks, Raphael swooped his mouth down on hers.

Hard. Hungry. Hot.

Thumb on her chin, he pressed and Pia opened with a deep groan that reverberated through every nerve ending.

She'd been dreaming of this fevered desire between them, of seeing that dark glitter in his eyes, of the handsome, gorgeous, sophisticated Raphael wanting her beyond any other woman.

All the reasons she shouldn't be desperately clinging to him were reduced to ashes. All the misgivings and doubts she'd harbored about feeling so much for him evaporated into mist by the heat between them. The rasp of his hair-roughened wrists under her palms, the rapid beat of his pulse against her skin, short-circuited her last rational thought.

His thumbs pressing oh, so firmly against the corners of her mouth, again and again, he dipped his mouth over hers, never resting, never fully giving her what she wanted.

On the next dip, he swiped the seam of her lips with his tongue and Pia melted into his body. Her hands rose to his shoulders, pleading with her touch. Wrapped around his nape, conveying her need for more, she sank blissfully into the rough swathe of his hair, an intimacy she'd been craving for so long.

A fine tremor ran through his body. "Let me taste you, *cara mia*. Let me show you how much I want this, no, how much I *need* you."

Pia opened her mouth under his, his words lighting a fire in her very blood.

The taste of him exploded in her mouth. Her lips stung when he rubbed his against hers and then cooled them off with a lick. His teeth sank into the cushion of her lower mouth, sending sharp arrows of pleasure down her body, and then he soothed the hurt with a puff of air.

Again and again, he plunged his tongue inside her mouth, a silky slide against her own, an erotic invitation to play with him one moment, a divine promise the next.

"Raphael, I...oh, please," she sobbed when he pulled his mouth away from hers.

Tall and arrogant, he stared down at her with glittering

eyes. His nostrils flared, his customarily mocking mouth swollen lush.

She would have dropped to the floor like a puddle of feelings if his hands hadn't anchored her. Even there, his hold was less tender and more aggressively possessive.

A sharp laugh fell from his mouth. "I can give no sweet words. I will make no promises, Pia. Do you still want me?"

CHAPTER TEN

KNEES SHAKING, PIA drank him in. His black shirt unbuttoned to his chest, jeans hung low on his hips, he was a
dark fantasy come to life. His rough hair stood up, thanks
to her fingers, but it was his penetrating stare that took
her breath away.

The depth of desire in it singed her skin.

His gaze was more questioning and combative than
anything her imagination could have conjured.

But this was Raphael, so ruthless and yet so tender at
times. There was nothing sweet and romantic about him.
Nothing sensitive and cajoling about him.

His gaze swept over the naked length of her legs, the
pulse skittering wildly at her neck. Her sex clenched, hard
and sudden, at the masculine possessiveness written across
every inch of his proud face. "No words, *cara mia*?"

And the truth of him as he stood there, as he stared at
her with absolute desire etched into taut features, darken-
ing those deep-seated eyes was more real, more telling than
any sweet words he could have given her. She hadn't felt a
millionth of this wonder, this ever-present thrum before.

Months with Frank couldn't measure up to a moment
with Raphael.

"I know you, Raphael, and I want you," she said simply.

With rigid movements that spoke of his control, he
picked her up.

Pia wrapped her hands around his neck, touching the

base of his head with the tips of her fingers. Every inch of him was a pleasure point to her seeking, searching fingers.

She hid her face in his chest. Heat from his skin filtered through his shirt, and warmed her cheek. The thundering beat of his heart matched hers and calmed something inside of her.

Her breath fled her body afresh when he crossed into his bedroom to Raphael's vast bed and laid her down. Dark gray sheets and curtains made the room utterly masculine. His gaze drinking her in, he pulled his shirt off in one smooth movement.

The strong column of his throat and the width of his shoulders made her chest rise and fall. Taut, gleaming olive skin stretched tight over lean musculature greeted her. Sparse hair covered his defined chest, arrowing down over his abdomen and disappearing into his jeans.

Low-slung, those pants revealed narrow, defined hips.

But it was the front of his pants, showing unmistakable evidence of his desire, that caught Pia's rabid attention. His shape and size was clearly identifiable even like that.

A rush of wetness slid between the folds of her sex. Pia crossed and uncrossed her legs, a restless slithering in her skin as she heard his rough exhale.

"What does looking at me do to you?"

She jerked her head up. Heat built in her chest and began flowing up her neck and cheeks. His fingers fluttered over the waistband of his jeans and intense curiosity thrummed in her blood.

She was about to work up the courage to touch him when he spread her legs shamefully wide and stepped between them. The naked glory of his chest muted any words Pia was capable of uttering.

With a hard pressure, Raphael pulled at the base of her neck. "What happened when you looked at my arousal,

Pia?" He breathed the question into the crook where her neck met her shoulder.

Wrapping her hands around his midriff, she hid her face in his chest again. Everything she was feeling, everything he said, this moment so thick with desire, it was such a profusion of sensations like she had never imagined. "Please, Raphael... I can't speak it. I can't..."

With a hard laugh that sent shivers down her spine, he took her mouth in a ravishing kiss that plundered beyond just her lips. It was as if with every kiss, he was stealing away parts of her.

Pulling away from the languorous weight of his kiss, she tilted his head down so she could look at his face. His lips were swollen this time. His nostrils flared, his jaw so rigid that Pia caressed it tenderly.

She drank him in, from the small scar on his upper lip to the small mole near his eyebrow.

"I'm sorry I... I can't give words to what I feel. I..."

"Nessuno." A forbidding look descended in his eyes. "Never be sorry for what you are, Pia. Not with me. Never with me. I forbid it."

His thunderous expression made her smile. His arrogance that he could just forbid her from feeling stuff! "But I heard that men like women to be adventurous in bed." She loved being with him in this moment. The promise of their near-naked bodies was heady, her desire for him thrilling. But it was the peek inside of Raphael's head, this insight she was getting into the core of the man that Pia relished the most.

His fingers gripped the collared edges of her shirt, "I do not care what you heard or were told, Pia. Your diffidence only makes me realize how much you must want to let me do this."

She frowned. "Do what, Raphael?"

The ripping of the buttons on her shirt was the answer to her question.

She gasped at the coldness of his palms as they cupped her small breasts. He pushed her and she bowed back, her trust in him complete. His mouth buried between her breasts, Raphael punctuated his kisses with words. "What I want from you, what will pleasure me, I will teach you, *si*?"

"I want to please you," she whispered softly.

His eyes flared hotter. "You will." Pursing his mouth, he nipped her flesh, leaving a wet trail. "And what will pleasure you, what will send you over the edge, we will discover it together."

"*Si*," she said, floating on a cloud of sensation and never wanting to come down.

In return for her surrender—or was it reward?—he separated the edges of the shirt and pushed it off her shoulders. It hung at her elbows, baring her to his drinking eyes.

They darkened impossibly as he stared at her small breasts with their plump nipples painfully distended.

No man had ever seen her like that and Pia couldn't bear the potency of the moment, of things that she hadn't even considered. Of things she had already given over to Raphael by giving him this intimacy.

He pressed a reverent kiss to her midriff, his large hands easily spanning her waist, then a trail of hot, wet kisses up and down, from her navel to her pubic bone.

The cool sheets were a welcome contrast against her burning skin as he busied his fingers with her breasts.

He licked the aching tips as if he were testing their rigidness, their plumpness. Soft flicks, long, leisurely flicks, his gaze telling her without words how much he liked the taste of her. Gauging with those piercing eyes what she liked.

Pia arched her chest into his mouth, pressed her fingers into his nape to keep his mouth at her breast, and then flushed at her own shameless abandon. Eyes dark, Raphael noted it. She closed her eyes.

Every sensation was magnified a million times. A running kaleidoscope of colors burst behind her closed lids, as if her every sense was on the verge of explosion, of new birth.

The rough, sucking sounds he made with his lips, the Italian that emerged from his mouth drove Pia wilder, hotter, wetter between her thighs.

And suddenly his mouth was gone, leaving her desolate. Her eyes flew open, her breath serrated.

His eyes gleamed with possessive wickedness, a feral satisfaction. "I wish I could show your face to you now, *mia cara*. Your eyes are so wide that they drown your face, your mouth is pink and swollen from my kisses, your skin is trembling and marred already with my attentions…

"Shall I carry you to the mirror, Pia?" His eyes held hers, a thousand unsaid desires in them, dark fantasies she could see them both drowning in. There would be nothing of her that he didn't touch, that he didn't take. Nothing he didn't own. "Shall I show you what I see? How beautiful you are?"

She opened her eyes, saw his nostrils flare. And blushed hot when she sensed the scent of her arousal thick in the air. A muscled leg thrown over her thighs, he leaned over on an elbow.

"There is nothing shameful about what you feel for me, *tesoro*. About what you need from me." His mouth closed over the turgid nipple and pulled, and Pia jerked. She clutched her thighs tight as sensations zoomed and coalesced there. As if there was a direct connection between her nipples and the shockingly wet place between her thighs.

His broad palm descended between her thighs and when

Pia squeezed them again under another pull of his wicked mouth over her nipple, he was there, giving her the pressure she craved.

His fingers opened her up, a wicked smile curving his lips. Holding her gaze captive, his sculpted mouth blew on her hot, wet nipple, and his fingers drew mesmerizing circles over her folds, stroking, petting, spreading the dampness.

And then his finger was inside her, stretching her.

Spine bucking off the bed, Pia gasped at the sudden invasion.

"You've never done this before?" he asked softly, as if he was afraid to scare her off.

Pia couldn't even answer, for every ounce of her brain's rationale was busy processing the caresses of his thumb. Somehow, dear God, he'd found that spot that seemed like her entire being was centered there even as he pumped in and out with his other fingers.

Pressure drew her body tight, like a bow stretched too much. "I would like an answer, *mia bella*."

Pia shook her head frantically chasing the speed she needed, arching her lower body into his hand. "No. *Per favore*, Raphael…"

"Anything you want, *bella*."

And then his thumb settled there, pressing and stroking mindlessly until Pia writhed against that touch, frantic in her own skin.

It was science, it was hundreds of years of evolution and yet what Raphael did to her felt like magic. As if what happened between them couldn't be explained away by a theory.

The world dissolved into pure sensation as he stroked her just the way her body needed it. Unbearable pleasure broke over her in cresting waves, building one over the other, throwing her out into the space and then gathering her back into herself, but a different version. And when she fell back to the ground, Raphael was there to catch her with his warmth, his endearments and praises, with his arms.

Desperate to keep touching him, desperate to keep the connection even as those powerful tremors in her lower belly ebbed, Pia pushed back a lock of hair that had fallen forward onto his forehead. Realizing the possessiveness of the action, she stilled.

"Touch me, *bella*. Anywhere you want."

With a sigh, Pia greedily ran her fingers over his taut form.

He prowled over her on all fours and she reveled in the feral hunger stamped over every tight muscle, every jutting bone. She wanted to shatter his control. She wanted him as delirious with pleasure and need as she was. She slid her questing fingers over the rough silk of his bare back, loving the grooved line of his spine. He smiled against her neck, interrupting the kiss he'd been pressing there.

Dark eyes held hers captive, a stark honesty to them. "You wear everything on your face, you tell me in beautiful, honest words what I do to you, your body sings for me when I so much as brush the tip of my finger against it…" Slowly, as if he were a jungle cat, he shed his pants and boxers.

How had he known what she had needed to hear? How did he know that she wanted to please him, if it was the last thing she ever did?

He brought his body down over hers until they were flush from shoulder to thigh to foot.

Pia grasped his back with both hands, drowning in a surfeit of sensations—his angular hips cradling hers, muscular thighs pushing her into the bed, his hands kneading hips and cupping her buttocks. "Do you see how desperately I need you?"

In reply, she slid her hands to his hips. Hard muscles,

velvet rough skin, hair-sprinkled limbs so different from her own and yet so perfectly complementary and then there was a litany of Italian from his mouth as she touched and stroked everything. She kneaded his buttocks shamelessly, traced his flank with questing fingers, touched and stroked every inch of tightly honed muscle.

And with each innocent touch of hers, he turned harder, and tighter, his rock-hard erection swelling in the groove of her thighs. The hard, velvet length, the sheer size of him made her mouth dry.

Her heart picked up pace as he kissed the rim of her ear and whispered, "Spread your legs for me, Pia."

Head bowed into his chest, Pia did. A jolt of sensation spread outward when he rubbed his shaft along her sex. Her breathing hitched to a faster rhythm and soon Raphael's joined hers. His one hand clasped both of hers above her head while with his other hand, he rubbed himself in her wetness.

"You're so perfect for me, Pia." Another slide, another shiver. Another sigh from her mouth. "As if you were made for me."

Slow shivers built in her spine at the slick slide of him against her. Even oversensitized from her climax, a whisper of sensation pooled again at her sex. And then, suddenly, he was inside her in a hard yet somehow smooth, unsuspecting movement.

Her spine bucking, Pia gasped at the invasion. Nails digging into his shoulders, she tried to buck him off but he remained lodged inside her.

It was as if there was a hot poker inside her. His body incredibly rigid, his muscles tense, Raphael whispered words against her temple, her eyes, her nose. Fervent promises to make it better, feverish endearments as if he couldn't bear to hurt her. "Look at me, *cara mia*. I promise you the worst is done."

Pia opened her eyes, terrified of showing him what she was feeling. Of making him think she didn't want this, didn't want him. But such a warm smile dawned in his eyes that it drove away her misgivings. "You're the science teacher, *si*?"

Her sex spasmed as if to remind her and he sank in a little more. "I'm sorry, Raphael. I... I didn't mean to..."

"No sorries between us, Pia. Not when I've to hurt you a little more before I can give you pleasure."

Tiny beads of sweat gathered on his forehead. His skin was like damp velvet under her fingers. He looked as if he was hewn from some rough stone, so stark were the bones of his face. He was exercising immense control, Pia realized, and felt like a big coward. "I don't care how much it hurts, please move."

"Kiss me, *cara mia*. Like you mean it," he added with a taunt.

Unclenching her fists, Pia took his mouth in a soft kiss. Hands in his hair, she pulled him down, angling his mouth the way she wanted it. It was the first time he let her drive a kiss between them. Liking the way he growled under her touch, Pia slid her tongue inside his mouth in a silky sweep that made him groan deep in his throat.

She peppered his jaw with urgent kisses, licked his neck like a cat, and then dug her teeth into the groove of his shoulder. A timely epithet flew from his mouth even as his hip jerked, sending sensation spiraling down her spine.

And just like that, slowly, her body got used to his invasion inside of her. She softened and stretched around him, a slow pulse of pleasure spiraling out from there. When he moved within her in soft, slow strokes, it was as if there was a poem of pleasure being written inside her. As if she were being taken apart and remade again within Raphael's hands.

Trusting some unknown instincts, Pia wrapped her legs around his back and he groaned his pleasure.

She'd always wondered at the raw intimacy, at the lack of inhibition that had to go hand in hand with sex, had always cringed at revealing herself like that. Yet nothing in the world felt more natural than being beneath Raphael, than meeting his eyes and sharing the pregnant moment, nothing more perfect than the sweaty shift and slide of their bodies against each other with pleasure billowing in their wake.

His hands under her buttocks, he lifted her until every hard stroke rubbed against her clitoris. Soon, the pressure built again until Pia came in a cataclysm of pleasure.

And he watched her, every nuance in her face, as if he owned her. With an intensity that sent aftershocks through her pelvis.

"You feel like heaven, *tesoro*, and I have to move," he said in apology.

Pia touched her fingers to his forehead, and the lock of hair that was always falling down. "I'm yours, Raphael," she whispered, her heart overflowing.

Her name on his lips, her body held down tight, Raphael thrust faster and deeper inside her. She felt his spine lock. With a guttural cry that she'd forever remember, he spent himself inside her.

With his hands tight on her hips, his heavy weight pressing onto her, her body felt as if it was being thrown around by a storm. Her breathing matching his rough rhythm, Pia couldn't let go of him.

Morning light was beginning to seep in through the curtains, bathing their bodies in an orange glow. He was hard and heavy over her, but deliciously so. Hadn't she heard some of her colleagues whisper that men always pulled away after they were *done*? That they didn't like clingy women?

She very much wanted to cling to Raphael, to breathe in the musky scent they made together, to soak in the wonderful warmth of his body. But she didn't want him to think she was getting all gooey and sentimental over what they had done, even though it was exactly what she was feeling.

Her heart dipped as he moved away from her. She scrunched her eyes tight and felt his eyes on her back. The sheets slithered around her, and she heard his soft tread on the floor. A sharp ache—one that rivaled the one in her body—filled her heart.

Raphael wasn't given to tenderness or sweet words, she told herself.

She didn't know how long it was—it felt like an eternity—before she felt him tugging the duvet from her tight fingers.

"Raphael, what are you—"

"Shh, let me."

When his hand reached her thighs with a cold washcloth, Pia flushed. "Raphael you don't have to—"

"*Si*, I do." His gaze held hers, a wealth of words that he wouldn't say in it.

Looking away from him, heat crawling over her cheeks, Pia gave herself over. With a gentleness that brought tears to her eyes, he finished cleaning her up. And then he was back in the bed before she could arm herself against the onslaught of emotions crowding her.

A warm glow fanned out in the regions of her heart. She ran her fingertips over the back of his hand, absently stroking the veins. The scent of their intimacy was a warm blanket around them.

The sudden realization that she could spend eternity like this hit her like an electric charge to the heart. He didn't want eternity. God, he didn't even want a few months.

"Turn around and face me."

When she stiffened, he pressed until she was on her

back. The smallest movement made her aware of the soreness between her thighs.

With his hawk-like gaze, Raphael caught it. A furrow came on between his brows. "Do you still hurt?"

Pia blushed, and then shook her head. Then she saw the uncharacteristic hesitation in his eyes. From everything she'd learned about him, she knew Raphael didn't do intimacy.

He tipped his head and took her mouth in a soft, tender kiss that made her chest ache. She would never tire of his kisses or that look he got that said he wanted to kiss her. He pulled her closer to his naked body and tucked his arm neatly under her bare breasts. Pia stiffened and tried to pull the duvet up.

A tussle resulted. She huffed. He growled. They made a compromise and pulled the duvet up over his arm while his hand cupped her breast.

"I like having you in my bed like this, knowing that whatever everyone else sees, I know the real, passionate you, *exploding like a firework*." He said it softly as if to let her get used to it. "Only me, *cara mia*." A long sigh left her and Pia settled into his embrace.

"Raphael, we need to talk—"

"No, what you and I need is sleep. Hours and hours of it. We'll only wake up when you're not sore and I can be inside you again. Until then, sleep, *tesoro*."

And just like that, Pia fell asleep.

The loud peal of Raphael's cell phone startled Pia awake. It took her a few seconds to orient herself but the soreness between her legs brought back awareness of the previous night.

She felt Raphael's kiss against her shoulder, and then his groan as the phone started again. The sheet held tightly with her fingers, she turned around to face him. Sleep mussed, he was even more gorgeous in the morning sunlight.

With a gentleness that stole her breath, he pressed his thumb against her lower lip. "You are good?"

She nodded, unable to find words that could sum up the glorious feeling in her chest. And then, because she knew he couldn't ignore whoever it was indefinitely, and because she didn't know when she'd get a chance again, she pressed a kiss at the hollow of his throat and licked his skin.

He groaned, kissed her hard, and then picked up the phone.

Within seconds, the gentle lover disappeared.

With two rapid-fire sentences he finished the call, whipped out of the bed and padded, utterly naked, into the bathroom.

Hearing the shower run, she quickly pulled his T-shirt on and sneaked down the corridor into the other bedroom. She'd barely finished her shower and pulled on another of his shirts when he walked in, a scowl on his face.

His jet-black hair was wet and dripping. Undone shorts hung low on his hips. Pia swallowed the jolt of lust that hit her low in her pelvis.

Before she could blink, he picked her up in his arms and dropped her on the bed in his own room. "I told you we're going to sleep around the clock."

Pia laughed and pushed her wet hair out of her face. She didn't know whether to be mad or glad about his possessiveness. "I just… I've never been in a relationship like this before and with you everything's muddied." She smiled when he joined her on the bed and sat up with her tucked between his legs. "I didn't want to assume."

"This is not an affair, *si*? What it is, we'll figure out later."

Turning in his arms, she kissed his mouth full on. It

was a good minute before she let him go and by then they were both breathing hard.

"Raphael, who was that on the phone?"

"My lawyer. He's heard from Allegra now that she's out of the clinic."

"Your ex is out? How is she?"

"Apparently, she worked through the entire program, is certified to be drug-free and has her addictions under control, no boyfriends in tow, and is desperate to see Alyssa."

Pia wanted to ask for more information, dying to know about the woman who had once worn his ring. She rubbed her finger, and then dropped it when she realized what she was doing. "I heard your mother say she was extremely beautiful."

She cringed the moment the words were out but Raphael barely seemed to note the wistful tone in her voice.

"She's extremely beautiful, the life of every party," he replied with a faraway gaze, "and every man she knew wanted to possess her. I had the biggest bank account among the fools who pursued her and so she chose me."

"You can't believe she chose you just for that," she said, shocked by the depth of his cynicism. "You're a very—" He arched his brow and she flushed. "You know your appeal, Raphael. Modesty doesn't suit you."

"It was my pocket and my power that attracted Allegra. Not that my looks didn't help. Actions speak louder than words however much she professed to love me. All her behavior, that I was too besotted to see then, proved how much she cared for the status of being Raphael Mastrantino's wife and not at all for me and our marriage."

"So you have no culpability at all for its failure?"

"Not everyone wants to shoulder blame when it's not theirs. Frank took advantage of you. It's not your fault."

"But you loved her, didn't you? When they think I can't hear them, or maybe because they want me to hear it, people dissect your marriage. They talk about how you pursued Allegra for three years. They call it the match of the decade."

Trust Pia to drill down to the matter.

There was never judgment in Pia's tone. He wrapped his arms around her and pulled her tighter against him. He knew himself and yet every time Pia delved deeper, he found something new.

Not always good things, but things he hadn't known.

Jaw tight, Raphael pored over her question.

Had he loved Allegra?

Not that he'd had eyes for anyone but his stunning ex. He had been thinking with something other than his head.

Drunk on his success with Vito Automobiles, puffed up with power, he'd decided she was the perfect candidate long before she had set her sights upon him. He had pulled his family from scandalous ruin and bankruptcy and all that had been missing was the perfect society wife to complete his ascent.

"No, I didn't love her. And in hindsight, I wreaked even more damage on her than her mother had done with her affairs and her neglect. I should have never married her. She needed someone softer, kinder and I...all I wanted from her was a trophy wife."

He laid his head back against the headboard. *Christo*, of all the times to realize his faults. He couldn't soften toward his ex now.

"Isn't it good for Alyssa that her mother's worked through the program?" came Pia's tentative voice.

He shrugged. "It doesn't matter. I forgave her when she had affairs behind my back. I forgave her when she lied to me about—"

A hard gleam entered his eyes. But Pia was beginning to see beneath that hardness. Beginning to understand that

Raphael felt things deeply. More than even he understood. That he was just good at burying it all.

She pressed her face into his chest, feeling an overwhelming tenderness for him. And waited.

"I found her high at the house once with Alyssa barely a month old. Gio and her mother, even mine, they all pled her case. They said that addiction is like a sickness, that she didn't know any better. But she's an adult who's responsible for her actions. I won't forgive that. She's not getting her hands on my daughter in this lifetime."

"That sounds so final," Pia said, before she could stop. "Are you protecting Alyssa? Or punishing Allegra? Is it even about Allegra, or is it about your father?"

He looked so furious then that Pia braced herself for a cutting reply. She'd gone too far. Worse, they both knew she'd unwittingly struck on the truth.

"Only you could look beneath my anger for a junkie ex, Pia."

Something in his tone tugged at her. She longed to wrap her arms around him and hold him. To tell him that caring for someone was not weakness. That he wasn't invincible, whatever the world led him to believe. "I just… I think you've never forgiven your father for what he did."

He looked away but didn't deny it. "He had been my hero for so long. And then suddenly, one day he was gone, without a word."

And he'd left Raphael alone with a burden that would crush most seventeen-year-old boys. A burden he'd used to fuel his own ambition. A burden that his mother had continued to put on him.

"Raphael—"

"It's all in the past, Pia."

He took her mouth in a hard kiss that sent little waves of pleasure through her body. When he pulled her beneath him, when he rocked into her with the utmost tenderness because he was worried she'd be sore, when he kissed her mouth with warm languorous strokes, she gave herself over to him.

He loved her slowly, gently this time, as if she were breakable in his rough hands. He told her in sweet Italian what she did to him. But as their climaxes hurled them into ecstasy, as he tucked her under his arm, an ache unlike any she'd ever known settled in her chest.

Raphael might think it was in the past, but the mark was still there.

The anger, the hurt, were both still there buried under a hard shell.

He would never let himself weaken, never care again.

Pia knew it as surely as she did that she felt something more than attraction for him. Something more than admiration. And the scariest part was that she didn't know how to stop it.

CHAPTER ELEVEN

PIA DIDN'T SEE Raphael for another two weeks.

He wanted her. But whether he'd have acted on it if he hadn't been shaken by Gio's sudden heart attack, if he hadn't been vulnerable, was a doubt that gnawed at her constantly.

She was more aware of her body now than she had ever been before—aware that anytime she thought of them in that huge bed, her sex became damp and her breasts tingled; aware that anytime she caught even a hint of that aqua-based cologne her skin prickled; aware that when she touched herself when she was showering or when she was finding sleep hard to come by, her body ached for a more purposeful, knowing touch. Ached for him.

He hadn't forgotten her, that was for sure.

Because for every day she hadn't seen him, he had sent her flowers, a diamond bracelet by an up-and-coming designer whose pieces had year-long waiting lists, so Gio had informed her. She was determined to return it, but then came a brand-new coffeemaker with endless capsule refills because she'd been complaining that Italian coffee was too strong for her. And then one day, the present that had her heart thumping against her rib cage arrived: a high-end set of carving tools and a particular type of wood that she'd told him she couldn't source anywhere in the world.

Her heart warmed at the thoughtfulness of his gifts,

highlighting the contrast from when it had only been a pretense.

She didn't want things with Raphael to be over. She wanted more of his kisses and his hot caresses, his warm smile that only she brought out, and just more time with him.

She wanted a relationship with him.

But after the second week of still no Raphael, mild resentment and a gnawing anxiety settled on her. Especially when his mother took it upon herself to visit Pia and slyly let it drop that Raphael was dealing with matters relating to Allegra, who had briefly visited Alyssa two days ago.

More than once, Pia caught a hint of suggestion from Portia as to how hard Raphael had worked to build Vito Automobiles to what it was today. And how much Gio himself owed Raphael.

All she cared about was that he'd been so close and hadn't dropped by to even say hello.

At least her application to a prestigious online university to get her master's degree in education had been accepted—a dream of hers for so long. No sooner had she received the email than he had sent her a brand-new laptop, a box of chocolates, a pair of her prescription glasses because she'd told him she kept losing her first pair and misplacing the spare.

When Pia had laughed for two minutes straight, Gio had been utterly puzzled.

So most afternoons, Pia settled down in the veranda with her laptop and lesson plans while her grandfather napped. Afraid of creating even the smallest ripple through Gio's precarious health, she had abandoned her plans for leaving Italy for now.

So it was fifteen days later that she found Raphael standing in the courtyard with a glass of white wine in his hand.

He cast a tall shadow in the afternoon sun, his broad shoulders tapering into a lean waist and muscular thighs, the very ones that had cradled her. There had been such power, such strength in him and yet he had been so gentle with her. That she knew his body with such intimate knowledge sent a strange thrum of power flowing through her veins.

Not that she had any illusion that he belonged to her.

She doubted Raphael would ever truly belong to any woman. And yet, seeing him stand there, Pia could only feel tenderness for him. As if somehow she could bring a new facet out of this hard man. As if she could give him something he didn't have or hadn't known before.

She sighed and trudged up the steep path. His hair, grown overlong, curled over the collar of his shirt. A pang beat through her chest as she noticed the dark shadows he sported under his eyes.

Wineglass raised to his mouth, he froze when he spotted her. That intense stare of his made her pulse flutter, that familiar feeling of excitement and anticipation singing through her veins.

His dark eyes swept over her with such lingering hunger that Pia instantly knew that he felt this thing between them just as strongly as she did.

Sweat had gathered over her forehead and her neck for she'd been walking for almost an hour. Her hair was a nest around her face. She wished she'd worn anything but another pair of old jeans and a collared T-shirt.

Then hated herself for thinking that.

"Hello, Pia."

Pia walked around him, the clamor of her heart far too much to stand being near him right then, and poured herself a glass of ice-cold water. Only after she took a fortifying sip did she lift her gaze and meet his.

"Hello, Raphael."

The table stood between them, yet nothing could dilute the awareness singing in the air between them, or his displeasure. His fingers gripped the wine flute so tightly that she was afraid he would break it and hurt himself.

"You didn't come to the phone when I asked for you."

She shrugged while her grandfather watched them as if he were at a tennis match. "I just…it wasn't a good time to talk on the phone," she said.

"All five times that I asked for you?" His tone rang with disbelief. His gaze lingered on her lips, searching, seeking.

There were a thousand questions in that simple sentence and Pia couldn't answer all of them in front of Gio, even if she had the answers.

"I've been busy. Studying. I enrolled in a wood carving class in the village. Also thank you so much for the new tools and the wood. And the laptop. And my new glasses. I appreciate all the gifts," she said lamely.

He carefully put his wineglass down and folded his hands behind him. "Do you?"

She hesitated at his combative expression. "Yes."

"Tell him about the man you met when you went out to the *trattoria* the other night," Gio urged. "You're seeing him again, aren't you?"

Like a hound scenting prey, Raphael walked past the table toward her. "Who is this man?"

Pia glared at Gio. Really, she didn't understand Gio sometimes. Of all the hundred things he could've mentioned to Raphael her non-date was what he told him? "Just a guy I met at the café."

"Is he a local? Does everyone at the café know you're Giovanni's granddaughter? Why didn't Emilio tell me?"

"So Emilio is spying for you?"

"Emilio keeps an eye on Gio and now on you too."

"I'm not answerable to you. You're going to let him

question me like that?" She appealed to Gio when he finally put the phone down.

"Raphael," her grandfather said in a mock warning.

While she had been taking her stand, he had moved closer. The familiar scent of him—musk and heat—had her knees trembling beneath her. Pia clutched the table when he reached out a hand and brushed her cheek.

His hand pushed at a lock of hair behind her ear, while with the other he cupped her hip and pulled her forward. Her pulse racing, her body turned traitor, dipping toward him as if he were her true north.

"Are you trying to make me jealous, *tesoro*?"

Staring into his eyes, Pia forgot the entire world. "You're the one who jumped to conclusions. And I would never do anything so low."

"You wouldn't?" He looked at her as if she were the answer to a lot of questions. A thumb traced her jawline, resting at the corner of her mouth. "You still haven't told me anything about him."

"Christ, Raphael. He's a waiter at the café in the village. He saw me with some tools, we started chatting and it turns out carpentry is his hobby. We started talking, found we had a lot in common and when he told me about the class, I enrolled in it. That's it. I made a friend. Sometimes, we hang out at the café. I didn't know I was supposed to send you a day-to-day summary of my movements. I didn't know I wasn't allowed to make friends. Am I so untrustworthy? Am I answerable to you?"

"No, *cara mia*. Not answerable, and not untrustworthy, but you're…"

"Naive and foolish?"

"Innocent." How she was beginning to hate that word! "I do not care who you make friends with as long as the only man you let hold you like this is me."

"Raphael, please, can we—"

She never finished the sentence because he pressed his mouth to hers in a soft buss and she was instantly lost. Every slumberous nerve ending leaped to life.

Oh, how could she want him so madly and be so mad at him at the same time?

His lips were so soft and yet hard, so familiar and yet there was something new in his every kiss. She could spend a lifetime in Raphael's arms just savoring the taste of him, learning what he liked, discovering what she needed. Twining her tongue with his, Pia poured her heart and soul into his kiss.

When he held her like that, when he looked at her with such tender desire in his eyes, desire and love didn't feel so different. What resonated in her body seemed to calm the clamoring in her soul. When Raphael was near, everything in her lined up.

"*Maledizione*, but I have missed kissing these soft lips," he whispered into her mouth, sending arrows of pleasure to scandalous places. "Tell me you missed me, *cara mia*. Tell me you lie awake like me in the middle of the night wishing for my body, like I did for yours."

Vining her hands around his neck, she sank into his hard body. Soft groans rumbled from their mouths as, thigh to thigh, their bodies fit perfectly against each other.

Pia had no idea how far she would have gone, if he hadn't pulled back. It took her a few minutes to realize through the sensual haze that Gio had spoken.

She burned with embarrassment. Yet her grandfather ignored her completely, as if the responsibility of it solely lay at Raphael's feet. "Gio, it's only—"

Engaged in some macho one-on-one with Raphael, her grandfather wouldn't even look at her. "Pia, I would like to speak to Raphael alone."

She'd never been dismissed like that ever in her life before. "Not if you're going to discuss me," she said, frustration bleeding through her words. "Nonno, I know you worry for me and I didn't make it easy by trusting Frank but I can take care of myself and this is really not anyone's business but—"

"That cheating man is not my concern, Pia. Knowing what is at stake, knowing my worries and my plans for you, what my godson does with you *is*. Raphael, this has gone on long enough. Will you do the right thing or shall I—"

"Calm down, Giovanni," Raphael said softly, a hint of steel in his tone. "The status of our relationship was hardly crucial when you were lying in the hospital bed."

"And now?" Gio taunted.

Raphael replied in that same cutting voice that sent chills up Pia's spine. "Leave it to me."

Pia stared from one man to the other, feeling as if she were standing on ground filled with land mines. A sudden grin transformed Gio again to that loving, but cantankerous old man. Dread pooled in Pia's belly. "So, you two will be married soon?"

Words came to her lips but Raphael's grip around her waist tightened.

"As soon as I can manage it, *si*," Raphael replied, and Pia went utterly still.

It was as if someone had pulled the rug from under her. As if someone had punched her in the stomach in the dark.

Contrary to what would be expected of an eighty-four-year-old man who had just had two heart attacks in one year, Gio laughed heartily. "This year, Raphael." His bushy eyebrows scanned Pia's face. "You'll be happy with him, *piccola*."

Whatever protest Pia was about to make died at the transformation in his face. How could she do anything to ruin the happiness in his face? "Nonno, I'd like to wait until you're better before we even talk about the plans."

Gio nodded magnanimously. "I remember how glorious

it feels to be young and in love, but remember what happened with Lucia and me." He pulled Pia into his arms, gave her a kiss on her cheek, his eyes glimmering with tears. "Lucia would approve of who I found to look after you.

"Too much *excitemente* for an old man, *si*? I will go rest now."

Who I found to look after you...

The words left a chill on Pia's skin. There was something so very wrong with it but she couldn't put her finger on it.

The moment Giovanni's silver head disappeared behind the doors of the house, she jerked away from Raphael.

Just when she was beginning to accept that she wanted a relationship with Raphael, the idea of marrying him, the idea of being his equal, his lover, his wife sent her into a swirl of panic.

"Pia, wait."

"No, Raphael. I need to—"

She tried to slip away, but he captured her wrist and tugged her closer. Her legs tangled with his, her chest rasping against his. The man had the most beautiful black eyes. And when they focused on her like that, she was afraid she would melt from within. That she wouldn't be able to refuse whatever he commanded of her in that arrogant tone.

"Let me explain, *cara mia*. You will—"

Chest rising and falling, Pia faced him. "Don't call me that."

His fingers crawled to her bare arm, the length of them wrapping around it. "I will call you whatever the hell I please."

There was a possessive intensity to his words that shivered over her skin. He wasn't mocking her now and something clearly had upset him too. Not that he would ever admit to it. "But I'm *not* yours to call whatever the hell you please," she countered softly, staring into his eyes.

They flared infinitesimally, and Pia felt a surge of satisfaction amidst the panic. Did he really think she had no spine? "I didn't protest in front of Gio because I didn't want to upset him. Because I tried to understand that he called your honor into question. Clearly there's something going on between you two."

Inscrutability again. What were Gio and Raphael planning that she wasn't supposed to know? She hoped it wasn't another protective measure. "I've never seen you so upset before."

She fisted and unfisted her hands. "I hate lies. I hate deception of any kind and it is my grandfather we're deceiving."

"It's only deception if it's not true."

She flinched and stopped her frantic pacing. But he wasn't joking. Dear God, he looked absolutely serious! "I've not agreed to marry you. And I don't remember you asking me. So of course it isn't true, and ergo it is deception."

"If the lack of a proper proposal upsets you…?"

A hysterical laugh fell from her mouth while he stared at her with an inscrutable expression. "Stop saying I'm upset. I'm not upset. I'm just stating for the record that we don't even have a relationship."

"No?" His fingers clasped her bare arm and her breath fell out of rhythm instantly. "So you go around sleeping with men for the fun of it?"

"There's nothing wrong with sleeping with a man for the fun of it. Sex should be fun and positive and tender and breath-stealing, shouldn't it?"

A wicked gleam danced in his eyes. "I am pleased to have left you with such good impressions, *bella*. I agree that sex should be fun and positive and should be had whenever one wants to." Heat arced between them, his fingers crawling into her nape. A sultry invitation glimmered in his eyes.

On a soft whimper, Pia closed her eyes. Images of their long, sweaty limbs tangled in gray sheets, the sinuous whispers of their skin sliding over each other, Raphael moving inside her like music—the sensations inundated her.

"But we're not discussing the sexual mores of twenty-first-century women, are we? We're discussing you, Pia. I know that what happened the other night is not a small thing for you."

"No. But one night's incredible sex is not the basis for marriage either. You could have told Nonno that we're just…we're just…"

"Whether now or in a few months' time, we have to face this question, Pia."

"Maybe so. But you said you didn't want a relationship with a woman, much less to marry one."

"You think I took you to bed, took your virginity, without being prepared for the consequences? Do you honestly think we could have a red-hot affair under Gio's nose, and then go our separate ways? Turn the clock back to become polite acquaintances who have already shared lovers' intimacies? Will you be perfectly all right when you see me with a new woman?"

"Yes." She called his bluff while her heart thudded. "I'll be fine. We should stop now. Before all those scenarios could become true. Before one of us gets hurt."

Jaw clenched tight, he stood in front of her. "Is that right, *bella mia*? You have zero interest if I take another woman to my bed? If I push inside of her wet heat like I did with you, if I send her into ecstasy with my body and my fingers like I did you? If I—"

Pia cupped her hand over his mouth, unable to hear anymore. "I don't know how one night of sex has transformed into this. We don't suit each other. I'm not beautiful or sophisticated or any of the things that your other… your usual women are.

"And you…"

"And I what, Pia? Tell me how I do not suit you."

"You don't believe in love."

"You thought you were in love with Frank."

"You'll never let me forget that mistake, will you? You think I'm a foolish idiot. Why would you even want me as a wife?"

"I do think you're naive. But it is what attracts me to you. You're unlike any woman I've ever known. You're honest and open. You don't care about external trappings. Just as you know you can trust me, I know I can trust you with myself and even with Alyssa. We burn when we come together and if you put love aside, you and I want the same things out of marriage."

"Like what?"

"Fidelity, respect and lots of babies."

"You truly want more children?"

"Yes. Especially if they'll be nearsighted and smart and beautiful like you are."

"I have to think about it. I need more time. I need…"

"*Si?*"

"I want to spend time with you."

"I'm more than happy to do that."

She blinked. "You are?"

"*Si,* Pia. Usually when a man is attracted to a woman, and he wants to do all sorts of deliciously wicked things to her, and is determined to persuade her to walk down the aisle to him, he wants to spend time with her. He wants to be the one who brings her favorite things, he wants to be the one who makes her cry out with pleasure, he wants to be the one who gives her babies…"

Pia threw herself at Raphael, glad that they were finally

on the same page. "Although I don't think we should sleep with each other again too soon."

He looked thunderous. "What kind of a condition is that?"

"I go into this dreamy state where I can't think logically when we make love. I…what I'm saying is…you have too much power in this relationship if we have sex."

A hard, harsh laugh fell from his mouth. "You think you don't have any?"

A vein pounded in his temple as she pulled him toward her. Joy blooming in her chest, she wrapped her arms around his waist, ran her hands over his muscled back and down. How she loved the way he felt in her hands. When she slipped her hands lower to his buttocks and tugged, his arousal grazed her belly. "Do you think I do?"

Jaw tight, heat scouring those sharp cheekbones, he raised a brow.

"See, I didn't even know I had it." When he'd have slammed her body into his to cradle his arousal, Pia pushed back at his shoulders. "No, let me touch you as I please."

"You're playing a dangerous game, *cara mia*. It's been two weeks and I know if I touch you, you'll be wet for me."

Pia blushed, the dampness between her thighs confirming his arrogant confidence. "Yes, well, we already agreed that you can melt me like an ice cream on a summer day with one look, *si*?" She ran her hands up his back and sank them under his collar.

She petted him as if he were her very own wild animal. He growled when she rubbed herself against him. On purpose. Heat blazed in his eyes.

She was playing a dangerous game, and yet she'd never felt more alive. "Stay still for me, won't you, Raphael?"

His explicit Italian—about what he'd like to do to her instead—sent heat pooling in her lower belly.

Sinking her fingers into his hair, Pia kissed the corner

of his mouth. The scratch of his stubble against her lips was heavenly as she peppered that arrogant jaw with soft kisses. "I don't even know what I like and don't like yet."

"Let me participate and I'll give you the different options, *bella*. You love experiments, don't you?"

Laughter bubbled up her throat even as she nibbled on his lips as if he were her favorite treat. He tasted of wine and masculinity and seduction and it went straight to her head. And her buckling knees.

When she traced that lower lip of his that drove her wild, he sucked the tip into his mouth and released it with a pop. A whimper escaped her mouth, her nipples suddenly sensitive against her bra. On the next breath, his fingers crawled into her hair, held her tight, and he took over the kiss. Hard and demanding, he plunged his tongue into her mouth. Rising to her toes, angling her mouth, Pia gave back as good as she got.

Their teeth banged. Their lips nipped and bit.

His thigh lodged between hers, hard muscle rubbing against the apex of her sex. Just where she desperately needed it. "*Dannazione*, Pia." His forehead leaned against hers, his warm breath feathering over her face. "Come to bed, *cara mia*. I will happily show you how much power you have over me. We could spend all day in bed and by nighttime, you would know whether you like me above you, or under you or behind you.

I will show you how to use that sweet, deceiving mouth to drive me to the edge. I will show you what I can do to you here—" he emphasized by rubbing at the spot that ached for his attention "—that will…"

A rush of wetness filling her sex, Pia drew a sharp breath. And stumbled away from Raphael. The man could seduce her just with words.

And like her, he was breathing hard. His pupils dilated, his nostrils flaring, as if he had just engaged in a physical fight. The front of his trousers was tented and when her gaze lingered there, his growl was feral.

Raphael undone—or at least close to—was the most glorious sight she'd ever seen.

Swallowing away the longing burning through every inch of her, she slowly wiped the moisture from her lips with the back of her hand. "I know you want to spend the day with Alyssa and I have to study. But I've been dying to see one of the cars you've restored," she added. Proving to herself that she could affect him just as much as he did her was a small victory. But having won the battle, she wasn't really interested in the war.

A vein pulsing in his jaw, he stared at her for so long that Pia wondered if she had pushed him too far. "Friday evening."

When he passed by her without touching her again, her heart sank.

"And Pia?"

"*Si*, Raphael?"

"You *will* be my wife, and I know how to exact retribution."

CHAPTER TWELVE

TORTURE BEGAN TO take on a new personal meaning for Raphael over the next month, thanks to his unofficial fiancée's unwillingness to let him give them both what they desperately needed.

If he had thought Pia biddable, she had proved he was utterly wrong. *Dio mio*, under the naive, smiling, ready-to-please demeanor was a core of steely stubbornness.

When she'd said she wanted to spend time with him, she'd meant it. And not in his ex-wife or mama and sisters kind of way, where what they wanted was for him to show them off in their designer gowns, the latest of Milan's haute couture fashion, at parties, and theaters. Where they could show off their connection with Raphael Mastrantino, CEO of Vito Automobiles, a man with powerful friends.

With them, it was always about the glitter he could add to their standing in society. It was the veneer of power that spread to them when they could claim a connection to him. It was what Raphael could provide and nothing else.

But with Pia, *Dio*, when she'd said she wanted to spend time with him, she'd meant she wanted time with him. Learning about him. The two of them *hanging out* with each other.

It had become Raphael's favorite phase in all of the English language.

She had insisted that he show her the vintage car he

was restoring currently. So Raphael had taken her to his house in Como one afternoon. What he'd expected was for her to ooh and aah over it, and then expect him to show her the sights of Como, the only village along the lake she hadn't seen.

Instead, driven by Emilio, Pia had arrived in the cutest overalls he had ever seen. Uncaring of the fact that her hands could get greasy or that her hair would be messed up—though Pia's hair was always messy and he loved it like that—she had crawled under the hood with him, asking him to explain what it was that he was currently doing.

Talking about the chassis and suspension while the scent of her curled in his muscles, her hot breath stroked his cheeks—he had never had a more diverting evening.

They had ended it with a glass of Chianti and mac 'n' cheese that Pia had cooked in his kitchen, having informed him that that was the extent of her culinary abilities.

Having never spoken to another soul at such length about his passion, Raphael had spent most of their dinner in quiet rumination and with a burning need to peel the overalls off her lithe body. To kiss and lick every inch of her silky curves.

Sharing even silence with Pia was wonderful.

They had ended the night, because she had a test early in the morning, with a soft kiss that had left him with blue balls. But also with a thread of quiet, incandescent joy he'd never known before.

Another time, she had invited him to sit through her class, and then made him model for her first face carved from wood, because as she had put it, he had classically handsome features with a bold nose and an arrogant chin that would lend itself to that particular type of wood.

He had sat still for almost an hour while the minx had worked with her hands, only to find her dissolving into giggles when he'd asked her to show him what she had so far.

"*Mi dispiace*, Raphael. I'm so bad at this, I've made you into a monster," she had sputtered amidst her laughter. "I'll ask Antonio to sit for me next time." Of course he had said no, to which she had responded by crawling to him on her knees, tracing those blunt-nailed, callused fingers over his nose, temple and then over his lips. She had then taken his mouth in such an erotic kiss, swirling tongue and biting teeth and all, that Raphael had been harder than the block of wood, and said, "I can't bear to ruin this gorgeous face, Raphael."

Since he was busy with work and Allegra's custody suit, and she was busy studying and carving and meeting the new friends she had made, all they could manage one week was two evenings spent together holed up in Gio's study, which he had been far too happy to give up.

While Raphael had spread out his paperwork on the vast mahogany desk, Pia had settled her textbooks around the sitting area. It was the most enjoyable quiet evening of his life. The sight of Pia with her glasses perched on her nose, studious concentration furrowing her brow, had driven him half-crazy.

The thought of spending the next fifty years in such close quarters with her was surprisingly exciting. He imagined looking up from his work to find her gaze on him with a slight smile, sitting in comfortable silence but with an ongoing sizzling awareness; the absolute knowledge that it wouldn't make a difference to Pia if his assets grew another billion or not, or if he lost most of it with some bad decisions like his father. The trust that she would never stop looking at him as if he were the most perfect man she had ever met—it filled him with the desire to wrap his arms around her and never let go.

Locking the door against any servants, uncaring that

he was dishonoring her under Gio's roof, he had crossed the room, knelt in front of her, pulled her hair from the tight braid she had forced it into and drunk greedily from her welcoming mouth.

He'd meant to keep his word. He'd meant to let her come to him, to give her the time she'd asked for. And yet, her responsive moans had had him spreading her legs wide, pulling up the long skirt she had worn that day, and then kissing his way up the silky skin of her thighs, all the way to the damp center of her sex.

He had tasted her desire for him while she had sunk her fingers into his hair, gasping and moaning, scandalized by his actions and yet thrusting against his ministrations until she was falling apart against his mouth while digging her teeth into his lower lip. The most potent masculine satisfaction had surged through him when she had collapsed into his arms, limbs trembling.

Cheeks pink, breath serrated, hair in wild disarray and her eyes, those wide, deep brown eyes glittering with an emotion he didn't want to give a name to. *Dio*, she'd been the wildest, the most beautiful thing he had ever seen.

Fingers sinking in his hair, she had guided his mouth down to hers for a quick press. "I didn't know I could feel so much pleasure that I could happily die from it."

"You're not dying until I have punished you for your no-sex rule," he'd said, sinking his teeth into the rough cushion of her palm.

"Poor Raphael, it has been, what? Three weeks?"

A soft flick at the center of her palm with his tongue. Like a spark plug when combusted, she immediately slithered in his lap. "Five weeks and four days, you minx."

She had crawled to her knees, stroked her palms up his chest, cheeks flaming pink and with the most mischievous grin said, "Raphael, can I...?"

He hardened into stone. Her hands on his thighs, yes, but the shy desire, her hesitation, got him every time.

"Can you what, *cara mia*?" If she had asked the world of him, he would have agreed.

Her face burrowed into his chest, her fingers drawing mesmerizing lines on the back of his neck. "I… I want to return the favor."

He swallowed the jolt of lust that shot through him. "What favor?"

"I want to do to you what you did to me just now," she had finally whispered at his ear. "I want to make you lose control too."

How he hadn't combusted right there, Raphael had no idea. Wedged against the taut curve of her buttock, his erection had twitched in his trousers at her innocent suggestion.

"Are you agreeing to marry me then?" he'd taunted instead.

He had no idea what she'd been about to say because his infernal cell phone had rung, disrupting the pregnant moment.

Somehow, what had begun as a convenient arrangement had morphed. It wasn't just the prize of finally owning Vito Automobiles that lured him anymore. It wasn't the convenience of returning all the favors Gio had bestowed on him by marrying Pia. It wasn't taking on the responsibility to protect her and Gio's wealth.

It was Pia herself.

He knew as surely as the beat of his heart, while he waited at the center in front of Teatro Alla Scala for her to arrive for her special opera night, that he wanted Pia in his life.

He wanted the woman who looked at him as if he were the world to her. And in return, he would give Pia everything she could ever want, everything that he was capable of giving.

* * *

Pia stepped out of the limo on a side street, an unnecessary indulgence Raphael insisted on, and walked the last few steps to the front of the historical opera house Teatro Alla Scala and gaped with her mouth open. She could have just as well caught the light rail, but of course he wouldn't listen.

Glad that she had worn her soft silk emerald-green dress that made Milan's humidity bearable, she looked around herself. Typical of the busy city's evening, Piazza della Scala was busy and noisy, mostly with tourists. Locals, she'd learned, had already escaped to the beach, especially as it was the weekend.

She had barely breathed in the architectural marvel all around her when the hairs on her nape stood up with that familiar prickle. Turning around, she spotted Raphael instantly among the elegantly dressed men and women in front of the famous opera house.

Tall and wide and impossibly gorgeous, he stood out. His shoulders looked broader than ever in the handmade suit, his looks even more breathtaking in the magnificent lights of the square.

Clad in a black suit with a white shirt underneath, hands loosely tucked into his trouser pockets, he was leaning against a pillar and watching her with a curious smile playing around his lips. As if knowing that she wanted to linger, he crooked a finger at her.

That playful arrogance, that wicked promise in his eyes sent a shiver down her spine. He looked good enough to be devoured. And he looked at her as if he was ready to devour her.

It had been a whole long, utterly miserable ten days since she had last seen him, ten days since he had sent her into spasms of unbearable pleasure with his mouth at her most private place. Just thinking of that scandalous moment, the pleasure that had filled her sent blood rushing to her ears.

And he knew. Even across the ten feet or so that separated them, she could see the gleam of that hunger in his eyes, sense the attraction arc between them.

Heart beating a thousand beats a minute, aware of more than one woman stumbling to a stop at the breathtaking sight of him, Pia reached him.

He is mine, a part of her cooed in joy.

Holding her at arm's length, he swept that possessive gaze over her arms and shoulders left bare by the thin straps of the dress. A much-needed breeze wafted by, revealing the thigh-length slit in her dress. She saw him swallow as a partial view of her toned leg flashed and she was fiercely glad for swimming all those hours and keeping herself fit.

And then his arm was around her, his mouth at her ear. "I do not like any other man getting such a good view of your legs, *cara mia*. They are only for my pleasure, to be wrapped around my hips while I move inside you." His hand rested possessively on her waist as if to warn off any approaching man. "I think I like you all covered up in your jeans and my shirts."

Luckily, Pia wasn't required to respond as the ushers were showing them to their seats on a balcony, which she was delighted to find was an individual room with a private coat closet across the hallway from the box.

While Raphael exchanged words with the usher, Pia took in the historical circle-style theater that she'd heard so much about. The energy of the place was incredible. Gorgeously decorated in gold and stunning red velvet, the *teatro* was everything she'd hoped it would be. Pushing up her glasses, she began to people watch, because the women and men were dressed in elegant designer outfits that would probably rival the costumes themselves.

When Raphael tapped on her shoulder and showed her to a seat, Pia smiled sheepishly. "I'm sure my enthusiasm must look very *provincial* to you. But Nonni described this very theater to me so many times and all the wonderful productions she had seen here before she left Italy that I can't believe I'm finally here.

It feels as if I have waited forever to see this. I think she wanted me to come here too." Tears filled her eyes, a sudden ache filling her to her very soul.

She knew Lucia had come here with Giovanni once. The special friend her Nonni had always mentioned with melancholy in her eyes could be no one else. And yet, soon after, they had had a big row, and Lucia had fled Italy while Gio, in a fit of anger, had engaged himself to a heiress.

Suddenly, that Raphael had brought her to the same theater, to the same opera, struck a chord of fear through her. She shivered, and instantly Raphael pulled her into his embrace.

Pia hid her face in his chest, embarrassed by her irrational fear. This was ridiculous. She and Raphael were different from Gio and Lucia.

For one thing, they were older and wiser. They understood each other much better. And yes, at every chance possible, Raphael stubbornly claimed that he didn't believe in love while she still did. But hadn't he shown her that he cared for her in a million ways over the last month and a half?

Weren't actions worth more than words?

Despite his cynicism because of his marriage to Allegra, despite his hardened exterior from having to raise his family from sudden calamity to prosperity, wasn't his desire to marry her based on loyalty and respect? Didn't it prove that somewhere in his heart Raphael did care for her?

The man who had so ruthlessly accused her of being

an impostor and a cheat the night of the ball, the man who had threatened to cut his ex-wife out of their child's life, Pia would have never expected him to consider marriage at all.

But it was he who had accepted the consequences of their night first. He who hadn't hesitated even for a moment over the step they would have to take for the future.

What she felt for Raphael—she was so scared of calling it love—was so much more complex than what she felt for Frank. Frank had only pandered to what she had so desperately needed at that time in her life whereas Raphael could be infuriating and arrogant but he would never lie to her.

He would never deceive Pia, would never make her feel as if he needed an added incentive to be with her, to somehow make up for her plainness and her shyness. For the glitter she lacked.

So what if he would never admit in so many words that he loved her? Wasn't what they had better, more real than some notion of love she had cooked up in her head?

His abrasive palms covered her bare arms and moved up and down. "Your skin is ice-cold, Pia. What is it?"

"Nothing. Thank you so much for this, Raphael."

"Never apologize for your enthusiasm for everything in life, *cara mia*. Haven't I convinced you yet that your pleasure, in all things, leads to mine?"

Pia blushed and cast a confused gaze at the empty seats in some of the private rooms for the opera was about to begin soon. "Antonio told me this particular production of *Rigoletto* had been sold out months ago." She sat down next to Raphael and adjusted her dress. "Do you think they're late?"

"I asked a friend of mine to buy as many tickets as he could on this level."

"But why?"

"Because I wanted you all to myself. And I wanted this night to be special for you." Pia gasped as only now she noticed a bucket of champagne on the table and a small velvet box in his palm.

Her heart thudded. Her mouth went dry as he opened the box and pulled out a magnificent princess-cut diamond with tiny emeralds around it, set in a simple white-gold setting.

"Pia Alessandra Vito, will you be my wife?"

"Oh." It was all the sound Pia could make, all the response her brain could come up with. Because just as she knew this theater, she knew of this ring too.

It was the ring with which Giovanni had proposed to Lucia. The ring that Lucia had sent back to Gio after their fight. Another tremor slid down her spine as she stared at it.

Something about this ring made fear bubble up in her. "Pia?"

She jerked her head up, met his gaze and the desire she saw there fragmented her silly fears. "I'm sorry. I... Gio gave this to you?"

"Si."

"When?"

A shadow fell over that dark gaze. "Is that important?"

The impatience brewing in his carefully controlled tone told Pia how insensitive she was being. Heart thundering, she extended her left hand to his and smiled. "Yes, I will be your wife, Raphael."

With a victorious smile, he slid the ring onto her finger. Pulling her down to his lap and sinking her hands into his thick hair, Pia poured herself into his kiss. His mouth was warm and fluid over hers. They kissed softly, slowly, nibbling at each other, playing with their tongues, until passion was simmering in their very blood. With an arch of her back, restless with need, Pia wiggled in his lap. The length of his hard erection caressed her buttocks, sending a groan from her lips.

With a chuckle, Raphael pushed her off him and settled her in the next seat. Still in a haze, Pia gazed widely and he brushed a kiss over her temple. "If you wiggle anymore in my lap like that, *cara mia*, I will shame myself and then we'll have to leave before you see this grand production of *Rigoletto*. And then you'll not forgive me for spoiling your evening."

A hush fell over the theater and the red curtains were pulling aside when Pia murmured, "I think I would forgive you anything, Raphael. As long as you keep kissing me like that."

Raphael gently tapped on Pia's shoulder while the audience clapped thunderously at the end of an outstanding performance of *Rigoletto*. This particular story wasn't a great favorite of his but even he'd been moved by the top-notch performances and the intricately detailed sets.

Or maybe it was the woman he had shared the experience with. The woman who now belonged to him, body and soul. For a man who had vowed never to marry again, it was a bit of a shock to realize he very much wanted Pia's soul to belong to him too.

A savage sense of satisfaction pounded through his veins, made even hotter by the magnificent drama they had just seen. Not even the pride he had felt when he had made his first million, or when he had bought back the house his father had lost to creditors, could parallel his sense of possessiveness as he stared at the diamond glittering on Pia's finger.

She hadn't come to Teatro Alla Scala on his arm because it was the "in" thing to be enjoying high culture or to be seen in designer outfits, but to immerse herself in the drama played out on stage. She had tears in her eyes because she could see the majesty of the theater through her Nonni's eyes and relive it for her.

Pia had watched transfixed, every emotion portrayed on the stage reflected on her own face.

And watching her, understanding the depth with which she felt things, Raphael couldn't help but be moved. Couldn't help but feel a strange turmoil that he couldn't calm.

They emerged from the theater into the pulsing energy of the pedestrian square. Something feral throbbed in his veins and since he didn't want to scare Pia, he offered, "We're mere steps from the Duomo. Would you like to get a gelato to cool off? Or a coffee, which by the way I should remind you is an *espresso* in Italy and not the watered-down junk you call coffee?"

She turned to him and the candid emotion he saw in her eyes rooted him to the spot. "Not tonight, thank you. Nothing could top that performance."

As if it were an uncomfortable, unwanted weight, she twisted the ring on her finger. She had fiddled with it self-consciously during the performance too.

"Pia, if you do not like the ring, we will get you something else. I could not refuse Gio in that moment but I will absolutely understand if it does not please you. I want you to have whatever you want, *cara mia.*"

"No, of course I love the ring, Raphael. Nothing could make this night more glorious than it already has been."

"Then let's finish it with some of the calamari you like so much. With Gio visiting his sister today, I'm sure you've forgotten to eat." He let his gaze settle on the upper curves of her breasts.

It was the first time Pia had worn something so silky and revealing. And it was driving him crazy.

"Because I can't afford to lose any of the few curves I have?"

The vulnerability in her eyes snagged at him. "Because

you're now mine to protect. I wish I could show you how perfect you are to me."

"I think I'm beginning to believe it."

"Bene." He inclined his head, waiting for whatever was in her head to come to her lips with bated breath, for he knew only one thing made Pia so self-conscious.

Even white teeth digging into her lower lip, she adjusted her clutch, and then looked up again. That hint of hesitation in those eyes pierced him. And made him wild with desire, for he knew what it meant. "I just want to go home."

But he still waited. He wanted to hear those words from her mouth. He wanted her surrender. He wanted her to choose this, him. Again and again. He had a feeling that even a lifetime wouldn't be enough. "I will take you home then."

"No."

Covering the distance between them, she laced her fingers with his, pressed her body to his in a side hug that sent a shudder through him. If they lived a hundred years together, he would never get used to how freely she expressed her affection. How easily and naturally it came to her to show what she was feeling. That diamond sparkling brilliantly on her finger reminded him that the generosity of her spirit was his too now. His to guard from anything that could hurt her. Including himself.

A weight unlike any responsibility he had shouldered so far in his life.

She made a moue of her mouth, and then completely negated the saucy effect by pushing her glasses up on her nose.

He chuckled.

"I don't want to go back to the estate and I don't want a gelato."

"No? What are you interested in then, *bella*?"

A soft kiss on his cheek. Her breath fluttering over the rim of his ear. And then those warm brown eyes pinned him.

"You." There was no coyness in her gaze. No sultry invitation. No feminine arch of her body or fluttering of her eyelashes. Just pure, artless need. "Tonight, I want you, Raphael. Just you."

CHAPTER THIRTEEN

BY THE TIME she and Raphael rode the glass elevator to his ninth-floor apartment, Pia's nerves had stretched to breaking point. Desire was a live wire left unearthed between them as they sat at the ends of the seat in the taxi, speeding through the seven or so miles to his apartment in the affluent fashion district, a world away from the busy nightlife through Corso Venezia.

Raphael's cell phone gave that shrill ring the moment they stepped inside and Pia almost jumped out of her skin.

His hand at her lower back, Raphael steadied her. His own pithy curse when he looked at the screen painted the air blue. "I have to take this call."

While Pia stood there in the middle of the huge lounge, her pulse ringing like a bell all through her body, Raphael returned, after only a few minutes. His mouth took on that hard cast that she didn't like. Another darker tone added to the awareness sizzling between them.

She thought they'd grown comfortable with each other over the past few weeks, that they had crossed a milestone in their relationship, had gotten closer emotionally too.

Yet it seemed that all it took was one of them to give voice to this need between them, to express desire for sexual intimacy—she blushed when she realized that was what she had done—and every word became explosive, every look rife with promise.

"Who was that?"

He shrugged off his suit jacket, carefully folded it and left it on the chair. "Nothing important."

Struggling to keep her dismay off her face, she said softly, "That's what you say when you don't want to tell me."

His fingers stilled on his shirt buttons. "I don't want to tell you because it's not important."

"And yet, it made you curse like that? I've seen very little that causes you to lose your arrogant confidence. I know you're used to keeping matters close to your chest, that you probably never had a chance to confide in any—"

"It does not concern you, Pia. *Bene?*"

A sudden prickling heat behind her eyes, Pia simply nodded.

Raphael exhaled harshly, the tight line of his shoulders relenting. His hair, already messed up by Milan's humidity, became a little wilder when he pushed his hand through it. "I did not mean to be short with you." A sigh that made that broad chest rise and fall. "*Mi dispiace*, Pia."

Whatever hurt she had felt, his genuine apology instantly placated it. The matter was nowhere near resolved, she knew. It was her right as his future wife, it was her deepest wish that he share everything with her. But Pia had enough patience to wait. In every way, Raphael had proved that he was worth waiting for. "It's okay, Raphael."

"You mean it, don't you?"

"*Si.*"

His dark eyes, liquid with desire, swept over her. "I knew there was more than one reason I wanted to marry you."

Swallowing away her own anxiety about what was coming, she wanted to do something bold but in the strange mood he was in, it was hard to hold on to her newly discovered confidence.

"Would you like something to drink? I have some nice Chianti."

Despite the thick tension in the air, Pia smiled. She loved that he always remembered those small details. From the most trivial to the most important, he was always looking out for her. Part of it, she knew, was his nature. That sense of responsibility that had fallen on his shoulders at a young age had never quite left him.

He was one of those alpha males who walked into a situation and immediately took charge of it. Protected the innocents and chased away the threats. And remained aloof even amidst a crowd.

Part of his protective instincts toward her were also because she was Gio's granddaughter. And he was big on loyalty.

But a small part of it, she hoped, was because of what she meant to him. Was because of who she was.

She covered the few steps between them, until the tips of her breasts were barely grazing his chest. "I feel like I'm already drunk. So no thank you."

He grabbed her wrists and pushed them behind her until the front of her was pressed deliciously up against his hard body. "Always so polite." His mouth flicked a silky, wet trail from her jaw down to the crook of her neck. He sucked her skin rough and hard. Pia jerked as wetness rushed between her thighs. She couldn't even clench them because he had jammed his hard thigh between hers. "Raphael, wait…"

"Always so ready to forgive and forget. Always so generous."

A keening moan rose from her throat as his wicked tongue softly licked the hurt he had inflicted with his teeth. Pain and pleasure fused, love and desire roped together and ran hot like a cocktail through her blood.

Somehow she managed to pull back, clasped his jaw

and forced him to meet her gaze. "Raphael, will you not tell me what has made your mouth become hard again?"

His hands started torturing her then, stroking up and down her back, kneading her hips, cupping her behind until his arousal pressed against her lower belly. Her temperature shot up ten degrees at the least. "My mouth becomes hard?"

"Yes." She moaned when he rubbed it against her. "And you get that look in your eyes." With a half sob, half smile, she caught his hands with hers. "You have just asked me to be your wife and I accepted. You cannot hide things from me now. I want to share everything, Raphael, the good and the bad, with you.

I want to be here when you need me, just as you were there for me when I needed you."

She had no idea if she had gotten across to him. But when he raised his head and looked down at her, there was a dark glitter in his eyes. "There is something I need from you tonight. Will you give it to me?"

"*Si*. Anything."

"Undo my cuffs."

Taking his left wrist in her hands she undid the cuff links. And then repeated the same with the other hand. He unbuttoned his shirt and threw it off those broad shoulders. The sight of his lean chest with all his skin stretched taut over it made Pia tremble.

"Take off your clothes for me."

Instantly, Pia froze. "Here?"

"Here. Now."

"You did say anything," the devil said, taunting her.

She tilted her head. *"Bene."*

If this was what he wanted, then he would get it. She held his gaze, letting the slumbering heat in it drive her. She trusted Raphael with everything she had in her, so her shyness, her insecurity about her body, was nothing but a small barrier to cross.

She moved her hand to the zipper hiding on the side of her dress and pulled it down. The quiet rasp of it was loud in the silence.

Her movements were clumsy when she pulled the straps down. Dark eyes watched her the whole time and flared when the silky material fell to her hips and her breasts were bared. Pia shivered, less from the breeze that flew over her heated skin and more from the dark hunger in his eyes.

Her breasts felt heavier, the nipples turning into aching points as his gaze lingered there with barely hidden fascination.

"Push it down all the way. And step out of it."

Pia did as he bid, the last of her shyness leaving her at his quicksilver reaction. He was right. She had just as much power as he did in this situation. Her dress whispered to the floor, and still in her heels, she kicked it away.

She lifted her chin, daring him to go on, even as a thousand butterflies danced in her belly. His gaze moved from her breasts to her midriff and then lower. The flimsy white underwear she wore did nothing to hide her from him.

"Are you wet for me?"

Heat burst inside of her like a hot geyser, spreading to every nerve ending. "Raphael, *per favore…*"

"I wish to know, *bella.*"

"I'm ready for you. I was ready for you when I saw you leaning against that pillar. When the Duke mercilessly seduced Gilda. When Rigoletto hired that assassin. When Gilda sacrificed herself for her unscrupulous lover. There, are you satisfied? Can you please take me to bed now?"

"Not yet." A silky smile curved his mouth. It seemed he was bent on pushing her to the edge now. "Come here and undress me."

She blinked.

He raised his brows. "I would like to be naked now, Pia."

She would not admit defeat tonight.

She walked toward him, stopped when the scent of him coiled through her veins. His trousers did nothing to hide his need for her. Swallowing, she set her fingers to work undoing his fly and then sliding them under the elastic band of his boxers pushing both of them down.

The turgid length of his erection sprang free, the soft head flicking her palm. Her sex clenched, and a gasp emanated from the depths of her.

It was all she could do to pull her gaze away from it and lift it to his face. He stepped out of his trousers and flicked them to the side with his feet, bold and utterly masculine. "Remember what you offered that night in the study? Is it still on, Pia?"

Just the thought of it made her skin tighten over her muscles. "Yes, the offer is still on."

Holding his dark eyes, she sank to her knees. His erection lengthened even before she touched it, sending a surge of power through her. Whatever it was that he thought she was not equal to, she would prove him wrong.

She was more than enough woman for Raphael Mastrantino.

"I want to make every fantasy of yours come true, Raphael. So you have to tell me if I do this right or wrong, *si*?"

Raphael's heart pounded in his chest as Pia obediently sank to her knees. *Dio mio*, he'd been angry at Allegra's latest trick to get custody of Alyssa.

After all her affairs, to claim that he was not a suitable father... His mood had instantly darkened. And when Pia so innocently offered to share his worries, he had worked himself to a dangerous edge.

He had only issued his command as a dare. As a way for

him to fight the all-encompassing emotion he was beginning to recognize in her gaze. To bring this thing between them back into his control. Because, sometime between beginning the evening with Gio's ring in his pocket and ending it with Pia telling him that she wanted *just him*, something had changed.

Even with Allegra's ridiculous claim, he still had everything he had ever wanted. So where was this dread in his heart coming from?

Any further thought on the matter shredded into nothingness when Pia took him in her hands and closed her calloused fingers around his shaft. His breath left him in a sibilant hiss when she stroked his rigid length in slow, cautious, almost-feathery movements.

Hair like a golden cloud around her face, the line of her spine a sensuous path, she had never looked more beautiful.

His nerve endings fired at her inexperienced, innocent touch, more than with any practiced lover's caress.

He looked down, hoping that the wide-eyed innocence of her face would smash his dark mood. But instead he found her opening that pink mouth wide and dipping it toward his erection.

His heart thumped against his rib cage.

Her small breasts with their pink-tipped nipples. Her toned thighs tensing at her stance.

It was an image that made him far readier than he wanted to be, after a month of deprivation.

At the first slide of the welcoming wet warmth of her mouth over his length, his hips thrust forward. A thrill ran up the back of his thighs pooling in his groin. He cursed hard and long, sweat beading along his skin.

The sound of her soft sucks sizzled amidst his harsh breaths.

Dio mio, had she any idea how she was destroying him?

A soft gasp fell from her mouth as he thickened a little more. Fingers delicately wrapped at the base of the shaft, she looked up at him, liquid desire making her eyes look like warm inviting pools.

"Am I pleasing you, Raphael?" *Christo*, even her question was artless. She did really want to please him. Not as a challenge, not for a dare. Not to prove to herself or to him that she had power over him.

But for the simple reason that his pleasure mattered to her. This intimacy between them meant something to her.

More turned on than he had ever been in his life, he sank his hands into her hair and guided her mouth the way he wanted it. Told her how much pressure he wanted and where he wanted it. Told her to use the slide of her silky tongue against his length.

As if she was one of her dedicated pupils that she often talked about, Pia followed his instructions to the letter. Soon, he was reaching the edge and the last thing he wanted to do was terrify her by pushing this into something else. He knew what it had taken her to accept his challenge. What she'd had to overcome because she wanted to please him more.

And that blunted the edge of his desire more than anything else. Wrapping his fingers around her wrists, he pulled her up roughly, lifted her in his arms and carried her over to the bed.

Warm skin, and trembling muscles, she was a lush invitation. And his for always. Every night and every day, she would belong to him. And he would touch no other ever again.

The realization made the moment even more poignant, raised it from just sex to something else.

She moaned as he joined her on the bed and covered her body with his. Protested with her nails on his back when he took her mouth in a leisurely kiss. Bucked up when he skimmed his mouth over her taut nipples without taking them into his mouth.

Her soft mewls goaded him on and on.

Flipping her pliable body easily, he separated her legs until she was straddling his arousal. Her spine arced under his touch as the softest, hottest part of her pressed against his erection.

She was damp and ready for him.

"I need you, Raphael, now," she breathed, writhing her body over his. With her eyes closed, her unruly hair flying around her face, her high breasts beckoning him, she was a potent invitation.

Slowly, softly, he brought her down on him so she could feel every last inch of him. He spread the lips of her sex with his fingers, the sight of her taking him in incredibly erotic.

Her low moan made him lose the last bit of control. He wanted her far too much and found himself thrusting, hard and rough, up into her snug sheath until he filled her completely.

Her shocked gasp rent the air.

"Pia? *Cara mia*, did I hurt you?"

Spine still arched sensuously, she bent toward him until the peaks of her breasts rubbed against his chest. Her eyes were glazed, a soft smile spreading her mouth. "*No.* I just forgot how it feels when you're inside me. And this way…" She flexed her hips in an age-old feminine rhythm and he sank deeper with a muttered oath. "This way…you feel like you're everywhere."

She took his hand and brought his palm to her heart, where it thudded. Her skin was damp to his touch, the scent of her arousal coating the very air he breathed.

Her eyes, crystal clear in the soft light of the evening, pinned him. "You're here, Raphael, in my heart too. Did you know? Somehow, you have made me fall so utterly in love with you."

Everything froze inside Raphael as his brain struggled to process those heartfelt words. Words he thought he was ready to hear, words he had even thought his due because that was the only way Pia would enter a marriage. Words he hadn't realized would steal the breath from him, would knock him out at his knees.

Mere words had never meant anything to him before, so how could it feel like hers could pierce him clean to his soul?

With a glorious smile, Pia pulled herself up and ground down on him. Sending pleasure pulsing through his groin. Her declaration rang in his ears as his body drove deeper, faster, again and again into her slick wetness.

Her moans surrounded him as he pulled himself up and stroked her swollen clit with every thrust. Something let loose within him, and he wanted to wring every ounce of pleasure from her body.

He wanted to give her this, because it was the only thing he had to give.

Soon, she was exploding around him, her muscles clenching him and releasing him in a cataclysm of pleasure. It spurred him on to his own mind-blowing climax.

But still she was not done. While his lungs struggled to draw air, she bent over and pressed a damp kiss to his mouth. The scent of her and him and sex was a potent cocktail in the air, a heady drug that he wanted every night.

"*Ti amo*, Raphael," she whispered, with a shy smile. Before Raphael could even wrap his mind around her words, around the truth of it shining in her eyes, she fell asleep on his chest, with him still lodged deep inside her.

Raphael woke up when dawn began to paint pink fingers over the sky. With a warm, silky-soft body tucked up into him as if it was made for him. As if she was the part that completed the puzzle that he hadn't even known was incomplete.

Sinking his free hand into her thick hair, he gently pushed it back from her face. Long lashes drew crescent shadows under her eyes, which sported dark circles. Had she been studying for some infernal test again? Had he tired her that much with his relentless need for her?

It seemed as if her words had unlocked some fathomless desire in him, for the more he had her, the more he wanted her.

Even in sleep, her face lost none of its artless charm. Something snagged in his chest as she burrowed deeper into his arms. *Maledizione*, but her trust in him was absolute, limitless.

Having never been on the receiving end of such unconditional, nonjudgmental emotion, he didn't know how to handle it. A part of him wanted to distance himself from her, wanted to slam the door on whatever she had opened between them.

He wanted to wake her up and say, *Demand something from me. Ask for something in return.*

If she didn't, he felt as if he would never know the value of what she was giving him. As if he would never recover his balance in this relationship.

She wriggled again with a soft huff, and his body came alive.

His arm was tucked under her breasts, her head in the groove of his arm. The lush curves of her buttocks pressed against his groin invitingly and his erection twitched and lengthened in greedy response.

He let his gaze linger over her naked body. And felt a jolt of shame when he saw the imprints of his fingers over her hips and inner thighs. *Dio*, he was a civilized man, not an animal. And yet, the thought seemed to have no control over his libido.

Careful not to wake her, he pulled his arms from under her and slipped out of the bed.

After a quick shower where the innocent enchantress had once again sent his lust into overdrive, where he had quite mercilessly pounded into her already-used body, he had barely toweled her dry before she had fallen into a deep sleep.

But even as those long lashes had been fluttering closed over luminous eyes—how had he never realized how big her eyes truly were behind those spectacles?—and her breath had been slowing down, she had kissed him softly. Slowly, as if in his mouth lay the key to her dreams.

Her cheeks had been pink, her eyes shining with that love she so easily whispered about to him.

Just you.

No two words had ever caused such a powerful longing to rush through his body. Struck such deep fear into him.

He hadn't been *just Raphael* in a long time, if ever.

He had been a scholarship engineering student at university, a son who had lost his father amidst a financial scandal and not allowed time to grieve, a young man who had suddenly become responsible for the pampered lifestyles of his mother and sisters, a man driven by ambition to wipe clean the scandal associated with his father's death, a protégé under the genius of Giovanni Vito, and then finally a CEO who had chosen and pursued the most beautiful, the most glittering, insubstantial butterfly of a woman to be his trophy wife.

But the way Pia looked at him, with startling emotion from the depths of her warm brown eyes, for the first time since he had accepted Giovanni's unspoken challenge, unease settled in his chest.

If all the trappings of his wealth and status were removed, if his ambition and his driving need not to become his father or share his fate were removed, then who was he at his core? Without the shame he felt for his father's failure, the bitterness brewed for years by his mother's care-

less callousness, the cynicism he had developed in order
to bear Allegra's affairs—who was he then?

Had Gio ever wondered if that man was good enough
for his precious Pia Alessandra Vito?

CHAPTER FOURTEEN

NOTHING, IT SEEMED to Pia, had gone right the day of her engagement party to Raphael.

The mid-October day had dawned sunny enough, with just the right amount of chill in the air. Pia's usual breakfast with Gio on the small veranda, the perfect start to her day, hadn't happened because he'd been interrupted yet again by a call from one of his sisters and he'd left immediately.

Pia had begun to dislike Thea Rosa quite a bit, for she seemed to delight in torturing Giovanni with all kinds of escapades at her old age.

So she'd breakfasted alone. All her misgivings about Raphael had grown into an insurmountable obstacle.

The toast she'd had sat in her tummy like a piece of lead, hard and unforgiving. And since she hadn't been paying attention, she had accidentally spilled hot water over her fingers and scalded herself.

What, or rather who, she really wanted was Raphael. They hadn't seen each other for a fortnight and Pia felt quite a juvenile resentment that his business always seemed to take him away when she needed him the most.

Just as he'd been unavailable the day she'd realized her period was three weeks late and had freaked out. After the first night with Raphael, she'd immediately gone on the pill. He was the one she wanted to freak out and panic with, since he partly shared the blame if she were pregnant. But no, Raphael had been in blasted Tokyo negotiating a new trade agreement between Vito Automobiles and a Japanese manufacturing company.

Instead, she'd had to beg Emilio to drive her to a pharmacy at least twenty kilometers from Gio's estate and Como where Raphael lived, to buy a pregnancy test. And then she'd performed the test in secret, because she was terrified of a servant finding out and telling Gio before she'd had a chance to process it and told Raphael.

Fortunately, the test had been negative.

Yet Pia had sat in the restroom for half an hour, feeling an inexplicable but violent urge to cry.

What she'd wanted then was the solid, comforting presence of the man she loved. The man who it seemed took care of every small thing for her.

On his return from Japan, Pia had broached the subject of his cutting down at work, and had received the most piercing stare leveled at her. He hadn't shut her down as he usually did but he hadn't responded to her suggestion either. Even Gio had backed her, saying he could delegate more.

"My father delegated, he trusted people he shouldn't have and his business sank within two years," had been his reply.

Since she didn't want to hurt him, and his father had always been a touchy subject with Raphael, Pia had left it at that.

She had let a lot of things slide, she realized now, but weren't those the growing pains of a new relationship? Pia had learned that Raphael, even after being married once, rarely, if ever, shared his thoughts with anybody. He was used to going it alone, used to that role of problem solver so much.

But the more they saw of each other and the more they had planned their engagement, the more Raphael had begun retreating from her. He'd become the stranger she had met that first night, brooding and unapproachable, except for the fact that she was allowed to sleep with him now.

Like clockwork, he either brought her to his apartment, kept her up until dawn—not that Pia wasn't just as voracious for his touch, for his possession—or he came to her at Gio's house, long after Gio and the staff had gone to bed. Usually, he found Pia studying or working on her toys.

When she was, he shed his shirt and shoes and waited for her to finish—as if she could make sense of a single line when his mere presence fried her brain. And then he took her to bed.

And every time, he made love to her—whether tenderly or with a fierce passion that left her sore for hours later—Pia couldn't stop the words of love tumbling from her mouth. Because it was only there she found the Raphael she had fallen in love with. Only there that he opened up to her. Only there was he not a stranger.

Three weeks later now, her period had started, and then stalled after a day. Pia had no choice except to ask one of Raphael's sisters to recommend a gynecologist and claim a ghastly yeast infection to silence the instant speculation written on all four of his sisters' faces as well as on Portia Mastrantino's.

Raphael was out of town. He wasn't flying in until a couple of hours before their engagement party. And again, Pia found herself battling the most inexplicable urge to cry.

No, not inexplicable anymore, if she were honest with herself.

Something had changed, she now realized since the night at the opera. Since Raphael had received that phone call? Since she'd agreed to marry him?

No, since she had told him that she had fallen in love with him.

It clicked like the missing piece of a puzzle that had been tying her up in knots.

That was it, the moment when everything had changed. The moment Raphael had begun withdrawing from her.

Why? She hadn't demanded anything of him. She had never said it with an expectation that he would reciprocate. She had only said it because she loved him. God, she loved him with everything in her and she wanted him to know it. She wanted him to know that she appreciated him, that she understood why he would probably never say it back. That she loved him just as he was.

Had he lost interest in her because of that? Had her appeal dimmed as a result?

She had heard talk among his mother and sisters that Allegra was back in Milan. That he'd been seen with her at a new restaurant. For a split second, Pia's faith in him had wavered. Even when she prodded, he barely said two sentences to her about Allegra.

Did he want to be back with his ex? Had she paled in comparison to the famed beauty?

No, something in her whispered.

Raphael was not some fickle boy she had a crush on. Raphael would never break her trust in that way. He thought her naïveté, her lack of sophistication was attractive. That it made her unique.

Yet, all afternoon, the question of his withdrawal gnawed at her soul.

Her fingers burning, her stomach in a constant knot, Pia watched in dismay as a small battalion of workers arrived in the huge open area in front of the house and began putting up a snow-white marquee of humongous proportions.

Fifteen minutes later a party organizer, an army of catering vans and then another crew of workers to decorate the tables arrived.

She hurriedly called to Portia, who had put the party

together, that there must be some mistake. Only to be informed that there wasn't. Two hundred and fifty guests were arriving to celebrate Raphael Mastrantino's engagement to Giovanni Vito's granddaughter.

The board of Vito Automobiles and all of their families, major shareholders, Gio's extended family, all of the million Mastrantino cousins and their families—it seemed the entire world wanted to see Raphael and his new fiancée.

"They all want to make their nods to Raphael. I mean, they always knew this would happen, but now it is more… definite, *si*?" Portia had said over the phone.

When Pia had whispered that she didn't actually understand, Portia said "When Gio declared you his granddaughter and his heir, it created problems for my Raphael."

"But why?"

"Because Giovanni and Raphael both own thirty-five percent each of VA's stock. With your appearance, it became clear that whoever married you would inherit that stock. So there were some who thought Raphael would not remain CEO for long. My son is a ruthless businessman and not everyone likes his principles, his practices. Some thought they would betray him and make good with the man Gio chose for you." Knuckles white, Pia gripped the phone, nausea rising through her throat. "But now that Raphael is marrying you, everyone wants to cook favor with him again."

The phone dropped from Pia's hand and clattered to the ground while she grappled with the truth.

Pia heard Portia's stilted English still coming from the phone, saw the decorators pull out rare orchids in droves, and it was all a haze as she walked back to her bedroom.

Now that Raphael was marrying Pia, there would be no contest for the CEO position. With 70 percent of the controlling stock in his hands, no one would ever again rival Raphael's powerful position. No one would ever take away the most valuable thing from Raphael—his wealth, his status and more than anything, his power.

For that was the only thing that defined Raphael Mastrantino.

And that power was the only reason he had proposed to Pia.

Because, she knew without doubt, Giovanni would have given Raphael Vito Automobiles for only one thing in return.

A ring on her finger.

With Gio nowhere to be seen, and family members—both Vitos and Mastrantinos—arriving as early as four, Pia found no respite anywhere in the house. Not that she could escape the misery of her own thoughts if she were alone.

At the risk of seeming churlish to Portia and Raphael's sisters, she had refused to dress for the party. At least not until she saw him. Not until she cleared up this matter with him.

Dressed in jeans and a sweatshirt of Raphael's that she had borrowed from his apartment one night, she was about to bolt to a café in the village when someone grabbed her and pushed her into Gio's study, thankfully empty of well-meaning relatives.

Raphael stood leaning against the door, devouring her as hungrily as she did him.

The sight of him hit her hard, sending such a pulse of longing through her that she swayed. His clothes for once weren't perfect, his eyes sported dark circles.

And yet he was so dear to her heart. An extension of herself.

Other things were more important to him than her. Even that she had accepted. But if the very foundation, the existence of their relationship was because she was Gio's heir—could she live with that?

"Ciao, bella."

"Did you just get back from Tokyo?"

"Not ten minutes ago."

"Raphael, we have to—"

Not a word emerged from her mouth before he slammed her into the door none too gently and his mouth covered hers. All her misery evaporated under the hungry onslaught of his lips.

"Dio, I have missed you, I have missed this body and now the bloody house is crawling with cousins and aunts." His lips fused to hers, his hand crawled under the sweatshirt that she was wearing.

Filling his hands with her breasts, he growled his approval at her braless state. Past the point of no return, even knowing that this passion would only make things worse when she confronted him, Pia couldn't stop him. Couldn't stop herself from mindlessly rubbing up against him. Couldn't stop herself from stealing this incredible pleasure, this closeness with him.

"I missed you too." She pulled at his hair and bit his lower lip, frustration making her reckless. "I needed you, Raphael, God, how I needed you." A strangled cry escaped her when he rubbed his whiskers against her nipple, and then ensconced it in the wet warmth of his mouth. "I hate your job. I hate that you're never there when I need you. I hate that—"

His teeth tugged gently at her nipple and Pia lost rational thought.

As if sensing her own edgy need for him, a torrent of Italian fell from his mouth. He praised her, he told her in elaborate detail how much he had missed her, how he had taken himself in hand one night in his hotel room imagining it was her mouth again. Pia was sobbing by the time he unzipped her jeans and then his trousers, begging shamelessly for him to do all the things he was promising by the time he lifted her up against the door.

She wrapped her legs around his hips and he drove into her wet heat.

Guttural groans colored the air.

Head thrown back, arms vined around his neck, Pia gave herself over to the incredible sensation spiraling through her pelvis as Raphael plunged and withdrew with sure, fast thrusts.

And lost in the indescribable pleasure, lost to the magic he wove, she couldn't stop the words. "I love you, Raphael…and I hate you for what you're doing to me."

His sweat slicked body stilled around her, his dark eyes staring at her with shock. Tense muscles jutted out of his shoulders.

"Pia?"

But far too gone now, Pia buried her mouth in his neck and bit him, urging him to move.

On the next thrust up, he kissed her. Tongues tangled, teeth bit. And he moved inside her, with desperately hard thrusts, without the finesse she had come to know from him.

They exploded together within seconds of each other, their harsh breaths a symphony in the silence.

With her body's utterly explosive climax came Pia's tears, releasing everything she had been holding on to so tightly for weeks, afraid that if she voiced it, it would all fall apart.

She pushed at his shoulders and Raphael pulled out of her and slid her down to the ground gently. If he hadn't held on to her, Pia would have slithered into a heap on the floor.

The scent of him curled around her. Made her body and mind automatically think he was hers. That he would never deceive her.

God, she was a naive idiot.

With gentle movements, he straightened her clothes. Pia jerked away from his touch. A guilty flush scoured his cheeks as he took in her actions. His mouth tightened, deep grooves etched around it.

"Please, let me go."

He stared at her tears, as if he were fascinated by the sight of them. And sighed. *"Bene."*

She buried her face in her hands. She was aware of every breath of his, of the shift and slide of his muscles as he pulled up his legs. She wanted to burrow into his embrace and sob like one of her students.

But how could he erase the hurt when he was the one who had caused it?

"Pia, was I rough?"

The tenderness in his voice almost broke her. "No." The aftermath of her climax still made her body clench. "Yes, but I wanted it just as much as you did. I'm not breakable."

His rough exhale said he'd been horribly worried about her answer. His worried gaze said he found no solace in it. "Not breakable, *cara mia*. Fragile." He stared at his own hands as if looking for answers as to how to handle her there. He fisted them and she knew it was to stop himself from reaching out to her.

That he knew something was wrong between them offered no relief to the ache in her chest. Why hadn't he fixed it, she wanted to ask. Wasn't that what he was good at?

He ran a hand over his face. "Pia, whatever it is that's bothering you, we will work through it. I… I admit that I have a problem with delegation at work. And I'm willing to find some middle ground."

"It might be a little late now," she said, hating the dejection in her voice.

He stilled. "What do you mean?"

"Why are you tender with me only before or after sex, Raphael? Why do you hide away, closet your emotions, shut me down when we're not engaged in intimacy?"

This time, she definitely didn't imagine the guilty look in his eyes. "You're imagining things. I told you I'm not a man of sweet words."

She snorted. And the bitterness in that sound appalled her. Was that what he had done to her? Had he achieved what Frank hadn't? How could it be love when it hurt so much? "Please don't insult my intelligence. You blow hot when it comes to sex and then cold the rest of the time. You twist me in knots. I'm not allowed to comment on your work life—"

"I just admitted that I have a problem."

"I'm not allowed to talk about what is going on with Allegra. I'm not allowed to mention your father. Damn it, Raphael, I know half the things that are going on in your life because of your mother."

He cursed hard and long. "She has upset you. I should've known. Pia, there's nothing between me and Allegra. Do you have such little faith in me?"

"She did not upset me. *Your* actions did. God, Raphael, when were you going to tell me that you're using our upcoming wedding, using me to deny Allegra even visiting rights to Alyssa? You want me to be a mother to your little girl, but I'm not allowed a say in it?"

"I will not force you to be a mother if you don't—"

"I love your daughter!"

"Then what is the problem?"

"It's your assumption that I will play along with whatever you have mapped out for us, your inability to include me in anything important in your life. All you want from me is sex. It's the only reason it took me this long to figure it out."

"Figure what out, Pia?"

"That you began retreating from me since I told you I loved you. I guess the guilt was too much for even you."

"What guilt?"

"The guilt of making me fall in love with you, the guilt you feel when I look at you with adoring eyes, the guilt of hiding the fact that you only asked me to marry you because I come with a hefty stock option in Vito Automobiles."

She thought he would explode with anger. But his silence only confirmed his guilt. It skewered the last ray of hope she had nourished that there would be a different explanation, that there could be another reason.

Some fantasy that she hadn't known she had bought into that gorgeous, powerful men like Raphael Mastrantino could fall for plain, geeky, shy nobodies like her.

And now she was pathetically self-pitying too.

"Pia, I was attracted to you from the first night. And you to me." The resignation in his voice delivered the final crack against her heart. He wasn't even denying her allegation.

"According to your mother, you attract more than half the female population in Milan, if not Italy. But I don't think you'd consider marrying them all."

"No. I admit that when Gio proposed it—"

"Of course Nonno talked you into it." She banged her head into the door behind her. The urge to do violence instantly died when her head pounded.

"*Dio mio, Pia!* Stop acting like a child!"

"When have you or Gio treated me like an adult? I obviously don't inspire him to high levels of confidence in myself. Clearly, he knew that it was a facade. Was it the stock that worked finally? Or was it the fact that with the stock in hand, as the uncontested CEO of VA, you've reached heights that your father never could. You could prove to yourself and the world that you're not him. That you could never be weak like him. Have you sold yourself to Gio just to prove that you're incapable of loving, Raphael?"

Raphael pushed up to his feet with an athletic grace she loved and hated and pulled her up with him. When she'd have pushed away from the door, he caged her there with his body. The scent of their intimacy was still thick in the air, a potent mixture that made longing rush through her. "The only thing Gio sought to do was to protect you…"

"From the likes of Frank, *si*? Because I'm naive and plain and will fall for any sweet-talking rogue, like I fell for you, *si*? I get it. He could have just tied up the stock in your name, couldn't he? He could have told me not to fall for anyone because it is only the Vito fortune that is valuable about me."

"Pia, that's not true."

"That's what your actions have made me believe, Raphael," she said softly. "That's what hurt the most. He didn't have to barter me to you as if I were cattle he couldn't wait to get rid of."

Raphael cursed. "He did that because he thought I needed you too."

"Then he is a foolish old man. Because you don't need anybody, least of all a naive idiot like me. Congratulations, Raphael, you have the company, you have the world's adoration, and you have proof that you'll never give something as weak as love any place in your life, like the rest of us. But you've lost me."

Tears catching her throat, Pia pushed away from him.

"Do not walk away from this. Talk to me. Tell me what you need from me. This is the night of our engagement party. There are two hundred people arriving even now."

"All these weeks I was desperate to hear those words from you. I was… I really needed you, Raphael. You will protect me from the big bad wolves of the world. You will triple and double my stock value in VA. You will ply me with expensive, breathtaking gifts. You will seduce me long into dawn. You will pleasure me until I don't know my own name. But you can't love me, can you? You were right all along. It's just not in you." Poison spewed from her lips and Pia couldn't seem to stop herself. And for this, for turning her into this, she truly hated him. "I thought it was only words you weren't capable of."

"I understand that you're upset. But you're being far too cynical about it."

"Shouldn't you be happy that I see the world now as you see it?"

"Nothing has changed."

"No, everything has changed, Raphael. Don't you see? *I* have changed. My perception of *you* has changed. In my eyes, you're no better than Frank."

He reared back as if she had hit him. His nostrils flared, his jaw became tight. "You do not mean that."

"He cooked a friendship with me, pretended to love me because I was an easy mark he could siphon cash out of. You proposed marriage, you bought me with a ring for the same reason. Ergo, you are just like Frank."

A paleness seemed to pool beneath his olive skin. His hands folded, he shrugged. "If you can think that of me, you're right. There's nothing left between us to fix."

Tears clawed up her throat, but she was damned if she would cry again in front of him. Her chest hurt, her limbs trembled. And suddenly Pia knew why it hurt so much, why it felt as if a part of her was being wrenched away.

Why even the worst words from Frank hadn't given her a millionth of this pain. Why it was utterly important that she preserve her pride in front of Raphael while she had flailed like an idiot in front of Frank.

Because his betrayal felt like he'd taken her heart and pounded it into pieces. Because it felt like she would never stop loving him and yet she could never bear to live with him.

She wrapped her arms around herself. "Please tell your cohort that the engagement is off. I can't bear to be near you right now. Tell Gio that I will see him again when he stops hanging that stock sign around my neck for every eligible man to look over. Maybe Gilda didn't sacrifice herself for love, Raphael. Maybe she just wanted freedom from the Duke and her father. And that was the only way she could have it."

CHAPTER FIFTEEN

YOU'RE NO BETTER than Frank.

Weeks after she had spoken them, Pia's words burned holes through Raphael's head.

For the first week or so, he had held on to the anger.

How could she even think that he was the same as that bastard who had deceived her, who had used her for his greed? If he was so low in her estimation, there was no point in them continuing the relationship.

By the third week, his anger had drained away and all that remained was a gnawing sensation in his gut. A burn in his throat. *Dio*, her accusations were a nail continually scraping at his flesh.

But even beneath the hurt, he knew the dread that she was right. At least from where she stood.

He could hardly sleep for the regrets that ate through him all hours.

Even after Frank had hurt her, Pia had never wished him harm. But she'd been so angry, so cynical that day.

So hurt by his actions…

His first thought of even having a relationship with her had begun with Gio's proposal in mind. That he had felt guilty about it, just as she had perceptively realized, was also true.

As days had flown by in the buildup to their engagement party, and the more they were entrenched in each other's lives, the more he had realized that she deserved so much that he could not give.

It was why he had withdrawn from her. Why he had struggled for the first time in his life with the idea that he was inadequate for the role he wanted to play. Nothing and no one had ever prepared him to receive such unconditional acceptance, such unadulterated affection.

And instead of telling her the truth, instead of admitting to his mistakes when she had confronted him, he had pushed her away.

I needed you, Raphael, so much.

The most important person in his life, and he hadn't been there for whatever it was she had needed from him.

He wanted to cherish Pia; he wanted to give her everything she wanted. *Dio mio*, he wanted to be able to love her.

No, not just be able to…

He did love her. He'd been so caught up in his own insecurity that he hadn't realized that he wanted her happiness above everything else in the world, even above his own.

Instead of telling her that, instead of sharing his crisis of faith in himself, he had alienated the best thing that had ever happened to him. Crushed the heart of the one woman, the only person who had seen the real him, who had loved the true him.

I want you, Raphael. Just you.

This time, her words filled him with elation, with energy. This time, instead of pulling away the ground from underneath him, he realized how fortunate he was to have found Pia.

How incredible it was that such a generous woman had seen something in him that was worth loving. That he had been given a chance to love her in return, to spend the rest of his life knowing that whether he succeeded or failed at another business venture, whether he remained hard and unyielding or not, Pia would always love him.

That was how she was made.

And, *maledizione*, he had hurt her for loving him.

Refusing to waste another moment, Raphael choppered himself to Gio's estate instead of being stuck in traffic.

"She's not here," Giovanni mumbled from the sitting lounge even before Raphael could ask the question.

Gio looked tired. Raphael took a seat next to him, his throat closing up. "I ruined it all, didn't I?" He buried his face in his hands. "I… I should have never interfered. I shouldn't have forced—"

"I never intended to hurt her, Gio. I have been a fool, ten times everything you told me I was becoming. But I didn't listen."

"You see, you and I both misjudged Pia. We thought just because she's soft-spoken and generous to a fault, she needed us to look after her, to treat her as if she were a child. But she is tougher than even my Lucia, I think. Only a strong woman could forgive the hurt we caused her."

Raphael jerked his head up. Hope burned a hole through him. "What do you mean? Is she talking to you again? Has she come back from her…*friend's* house?" He almost choked on that word.

That she had moved to her carpenter friend Antonio's house had been a physical blow.

Even split up as they had been—permanently, in her mind—he knew Pia still loved him. That Pia would never just fall out of love with him.

Still, every time he had thought of her sharing a small studio with him—and it had been every waking minute— a possessive urge to throw her over his shoulder and bring her back to his apartment had overpowered him.

"*Si*, she has returned. She said she was too worried about me but it didn't mean she has forgiven me. I am worried about her."

"Why?"

Gio didn't quite meet his eyes. "I promised her I would stay out of this mess between you and her." He sighed. "So I didn't send for you even though... I cannot say more, Raphael. Are you here to fix your mistakes?"

"*Si.* And to beg her to forgive me, if need be."

"But she's very hurt. If you do not love her, you will do it again."

"Giovanni, trust me this time to get it right. *Per favore.*" Yet Gio stared at him doubtfully. When had his reassurance not worked for Gio? What the hell was he not saying?

Had he lost Pia?

He shot up from his seat, his nerves shot to hell for the first time in his life. "Where is she?"

"In her bedroom. I'm sure her nap is done."

And since when the hell had Pia needed to nap in the afternoon? The woman was either studying or carving or walking or making friends or learning Italian.

He was already at the foot of the steps when Gio's words stopped him. "Remember what you did and how much she has to forgive. Do not get angry. Do not let your ego get in the way."

Gio's warning ringing in his ears, Raphael took three stairs at a time, pushed open the door to Pia's bedroom and strode in.

She was standing leaning against the wall, looking out into the balcony and turned immediately when he closed the door behind him with a soft thud.

And paled when her sleep-mussed gaze found him.

Something was different about her, he would have known even without Gio's cryptic warnings.

She seemed to have shrunk three sizes in just a few weeks. Not that she had much weight to lose to begin with. Her hair was piled in that knot tightly over the top of her head and it pulled her skin tighter over her features.

Dio mio, she looked as if a hard breeze could blow her over.

Had he done this to her?

"*Christo*, Pia, what the hell have you done to yourself?"

He rushed to her, desperate for action, desperate to set things to rights.

But she moved back from him, her chin stubbornly tilted. Her mouth narrowed. Only her eyes, her gorgeous brown eyes reflected her emotions. "I would appreciate it if you didn't talk to me as if I were an imbecile. Or better, please leave, if that's all you have to say."

He couldn't bear to have her look at him like that.

Couldn't bear the idea of something being wrong with her. Nausea filled his throat. "Are you ill?" The thought of some unnamed disease doing this to her threatened to take him out at the knees.

"Did Gio ask you here?" Fury flared in her gaze at the thought. "Christ, I told him never again. I told him he wasn't to breathe a word to you and he swore…"

Raphael pulled her roughly into his arms, his heart beating so hard he could hear it in his ears. "*Dio mio*, calm yourself. Gio didn't ask me. I came of my own accord. I came to ask him about you. I came because I couldn't…" He drank her in. "Pia, are you sure you're not ill?"

"Stop saying that. You don't have to make me feel worse than I already do. I know I look a fright…"

"Get over yourself, will you? You are beautiful to me. Always. But it's true that you look like you'll break apart if I press hard."

Some of his panic must have come across because she sighed. A wariness entered her eyes. Still, she stepped back from him. "I'm not ill. Just…" A shrug and she looked away. "What are you doing here? Please Raphael, just for once, respect me enough to leave me alone." Sudden tears filled her eyes. "Seeing you like this…you have no idea how hard it is for me.

I have some things to think through, some decisions to make. Then we can talk, *si*?"

He inclined his head. A lead weight sat on his chest. "But I have something to say to you. Will you hear me out?"

"*Si*. As long as you give your word that you won't touch me."

He swallowed the punch it was to his chest and nodded. *"Bene."*

Taking her hands in his, he pulled her to a sofa, then released them. Then went on his knees in front of her. The tears she had valiantly tried to hold back fell over onto her cheeks. And she sniffled.

"Please, *bella*. Do not cry. That I did this to you…" Even his throat was burning now. "Pia, I adore you from the bottom of my heart."

She shook her head and he said, "Just one chance, Pia. Let me finish. I…yes, it was Gio who…maneuvered me into this. You were right. He dangled everything I wanted in front of me. I resisted as long as I could and it was hell for me. But the night of his heart attack, I just couldn't deny it anymore. You were right. I felt the inevitable weight of your responsibility on my shoulders. With Gio looking like he did… I couldn't walk away anymore.

"Everything you said about it is true. But Pia, even if he hadn't, there was a connection between us from the first moment. Not just attraction, *cara mia*. Something that went deeper than that. Even with my jaded view of the world, I knew how incredible you were, how giving. Giovanni was right when he said I needed you in my life, just not the other way around. Only I didn't want to acknowledge the connection. I didn't want to see anything deeper at that time. How could I? I have never known a connection like that before.

"Given enough time, I would like to believe that I'd have come around to the same idea. I have to believe that I would have recognized how precious you are. Seen how much happiness, how much peace you brought into my life. Your love humbles me, *cara mia*, reminds me of what is important in life. Strips everything from me and leaves the core of me stronger. And I would spend the entirety of our lives, an eternity, making you happy, if you would give me another chance."

Breaking his word, he kissed her knuckles. He buried his face in her chest. Her heart thudded near his mouth, the scent of her settling deep in his pores. With Pia, he was home. "I love everything about you, *cara mia*. Every inch of you. Every smile of yours."

"I want to believe you, Raphael. I missed you so much too."

It was as if a weight lifted from his chest. He pressed kisses from her wrists to her shoulders and then across her neck, joy filling him to the brim. "Then marry me, Pia. Marry me because I can't go another day without seeing you, without holding you, without kissing you. Marry me because I want to be yours. Pia's Raphael—when I'm with you, I'm the best of myself."

When her tears gave way to sobs and she fell into his arms, Raphael held her tight and uttered useless phrases for he could not bear her pain.

"You made me doubt myself. You made me hate myself. Love should not do that," she whispered, between hiccups.

He clasped her cheeks and stared into her eyes. "*No, cara mia*. It should not. There's nothing in the world that could put a price tag on you. I fell in love with you long before I realized it. I would not change a thing about you, Pia. You have to believe me."

She nodded and wiped her cheeks, sudden resolution in her movements. "Then I have to tell you something too.

And you have to promise that you will tell me what you feel. That whether you get angry or furious or hurt, you will communicate with me. That you won't just shut me down."

Heart beating rapidly, he nodded. "Pia, you can tell me anything."

She drew in a long breath. "I'm pregnant."

He felt dizzy, as if someone had robbed all the air around them. Questions pounded through him, like flies buzzing, and beneath that, a crushing sense of void in his gut.

This was what Gio had been talking about. *Christo*, how long had she known? How long had she been hiding the truth? How long would she have kept it a secret?

"It is yours," she said so softly that his head jerked up.

He gritted his teeth, trying to corral the hurtful things that wanted to get out. "For all my sins, Pia, I never doubted your loyalty, your love."

The betrayed look in his eyes made Pia wish she could change the circumstances. She had never wanted to be the one who deceived him, never wanted to see that disillusionment in his eyes, but if she had told him, with what she'd learned since about Alyssa... All she had held on to was hope.

He was processing it, she knew, running through the emotions. Breath braced, she waited, hoped he wouldn't just cut her off again. Even a furious explosion was preferable to him shutting her down.

"How far along are you?"

"Almost ten weeks. I think it happened that first time."

"I wore a condom."

"They are not foolproof. Raphael, I know it's a shock but—"

He stood up, a sudden energy to his movements. "What was the decision you had to make? Things you had to think through?" Whiteness emerged under his skin. "*Dio mio*, were you just going to leave Italy without telling me, like Lucia did to Gio? Was that my punishment for hurting you, Pia? Is that all your love means?"

Pia wrapped her hands over his shoulders, willing him to look at her. "Raphael, please listen to me. I… I wasn't going to go anywhere. I would have never left Italy without telling you, even if I wasn't pregnant."

His fingers manacled her wrists, emotion tight in his features. "Then why the hell didn't you tell me?"

"Because if I had told you, you would have insisted on us marrying."

"Of course I would have. Do you want our child to be illegitimate?"

"I don't care for that label, seeing as my father carried it his whole life. I love you with everything in me, Raphael. I will love you the rest of my life. But to be married to you knowing that we were together for our child, knowing that you were doing it to protect me and the baby, to be another responsibility to you, it would've killed any love I felt for you…" She shuddered. "I couldn't live like that."

"What if I had never come back, Pia?"

"After my initial anger faded, I couldn't help but hope. Gio told me about how Alyssa wasn't even yours."

When he cursed, she bade him to look at her. "I was the one who held her first. The one she bonded with, the one who she asks for when she has a hurt. She's just as much mine as she's Allegra's. It doesn't matter that biologically I'm not her father."

"The only reason Gio told me, I think, is to give me hope. And he was right. After everything she did to you, that you could love that little girl so much made me hope, Raphael. It told me that I hadn't made a mistake again. It told me that you could love me. And when Gio told me that you had reconsidered Allegra's requests, that you had agreed to supervised visits, it made me fall in love with you a little more."

"I did it after our fight, when I realized how much I had hurt you. Allegra and I hurt each other throughout our marriage. If there was any chance for you to forgive me, to love me again, I realized I needed to be a better man. For you, Pia. You bring out the best in me, *cara mia*."

Pia felt as if she could fly, as if the happiness rushing through her would consume her.

Sinking her fingers into his hair, she pulled his head down and kissed him. His taste sent a familiar pang through her, released an incredible joy.

He loved her. He loved her. She wanted to shout the words to the world.

He pushed away from her, his breathing rough, his gaze still hurt. "Is this what you needed to talk to me about?"

She nodded, glad that he was talking, working through his emotions with her. "The first test was negative. Then I had some—" heat piled over her cheeks "—bleeding for a day. I thought it was my period finally. But apparently some women bleed even when pregnant. Finally I went to see a doctor and she confirmed it."

He hugged her tight, so hard that for a few seconds Pia couldn't even breathe. "And now? Has it stopped? Is it a danger to you or the baby?"

"No. I still can't keep anything down, which is why I lost so much weight and I have to call her if anything happens."

Raphael sighed. He should have been there with her. "When did you see the doctor?"

"The day after we...the day after everything fell apart."

Lifting her into his arms, he sat down on a chaise and pulled her into his lap. His hands crawled to her midriff, and sure enough, he could feel the barely there curve of her stomach. A wash of contentment settled over him. "It has been rough on you?"

She nodded and burrowed into his chest. "I have been suffering through this horrible nausea. For a while there, I couldn't eat even a cracker for fear of…" She cringed and he smiled.

"Will you forgive me? For not being there when you needed me."

Smiling, she kissed his jaw and then his mouth. "Raphael, I love you from the bottom of my heart. There's no need for forgiveness if you truly believe that you want to spend the rest of your life with me."

"You still doubt me?"

The minx shrugged.

He pushed to his feet and carried her to the bed. He crawled over her, joy beating in his chest. "Then I will have to spend the next few months convincing you that I do. That without you, my life is barren, hard, cold."

"Are you sure you aren't talking about your bed?"

"That too," he whispered before taking her mouth in a hard kiss.

His world for the first time in his life was complete. His family was complete. And he felt utterly loved for just the man he was.

* * * * *

To the memory of my dear dad—Robert 'Jim' Giblett—
who didn't get to see this one finished
after many hours on the phone listening to
me making up these stories, laughing in the right places
and telling me I could do it when I thought I couldn't.

Life isn't the same without you, Dad.
You were everything to me,
your Lucy/Kareena

CHAPTER ONE

'I'VE FOUND YOU a girl,' was the unexpected news his grandfather greeted Nik Voronov with cheerfully. 'She's local, so you'll have to come down.'

The key words, Nik suspected, were, *You'll have to come down.*

His conscience pricked. He hadn't set out ten years ago, when he'd founded his company, to work twelve-hour days and seven-day weeks, but he did. He had the world on his shoulders, and his grandfather more of late on his conscience, and balancing the two was hard.

Nik lowered his head as a gust of wind buffeted him on the approach to the complex of site buildings where he had an office.

Around him was the site where his company, Voroncor, were sinking down exploratory equipment and mining kimberlite deposits from the rich Siberian earth. Work went on all year round, and because it was January everything was white except in patches where the ashy black earth showed through.

At least the wind had died down and he could see what he was looking at. Three years' hard work to pull this reserve into the Voroncor fold.

'Is that right, Deda?'

'Her name is Sybella and she has everything a man could want. She cooks and cleans and she's wonderful with children!'

The triumvirate of qualities guaranteed to ensure a man a good life, according to his seventy-nine-year-old grandfather.

Nik was well aware he could remind the old man he had

a chef on the payroll, cleaning staff for all four of his international residences and no children to speak of. Moreover, no woman in the twenty-first century would view cooking, cleaning and raising children her sole responsibility.

But he'd be wasting his breath and it wasn't the point.

Tactfully he rolled out the line he'd been using since his grandfather became actively interested in his personal life, which had—not mysteriously—coincided with the loss of his own wife, Nik's adored grandmother.

'When and if I do meet the right woman, you'll be the first to know, Deda.'

His grandfather harrumphed. 'I've seen you on the Internet with that model.'

The Internet? The last time they'd spoken the old man was using the tablet he'd got him as a tea tray.

But he knew who his grandfather was referring to.

Voroncor's sister company Voroncor Holdings had bought out a retail corporation and Nik found himself in possession of some premium retail brands, including the fashion house Spanish model/actress and 'it' girl Marla Mendez was currently spruiking for.

The lady had pursued him around the world seeking his investment in her personal project, a lingerie line, not exactly his field but he had a personal reason for stumping up the funds that had nothing to do with Ms Mendez herself. A few photographs of them together at events had been enough for the tabloids to seize on the idea they were personally involved. He saw no reason to set his grandfather straight.

'That woman is not right for you, Nikolka. There is something hard about her. She would not be good with little children.'

Nik considered reminding his grandfather he had no children, but he suspected that was Deda's point.

'Sybella works with children,' his grandfather added helpfully.

No surprises there.

'I think you should come and see her at work. I think you would be impressed, *moy mal'chik.*'

There was a long pause as Nik shouldered his way down the corridor and into his office, signalling for a coffee as he passed one of his admin assistants.

'Did you hear me, Nikolka?'

'I'm here, Deda. How did you meet her?'

Nik began pulling off his gloves, idly glancing at the information he'd asked for on the screen of a laptop another assistant silently opened in front of him.

'She lives down the lane from the Hall, in the village. She's a tenant. I believe she pays you rent.'

Vaguely Nik remembered some old English custom of the squire having first rights to local virgins. He held fire on mentioning it to his grandfather.

When he'd bought Edbury Hall a year ago he'd flown over in a helicopter. The village below had been merely a small sea of roofs swallowed up by the encroaching forest. His attention had been on the magnificent Elizabethan 'E', its outbuildings and the undulating pastureland around it.

His lawyer had done the groundwork and put everything in place. The purchase was a good investment, and it currently housed his grandfather while he was in the UK undergoing tests and treatment for a variety of complaints set off by his diabetes.

Nik hadn't paid much attention to a lane, or the village, or the fact he had tenants. His admin dealt with that.

'What are you doing consorting with the tenants? That's not your problem, Deda. You're supposed to be relaxing.'

'Sybella comes to the house to keep me company and help me out with a few secretarial things.'

'You have staff for that.'

'I prefer Sybella. She is genuine.'

'She sounds great,' Nik said mildly enough, making a mental note to ask a few questions of the house staff. He didn't want his grandfather's kindly nature being taken advantage of.

'We have a busload of children from all over the county once a month, up to thirty at a time, and Sybella is un-flappable.'

'Unflappable, good to know.' Nik indicated he had what he needed. Then his head shot up. 'Busloads of—what? Hang on, Deda, where is this?'

'At the Hall. The children who come to see the house.'

Nik stopped finding this amusing. 'Why are busloads of children coming to the house?' But he already knew.

'The Heritage Trust show them around,' Deda said cheerfully.

The Heritage Trust. The local historic buildings pres-ervation group, who had kept the Hall open to the public since the nineteen seventies.

His purchase a year ago had shut all commercial ac-tivities at the Hall down. There had been a picket at the end of the drive for a week in protest until he'd called in the police.

'This is not what we agreed, Deda.'

'I know what you're about to say,' his grandfather blus-tered, 'but I changed my mind. Besides, no final decision was made.'

'No, we talked about it when you moved in and we de-cided to leave the matter in my hands.'

'And now it's in Sybella's,' his grandfather said smugly.

Sybella.

Nik couldn't help picturing one of the matronly women who had picketed the drive, in her husband's oversized hunting jacket and wellington boots, face like the back of a shovel, shouting about British heritage and marching a troop of equally appalling kids through his grandfather's home. When she wasn't going through Deda's papers and possibly siphoning his bank account.

This was not what he wanted to hear. He had a new pipe starting up in Archangelsk, which would keep him in the north for much of this year. Business was expanding and he needed to be on site.

But now he had a new problem: a white elephant of a property sitting up in the English Cotswolds he'd been ignoring for too long, currently housing his grandfather and apparently the local historical group.

Nik didn't have time for this, but he knew he was going to have to make time.

'And what does this *Sybella* have to do with the Heritage Trust when she's not cooking and cleaning and herding children?' he asked tightly.

His grandfather chuckled and delivered the coup de grâce. 'She runs it.'

CHAPTER TWO

THE PRESIDENT OF the local branch of the Heritage Trust stood up, removed her glasses and announced somewhat dolefully to the committee members assembled that a legal document had been lodged this morning at the trust's London office suspending any further activity of the trust in the Hall.

'Does that mean we can't use the empty gatehouse as a visitors' centre?' Mrs Merrywether wanted to know. 'Because Sybella said we could.'

A dozen grey heads turned and Sybella found herself sinking a little lower in her chair, because she had indeed waved a letter around last month claiming they had the right.

But dodging responsibility wasn't her way.

'I can't understand why this has happened,' she told the meeting, feeling very guilty and responsible for the confusion that had gripped the room. 'I'll look into it and sort it out. I promise.'

Seated beside her Mr Williams, the retired local accountant, patted her arm. 'We know you will, Sybella, we trust your judgement. You haven't led us wrong once.'

There was a hum of agreement, which only made Sybella feel worse as she packed up her notes and made her usual early departure.

She had worked hard for twelve months to make Edbury Hall a place of life and activity for its new incumbent, Mr Voronov, and continue to earn its keep for the village. While this house might personally remind her of some grim stage set for a horror film starring Christopher

Lee, the Hall also brought in its share of the tourist trade and kept the local shops turning over.

If this all collapsed it would affect everybody. And she would be responsible.

Rugging herself up in the boot room for her dash home, Sybella fished her phone out of her jeans back pocket and rang her sister-in-law.

Meg lived in a jaunty little semi-detached house on a busy road in Oxford, where she taught art to people with no real aptitude for painting and belly danced at a local Egyptian restaurant. She took off and travelled at the drop of a hat. Her life was possibly the one Sybella would have gravitated towards if life in all its infinite twists of fate hadn't set her on another course, with much more responsibility and less room to move. Sybella considered Meg her best friend.

'It's the letters. I should have known,' she groaned after a brief rundown on tonight's meeting. 'Nobody writes letters any more.'

'Unless you're a lonely seventy-nine-year-old man rattling around in a big empty house, trying to fill it with people,' said Meg.

Sybella sighed. Every time something new occurred at the Hall Mr Voronov gave the same advice.

'Just write to my grandson and let him know. I'm sure there will be no problems.'

So she had. She'd written just as she'd been writing every month for the past year detailing events at Edbury Hall.

Because she'd been too damn timid to face him on the phone.

She'd let her native shyness trip her up—again—and this was the tip, Sybella suspected, of a huge iceberg that was going to take her little ship out. She said as much, leaving out the bit about being a timid mouse. Meg didn't cut you slack for being a mouse.

'My ship, Meg. My ship of fools, me being the captain!'

Meg was silent and Sybella already knew what was coming.

'You know what this is a result of? That weird life you lead in the village.'

'Please, Meg, not now.' Sybella shouldered her way out of the boot room. The corridor was dark and faintly menacing, although she suspected anyone coming across her would probably run the other way. She was wearing her Climb and Ski gear that was packed with a substance that was supposed to keep you warm and dry in the Arctic. It wasn't particularly flattering to a woman's figure and it also inhibited natural movement. She was aware she currently resembled a yeti.

Meg was persistent. 'You hang around with all those oldies…'

'You know why I volunteer with the Heritage Trust. It's going to get me a job in the end.'

Sybella made her way to the servants' entrance, from which she could slip unnoticed out of the house, cross the courtyard and disappear through a space in the hedge that led to the lane that wound down the hill to the top of her road.

'Really? You've been doing unpaid work for them for over a year. When does it pay off for you?'

'It's work experience in my field. Do you know how difficult it is to get a job with just a degree?'

'I don't know why you won't move down to Oxford with me. It's bristling with opportunities.'

'Your parents are here,' she said firmly. She was always firm when it came to her daughter's well-being. 'And I'm not removing Fleur from her home.'

'It's a two-hour drive. They can see her on weekends.'

'Who is going to look after her while I'm at work? Think of the practicalities, Meg.' God knew she had to. If she hadn't been so busy juggling all the balls life had thrown at her she might have thought through those practicalities with a little more precision at the Hall.

'Fair enough,' conceded Meg. 'But you've put a lot of eggs in that house of horrors basket.'

'Yes, because I have a growing daughter who has her roots in this village—a village with no other job opportunities in my chosen field. I've tried Stansfield Castle, Belfort Castle and Lark House. None are interested in someone with lots of education but no on-the-ground experience. Without Edbury Hall, Meg, I'm stuck!'

'So in the meantime you're writing letters to a man you're never going to meet. Should I ask about your love life?'

'What has my love life got to do with the letters?'

'I think if you had a boyfriend you wouldn't have all this extra time to sit around writing letters and sealing envelopes. You'd be like the rest of us and use freaking email.'

'It wasn't extra time. It was extra *effort*. Besides, I do use email. And I'm not looking for a romantic relationship, Meg Parminter.'

'I don't know why not. My brother's been gone six years. You can't keep hiding away in Mouldering Manor with those oldies, Syb. Seize the day!'

Given her days were quite long, what with her part-time archivist job at the town hall, her volunteer work with the Heritage Trust and sole responsibility for her home-schooled five-year-old daughter, Sybella wasn't quite sure which part of the day she wasn't seizing.

Besides, the idea of taking off her clothes in front of a man after six years of not having to endure that specific kind of embarrassment with Simon was not an encouraging one.

'You know that film you love, *The Ghost and Mrs. Muir*?' Meg asked. 'Do you remember at the end when her daughter comes home all grown up with the fiancé? One day that will be Fleur, feeling guilty because she's got a life and you haven't!'

'I will have a life,' Sybella shot back, confident at least on this point. 'I'll be in the midst of a brilliant career as a curator and very fulfilled in my life's ambition, thank you very much.'

'Okay, maybe that analogy doesn't work in the twenty-first century,' Meg grudgingly allowed. 'But are you really going to wait another twenty years before you pull the "take a detour" sign down off your bed?'

Sybella pushed open the heavy wooden door and made her way outside. She blew out a breath and watched it take shape in the air.

Blast, it was cold.

'It's not a priority for me, Meg.'

'Well, it should be!'

Sybella looked around to make sure no one was lurking in the bushes to overhear this.

'I really don't want to discuss my sex life, or lack of. I'm just not interested,' she said firmly. 'There, I've said it. Not. Interested. In. Sex. I am, however, very interested in what I'm going to say to Mr Voronov's grandson when he prosecutes us!'

Which was when she noticed a pricey-looking off-road vehicle coming up the drive, followed by another and another.

Mr Voronov hadn't mentioned guests. She was familiar with his schedule, given she came and gave him a hand with a few things he refused to entrust to the personal assistant his grandson had engaged for him.

She told Meg she'd call her tomorrow and stowed her phone, pulled the ski mask down over her chin to repel the cold and headed out across the drive to see what they wanted.

Nik parked in the courtyard, slammed the door behind him and crunched through the snow to open the boot and retrieve his overnight bag.

He'd never seen England's little tourist Mecca from this vantage point. Driving in, he thought it looked very much as if he'd stumbled onto the film set of the dramatisation of an Agatha Christie novel. Or maybe it was a recreation of Shakespeare's youth because if he wasn't mistaken, as the road had opened out into the town square, there had been a maypole.

Sticking up like a needle without a thread.

Everything else was under a ton of snow and ice.

He glanced up at the looming walls of Edbury Hall, with its multifaceted windows and grey stone. Snow drifts had made clumps of the carefully tended hedges and topiary.

It was a picture postcard of Ye Olde England.

No wonder those crackpots and loonies from Edbury's branch of the Heritage Trust were bombarding his offices in London every time something got raised or lowered on the property.

He sensed rather than heard movement coming up behind him.

Good. Someone around this place was doing their job.

'Here.' He bundled the luggage at the rugged-up figure hovering at his shoulder. Then he slammed the back of the vehicle closed and hit the lock device on his keys.

He turned around to find the help was staggering under its weight. Which didn't last long because the next thing he knew the guy was lying flat on his back in the snow.

He waited. The man wasn't getting up. He did, however, stick a gloved hand in the air and wave it around. He also made a noise that sounded like a cat being drowned in a barrel. Nik liked animals; he didn't much like incompetence in people.

Which was when he noticed the black ski mask under the hood of the guy's coat and Nik lost his easy stance, because in Russia personal security was often a matter of life and death, and right now instinct was telling him this guy was not one of the people he had authorised to work for his grandfather.

He grabbed the interloper by the scruff of his coat and heaved him to his feet.

Sybella tried to cry out but her voice box was currently lodged somewhere in the snow after the impact of hitting the ground.

She found herself being lifted by the scruff of her neck until she was almost hanging, her parka cutting up under her arms, the toes of her new boots scrambling for purchase.

'Give me your name and your reason for being out here.'

Her assailant had a deep, growly baritone that corresponded with his size. His rich Russian accent meant he probably had something to do with the current owner of this property. Given his size and strength he was possibly a bodyguard.

He was also clearly a bear.

'*Imya?*' he barked out when she didn't immediately respond.

'There's been a mistake,' Sybella gasped through the fine wool barrier formed by the ski mask over her mouth.

'What are you, journalist, protester, what?' He gave her another shake. 'I'm losing patience.'

'Put me down,' she pleaded. 'I don't understand what's happening.'

But even to her ears her plea was muffled into incoherence by all the wool and the wind.

Nevertheless, he dropped her and she landed heavily on the soles of her boots. Before she could react he whipped back the hood of her parka and gathered up a handful of her ski mask, yanking on her hair in the process. The ski mask came away and with it her long heavy flaxen curls. Freed, they began whipping around her face in the frigid wind.

His arms dropped to his sides.

'You're a woman,' he said in English as if this was entirely improbable. His voice was deep and firm and weirdly—given the circumstances—reassuring.

Sybella pushed the wildly flapping hair from her eyes and, finally able to be understood, choked out a little desperately, 'I was the last time I looked!'

He stepped in front of her, and if she didn't suspect a little brain damage from all the pushing and shoving, she'd think it was to shield her from the wind and elements.

'Did I hurt you?' he demanded, his head bent to hers.

'N-no.' Scared the life out of her, but she was in one piece.

At least she no longer felt in danger of ending up on her bottom again. She was also staring, because you didn't see men like this every day in Edbury.

He was a good head taller than her and she couldn't see around his shoulders and up close he had slightly slanted grey eyes, thick golden lashes, high flat cheekbones and a strong jaw stubbled in gold. He was gorgeous. His mouth was wide and firm and she found her attention constantly returning to it.

'What are you doing out here?' he demanded.

She could have asked him the same question.

Trying to gather her wits, Sybella took her time checking the seams on the arms of her parka. They appeared intact. Seams, that was. Apparently the fabric could withstand being dangled by a bear, but not the ingress of water. She was soaked through.

And cold.

'I asked you a question,' he repeated. He really was very rude.

'Minding my own business,' she said pointedly, making a show of brushing the snow off her cords to cover the fact her hands were shaking.

'Never show them you're rattled' was one of the few useful lessons a draconian English public boarding school education had taught her. Also, 'be the one asking the questions'—it made you look as if you knew what you were doing.

'Maybe the better question is what are you doing here?' Pity her voice shook a bit.

'I own this house.'

Her head shot up. 'No, you don't. Mr Voronov does.'

'I am Voronov,' he said. 'Nikolai Aleksandrovich Voronov. You are talking about my grandfather.'

Sybella's knees turned to jelly and a funny buzzing sound began to ring in her ears.

'Kolya?' she said a little faintly.

His eyes narrowed and Sybella felt as if she'd been knocked over in the snow for the second time tonight. Somehow, some way, she'd got this all wrong.

He looked her up and down.

'Who did you say you were?'

CHAPTER THREE

IN TROUBLE, THAT was who she was.

'I asked you a question,' he repeated.

Yes, he had, and he expected an answer, she interpreted from the way he just stood there, arms folded, on closer inspection less like a bear and more like some angry Norse god.

'Speak,' he commanded.

She literally jumped but then her training kicked in. She handled tour groups of small children regularly and knew one had to establish rules and boundaries if chaos wasn't to ensue.

'I think you need to calm down,' she said shakily, aware her heart was beating so fast she should probably take her own advice.

He took out his phone.

'Wh-what are you doing?'

'Ringing the police.'

Oh, that wasn't good.

Sybella didn't think, she just made a snatch for his phone. It wasn't the cleverest thing she could have done, but once the area's constabulary were involved this would be around the village in a flash. Her parents-in-law already thought she wasn't handling her life to their satisfaction. It would be another reason why she and Fleur should move in with them.

He held the phone just out of her reach, which was easy for him, given he appeared to be a god stepped down from Asgard. Sybella wouldn't have been surprised if he'd grabbed a stake of lightning while he was at it. Only he was looking down at her as if she were a puppy with muddy paws that had suddenly decided to jump on him.

It was beyond frustrating.

'Please,' she tried again, 'this is just a misunderstanding.'

'*Nyet*, this is trespass. I want you off my property.'

Sybella shook her head in disbelief. 'Are you going to let me explain?'

'*Nyet.*'

She stepped up to him and laid her hand on his forearm. 'Please, you have to listen. I'm not a trespasser.'

He frowned.

'I've never trespassed in my life. Not knowingly.'

Which was when the committee members of the Heritage Trust appeared out of the side entrance of Edbury Hall, humming like a hive of wasps.

Sybella's heart began to beat so fast she seriously thought she might pass out.

'Who in the hell are they?' he demanded, because clearly nothing was getting past this guy.

'The Heritage Trust committee,' she croaked. This was a disaster! She had to go and warn them.

Turning quickly, she didn't notice the bag at her feet until her boot caught on it and Sybella found herself for the second time tonight arms extended, launched head first for the snow.

Strong hands caught her around the waist and literally lifted her, this time bringing her into contact with his big, hard body. Instinctively she wrapped her arms around his neck. It was the wrong move. Sensation zipped through her body like an electrical charge and it dipped right between her legs.

Sybella panicked and tried to pull away but he had her held tight.

'Stop wriggling,' he ordered gruffly and she stopped. Mainly because her face was dangerously close to his and a part of her was finding the physical contact thrilling.

'Can you—just—look, stop holding me!' She was mumbling this into his bare neck, because apparently he thought hugging her to him was a good idea.

It wasn't. Even with the layers of fabric between them she'd been a man-free zone for so long it was like landing on planet Mars and discovering there wasn't enough gravity to hold you down. Worse, he smelt awfully good, manly in a way she had forgotten, and, combined with his warm solidity, she was beginning to enjoy all the contact.

Not interested in sex? She'd clearly sent a message out into the universe and the sneaky gods had sent down one of their own to make a liar of her.

'Please,' she begged, turning her face to meet his eyes, which was a mistake because he was looking back at her and they were dangerously close.

She could see how thick his golden eyelashes were, and his eyes had seemingly soaked up the colours around them like the Northern Lights she'd seen on a documentary about the Arctic. She could have sworn a moment ago they were icy grey.

Her panicked breath caught and everything telescoped down to his amazing eyes before his gaze swooped to her mouth. He looked as if he was going to kiss her or was that just her idea?

Panic renewed, Sybella began to thrash about in earnest. 'Please let me go before this all gets out of hand!'

On the contrary, Nik was confident he had it all in hand.

He would deal with the small tide of humanity edging towards them, and then he would find out why there appeared to be no security at all in operation at his grandfather's home.

But first he needed to deal with what he had in his arms, the problem being he wasn't sure what that was. He'd turned his head to find something other than what he'd first imagined. She had a vivid face, eyes that seemed to be searching his and the kind of sensuous full mouth that gave men creative thoughts. She also smelt of flowers, which was distracting him. He set her down in the snow.

'Do not move,' he told her.

He went around to the cab of the SUV and turned on the headlights to high beam, capturing the dozen rugged-up intruders like a spotlight on a stage.

'I'm Nikolai Aleksandrovich Voronov,' he said in a deep voice that didn't need to be raised. On its own it carried across the front façade of the house and possibly beyond. 'If you're not off the estate in the next two minutes, I'll have you all arrested for trespass.'

He didn't wait to see what they would do. He knew what they would do. Scatter and run.

Nik hoisted his bag over his shoulder and gave his attention to the unhappy girl, standing there encased in what looked like cladding. In the dark she no longer looked like the sensual siren he'd imagined a moment ago and was back to being the abominable snowman.

'You can go with your friends,' he said with a curt nod, before turning his back on her.

Sleet was falling more heavily as he approached the house.

He used the side entrance lit by lamp posts that glowed through the snowy gloom like something out of *The Lion, The Witch and The Wardrobe*, a book his Anglophile grandfather had given to him when he was a boy. No wonder the old man loved the place. Nik saw only an investment and right now a heavy oak door he pushed open with his shoulder.

He was aware he'd been followed, alerted by his companion's crunching footsteps over the stones and her hitching breath, because clearly the woman was out of shape with all that extra weight she was carrying.

He waited for Rapunzel because he wasn't in the habit of closing doors in women's faces. Another glance reinforced what he already knew. She was tall, abetted by a pair of what looked like hiking boots, and the parka and trousers gave her a square look not identifiable as female in the dark.

'What do you want?'

She had planted herself just inside the threshold.

'To explain.'

'I'm not interested.'

She stepped towards him, clearly reluctant, the light falling full on her.

She was wearing the ski mask now as a beanie, most of her astonishing hair caught up inside it. She had full cheeks pink from the cold and her hazel eyes he'd already established were bright, but it was her lush pink mouth that drew the eye.

'Actually, about that…you probably do want to talk to me.'

Nik had it on the tip of his tongue to tell her while she looked like a Christmas angel he wouldn't be changing his mind.

Instead he gave her a moment to clarify.

'I work here.'

She was staff? Why in hell hadn't she said so?

'I'm Sybella,' she said. 'Sybella Parminter.'

Nik took a moment to reconcile the girl standing in front of him with the woman with the wellington boots and the face like a shovel. He'd underestimated his grandfather. The old man had rigged a honey trap.

Nik crossed the floor to her in a few strides and, before she could react, reached behind her head and yanked off the ski mask.

Her hair tumbled out.

'What are you doing?' she demanded, lifting her bemittened hands to her head in a protective gesture, as if he might start pulling at her hair again.

It was exactly as it had looked in the snow, heavy and flaxen blonde almost all the way down to her waist. The electric light made it shimmer, or maybe he was just tired and even ordinary women were beginning to look like goddesses.

That fast a picture took shape of a golden angel ministering to his grandfather and putting ideas in his head about English heritage and great-grandchildren while she eyed the title deeds to the house.

'You can't just manhandle me,' she said, pushing back her hair self-consciously and eyeing him as if he were a wolf about to leap at her. He also saw the feminine awareness kindling in her eyes and knew exactly how he was going to handle this.

'Call me Nik.'

'Nik,' she said warily, taking a big step back. 'Well, I would like the opportunity to explain. If I could come back tomorrow?'

'I think you will stay where you are.'

'But you just told me to go.'

'Glad you're keeping up.'

She blinked.

'What were you doing outside?'

Sybella didn't know whether to run for her life or stand her ground. His pulling and pushing, not to mention the way he'd looked at her hair as if it were some kind of man snare, had left her unnerved. But she had people relying on her. She couldn't let them down.

'The Heritage Trust meet here on Thursday nights. I'm secretary. Assistant secretary.' She took a breath. Honesty was the best policy. 'I'm the only one who can do shorthand. We don't use a recording device.'

'You don't run it?'

'Well, no.'

He was shrugging out of his coat, looking around the entrance hall as if expecting minions to appear and help him. 'So you don't run it, you're the secretary. How long has this been going on?' he asked.

'A little under a year. Mr Voronov was kind enough—'

'For you to take advantage.'

'No, that's not—'

Sybella promptly lost her train of thought as the tailored wool slid down his arms and she discovered what had felt so solid outside when she'd been holding onto him. An expensive-looking charcoal sweater clung to broad shoulders and a long, hard, lean waist, apparently packed with bricks. Narrow muscled hips and long powerful legs filled out his dark jeans. By the time she reached his big, got-to-be-size-fifteen hand-tooled boots the tour had effectively rendered Sybella slightly dazzled and a whole lot mute.

She realised she'd just checked him out.

It was either her silence or the raptness of her regard that had him look up from shaking out his coat and give her that once-over thing men did, the subtle up and down assessment as to whether or not he'd consider sleeping with her...and Sybella had the humiliating thought he'd caught her staring and assumed she was doing the same thing.

Which she was. Unintentionally. Not because she was considering sleeping with him. Goodness, no. She hadn't *meant* to ogle him. It had just happened. But he didn't know that.

What made it worse was the Climb and Ski gear had currently turned her perfectly nice woman's body into a flotation device and the likelihood of him finding anything attractive about her was zilch.

'Care to tell me what you were really doing jumping out at me in the dark?' His eyes held a new awareness now that she'd pretty much flagged she found him attractive.

Sybella could feel her cheeks hot as coals. He made her feel like a teenage girl with a boy she liked. It was ridiculous at her advanced age of twenty-eight.

'I didn't jump out at you. You threw luggage at me!' He had moved across to the open boot-room door to hang up his coat. Sybella followed him, a tiny tug boat to his tanker.

'I expected to be greeted by staff,' he said.

She guessed that put her in her place. Sybella surreptitiously admired his rear, which like the rest of him appeared to be pure muscle, which was when he just tossed the grenade in.

'I also thought you were a man.'

And there went what was left of her self-image tonight.

'Wh-what?' she bleated, like a stupid lamb for slaughter.

'I mean, obviously you're not,' he said, frowning at her as if he'd just noticed her stricken expression and was assessing what it meant.

'No,' she choked, 'not a man. Thanks.'

'It was dark and you're wearing unisex clothing.' He was hanging up his coat, drawing attention to the flex of muscles along his back.

'This isn't unisex.' Sybella looked down at her considerable padded bulk. 'It's oyster-pink.'

His expression told her he didn't make the connection.

'Pink is traditionally a female colour,' she spelt out.

He continued to look doubtful.

She huffed out a breath. 'Look, this parka was clearly marked "Women Size L" on the rack,' she insisted. Then stopped.

Had she just informed him she was size large?

Yes—yes, she had.

'It was dark,' he repeated, and the frown was back.

He closed the door behind him, crowding her back out into the corridor.

When she picked up her bruised and bloodied self-esteem from the floor, Sybella would remind herself she was tall, wearing layers and a ski mask, and he was right—it was dark. Her throat felt tight, because it wasn't *that* dark.

Sybella only felt worse when he took the main stairs with an effortless stride that left her labouring as best she could in his wake, because by now she was not only wet through, the all-weather gear was making it difficult to move freely.

It begged the question how people climbed mountains in these things when she was finding a staircase hard going.

She was a little out of breath at the top.

'You need to get a bit more exercise,' he said, stopping to look down at her. 'You're out of shape.'

Really? That was what he had to say to her? The only time she ever got to sit down was on a quiet afternoon at the records office where she worked.

'Shouldn't you be on your way up to see your grandfather?' she said instead, no longer at all keen to explain anything to him. She just wanted to go home. Preferably to a hot bath where she could enjoy a little cry.

'He'll keep.'

He'll keep? What sort of grandson was he? Well, she knew the answer to that. The absent kind. She scowled at his back. If he hadn't been absent she wouldn't be in this fix.

Sybella followed him down the Long Gallery. She regularly conducted tours of this room, pointing out the features, recounting the history of the house. She suspected Mr I-thought-you-were-a-man wouldn't be very happy if he knew.

There were six Jacobean chairs piled up in the middle of the room, awaiting a home.

'What in the hell?' he said, circling them.

She opted for a cheerful, 'Don't you love these? Your

grandfather had them brought down from storage in the attics. We haven't worked out where to put them.'

'We?' He rounded on her. 'You're interested in the contents of the house?'

As if she were some kind of criminal. Sybella found herself backing up a bit. 'No, I'm interested in the past.'

'Why?'

A little flustered by the way he was looking at her, all suspicious and hard-eyed but making her feel very much a woman despite what he'd said, she found herself struggling for an answer. 'I don't know. I just am.'

He looked unimpressed.

She had to do better. She rummaged around for something he'd believe. 'If you grew up like I did in a very modern house in a relentlessly upmarket housing estate you'd see the beauty in old things too.'

He looked skeptical.

'It was the most soulless place on this green earth. I knew from an early age there had to be something better. More meaningful.'

Sybella took a breath, realising she'd told him a little more than she had meant to.

'Why does furniture have more meaning if it's old?'

'Because old things have stories attached to them, and the furniture that's survived tends to have been made by craftsmen and women. Artists.'

'You're a romantic,' he said, again as if this were a crime.

'No, I'm practical.' She'd had to be. 'Although I guess as a child I read books about other children who lived in old houses and fantasised that might be me one day.'

'Is that so?'

Nik was tempted to ask her if she could see herself in this house.

'It's not unusual,' she said defensively. 'Lots of children have thoughts like that, and I had a good reason to.'

Nik suspected he was about to hear a sob story. He was also aware if he gave her enough rope she'd probably happily hang herself. She was nervous around him and it was making her talk.

'I'm more curious about your interest in this house,' he growled.

'No, you asked me why I was interested in the past.'

He added pedantic to overweight and possibly a con-artist.

'Old houses, miserable childhood, check.'

'I didn't say I had a miserable childhood.' She looked affronted. 'I said the house was soulless,' she said firmly. 'We were the only people who had ever lived there. Which was ironic.'

'I'll bite—why?'

She tried to fold her arms, which was rendered difficult by the bulk of her clothing. 'Because the woman who raised me was obsessed with genealogy. Her genealogy, not mine, as it turned out.'

'You were adopted?'

She nodded, for the first time looking less communicative. Her pretty face was closed up like a fist.

He'd been fifteen when he was told his father was not his father, and Nik had always looked at his life in terms of *before* and *after*.

'When did you find out?'

She looked up at him as if gauging whether to tell him. 'I was twelve. It was when my parents separated.'

'Must have been difficult.'

'Yes,' she said. 'It was more difficult when they handed me back.'

'They handed you back?'

She was radiating tension now. 'Dumped me in a very nice boarding school and left me there for six years.'

He almost laughed. *That* was her complaint?

Spoilt upper-class girl still bemoaning her school years at what—going by her elocution—was an upmarket school. He wondered what else she had to complain about. And here he was, actually feeling sorry for her.

She was good, he had to give her that.

'Have you ever considered they were giving you a good education?'

'They gave me a very good education,' she said tonelessly, looking down at her clasped hands. She probably understood her bid for sympathy was going nowhere. 'But I saw them very rarely in the term breaks and now not at all. It was as good as handing me back.'

Sybella was pleased with her command of herself and that she could talk about her adoptive parents in a forthright way. He'd asked the questions; she'd merely answered them. No external emotion needed.

Only for all her firmness on the subject she could feel the cold running like a tap inside her and she would have trouble turning it off tonight.

'That is a sad little story,' he said, something in his tone making her think he didn't quite believe her.

She suddenly felt self-conscious and slightly annoyed. 'I guess it is. I don't know why I told you all that. I'm sure it's not at all interesting to a man like yourself.'

'You'd be surprised what interests me.'

Sybella discovered she didn't have anything smart to say in answer to that. But she couldn't help running her gaze over his broad shoulders, remembering how strong and sure he'd felt holding her.

His eyes caught hers and something flared between them. 'And what exactly interests you, Miss Parminter?'

Sybella knew what interested her, and it wasn't going to happen.

She could feel her face filling up with heat.

'It's Mrs,' she stated baldly in a desperate attempt to deflect whatever he might say next. 'Mrs Parminter.'

'You're married?'

There had been a current of awareness zipping between them from the time she'd been grappling with him in the snow, only Sybella didn't know that until this very second as it was sucked back to nothingness and what was left was a tense, awkward silence.

Sybella didn't know what to say.

But he did.

'Does your husband know you're out at night running around with other men?'

CHAPTER FOUR

WITH TOO MANY bad memories still beating around in her head something snapped inside Sybella, enough to have her hand arcing through the air.

Fortunately his reflexes were quicker than hers and he gripped her wrist, holding her immobile.

There was a fraught silence in which all she could hear was her pulse drumming in her ears. Then he said quietly, 'That was out of line,' releasing her arm so that Sybella could slowly lower it to her side.

'It's none of my business,' he added. Which was when she realised he wasn't talking about her trying to hit him. He was apologising for what he'd said.

The fight went out of Sybella, and with it flooded in the knowledge she'd almost hit another person.

Last year Fleur had pushed over a little boy in her social group and Sybella had sat down and had the talk with her. Physically hurting someone was wrong. Whatever the provocation, she must use her words, not her fists. And here she was, mother of the year, trying to slug a perfect stranger!

She'd had provocation all right, but that wasn't an excuse.

She needed to apologise to him but Sybella found herself struggling because he'd implied something, and he hadn't taken that back. Which was very different from saying it was *none of his business*.

'Six years ago my husband kissed me and climbed into his van and drove it out to the Pentwistle Farm,' she said in a low voice, 'and on the road between the farm and the turn-off he was struck by another car coming over the rise.'

Nik was looking at her with an expression she hadn't seen before in this man.

As if he were taking her seriously.

'So no, Mr Voronov, my husband has no idea what I'm doing nowadays—but I do. I wish I hadn't tried to hit you. I can't take that back. But you don't get to say things like that to me. I don't deserve your contempt, or do you just have a problem with women in general? I suspect you do.'

Sybella had no idea where all those words had come from or her ability to say them or even if they were true. But nothing had just 'happened' here tonight. It had been building since he'd held her in his arms outside in the snow and all the sensuality latent in her body had woken up.

She resented it, and she resented him. But none of that was his fault.

'I suspect I have a problem with you, Mrs Parminter,' he said slowly. 'But I am sorry for what I said.'

'You should be.' She held his gaze. She could see her words had affected him and she could also see some grudging respect in his eyes and that gave her the grace to say, 'I'm sorry too.'

She forced the apology out, because as wrong as her actions were she couldn't yet let go of them, or the feelings that had provoked them. None of this had made her feel better; she felt worse. She wrapped arms around her waist as best she could in her ridiculous parka.

He was looking at her as if she deserved some compassion. He was wrong. She deserved a good talking-to for all the mistakes she'd made in dealing with this house.

'You're cold,' he said. 'You need to take off your wet things.'

'I don't—'

'You can dry them in front of the fire, or I can have them laundered.'

'Please don't bother.' She passed a hand over her face.

'I'm going to take them back to Climb and Ski tomorrow for a full refund.'

'Are you all right?'

She blinked, taking her hand away from her face to find him watching her as if she might keel over. 'I guess so.'

Which was when her eyes filled with tears. *Oh, blast.*

Tired, wet, in some serious trouble over her activities in this house, and yet troublingly aware of Nik Voronov as a man and her own deficiencies in that area, Sybella wanted nothing more than to wriggle out of her wet things and cast herself down in front of the fire and sleep for a hundred years.

But she didn't get the fairy-tale option. She should be practising a better apology.

There was a rattle and clatter as Gordon, who ran the household, entered from a side door, wheeling the drinks trolley.

Saved by the man with the alcohol!

A long-time bachelor, Gordon was her ally in the house, having worked here for almost thirty years under the previous owner. He gave her a guarded look of surprise but didn't say anything. He was too good at his job.

Her host meanwhile had signalled to Gordon he could deal with the drinks.

Sybella wondered if she could just slip out with the trolley. But the fire lured her and she turned away to deal with her wet things, surreptitiously sniffing and wiping at her eyes with her wrist. She stripped off her parka and then her cords, feeling self-conscious in her tights but not exposed. They were of a durable denier and thick enough to act as leggings. Frankly, it was a relief to be able to move her body freely again.

She laid out her jeans before the fire and had just straightened up when a towel dropped over her head.

She gave a start but with a gruff, 'Hold still,' her host began to vigorously but not roughly rub dry her damp hair.

After an initial protest of, 'I can do this,' she gave in, because really he was impossible to argue with.

But this was her role. For five years she'd been the caregiver. It was disconcerting to find herself the one being cared for. And as his strokes became more rhythmic Sybella found herself going quiescent, some of the tension of the crazy evening leaving her.

It had been so long since her needs were seen to by someone else. She'd forgotten it could be like this. Even when Simon had been alive he'd been so busy with his new veterinary practice in the few months they were married they had seemed only to bump into each other at night in bed, and Sybella could feel her skin suffusing with heat because another man's hands were on her, if only drying her hair. But when she looked up and clashed with his grey eyes she was shocked into feelings so raw and insistent she barely recognised them as the gentle, awkward finding their way she'd had with Simon...

'That's enough,' she said, her voice a little rough with the sudden upsurge of feeling beating around in her.

He paused but then continued to dry her even more vigorously.

'If you collapse from pneumonia in a few days' time—' he said gruffly.

'You don't want it on your conscience?'

'I don't want a lawsuit.'

Sybella snorted, she couldn't help it, and she felt rather than saw him smile.

'I'm not a lawyer,' she said, 'and I don't have the money for a lawyer.'

'What do you do,' he asked, removing the towel so that her head came back and she could see him, 'besides haunt this house?'

She didn't miss a beat. 'I could give you a list?'

A slow grudging smile curled up his mouth, taking Sybella's entire attention with it. 'Why don't you do that?'

As if he had all the time in the world to listen to her life story. As if like before she'd spill her guts.

Instead she asked, 'Why don't you visit your grandfather more often?' It was the one thing that really bothered her, and it was more important than anything to do with the open house and how much trouble she would be in.

He reached out and gently smoothed the drying ringlets back from her face.

'I would have visited earlier,' he said, 'if I'd had any idea something so beautiful was here.'

Then his gaze dropped to her mouth.

She relived that moment in the snow and realised it hadn't been her imagination. There was a very strong attraction between them.

Only she didn't do things like this.

Given the last man to kiss her existed now only in her memory of him.

She wasn't even sure what she would do if he...

His mouth covered hers. He gave her no opportunity to back out, or overthink it, he just made it happen. One hand sliding around the back of her head to cradle her, the other at the small of her back. His hand was so broad he could span her waist from behind.

In a flurry of sense impressions, Sybella had never felt so delicate, so utterly aware she was a feeling, sensate woman and, as exciting and dangerous as this was, she felt completely safe in his arms.

Where he had been so rough with her out in the snow he was now showing due care and acknowledgement of her as a female, which put to bed his remark about mistaking her for a man and engendered a fluttery feeling inside her. It bloomed high in her chest and a swirling warmth gathered down below.

He brought her in close to his body and she felt the full hard, muscular strength of him and it was enough.

She gave way, her mouth softening under his, the entire lost art of kissing returning to her with some subtle but much appreciated changes.

His tongue touched, grazed, tasted, seduced and the feel of him was so completely male and so overwhelming in the certainty of his approach Sybella took what he gave her instinctively and with an utter disregard to where this might be leading.

Until all her doubts came rushing back in and she ducked her head.

'What's wrong?' he asked gruffly.

Apart from he was a stranger, and they didn't know one another, and she suspected given her activities in his house only trouble could come from this?

'I don't know.' She did know—she was feeling a bit too much and it had been so long and she no longer had any certainty in her ability to meet him as a sexually confident woman. But had she ever?

She wasn't ready for this.

Meg would say whatever sense of herself as a desirable woman had been shoved into the back of her wardrobe in a box along with her preserved wedding bouquet and all the plans she and Simon had made for the future. But it had happened before that. It had happened when Simon had briefly dated another girl and slept with her.

It was a little disconcerting to say the least to discover, gazing up at this intense, beautiful man, she had no idea where to go from here with him. But she did know one thing. She had to let him know what was going on in his house.

'I have to tell you something,' she blurted out. 'Edbury Hall is open to the public on weekends.'

Nik didn't immediately let her go. His hand was still curled around her sweet waist gloved in soft cashmere wool that made the most of her glorious curves above and below.

He could pinpoint the moment he'd stopped thinking clearly. It was when he'd seen her bending down by the fire, the most female-looking woman. She was the proverbial hourglass, and if there was a little more sand than was standard in that glass his libido didn't make that distinction. She had ample breasts and long, shapely legs, deliciously plump around her thighs and bottom, and in his arms she'd felt like both comfort and sin.

Which explained why his brain took a little longer to catch up, because his body was happy where it was, Sybella's curves giving him a full body press.

'Why is the house open to the public?' He forced himself to set her back. 'On whose authorisation?'

'Mr Voronov senior's, and—and yours.' Sybella's voice gave out, so the 'yours' wasn't much more than a whisper.

'Mine?' he growled, any trace of the man who had begun to kiss her and rouse such passionate feelings in her evaporating like the last patch of sunshine on a cold winter's day.

'You were sent the paperwork. I didn't just go ahead only on your grandfather's say-so,' she protested.

'I received no paperwork.'

No. She gnawed on the inside of her lip. Now she would have to explain about the letters. But she didn't want to be responsible for a further breach between grandfather and grandson. Family was important.

No one understood that better than someone who for a long time didn't have any.

No, it would be better if his grandfather confessed.

And what if Nik Voronov decided to blame her anyway?

Blood was blood, and old Mr Voronov might easily side with his grandson.

Sybella knew she had nobody to blame but herself and for a spinning moment she just started babbling. 'I don't see who has been hurt by any of this. Mr Voronov is a lonely man and he enjoys having people into the house…'

'And you have taken advantage of that.'

'No!' Sybella closed her eyes and took a breath. Arguing with him wasn't going to accomplish anything. 'I understand you don't know me,' she said, keeping her voice as steady as she could, given the escalating tension, 'and you say you're worried about your grandfather—'

'I am worried about him.'

'Well, I don't see any evidence of that given you're never here!'

Oh, she should have kept that to herself. And now he was looking down at her without a shred of give in him.

'I suspect you've taken my grandfather for a ride, and, if I find out that's the case, you really don't want me for an enemy Mrs Parminter.'

It was difficult not to take a step back.

She swallowed hard. 'Do you go through life mistrusting people?'

'When it comes to my family I don't allow anything past the keeper.'

Those words took the indignant air out of her because she guarded her little family too. His grandfather had become of late an honorary member of that family and for a moment she wondered if *she'd* got it wrong. Nik Voronov might genuinely care about his grandfather. If the shoe were on the other foot she would be suspicious too.

She tried again. 'Honestly, Nik, it's not what you think.'

'I think we can probably go back to Mr Voronov.'

He was making her feel as if she'd done something wrong.

Which was when she noticed he was getting out his phone.

'Are you calling the police again?' She tried not to sound despairing because, really, what were they going to arrest her on? Impersonating a married lady? Kissing a man she'd just met?

'I'm arranging a car for you. I take it you live in the village?'

It was no more than a ten-minute walk if she took the lane, but Sybella didn't intend to argue with him about the lift.

'If this is your organisation's way of drumming up support you can let them know that honey traps went out in the nineteen seventies.'

Honey trap?

He turned away and spoke rapidly into his phone in Russian.

Sybella wondered if being shaken about like a child's toy earlier had affected her hearing. It had certainly loosened some of her native intelligence.

What did he think, she was Mata Hari kissing men for state secrets?

Oh, boy, she definitely needed to get out of here.

Cursing her own stupidity, she pulled on her damp jeans and then bent down to reattach her boots. Everything was cold and unpleasant and would chafe but there was no helping that.

'I want you back here nice and early, let's say eight o'clock for breakfast,' he said from behind her. 'You have some explaining to do, and it will be in the presence of my grandfather.'

Sybella became aware he was probably getting a really good look at her wide womanly behind at this moment.

But everything was such a shambles—what was one more humiliation?

'Eight o'clock is too early.'

'Tough. Get an alarm clock.'

She straightened up. 'For your information I'll be awake at six, but I have a great deal to organise myself. You're not the only busy person in the world, Mr Voronov.'

He looked unimpressed.

'I am running a billion-dollar business, Mrs Parminter. What's your excuse?'

A five-year-old girl, Sybella thought, eyeing him narrowly, but he looked like one of those unreconstructed dinosaurs who thought raising children happened by magic. Besides, she was not bringing her daughter into this hostile conversation.

'The fact is I'm out of here tomorrow,' he informed her. 'Let's call this your window of opportunity.'

'To do what?'

'To convince me not to involve my lawyers.'

All the fight went out of Sybella. She couldn't quite believe this was happening. But she told herself surely old Mr Voronov would clear the air tomorrow.

'Fine. I'll be here.'

To her surprise he took his wool coat and handed it to her with a less antagonistic, 'You'll need this.'

Sybella looked at her Climb and Ski jacket she'd been unable to bring herself to put back on and self-consciously drew his coat around her shoulders.

The gesture reminded her of how kind he'd been drying her hair, how he'd made her feel cared for if only for a brief time. It was enough to make her want to cry, and she hated crying. It didn't change anything.

She turned away from him, his scent surrounding her inside the coat.

She spotted the bottle of brandy and on a whim picked

it up. After the events of this evening she needed it more than he did.

He didn't say anything and when she went downstairs to climb into the waiting car she was holding it to her like a safety blanket.

Stupid really, when she didn't drink. Stupid being in this car, when it would take only ten minutes or five minutes if she'd legged it. She brought her fingertips to her mouth. It still felt a little swollen and sensitive from all the attention. Stupid, probably, to have kissed him.

CHAPTER FIVE

'MUMMY, THERE'S A GIANT standing in our garden. What do you think about that?'

Given yesterday it had been an elephant under the stairs, Sybella didn't rush to call the fire brigade or police station or even Jack the giant killer.

When she did put away the bath towels she was folding and came into her bedroom, she found her five-year-old daughter was kneeling at the dormer window in her pyjamas, her big violet-blue eyes full of innocent curiosity for a world that produced fairy-tale characters in human guise.

Joining Fleur at the glass, she obligingly looked out. Her pulse hit a thousand and she stepped back and said a silent prayer. Then she leaned forward again to get a better look.

She became aware of Fleur watching her, waiting for a cue as to how to respond to this stranger at their door. Sybella shook off her astonishment.

'That's not a giant, darling, that's a Viking god.'

He was facing their door and in a minute he'd work out the old-fashioned bell-pull was indeed the bell—but it was broken.

Then he'd probably pound on the door until he broke it down.

'Mummy will go down and speak to him. Why don't you stay here with Dodge? You know how nervous he gets around boys.'

'Because they're noisy.' Fleur picked up her toy bricks and returned to fitting pieces together. Sybella wasn't fooled. Her daughter would wait until the coast was clear and make her way to the top of the stairs and peer down through the bannisters.

Sybella wouldn't have minded that option herself. Instead she took the stairs by twos, then stopped in front of the hall mirror and checked her face was clean. Clean but her eyes were shadowed with lack of sleep.

She'd been on the Internet late last night checking up on Nik Voronov and how much damage he could possibly do her. Given he was on the *Forbes* list, probably a lot.

At least she was wearing her work clothes: a white silk blouse, a knee-length caramel-coloured suede skirt and boots. Pretty respectable. She ran a hand through her yet-to-be-braided hair and went to open the door.

Then hesitated and looked at herself in the glass again, this time undoing her top two buttons.

There, just a hint of cleavage. It had nothing to do with making herself more attractive for the man who had called her a honey trap last night. It was about her own self-confidence as a woman.

She opened the door, and her self-confidence did a wobble and promptly fell over.

He was wearing a tailored suit and tie. He might as well have been wearing a surcoat and carrying a broadsword. She knew he'd come to take prisoners.

His eyes flared over her as if he were dropping a net and Sybella instinctively dug her heels into her shoes to keep herself from being dragged in towards him.

And just like last night in the snow it was his mouth she was drawn to. The wide lower lip, the slight curve at the ends that could go either way, like Nero's thumb, up or down, and decide your fate. She'd been kissed by that mouth last night and it had definitely been going her way for a little bit. But in the end it had all been a ruse to make her look as foolish as possible.

'Enjoy the brandy?'

The brandy? She hadn't known what to do with the

bottle when she'd got home so she'd stashed it in the linen closet.

It had occurred to her that Catherine, her mother-in-law, was regularly in and out of that cupboard when she babysat Fleur.

Sybella was forever coming home to freshly changed sheets, which she appreciated even as it drove her crazy.

Hiding spirits behind the bathroom towels, Sybella, dear?

A little devil she didn't know was in her made her say, 'Yes, thank you, I drank the lot.'

'Careful,' he said, his deep voice wiping away any comparisons with her mother-in-law, 'excessive drinking is a slippery slope to all kinds of illness in later life.'

'I'll keep that in mind.'

What did he want? Why was he looking at her in that way, his eyes trained on her, cool and watchful and somehow taking her clothes off?

'So,' she said, swallowing. 'How can I help you today?'

Nik eyed the two undone buttons.

'It's nine o'clock.'

'I told you my mornings were busy.' She made a gesture with her hand, wriggling her fingers. 'Serene on the surface, duck legs churning underneath.'

Nik's attention had drifted to her hair because it seemed to have grown more abundant overnight like some Victorian-era maiden. He suddenly found himself right back where he was last night. Wanting her.

He cleared his throat. 'My grandfather tells me you take tours of the house.'

She stood a little straighter. 'The third Thursday of every month, we have school groups in. Only in the west wing.'

'You bring people into my house?'

'I don't think your grandfather considers the house

yours,' she said, her fan of lashes flickering nervously. 'Really the house belongs to everyone in Edbury in a manner of speaking. There has been a manor house on this spot since the time of the Normans—'

'Fascinating.'

'It is fascinating!' She firmed her mouth. 'Your grandfather understands we're only caretakers of a place like this. That's why he agreed to open up the estate again to the public.'

Nik tried not to notice how her blouse hugged her breasts or her skirt flared over those rounded hips. 'I am more interested in discovering exactly why my property is being treated like a theme park.'

Sybella's heart sank. If this was his attitude there was no win for her here.

Only she noticed his gaze was roaming a little too far south of her face again and she could feel her body responding, the warmth rising up into her cheeks, the backs of her knees tingling.

'I'm not a theme park either,' she said flatly.

To her surprise a streak of colour rose over his high, flat cheekbones.

'And no one is treating Edbury Hall that way,' she hastened on, wanting to put the sexual awareness behind them where it belonged. 'It's more of an educational facility.'

He folded his arms. 'Who is paying your salary?'

'No one. Everyone volunteers.'

'Right.'

'No one's ever been paid at Edbury. All takings are funnelled back into other projects in the area.'

His gaze zeroed in on her. 'You're not an employee?'

She shook her head.

'Good, that makes this less ambiguous.'

'What do you mean "ambiguous"? What's ambiguous?' Sybella didn't like the sound of that.

He looked up at the lintel above her head and over the local stone that walled her house.

'You're also my tenant,' he spelt out, cool gaze dropping to hers once more. 'The lease on the Hall includes these weavers' cottages.'

'Yes,' she said feeling hunted, 'and I've never missed a rental payment.'

'Nobody said you had. But just as a hypothetical example, how would you like it if I turned this row into a tourist attraction on the weekends?'

'They are a tourist attraction.'

'Prostit?'

'People come from all over the world to photograph our cottages. Several film crews have been on site in this street in the past four years.' She folded her arms across her chest. 'I'm beginning to think you know nothing of Edbury at all.'

'You'd be right. I own the Hall for tax purposes.'

'I'm sorry?'

'I'm required to own a certain amount of property in the UK for tax reasons.'

She stared at him as if he'd announced he'd stolen the Crown Jewels and was currently storing them in the Kremlin.

'You must be joking? You've caused all this upset in the village because you want to cheat on your tax?' Her voice had risen exponentially.

Nik shifted on his size fifteens. 'I do not engage in illegal activities, Mrs Parminter, and I would be careful about what you say to me.'

She looked taken aback and retreated a little into the safety of her doorway.

Nik expelled a deep breath. He did not bully women, but every conversation with this girl turned into a confrontation.

'I'm not interested in your financial dealings, Mr Voronov,' she said, looking persecuted, 'any more than I enjoy being doorstepped at nine o'clock in the morning. Say what you've got to say and go.'

He looked her up and down, which she clearly didn't like. 'I've said it.'

'Good.'

She took another step back into her house and began to close her door. But he hadn't finished with her yet.

'Anything more you'd care to tell me before the lawyers get involved?'

She halted and then stuck her head out again. 'What do you mean "lawyers"?'

'I seem to have an echo,' he observed.

She pinned her lips together and those hazel eyes fixed pensively on him as she stepped reluctantly outside again.

'I—I hardly think lawyers are necessary.'

'Fortunately that decision is mine.'

Awful man. Why was he so set on blaming her for everything? And why was she still finding it difficult not to drink in every last masculine inch of him?

Sybella tried to find something reasonable to say but what popped out was, 'Why are you down here bothering people?'

He leaned in a little closer.

'I told you,' he said in that fathom-deep voice. 'I am visiting my grandfather.'

Sybella could have told him right now it didn't feel that way. After the events of last night it felt as if he were visiting her! For purposes that felt entirely too hormonal on her behalf.

'Well, perhaps if you'd bothered to turn up before now you'd know what was going on here,' she threw back at him a little desperately, 'instead of stomping around like a big bully and making everyone go through lawyers.'

'Given I'm based in St Petersburg, turning up isn't that simple.'

'Is that where you live?' The question just slipped out, openly curious, and Sybella knew she'd given herself away. Her stupid interest in him.

She could feel the heat rushing into her face.

'*Da,*' he said, and there was a silence during which Sybella remembered how much she'd told him about her life last night. The intimacy that had created.

'Well, maybe it isn't so easy for you to get down here regularly,' she admitted reluctantly, 'but your grandfather needs family around him at this time of his life.'

His eyes iced over. 'My grandfather is well taken care of.'

'Is he? Do you know he doesn't like his nurse? He doesn't trust her.'

Nik frowned. 'He hasn't said anything to me.'

'Perhaps if you visited once in a while you could talk to the people around him who matter, not the people you're employing, and you might have a better idea of what's really going on instead of making up these stupid stories and—and picking on me!'

'And you're one of the people who matter?' he asked.

'I don't matter, but I am here. I do see what goes on.'

Nik didn't like the picture she painted, that his grandfather was unhappy, that in some way he was failing.

Only her hands had migrated to her hips again, and he was finding it difficult not to be distracted by the way her chest lifted every time she made her point and the button holding back the mystery of her cleavage strained.

'Here's what I think, Mrs Parminter. You've been using my grandfather's kindness to benefit yourself.'

'Yes, you would think that.'

Sybella glared back at him.

The truth was so much more simple and delightful than anything this man could make up in his suspicious mind.

His grandfather had forged one of those charming inter-generational friendships with her small daughter.

Sybella had watched a lonely and reserved man come to life in the company of her forthright, imaginative Fleur, and the sight of Mr Voronov's white head bent over a book with Fleur's small dark one as they read together made every Thursday afternoon a treasure.

Fleur didn't come easily to reading. She was a child who wanted to be out of doors, climbing trees, chasing cows and getting muddy. All the things possible because they lived in the country. She was, in short, very much like her late father.

Simon had always struggled with reading comprehension and he wouldn't want his daughter to go through that.

His own father shared the same difficulty.

Mr Voronov was a godsend.

Furthering her career had been the last thing on her mind.

But she wasn't telling this man any of that.

She'd told him too much in her stupid confessional last night.

It was her business. It wasn't any of his.

'Frankly, I don't care what you happen to think. I am going to continue to visit your grandfather and there's nothing you can do about it!'

Sybella's soaring moment of satisfaction was short-lived.

'Mrs Parminter, let me tell you how it's going to be.' His voice had dropped to a calm dead certainty. 'Your visits to the house are over. You are to stay away or there will be consequences. Are we clear?'

'What consequences?'

'Legal consequences.'

The colour had gone; not a scrap of it remained in her face.

Nik waited to feel satisfied by that. He didn't. But he damn well wasn't taking ultimatums from this woman. Dealing with this had already taken up too much of his valuable time.

'Listen, I didn't mean for all this to get so out of hand,' she began.

'Are we clear?' he repeated in the voice he used on mine sites.

She trembled, visibly intimidated for the first time.

Nik could see the struggle in her face and his anger evaporated in a wink.

He'd spent the night with some fairly explicit sexual fantasies about this woman, and this morning he'd learned a lot of things that didn't make him very happy with her. It wasn't a particularly good mix.

'I understand perfectly,' she said, swallowing hard, making it clear with her eyes she didn't.

Unlike the last woman throwing ultimatums at him like plates, a Spanish model who had apparently never heard the word no before, Sybella Parminter didn't really seem to understand the way this was played. If she backed down, he'd give her a break. She wasn't backing down.

It was disconcerting because he'd just discovered he didn't like her looking bewildered and upset.

For the second time. Because of him.

He stepped towards her.

'Mummy!' A small person flew out of the house and wrapped herself around Sybella's legs.

Mummy?

Six years widowed. He wasn't good with kids' ages but this one fitted the time span. Sybella was immediately scooping her up, the little girl wrapping her arms and legs around her mother like an octopus.

'This is your daughter?' he said redundantly.

'Yes.' She turned away to go into the house and the child cast a look over her mother's shoulder at him as if he were an ogre in a fairy tale. She stuck out her tongue.

Nik found himself staring at a blue door shut in his face and with the uneasy suspicion he'd made a mistake.

CHAPTER SIX

SYBELLA DROVE AS fast as she was legally able along the familiar road from Middenwold Town Hall where she worked on Fridays, back into Edbury.

In a panic from work she'd rung and let Mr Voronov know she was coming and that she was bringing the letters.

Beside her on the passenger seat was the box of letters that would clear her name.

She didn't want to be responsible for a further breach between grandfather and grandson because family was important, but she didn't see that she had much choice. She couldn't put her kindly impulses towards Mr Voronov above the risk to her future professional reputation if her activities at Edbury Hall were publicly condemned.

She switched on her hands-free phone device as Meg's name came up and her sister-in-law's excitable voice filled the car.

'I can't believe you've got one in the village!'

Sybella cursed silently. If Meg had heard about it down in Oxford, it must be all over the village.

'We lay traps and snares and catch them that way,' she responded drolly, although she was in *so much trouble* it was no longer funny.

'What'd you use?' said Meg wryly. 'A net?'

'No, the possibility of a lawsuit.' Sybella breathed in through her nose and out through her mouth and told herself she shouldn't drive and panic.

'I don't think that's your main problem. So Nik Voronov actually stepped off his boat and onto dry land.'

'Boat? What boat?'

'His billion-foot-long superyacht—all Russian oligarchs have them. They live on them.'

'Where do you get this from?'

'I have my sources. I also have other sources. According to the village grapevine, the two of you were throwing some serious sparks last night.'

Oh, yes, there had been sparks, but they had definitely fizzled. Then a new fear gripped her. 'What do you mean "the village grapevine"?'

'Syb, *everyone* knows. I've had three phone calls and Sarah was banging on Mum's back door at seven o'clock this morning wanting to know if it was true you were having sex up against a SUV in the car park at Edbury Hall last night. With *a man*.'

'Well, of course I'd be having sex with a man,' Sybella huffed impatiently, even as she recoiled from the idea her mother-in-law knew. 'Not that I was, mind, I was just… holding onto him—and Sarah's been cutting my hair for five years. She should know me better.'

'You're missing the point. To half the village this morning you're just an exhibitionist floozy—Sarah's on board with that, by the way—but everyone else thinks you're legitimately on together. They think he's your boyfriend.'

'*What?*'

'It explains why you were able to get the Hall opened again with so little fuss.'

Sybella's mouth fell open.

'Now's not the time to panic,' advised Meg. 'This guy owes you—after everything you've done for his grandfather, and now he's compromised your reputation.'

'I doubt he sees it that way,' Sybella said, gripping the steering wheel and wondering how floozy was going to translate at the pony club and how she would navigate that with Fleur. Her friends were too little, but their mothers were not.

'He's closing down the house to the public, Meg. He came over and told me this morning. He warned me off ever going near the place again.'

'He came to your *house*?'

'He was very angry with me.' Sybella took a breath and swallowed to avoid sounding as vulnerable as she felt. 'Up until then I thought I could persuade him to keep the place open, appeal to his better nature.'

'Good luck with that.' But Meg was oddly quiet for a moment and Sybella got the impression she'd given something away. 'You like him, don't you?'

'No, don't be silly. He's not my type at all. He's—he's bearish.'

'Well, remember what Goldilocks did in the original fairy tale? She jumped out of a window never to be seen again.'

By the time she reached the Hall, parked and made her way across the crunching gravel, Sybella wished she could leap out of that proverbial window. She was also praying she'd find Mr Voronov alone. What if Nik had heard the boyfriend gossip? She wouldn't be able to look him in the eye after that. Although she guessed, when it came to the court case, it would be his barrister who was asking the questions…

So much depended on Nik Voronov being reasonable. Reasonable! She was so sunk.

Sybella was shown inside and as she reached the open sitting-room door she could hear male voices. Her knees gave out a little and she wondered if she could just leave the box of letters here and run…

'She has a kid. You could have mentioned it, Deda.'

'How was I to know you would take this much interest?' Mr Voronov sounded amused, his rich accent rolling the 'r's.

Sybella ventured a little closer.

'Nor did you mention the husband.'

'She's a widow. She was barely married when the poor boy's van was hit by an oncoming car. It's a sad story.'

'One you fell for hook, line and sinker.'

Sybella stiffened.

But Mr Voronov still sounded amused. 'Your cynicism will not win her over, my boy.'

Win her over?

'I'm realistic, and you, old man, need to stay still or this is going to hurt.'

Sybella didn't know what she expected to find as she came abruptly into the room but it more than niggled that if his eldest grandson was overprotective when it came to his legal rights, it wasn't translating into the kind of care the elderly man deserved.

What confronted her wasn't an angry Nik Voronov bullying his grandfather, but the younger man hunkered down in front of his grandfather's chair, deftly applying ointment to the abscess above his ankle.

'Sybella, *moy rebenok*, this is a surprise. Come and sit down. My grandson is looking after me today.'

'So I see.' It was not a surprise; she'd rung ahead to let him know she was coming. So now she was feeling a little set up.

Only Nik looked just as taken aback as she felt.

'What are you doing here?' he growled.

'Nikolai!'

'I've brought biscuits.' She held up the tin. 'My mother-in-law made them and sends her regards.'

'You didn't whip them up yourself in between all the dusting and vacuuming?' This was from Nik, who continued to lay a gauze strip over the wound and tape it up.

Sybella couldn't help noticing he was utterly competent at the task. It didn't exactly fit her image of him as the absent grandson. Clearly he'd done this more than once.

'I would, if I whipped them up at midnight,' she said, not sure of her footing here. 'My mother-in-law doesn't work. I do.'

Nik straightened up and Sybella was reminded all over again of his physical presence and how it could fill the room. He was entirely too dominant for her peace of mind.

It would probably be better for everyone if he left the village today, and quickly.

Only she kept remembering how his hands had felt against her skin, how gentle he'd been drying her hair and later kissing her, making all the lights turn on and leaving them on.

'Nikolka, I think you should take Sybella to lunch.'

'Oh, no, that's not why I'm here.' Sybella stumbled in her haste over the words and she knew she sounded rude but it was excruciating to think Nik might feel obligated to sit through lunch with her.

'I just wanted to deliver the biscuits—' she reached into her handbag '—and these. The letters you sent me, Mr Voronov, in your grandson's name.' She put them down on his side table. 'I would appreciate it if you showed him the documentation I gave you. He might be a little kinder on all of us.'

She glanced up at Nik, who was now standing dangerously close to her. Her whole body was vibrating like a tuning fork. She had to get out of here!

'This just proves we were in a correspondence, or rather I was with your grandfather, and everything I did was above board.' She couldn't look him in the eye or she'd lose all her courage.

'What have you been saying to her, Nikolka?'

'Nothing he didn't have a right to—given he had no idea what was going on.'

She went over and crouched down, putting a hand on

Mr Voronov's arm. 'I understand why you did it, but it's caused me a deal of trouble and upset your grandson.'

The elderly man covered her hand with his own. 'You cannot blame an old man for trying.'

Sybella rather thought she could, but she wouldn't.

'You really need to sort this out with your grandson, but whatever happens with the Hall, I'll continue to bring Fleur here for stories. That won't change.'

She glanced a little furtively at Nik, who looked as if he was about to say something, and straightened up, making her way to the door. Every step felt awkward but she couldn't be in this room a moment longer with Nik Voronov looking at her like that.

Sybella was almost at her car when she heard his heavy crunching footsteps.

'Sybella, we need to clear a few things up.'

'There's nothing to clear up.' Sybella tried not to sound breathless, a little dismayed at how everything female in her sat up to pay attention. 'We don't have anything more to discuss.'

He looked down at her as if he didn't agree.

'You know everything now,' she said in a tight voice. 'I'm pretty much an open book, as you can see.'

She thrust her chin at the small cigar box he carried in his hand.

'Let me drive you back to town,' he said.

'I'm perfectly capable of looking after myself, thank you very much.'

'You haven't done a very good job so far,' he said bluntly. 'You should have spoken up for yourself earlier.'

'Right. Good to know for future reference, but, if you hadn't noticed, I was thinking of your grandfather.'

She dipped her head as a tremor ran through her and without a word Nik put his arm around her.

It wasn't an invasive gesture, he was just there, and it

felt so good she found herself with her face against his shoulder, taking a few sustaining breaths because she had to end this in a moment. She couldn't be doing this with this man.

'I meant to me,' he said quietly against her ear. 'You should have spoken up for yourself to me.'

'Why?'

'Because I like to get my own way. But I'm human, Sybella. I could have got this wrong.'

She stilled.

'Besides,' he said, 'what was I supposed to do? Let this all slide? I had to get to the bottom of it. I owe my grandfather a duty of care.'

'No, of course.' Breathing deeply, Sybella extricated herself and he let her go.

She'd seen how tender he'd been with his grandfather, the bond between them. It made her feel graceless for her critical words to him. She'd clearly understood very little. And Nik was…well, overwhelming her. Sybella allowed that thought in for the first time. She guessed it was only to be expected. He felt so solid and dependable and she was so tired of being the solid and dependable one, and, besides, he made her feel like a desirable woman.

She couldn't remember Simon ever making her feel this way. Loved, yes. Cared for. But not this pulsing, breathless awareness every time he came near her.

She gave him a quick upward look. 'I should go.'

She opened her car door. He held it while she climbed in, but the hand she extended to reach for the ignition was shaking badly.

Nik knew this was down to him. He had this out-of-character urge to reassure her. He couldn't stand it that her lips were mashed together and seeing that tremor in her hand had him wanting to put his arms around her again, but she was clearly embarrassed.

Instead he said gruffly, 'I'll drive you—that way you won't end up parked up a tree.'

To his surprise she didn't argue. She let him take the keys with another subdued 'thank you'. He walked her around to open the passenger door.

'You have amazing manners,' she said, looking a little shy now. 'I guess it's a Russian thing.'

'*Net*. It's my grandfather's thing.'

'You are close to him, aren't you?' she said when he got in the other side.

'He raised me from the age of nine.'

She was looking at him curiously as he adjusted her driving seat to accommodate his long legs. 'I didn't know that.'

He never spoke about his childhood or his relationship with Deda to anyone, but there was something about Sybella that consistently had him relaxing his guard.

'They had a summer house on the Baltic. There were cherry trees along the drive so in spring it was like a tunnel of pink and white petals, and in summer Deda would take me sailing the fjords.'

'It sounds idyllic.'

He shrugged. 'It was a haven of sorts.'

'From what?'

'Boarding school.'

'We have something in common,' she said.

'I know.' He named the elite public girls' school she'd attended and then regretted it because she went stiff as a board again. 'I did a little basic research on you this morning.'

'Research?'

'You're in my grandfather's life. I have to check you out.'

She sighed. 'I guess so. What did you find out?'

'Don't worry, I didn't have your taxes hauled over.'

'I didn't know anyone could do that. Search into someone's background that easily.'

'It's just basic facts anyone could find on your social media page.'

'I'm not on social media.'

'No.'

'Then how—?' She broke off and shook her head. 'Don't bother, you're rich, you have your ways.'

'You probably know just as much about me from the Internet.'

'I know you have a big mine in the Urals. I looked it up. It looks like a vast crater.'

'You can see it from the moon,' said Nik.

'I won't ask you if you have a problem with your ego,' she murmured, and for the first time a small smile tipped up one corner of her mouth.

'I didn't dig it all myself,' he responded, trying not to get too distracted by the sudden desire to make her smile some more, 'but, yeah, my ego is pretty healthy.'

She exhaled a soft crumpled laugh and looked away, her cheeks a little flushed.

Nik couldn't rip his eyes off her.

'Your little girl,' he coaxed, 'what's her name?'

Her expression instantly softened. 'Fleur.'

'It's a pretty name.'

'My little flower,' she said.

'How old is she?'

'Five and a half.'

'I didn't mean to scare her,' he said, the words feeling outsized, almost as if he was blundering again.

'You didn't scare her. She's just not used to raised voices.'

'Yeah, I deserve that.'

She eyed him almost shyly and again he got the impression Sybella wasn't anywhere near as tough as she pretended to be—or maybe needed to be. 'Your grandfather is teaching her to read. On Thursdays, when I'm here to take tours. Afterwards Fleur and I have tea with him.'

And he had forbidden her to come to the Hall again. He wanted to ask her why she hadn't let him know this earlier, but then he knew he hadn't given her much of a chance.

He was revisiting every hard thing he'd said to her since they'd met. He was beginning to think Sybella Parminter didn't really want anything from anyone, she was so determined to do it all herself.

'What I said about the house. I'm not here to ruin your or your daughter's relationship with my grandfather.'

She nodded, focused on some point outside the car.

'But I can't have my grandfather's home turned into…'

'A theme park, I know, I heard you.'

He had a strong urge to pull her into his arms, but that wasn't going to go down well.

'Mr Voronov talks a lot about his grandsons.' She looked over at him as if trying to read his face. 'He—he seems very proud of both of you.'

'Possibly simply relieved the two of us have managed not to break any laws or tarnish the family name,' Nik said, the brief smile he gave her almost boyish, and Sybella's heart did a stumble. 'He's not the robust man he once was. When my grandmother Baba died it was sudden and unexpected. We were all left floundering.'

Sybella suspected Nik was including himself in that floundering and her susceptible heart did more than stumble, it completely softened.

'Deda went overnight from the man who adapted to anything to how he is now, sometimes querulous and unhappy and mostly set in his ways.'

Sybella privately acknowledged the older man could be difficult, but she suspected it was because he felt managed. 'Mr Voronov has spoken to me of his wife.'

'Baba was everything to him.' And perhaps to her grandson, Sybella thought, watching a sadness weight his expression.

'Why did he come here of all places?'

'His health required visits to a clinic in London. I found myself with no choice but to accommodate his wish to not live in the city. He was in a hospital bed when he put a copy of *Country Life* in front of me and pointed out the photograph of Edbury Hall, and I hadn't been in a position to say no.'

'But you wish you had now.'

He was silent for a moment and then said quietly, 'No, things have changed since I arrived yesterday. It's not that clear-cut any more.'

Sybella told herself he wasn't referring to her but it was difficult to hold his gaze when he looked at her like that.

Nik watched the shyness she worked so hard to keep hidden soften her features, her hands working nervously in her lap.

'I don't suppose we can sit here all day,' she said, 'or is that your intention?'

Nik laughed and she appeared taken aback, as if his amusement was something slightly shocking. Was he that bad?

'Where do you want to go?'

He expected her to say back to work, but she looked out across the gravel courtyard and said, 'I've got a window of an hour before I need to pick Fleur up. Why don't we just go for a drive?'

There was a wash of colour in her cheeks again. He knew he couldn't start anything with her, but it couldn't hurt to take a drive.

'Why don't we?' he said and started the engine.

Sybella directed him to Linton Way Forest and they parked under the oaks. She got out and they walked down the overgrown walking track that famously weaved in and over the hills.

She told him about the uses the village had for the estate, and he listened.

'We have tours on Thursday afternoons. People are free to look at the west wing on weekends. The pony club use the grounds once a month for the gymkhana. That's about it so far. It doesn't impact on your grandfather's private life in the house. In fact he often appears unannounced to talk to tourists himself.'

'What I'm more interested in is the financial benefit to your little organisation.'

Sybella looked genuinely surprised.

'The Heritage Trust is a charity. Any money goes back into preservation—no one is pocketing it. We all volunteer.'

Nik reached around to massage the back of his neck and Sybella tried not to ogle his biceps. She was aware of him physically in a way that was making it difficult to concentrate on the serious matters they were discussing.

Although something had changed between them, Sybella just couldn't put her finger on what it was. He was more willing to listen and she was incredibly conscious of him physically.

'How did you come to be involved with them?'

'I have a degree and a diploma in archives management I earned part time when Fleur was younger. I needed some work experience and the Heritage Trust is all that's available in the area so I volunteered. That was three years ago.'

'That can't have been easy with a baby.'

'No.' She slanted a shy look his way, because it was nice to have that acknowledged. Encouraged, Sybella plunged into the tough stuff. 'I met your grandfather when the trust approached him about opening the house. He took an immediate dislike to our president but he was rather taken by Fleur, who was with me, and invited the two of us to tea. I do tours now on Thursdays for various schools and Fleur and I take tea with your grandfather afterwards. It's become a sort of ritual between us.'

'He talks about you a great deal.'

Sybella chewed on her lip. 'Nice things, I hope.'

'Nice being the word. He wants me to settle down with a nice girl.'

Oh, yes, she'd seen those girls on the Internet.

'The thing is, Sybella, I work hard,' he said unexpectedly.

She could have told him she worked hard too, but she guessed he and the rest of the world put more value on his work.

She watched those long lashes sweep down, the irony in his voice only making him seem more impenetrable, and Sybella could absolutely see why very beautiful, sought-after women would make an attempt at breaching all that male beauty and privilege with the aim of being the one to stick up her flag.

'I don't have time to invest in someone else's life. I date women with a corresponding world view.'

Sybella just kept nodding because she wasn't sure why he was telling her this.

'My grandfather doesn't approve,' he said dryly.

'He's very good with Fleur. I guess he wants great-grandchildren.'

Which was when it all fell neatly into place.

'Oh, no,' she said.

'Exactly. You knew nothing of this?'

'It simply didn't occur to me.'

'You do fit the criteria,' he said, with a slight smile that had Sybella's head snapping around in astonishment. 'He told me you would cook, clean and be a wonderful mother to our children,' he added.

But not Nik's criteria. Beautiful and not looking for—what did he call it—an investment? Sybella wrinkled her nose. It was a horrible term. The antithesis of an emotion.

He was talking about his grandfather's criteria.

Which she guessed were somewhat less exacting. To do with being a mum and a homebody. What would he say if she told him she'd never planned to take on any of this, it was life in its infinite surprises that had laid down those roles for her?

That she still, deep down, thought of herself as the independent individualist she had always been.

Did he really think she was angling herself at him?

'I didn't stand around in the courtyard last night waiting for you because your grandfather put me up to it!'

'Good to know.'

So that was what this romantic walk in the woods was all about.

She was being given the message he wasn't interested. He clearly thought she needed that message. Sybella's stomach hollowed out.

Probably now was a good time to sort this, when her ego was still reverberating from his direct hit and she was feeling a bit numb.

'There's just one small problem I should probably alert you to before we go our separate ways,' she said with as much dignity as she could muster. 'After the other night a lot of people in the village think you're my boyfriend.'

'Boyfriend?'

Sybella could feel herself turning pink. This was possibly one of the more embarrassing moments of her life.

'It's not what you think. I haven't rushed about telling people you are.'

'I'm not thinking that,' he said slowly.

'The other night at the Hall when you were holding me, some of the committee members got the wrong idea.'

She looked up at him, biting the inside of her lower lip. 'It will blow over, but I thought you should be made aware of it.'

Nik did his best to repress his amusement. He cleared his throat. 'People do jump to some out-there conclusions.'

'I know, crazy, right?' Sybella began to talk faster, because now they were at the more awkward bit, but she had to ask. 'There's one other thing. There aren't many opportunities in the immediate countryside for curatorial jobs, and my CV isn't exactly bursting at the seams, and if it gets out what happened with the house being open to the public on false pretences and you shutting things down, I can't see anyone ever hiring me. Ever.'

'I see.'

'Reputation matters in this business.'

'Makes sense.'

'If you could see your way clear to not pressing any legal charges—'

'Sybella, I didn't have all the information to hand. I'm not going to make your life any more difficult than it already is.'

'Oh.' She said a silent prayer. 'Thank you. You're not nearly as scary as you pretend to be, are you?'

It was his turn to look vaguely bemused.

'I don't mean to offend you,' she rushed on, 'but you can be a bit intimidating. I suppose it's because you're so big.'

'There's that,' Nik drawled, not sure if she knew how adorable she looked babbling at him as if he had feelings to hurt and she was worried about having stepped on them. 'I also have a lot of financial clout. You'd be amazed, Mrs Parminter, how the world works.'

'I suppose I would,' she said, blushing. 'I should probably get up to speed on that.'

He almost idly wound the end of one of her ringlets around his index finger before releasing it. It was a gesture implying intimacy, touching her but not quite touching her, which made her think about when they had touched, when they'd kissed.

'No, don't do that,' he said. 'Stay the way you are.'

'Too tall, too opinionated, too fat,' she blurted out.

Oh. God. Where had that come from? Because there was nothing more attractive to a man than a woman who bemoaned her looks. At least in some far-flung universe they didn't currently occupy.

To forestall any opinion he might have about her round body or her interest in him, she bowled on, 'Sorry, I don't know where that came from. I guess all those women you date don't go on about their looks because they're so gorgeous it doesn't occur to them.'

Sybella took a breath and stared in disbelief into the middle distance.

There was this awful silence. She wondered if he'd think it was odd if she just ran off at this point, screaming, into the forest.

Instead she made a swipe of her watch under her long sleeve.

'Oh, goodness, is that the time? I have to pick up Fleur from communal play. She's got a birthday party tomorrow with her little friends. She's taking fairy bread, and I still have to pick up the ingredients.'

She didn't wait for his response but started hurrying away from him, back towards the car.

'Listen to me babbling,' she threw over her shoulder. 'You don't mind me driving, do you?'

His steady tread on the gravel mocked her hasty, messy retreat. She climbed in the car and waited, clammy with horror. Although he'd told her she wasn't his type, he knew now, if he hadn't already suspected, she was besotted with him.

CHAPTER SEVEN

SYBELLA SAT CROSS-LEGGED on her sofa, looking into the inquisitive brown eyes of her daughter's house rabbit.

'I committed the cardinal sin,' she told Dodge. 'I exposed every last one of my frailties in front of Nik Voronov. I may as well have told him no one has seen my good lingerie except the wash bag in the machine in six years.'

She answered herself with a question. 'Can you get more specific there, Syb?'

'I told him I was fat and lonely and pretty much desperate.'

'Why would you do that?'

'Because he probably dates glamazons and his grandfather wants him to date me instead and he basically told me that wasn't going to happen and I sort of went…crazy.'

'Well, you do go a bit weird with a full moon.'

'I don't think it was the full moon, although given not only am I talking to a rabbit, I'm doing the voice so he answers back, it might be. And now I'm not even talking to the rabbit, I'm talking to myself. I am so screwed.'

'I wouldn't say that,' said a deep voice and Sybella almost fell off the couch.

Standing in the doorway off the hall was her Viking god.

'How did you get in?'

'You left the front door unlocked and I heard voices. I used that bell-pull. Are you aware it doesn't work?'

Sybella's cheeks felt red hot, mainly because she'd been caught making an idiot of herself. In front of the one person in the world she couldn't bear to think any worse of her.

'I'm sorry but you can't just walk in here.' She eased herself off the sofa carefully, not wanting to alarm Dodge, who was now sitting up, peering at Nik, ears aquiver.

'You even apologise to intruders into your home,' he said as if she'd revealed some secret about herself, then a look of amusement crossed his face. 'Is that rabbit for real?'

'His name is Dodge, and he's a house rabbit, there's another one around, so please keep your voice down.'

'I wouldn't want to frighten the woodland creatures,' he said, lowering his voice, looking at her in a way that made Sybella weirdly think he was including her in that. He closed the door gently behind him so that suddenly her living area felt very small.

'What are you doing here?'

'I came to say goodbye. I'm leaving in the morning.'

Sybella was hit by a punch of utter disappointment. He was leaving? 'Oh.'

He wore a T-shirt and jeans, as casual as she'd seen him, only on him it looked like one of those ads in a glossy magazine where the guy was glowering sullenly at the viewer and toting some serious machismo, and usually there was a dangerous-looking motorcycle behind him. Yes, Nik Voronov appeared to have stepped out of those pages into her living room.

And he'd come to say goodbye?

'I read your proposal about opening the gatehouse as a tourist hub for the house and estate.'

Sybella was so busy swimming in disappointment he was leaving she didn't completely take it in.

"It's a sound proposal,' he said. 'I'm willing to talk about it.'

Now? This was good, he was staying—to talk about the Hall. It was a big step in the right direction—for the Hall.

Sybella did an internal eye roll. She really needed to get herself together around him.

'The truth is I'm under a bit of pressure with the old man.'

It wasn't what she expected to hear and it wiped all the nonsense in her head. He needed her help. He actually moved a hand over the back of his neck, the age-old posture of male admission he was willing to lay down arms. That alone spoke volumes about his feelings for his grandfather.

She melted. 'You really love him, don't you?'

He shrugged. 'He's my grandfather.'

Sybella thought of her lousy, self-interested parents and then shoved them back where they belonged, over a cliff and into the ocean of people who could break your heart if you let them.

'I'd like to speak to you about him, something personal. Can I sit down?'

He didn't wait for the invitation, but lowered himself onto the armchair, catty-corner from the sofa she was now inhabiting.

He leaned forward, resting his forearms over his broad knees, fixing her with that intent grey gaze.

She'd been entertaining so many romantic fantasies about this man over the last twenty-four hours, to have him in the flesh inhabiting her small living room had the quality of one of those.

'Where's your little girl?'

'Her aunty Meg is here for the weekend so she's having a sleepover with her at my parents-in-law's house. They live on the other side of the village.'

Something flickered in his gaze and Sybella could suddenly hear her heartbeat in her ears.

'You were going to tell me something…personal about you and your grandfather?' she prompted, aware her voice had a slightly airless quality to it.

He gave her a half-smile as if acknowledging the irony

of the 'something personal' when right about now everything about him being here felt personal.

'I am,' he said. 'It begins with my parents. They were childhood sweethearts, Darya and Alex, and had been together for a long time before they had a separation of about a year, and my mother got pregnant with me. She mustn't have thought that much of the guy because she rekindled her romance with Alex and he was apparently happy to call me his son.'

Sybella didn't know what to say.

'I don't have any memories of my mother. She had a rare kidney condition and died when I was still a baby. Papa raised me alone until he remarried. They were good years or so I'm told. I lived on a lot of film sets but this is in Russia. Alex always used the same people and the crew were like family. When I was five I got a very flashy stepmother and several months later a baby brother. Sasha. I'm sure you've heard about him.'

'Your grandfather mentions him from time to time. He seems to be in the public eye quite a bit.'

'My little brother is famous for his films and his parties, not always in that order,' Nik responded, but there was real warmth in his voice, as there had been when he'd spoken to his grandfather. Sybella was beginning to feel a little foolish about all her doubts. They were clearly a strong unit.

'Sasha was four years old when our father slipped on a ledge climb in Turkey. Papa was chasing a shot for a film he was putting together. He always took risks. My brother is very much like him.'

Nik's expression conveyed this wasn't necessarily a positive thing.

'I went to live with my grandparents after Alex's death. My grandfather was a successful businessman. I don't know if he's talked to you about that part of his life.'

'No, not really. We talk about family and books mainly.'

'His favourite subjects.' Nik was scrutinising her and she couldn't blame him. She was fast becoming the vault of Voronov family secrets.

'I'm not indiscreet, Nik. I won't talk about this to anyone.'

He smiled then. 'I wouldn't be sharing this with you if I thought you would. I'm telling you all this, Sybella, because it appears my grandfather has taken quite a shine to you, and he's told me how good you've been to him, and I behaved badly last night and I don't want to leave here with you thinking the worst of me.'

'But I don't,' she began, a little too anxious to assure him her feelings had changed. 'I saw how close the two of you are this afternoon.'

'I owe him so much,' Nik said simply. 'I only knew how much when I was fifteen and needed a blood transfusion and neither of my grandparents could help out. That was when Baba and Deda sat me down and told me the true state of affairs. I wasn't their grandson.'

'But you are,' said Sybella unbidden, and then flushed. 'I'm sorry, you don't need me to tell you that.'

'It's all right.' He was smiling at her and the effect of that smile was singing all over her body. 'So you see,' he said, 'we have something in common.'

'Have you tracked him down, your biological father?' She stopped, embarrassed. 'I'm sorry, that's another very personal question. You don't have to answer that.'

'No, I haven't met him.' He shifted and Sybella could see this weighed on him. 'I have his name. I haven't done anything about it. I don't know if I ever will.' He rolled those big shoulders. 'What about you? Have you gone looking for your real parents?'

Which was a neat way of diverting the conversation. Sybella wondered if he was even conscious of how everything in his body conveyed tension when he talked about his biological father.

'According to the records office, my father is unknown and my mother was a student who gave me up for adoption,' she answered. 'We got together when I was twenty. She came to my wedding. She remembers Fleur with birthday cards, which is something. I think it's hard for her to maintain relationships with people. She seems to have had a difficult life.' She looked down at her hands.

'I'm sorry I was dismissive about your adoptive parents the other night,' he said. 'I shouldn't have said what I did.'

She looked up. 'That's all right, it's forgotten.'

Nik was gazing back at her steadily, and this intimacy created by their mutual confessions was making Sybella feel something like the first steps in a friendship was springing up between them, only none of her friends were six-feet-six-inch Russians with Cossack eyes and a way of looking at her that made her think he might like to kiss her again.

'What a pair we make,' he said in that quiet, gravelly way of his.

Sybella dropped her gaze, suddenly immensely shy.

'What I guess I'm getting around to, Sybella, is that Deda has helped me through some difficult times as a kid, Baba as well. I owe them both a great deal. I'm cognisant I may have dropped the ball with Deda recently, but I want you to know he's in safe hands and why.'

Sybella blinked rapidly because she could feel ready emotional tears surging up.

Blast those pregnancy hormones. They'd arrived six years ago and never really gone away.

'I could see how close you were earlier today.' She dabbed at her eyes. 'I'm sorry if I implied anything else. I obviously didn't have the full picture and you weren't obliged to tell me. I mean, it's not as if we know one another.'

'I'd like to get to know you better.' His Russian accent was suddenly stronger and Sybella almost slid off the sofa again.

He would? Don't be stupid. He doesn't mean it like that.

'I would too.' She tried to think of something to avert attention from her burning cheeks. 'I can offer you something to eat. I was just going to mix up a stir-fry for dinner. Would you like some?'

Nik didn't hesitate despite having just eaten a full meal with his grandfather. 'Yes, I would.'

When she leaned forward to stuff her feet into slippers, as if to completely assure the direction of the evening, her breasts moved sumptuously against her top, giving him a glorious view of how generous Mother Nature had been.

'The kitchen's this way,' she said, straightening up as if nothing extraordinary had just happened, and with a shy smile she gestured for him to follow her.

Nik followed.

His gaze dropped to the fulsome curve of her bottom beneath the soft fabric of her drawstring pants. He'd never considered himself a connoisseur of the female bottom. But right now he was seeing the benefits of a woman with some heft in her pendulum. In fact he was pretty much transfixed by that sweet wobble and sway.

In the kitchen she had a bottle of Spanish red out on the counter.

'Can you get some glasses? They're in the cabinet over there,' she instructed as she began gathering her ingredients around her.

He found a couple of wine glasses and poured. He'd drunk worse.

Presently the place began to smell delicious from whatever was heating up on the stove.

Vaguely he remembered his grandfather mentioning Sybella's cooking skills, and he had to admit there was something about Sybella that made a woman being competent in a kitchen sexy.

He didn't do domestic scenes with women. He had a chef, or he ate out. His stepmother had been allergic to anything but restaurants, and until his grandparents had swept in and given him a home he'd eaten a lot of take-out.

So deep down he associated home cooking with stability and the love of his grandparents. But he wasn't one of those guys who clung to redundant gender roles. Which made this weird because underneath all that he was still the son of generations of conservative Russian males, and he really was enjoying watching Sybella cook for him.

'So you work at the town hall?'

'Yes.' She was busily chopping up apples but she gave him her shy smile. 'I'm the assistant archivist. You can find me in the basement with all the dusty files. We're putting a lot of things on the computer system but so much of what we handle is original documentation, dating back before the English Civil War, registers of births, deaths and marriages, land holdings, town maintenance. It's all there, and we keep the originals in the library for academics and the occasional documentary film maker. I chase things up for people three days a week.'

'This interests you, doesn't it, the past?'

'I like permanence,' she said, laying down the knife. 'It comforts me to know ten generations have lived here, in this house. People have been born here and died here, been married out of this house, triumphed and suffered and dreamed within its walls. I like old things, the way they soak up the lives of the people who have lived in them and with them.'

Nik remembered what she'd told him about being adopted, about being handed back, about her adoptive parents not being in her child's life.

This was important to her for good reasons. She'd pulled a bad hand as a kid, and, looking around her house, he could see she'd made more than a home with her daughter. She'd put down roots.

'So what plans did you have for the Hall before I bought it?'

She looked up in surprise, 'How did you know—?' She broke off and shook her head. 'You've been ahead of me all along, haven't you?'

'It's not difficult to work out.'

'Well,' she said, beginning to dice again, 'apart from turning the gatehouse into a tourist hub, we were planning on having open-day picnics in the grounds, but that was under the last owner. He was an American, you understand.' She cast an almost mischievous look at him through her lashes.

'Meaning a Russian is not big-spirited enough to get out of the way of English heritage?'

'No, no,' she said, laughing, and the sound arrested him. He'd never heard her laugh. 'I meant he knows the value of a buck. Edbury could be quite profitable.'

It was the last thing he'd expected Sybella to say, and he agreed with her. He'd been thinking along the same lines, but ruled a line under it. This was his grandfather's home; he wasn't dislodging him.

'It can't be done. Deda loves it here.'

Sybella put down the knife she was using with a clatter. 'Oh, my goodness, no, you misunderstand me. This wasn't my idea, it was your grandfather's.'

'*Prostit?*'

Sybella bit the inside of her lip. She was beginning to look forward to the moments when he spoke his language to her.

'Mr Voronov has been looking at literature from other local stately homes. We've been talking about what could be done here. To hold onto the heritage of the Hall to pass on to future generations. I thought you could be brought on board,' she said, then lowered her gaze because she was beginning to wonder if in a minute he'd warn her off going within twenty metres of the Hall again. 'We all care desperately about keeping the place historically intact for the future. And to be honest, Nik, I think it's given your grandfather a reason to get up in the mornings.'

Nik unfolded his arms. 'Why don't you tell me about it, then, your plans?'

'Truly?' she said.

Their eyes met and hers dropped first. She began dicing a little harder.

'Naturally it would take a lot of setting up. There are bylaws, not to mention the increase in traffic using local roads. We don't want the village being overrun by tourists. We get quite enough in the summer. Not so much Brits but busloads from overseas. Everybody wants to poke around in some between-the-wars version of England with its winding lanes and thatched cottages.'

'Says the woman who lives in one.'

She smiled and Nik felt something lodge behind his breastbone. This beautiful woman, who had blinked back tears when he'd told her about his parents, and dissolved in his arms the other night and now was preparing dinner for him, was smiling at him.

Those eyes stayed locked to his and he was suddenly only aware of the hard, heated consequences of being around her for the past twenty-four hours beating against the buttons on his jeans.

'Careful.' He laid a hand on hers where she was chopping up the apple. She looked down to see she'd almost nicked her finger. 'You're not paying attention,' he chided, stroking her finger with his thumb.

'No, I'm not,' she said with a small smile, those hazel eyes flitting to his shyly but with a look of unvarnished sexual yearning before they swooped down to his mouth, giving her away so entirely all he could do was remove the knife from her hand and wait for her eyes to lift again and dance to his.

He hadn't planned to make a move on her. He'd only known he owed her an explanation and an apology and the temptation of seeing her again had been too strong.

She had lowered her lashes and he was able to study her face, the boldness of her mouth, the soft, full curve of her cheeks. She was so damn lovely.

The heat from the pot had turned her cheeks pink and curled the fair tendrils escaping from her bun around her face. The fragrance of rosemary and basil, along with the olive oil from the pan, was on her fingertips and he was imagining those fingers touching his skin.

He wanted to lift her onto the bench, lay her down among her fresh ingredients and plunder her soft pink mouth until she was his.

'So your daughter is at her sleepover?' Nik heard himself ask as if they were having a general conversation.

Sybella nodded, not trusting her voice. She knew what the question meant. Telling him there was a fifty-fifty chance she'd get a phone call from Meg at around eleven and Fleur would want to come home would probably sink things where they stood.

She could surely keep these two halves of her life separate for an evening. He would be gone tomorrow and she would go back to keeping all those balls in the air.

But she didn't want to think about tomorrow. Just thinking about everything she had on her plate would surely close down her inner sex goddess completely.

She turned away from him abruptly and went over to the hob. She fumbled with the gas as she turned off the flame under the saucepan and pan, telling herself she could have this once. With this gorgeous man. Nobody needed to know.

Besides, it wasn't anyone's business…

Her breath caught as he put a hand around her waist and turned her and then laid a finger against her cheek and eased away an errant curl.

She gazed into his heated eyes and said, 'Maybe we can skip dinner.'

CHAPTER EIGHT

SHE TOOK HIS HAND, sliding her fingers along his, and he enfolded her slighter grasp within his own and she led him out of the kitchen into the narrow hall and to the foot of the stairs.

Nik saw a moment's hesitation in her, as she laid a foot on the first step and then stopped. Which was when he picked her up. She said something ridiculous about being too heavy but he'd already mounted the stairs and she was looking at him as if no man had acted like a Neanderthal around her, when he could imagine most of the men she met probably fantasised about doing this with her. But didn't make it past that first step. Her hesitation, the way she looked at him, told him this was not a regular occurrence in her life.

Her bedroom door was directly opposite the stairs and open. The double bed didn't look big enough but as he lowered her onto it he could see there was enough room for their purpose.

'Let me do this,' she said, before he could kiss her.

She was climbing up on her knees, tugging and pulling his T-shirt up over his head.

He was surprised by her willingness to take the initiative given her nervousness, but he wasn't complaining as he finished the job for her and tossed the T-shirt over his shoulder.

'I'm going to do this,' she said and he could have told her he wasn't going to argue.

She ran her fingers down his torso, exploring the definition of his muscles and tendons beneath the skin intricately converging to form that V below his taut abdomen, undoing a few of the buttons on his jeans.

Nik's breathing was already coming in snags as he watched her explore him with her fingertips. Her touch was so light, the expression on her face transfixed.

'Is this okay?'

She foraged under those loose buttons, meeting his eyes. 'Yeah, that's okay,' he said, swallowing as she slowly slid her hand over the length of him.

Nik sucked in a breath and went still, eyes lambent, the breath hissing between his teeth as she explored him with her hand.

When she was sure he definitely hadn't had enough she smiled and removed her hand and then slowly, enticingly began to move that same hand over the button fly of his jeans, opening it up.

'Are you trying to kill me, *dushka*?' he half joked, his voice hoarsened with the effort.

'That would defeat our purpose, don't you think?' Somehow that combination of her shy smile and her knowing eyes as she tugged his jeans down over his lean hips, taking his boxers with them, had the same effect as her hand on his erection.

She came over him, measuring him with her eyes, and lowered her head, her hair sliding forward to curtain her face as she licked him from base to tip.

Nik hissed and gripped the coverlet, fisting it as he fought not to disgrace himself. He was on a hair trigger; just watching her was enough to set him off.

She'd been so shy.

He really hadn't expected this…this sex goddess.

He tried to control the building reaction to her lapping, swirling pink tongue, the graze of her plump lips, and as she slid him into her mouth he knew he wasn't going to

make it if she went any further and he gently disengaged
her and deftly rolled her back onto the bed.

She lay there, smiling up at him as if she'd accomplished something she was proud of, as she should be, her
eyes glistening, her mouth wet, her breaths coming even
shorter as he slid one finger into the vee of her soft cotton
top, where it dipped into the valley between her breasts.

He went to strip her shirt off but she clamped her hands
over his.

'The light,' she said, blinking anxiously at him as if he
might say no.

He looked up at the overhead, a vintage frilled thing
that was currently lighting things up to his satisfaction.

'It's in my eyes,' she said, looking suddenly oddly flustered. 'Can we have it off?'

Only an idiot would argue with her at this point. He
bounded from the bed to turn the main light off. Sybella
had reached across and switched on the lamp. The room
was suddenly in shadows but Sybella was bathed in a dif-
fused caramel glow.

She looked positively feline and possibly the most sensual creature he had ever laid eyes on.

'Anything else you want doing?' he asked, coming
down beside her on the bed.

He ran his hands over her hips and behind to the curve
of her generous bottom still clad in satin something and
into her eyes crept a touch of tension. He snuffed it out
by kissing her hungrily, devouring the soft, sweet mouth
he'd been dreaming about for the last twenty-four hours.

He pushed her cotton top up over her breasts, lifting her
arms and arching over her as he slid the cotton free. She
was wearing a simple bra embroidered with pink forget-
me-nots and with her flaxen hair tumbling over her shoulders she looked like every fantasy he'd ever had.

'*Bogu*, you're beautiful,' he said, sliding one strap off her shoulder.

'Am I?'

'Gorgeous.' He tried to imbue the assertion with some of the reverence he really did feel, but it wasn't easy when all he wanted to do was fall on her like a sex-starved teenager who'd never been this close to a naked woman's body in his life.

'You're a bona fide sex goddess,' he asserted and she responded by wrapping her arms around his neck and coming up to meet him.

As their mouths fused he was no longer able to keep up this song of seduction and skill; he was just a man a little clumsy with lust.

He slid his mouth down her throat, licking over her cleavage, feeling her shiver against him in anticipation. He reached under her and released the catch of her bra and then slowly, with an intensity of purpose because frankly her breasts deserved worshipping, he peeled her pretty cups away.

He took his time to look his fill, feeling her eyes on him, her rapid, short breaths telling him she found this thrilling too. He took one taut pink nipple between his lips and licked. She gasped and bucked under him. He moved from one breast to the other, licking and sucking and moulding her, listening to her sighs and the little noises she made.

He untied the drawstring on her pants and hooked his thumbs under the sides of her satin knickers on the way down and peeled them both off, his hands actually shaking. She'd left herself as nature made her, the soft fair curls at the apex of her thighs as pretty as anything he'd ever seen.

He traced the seam of her sex with his index finger and she gave a little 'oh' as he lowered himself to kiss her there and inhale the heady scent of aroused woman. He licked her without warning and then again and she cried out and pulsed to her first orgasm, but he didn't stop, he went on and on until he wrung the last glorious ripple from her.

When he lifted his head and looked up she had her eyes half closed, her hair spread around her, the sensuality of her on full uninhibited display, and satisfaction thundered through him. She gave him a dreamy smile.

'What a little honeypot you are,' he told her and placed a kiss on her lower belly, where she was softer and she had a silvery pale tributary of zigzagging lines and some pinkish ones that hadn't faded yet, if they ever would.

Sybella watched him through her lashes. She didn't mind those tiger stripes—her baby had given her those. He traced them with his tongue and kissed her belly again, coming up over her with intent.

'Not a honey trap any more?' Her voice was smoky with satisfaction.

His grin turned rueful. 'I take it I'm not forgiven for that.'

Sybella reached for him, her hands smoothing over the warm breadth of his chest to curl over his shoulders where the muscles were bunched. She couldn't get enough of his body. 'Oh, I think you're forgiven.'

'Happy?'

She gave him a sly smile. 'Not completely.'

'I still have some work to do—what could the lady possibly want from me now?'

He settled between her thighs and Sybella had a blissful moment of being exactly where she wanted to be with exactly the right man.

He'd seen her body now in all its opulent glory and she was beginning to think just maybe the awkwardness with Simon hadn't been entirely down to her, because at no point in any of this had she wanted to be covered by a sheet. Nik was obviously, unashamedly devouring her with his eyes.

She could feel him hard and impatient, stroking himself against her. *Right there.*

Sybella shifted her pelvis to bring him to her but he was pulling away.

No, no.

'Where are you going?' she asked incredulously.

'I need to suit up.'

Sybella flopped back on the mattress, grateful one of them was using their brain.

Nik had pulled a couple of condoms out of his wallet.

She gave him a lopsided smile. 'You were confident.'

'I had hopes.'

'Hurry,' she urged.

Nik discovered his hands were shaking slightly as he rolled one on and she moved to take over.

'You really are going to kill me,' he said between his teeth.

'Well, like I said before, that would defeat our purpose.' She said it with a little smile on her face that grew as she slid her hands over his hips, coming up on her knees and then looping her arms over his shoulders.

He spread his hands around her bottom, enjoying the give of her, the softness, the sheer female voluptuousness of her body against his harder frame.

He was against her and she made a soft little noise against his throat. Nik didn't need the encouragement and drove home, the sheer size of him paralysing her senses for a moment and then his mouth was hot at her neck and he was sheathed inside her and Sybella sighed her deep-felt appreciation, turning her mouth to his as he kissed her, smothered her mouth with his, before lowering his head to suck on her breasts, leaving her gasping.

He positioned her with his big hands and thrust again

and again and when he thought he couldn't hold back she climaxed around him, the intensity of it tipping him over the edge. Conscious thought was a long time coming and when it returned to Nik they were lying in each other's arms, her eyes soft and no longer as curious as they had been when he'd first looked into them in the snow last night. She had her answer.

'Well,' she panted, her breath soft against his shoulder, 'that was…something.'

'*Da*, something.' Too fast, too urgent, just…sensational. He felt grateful, dazed and looking forward to taking that trip to heaven again.

Soon.

He stroked the hair off her face, feeling an unaccountable level of well-being he hadn't felt in years. Her skin was dewy with faint perspiration, her cheeks pink; she was fairly glowing.

His gaze moved over the rounded shapes of her sumptuous breasts and flagrant hip curved under his hand. He squeezed her softly, enjoying the flesh under his hand.

'You like looking at me,' she said, her fingers tangling in his chest hair.

'I'd be crazy if I didn't.' He touched his lips to the tip of her nose and then her eyelids and finally her temple. Nothing salacious, more in reverence for how tender she made him feel.

'I like looking at you.' She massaged her lower lip with her teeth, as if something else was on her mind. 'I always had…trouble taking my clothes off in front of Simon. I felt, I thought, I don't know, I wondered what he saw.'

He gave her a lascivious smile and she smiled back and then her eyes filled and overflowed with tears.

'Sorry,' she gasped, cupping her face with her hands, 'so silly. Don't mind me.'

She was so English. So polite in the oddest circumstances. She was a woman. She was emotional. She shouldn't be ashamed of it. It made him feel tender. So he reached for her and kissed her tears and murmured to her in Russian, which seemed to quiet her. Presently her shoulders stopped quaking and she lay still against him.

'You were very young when you got married,' he said.

She nodded against his shoulder. 'Only I didn't think I was. I felt like I'd lived a lifetime before I met Simon.' She raised her face to look at him. 'He was my first love. We met in my first year at university. But after a year he—we—decided to take a break for the summer. He was going on a dig in Athens—amateur archaeology was his hobby, we kind of had that in common—but I couldn't go with him. I needed to work, save some money, so it was a break in our relationship.'

Nik waited; he suspected he knew where this was going.

'The next term he wanted to get back together but he told me he'd had a sort of a fling with another girl. It was okay,' she hurried on, glancing at him as if daring him to condemn her precious Simon. 'We were split when it happened.'

But he could hear in her voice there had been no splitting as far as Sybella was concerned. She was loyal. He'd known her twenty-four hours but he'd seen her loyalty in action, keeping the crucial information about the letters from him to protect Deda.

'Then, you see, she was in a few of my tutorial groups so I had to spend the rest of the year seeing her several times a month. I got a little funny about it. She never said anything, I don't think we ever exchanged any more than the normal pleasantries, but she must have known.'

'Do you want me to comment or just listen?' Nik had a number of thoughts, all of them about her fool of a husband.

'Listen, I think.' She gave a soft, nervous laugh. 'I've

said all the critical things in my head and I said a few to Simon at the time. It's just, we got back together—obviously—but I knew something wasn't right. Even on my wedding day there was this niggle.'

'He was still seeing her.'

'Gosh, no, no! Simon wasn't that kind of guy at all.'

Nyet, and in Sybella's partial eyes probably never would be. Nik did his best not to take a dislike to her dead husband.

'He was very ethical. I mean, he didn't have to tell me.'

Nik wisely kept his own counsel. But the thought remained, I wouldn't have told her, I would have protected her from the knowledge. Then the next startling thought arrived: I wouldn't have gone to another woman.

Not when the girl was Sybella. She seemed to him a little traditional, the kind of woman who would expect fidelity. If the guy had loved her, he would have known that.

She eyed him, nervous once more. 'I know this will sound silly but I got a bit funny about my body. I got it into my head Simon didn't find me desirable.' She frowned a little, as if puzzling over the girl she'd been.

Now Nik officially wanted to punch her dead husband.

'You see, this other girl, she was very pretty and she was tiny, like a fairy tiny, and I'm not.'

Nik didn't know what to do with that. 'No, you're not,' he said.

She shoved him. 'You're not supposed to say that.'

He nudged up her chin to look at her, so incredibly lovely with her light-in-a-forest eyes and her pale pre-Raphaelite curls tumbling over her shoulders and those gorgeous breasts, and he knew in that moment what all men knew: they would never understand women.

'Listen, Lady Godiva, my interest in fairies ended around about the age of four. I want a woman in my bed, and I want her soft and warm and capable of giving as good as she gets—in and out of bed. Your Simon was young, yes?'

'Twenty-two when we got married.' Sybella's voice was soft and she was looking at him hopefully, as if he might say the very thing that was going to fix all this for her.

Nik wasn't so sure. He knew from personal experience how deep resentments could shoot those roots when they attached young. Rejection by your parents had to leave deep fault lines, and Sybella had just admitted hers. To him. As if he was worth her trust. But to respond in kind was something he couldn't do.

So he took hold of the surface problem and strangled the life out of it for her.

'I'd pretty much sussed it by twenty-two,' he said, meeting her eyes, 'but it can take some men a lifetime. Whatever package it comes in, Sybella, it's the woman inside who makes you notice her, who reduces you to an idiot and has you promising all kinds of things just to get her naked.'

Her mouth had fallen open slightly in the same way it had when he'd swooped her up into his arms earlier this evening and carried her up here.

Then her eyes began to kindle.

'You didn't promise me anything,' she said in a low voice.

He grinned at her. 'You should have asked, *dushka*.'

She was clearly trying not to smile.

'You're just saying that because you think it will get you laid again.'

'*Da*, there is that.'

The wounded vulnerability in her eyes had been replaced by the light he'd seen earlier.

That light was like a lighthouse beam guiding him right back to her and all that female lusciousness deep down she must know drove men mad.

'So how about it?'

And her mouth, which had become an instrument of both torture and pleasure to his body, curved up in a smile, carving that dimple deeply.

Bogu, he wanted to kiss that sweet mouth.

But she tucked her hand behind his neck again and brought his mouth down to where she wanted it, on her breasts.

Yeah, he'd died.

This was heaven.

CHAPTER NINE

Something gave a crack and the bed lurched to one side and then another crack and the headboard came away from the iron frame.

Nik sprang out of bed and, saying something in Russian, went around and checked out the situation.

'Should I get out?' she asked, not wanting to move in case it all collapsed.

'Hold still,' he grunted. 'I'll fix this.'

She gave a soft shriek as he dislodged the mattress base from the rest of the frame and Sybella found herself staring up at a ceiling that was significantly farther away than it had been a moment ago.

Nik carried the iron base in its two pieces out into the hall and leaned it up against the wall. Sybella watched him, craning her neck.

'You don't have to go, do you?' she called. 'The bed still works.'

Sybella screwed shut her eyes. *The bed still works?* Why didn't she say *I still work* and be done with it?

When Nik came back into the room he sized up the bed and then lowered the lean strength of his magnificent male body down beside her.

He shifted on the mess of twisted sheets and Sybella was suddenly very conscious of the lack of space in general, of how absurd this situation was in her small bedroom where she'd spent the last six years being nothing more than a harried working mum with no head space for what had happened here now.

No, space at the moment was definitely at a premium. His eyes were like dark onyx in the available light from the steadily burning lamp, and Sybella could see herself reflected in them but in a way she'd never really viewed herself before. This wanton creature who had revelled in her seduction of this powerful man, whom she'd pretty much brought to his knees—literally given a couple of the positions he'd held her in.

'I have to say, *dushka*,' he said in a gravelly voice, 'leaving is the last thing that's on my mind.'

He propped himself up, those big shoulders rising over her like cliffs, making it impossible to see over or around him, and Sybella found herself sinking under him again because this old bed, despite being a double, was really not made for two when one of them was six feet six. She enjoyed, however, that sensation of being rendered small and delicate and in thrall to him.

'You shouldn't have dragged me up here if you didn't want me to stay the night.'

'What do you mean I dragged you up here?'

'Lured me, then.' He gave her that slow, sexy smile and laid a kiss on her shoulder, her collarbone, the slope of her right breast, grazing dangerously close to her nipple. Little traitors sat up. She shivered as he brushed the underside of his unshaven jaw over one.

'You look like a wanton dairymaid—how could I resist?'

'Is that a reference to the size of my breasts?'

'Da,' he chuckled, brushing his lips over them, 'and your blonde hair and your dimples—and your roomy arse.'

'My what?' She hit his chest playfully as he slid his hands under her.

'More to get a grip on.' He laughed, doing just that. She'd never been more proud of her wide, womanly behind.

Then a thought hit her. 'I just imagined you'd be wanting to get back to your superyacht or whatever.'

He studied her. 'Superyacht?'

'Meg, my sister-in-law, has this theory that's where all the rich Russians live.'

'You've been talking about me?'

'Everyone in the village is talking about you.'

'I'm only interested in what you had to say.'

Sybella stroked his chest in seemingly idle circles. 'I said you weren't very happy with me.'

'I'm happy with you now.' He gave her bottom a squeeze.

She gave him a gentle shove.

'My yacht is about this big.' He measured it out to about an inch between his thumb and forefinger.

Sybella couldn't help it. 'Lucky for me that's only your yacht.'

'I could show it to you some time.'

'I thought you already had.' He smothered her giggle with a kiss and her blood began to hum again.

'I also have another estate in Northumbria,' he murmured against her mouth, and he named it and Sybella went a little pale.

'That's one of the finest castles in the north.'

'Too far and too cold,' he dismissed.

Sybella sat up, dislodging the sheet in her surprise. 'Then why did you buy it?'

'Tax purposes.'

'If you keep buying up my nation's history at this rate I'll end up working for you.'

'Would that be so bad?' He traced a line from her collarbone to her nipple. 'If we could keep doing this.'

Sybella's breath stuttered in her chest and not just because her breasts felt sensitive and responsive to him. Did he think they could find a way to keep doing this?

'Any more grand estates I should know about?' she asked, pulling at the sheet to cover herself again.

'No, just the two.' He kissed the exposed slope of one

breast and then the other, dislodging the covers so he could look at her while he played with them. Sybella was put in mind of a boy with a new toy.

'Real estate in London is more profitable. Russia isn't the safest place to keep all your eggs—' he spread his hands to cup either side of her breasts '—so I've got other baskets.'

Then mercifully he stopped talking about real estate and concentrated on their mutual pleasure.

When she opened her eyes hours later it was light. Nik was pulling on his shirt, and she sat up on her elbows, dragging the covers with her.

'What time is it?' She yawned.

'Almost nine.'

'I guess you should go,' she said half-heartedly.

'I should go,' he concurred.

He was looking down at her as if he still wanted her and Sybella's ego swelled a little more than it should, along with the plummeting feeling she was going to have to let him go and there didn't seem to be a clear-cut path for them, assuming he wanted one.

'When will you be back? In Edbury, I mean.'

Nik began reattaching his watch.

'I was thinking I could fly you up to London next weekend, if you could arrange someone to look after your daughter.'

Fly her up to London? She'd been thinking more along the lines of, When are you coming back to Edbury to see your grandfather? Maybe we could have dinner... Although given they'd already plunged in at the deep end dinner was always going to end here. So maybe London was the right option.

Only it sounded so illicit. And at the same time he was making plans for them, they didn't involve him stepping into her world, and she was a little taken aback by the impression he saw her daughter as an impediment.

'Fleur,' she said uncomfortably. 'Her name is Fleur.'

He smiled but he didn't say her name and a little part of Sybella curled at the edges like blight on a rose leaf.

'I guess I could come up to London. The thing is, I'm really only comfortable with Fleur staying with her aunty Meg or her grandparents, and I can't be away from her for more than a night. She's still so little…'

Sybella trailed off. He was getting out his phone. She guessed he wasn't really that interested in the logistics. It was her domestic life—not his.

He finished buttoning his shirt.

'Where's your phone?'

But he'd already spotted the chair in the corner where her soft patchwork carryall was slumped. Her phone lay on top of it.

She climbed out of bed, wrapping herself in the pale gold blanket, and drew close behind him to see what he was doing, although she had a pretty good idea and it made her warm inside.

'I'm programming in my numbers.'

His head was bent as she peered around him to watch what he was doing, a little confused about the entire procedure. It wasn't as if she had much experience with the whole casual dating thing. She'd only ever dated Simon.

'This way you'll be able to contact me if there's a problem.'

She was about to ask, *But what if there's not a problem?* when she heard it. Like a bat, she was on Fleur signal. It was a single muffled word. Then nothing for the count of one, two, three, four, five, six… And then the rattle of keys and her front door opening.

Battle stations.

She dived for her clothes on the floor, pulling up tracksuit pants and dragging a fluffy old jumper down over her head, flashing her boobs at him.

'They're back. You have to go,' she babbled, hunting around for his shoes. 'Listen, I'll head them off and get them into the kitchen and you come down and let yourself out.'

She shoved his shoes against his chest. 'Put these on and just stay there.'

Nik was caught by an unexpected wave of tenderness.

'Sybella.' He caught her arm and she gazed up at him with equal measures of annoyance and longing that had him wanting to prolong the moment. 'You are an incredible woman and you shouldn't doubt how sexy you are, or how lucky I feel after last night.'

She looked utterly transfixed, and in that moment he cursed her very young, very stupid dead husband.

Then a voice called out, 'Mummy!'

Sybella said something under her breath and he let her go.

As she came noisily down the stairs Sybella was convinced she had a scarlet 'A' painted on her forehead.

Meg was removing Fleur's coat and scarf. She looked up with a smile.

'I thought I'd bring her home and save you the drive, Syb. I have to be in Middenwold this morning anyway. Mum's having a tooth drilled and she says she can't drive herself home.'

'Mummy!' Fleur ran to hug her and be lifted. Sybella gave a little grunt. Her daughter was getting heavier by the day.

After some kisses Fleur was struggling to be put down. 'I want to show Aunty Meg my new shoes,' she complained, but Sybella had no intention of letting Fleur go up until the coast was clear.

'How about we go and put the kettle on first and make

some porridge?' She charged down the hall, making as much noise as possible. She dived for the radio and turned it up. A cheerful pop song filled the room with chants about love not hurting any more. Fleur began to bop up and down and Meg to dance with her.

By the time Fleur remembered her shoes the porridge had been eaten and at last Sybella was able to step into a shower and wash all of her extraordinary night off her glowing skin.

As she stepped out of the bathroom Meg was examining the broken bedstead Nik had arrayed at the end of the hall.

'How on earth did you do this?'

Fleur appeared with her new red shoes in either hand. 'It must have been the giant.'

A week from the day Nik had climbed out of Sybella's broken bed her name flashed up on his phone with a text.

For a moment he just rubbed his thumb lightly over the screen but purposely didn't read her words, aware of all the times this week he had called up her number only for his thumb to hover and then pass off. Indecision was not his way. He'd let the week get away from him and now he had a choice to make. If he didn't call her they could put a line under it.

He put his phone down to avoid temptation and picked up his drink.

'Problem?' His brother Sasha was watching him.

'Nichevo.'

They were sitting on the deck of his one-hundred-metre yacht, *Phantom*. The great beast was moored in the Adriatic, as it always was at this time of year, off the coast of Montenegro.

The centuries-old ramparts of the town of Budva, with limestone hills rising up behind it, was a starry backdrop of lights as the velvety evening dropped around them. The muted sound of thumping dance music heaved from the other end of the boat.

His brother, although long having given away the drugs and alcohol that had derailed him as an adolescent, seemed to need noise and activity around him. His parties on this boat were legendary. Nik had dropped in via helicopter to spend the evening comparing notes and swapping stories before he headed on to some talks and a symposium in Moscow.

'What are you doing with Deda?' Sasha asked, leaning back in his deckchair, resting his glass of fizz against his jeans-clad thigh.

Bare feet, Nik noted, the scorpion tattoo on his left ankle. His own were clad in hand-tooled moccasins stretched out in front of him. Kind of conservative, but he was kind of a conservative guy.

He eyed his phone again, wondering if she had a problem and he was ignoring it.

'When are you moving him out of that old pile?'

'I'm not.'

Sasha looked out across the water, in profile a muscle clearly leaping in his jaw. His brother liked to pretend he was chilled about everything that went down with Deda, but Nik knew better. He had missed those early years with their grandparents, forced to live with his mother abroad, and it made him diffident about interfering in the old man's life.

He saw himself as an outsider, the irony being Nik knew himself to be the one who didn't belong.

'He's happy with the public prowling around the place. To be honest it appears to have given him a second lease of life.'

'Looks like you're stuck with Mouldy Towers for the interim.'

Nik glanced again at his phone.

'What's her name?' Sasha asked, lifting his glass of fizz and ice to his lips. 'The woman whose call you don't know whether to take.'

Nik debated for a moment saying nothing. 'Her name's Sybella. She volunteers at the Hall.'

'So put it through to your office in London.'

Nik shook his head slightly. 'I slept with her.'

Sasha laughed out loud. 'Does that qualify as *droit de seigneur*?'

'*Nyet*, it means it's complicated.' Nik flashed his brother a quelling look.

'It's always complicated, man. Women as a species aren't happy unless they're raiding your head for what you're thinking at any given moment and then using it to crucify you.'

'Bad break-up with what's-her-name?'

'Just brotherly advice. I've never met a woman who didn't want full access to both your bank account and your darkest secrets.'

'Not Sybella.' Nik settled back, still nursing his phone. 'She mainly wants to keep the Hall open and for me to spend more time with Deda.'

'Oh, man, that's worse. She's already managing you.'

Nik frowned. 'It's not like that. It's complicated because she's got a daughter.'

'So? Has she got a nanny for the kid?'

'Even if she had the money for help it's not that kind of set-up. She's hands-on, home schools, community oriented. She's the whole package.' Nik shook his head slightly. 'Why am I telling you this?'

'So I'll talk you out of it. How long have you known her?'

'Forty-eight hours.'

Sasha obviously did his best to keep a straight face. 'That long?'

It had been enough time to get her life story, lose himself in the wonderland of her body for one night and find himself here on the deck of a yacht half a world away unable to stop thinking about her.

He downed his whisky.

'Why don't you stop overthinking it and show her a good time? You might find out she's more than happy to have a bit of a break from her packaged life. Is the kid's father in the picture?'

'She's a widow.'

'Then I don't see your problem. But if it bothers you that much move on. I've got a phone full of numbers I don't want. I can hook you up.'

'Really?' Nik raised a brow. 'You're farming out women now? Nice, Sasha.'

He ignored his brother, whose personal life was a car crash of beautiful girls and a man who walked away from the wreckage without a scratch, and stared meditatively at the tough glass, stainless steel and tiny circuit board he held in his hand that had revolutionised people's lives and made it hard for a guy to go to ground.

Surely he was doing the right thing keeping away?

He'd seen the photo on her bedside table, of the dark-haired, homely young man with an even younger, bright-eyed Sybella welded to his side.

That was what she needed. A man who would be there for her every day, not one who couldn't fix anyone's life.

He'd tried with his grandfather, but there was no bringing Baba back, which was all Deda really wanted, and Sasha was never going to forgive him for having the upbringing that was stolen from him.

Although Simon Parminter hadn't been there for Sybella in the end, he'd left her pregnant and with some hangups about her body that made Nik wish he could have set the guy straight.

Which was idiotic. If her husband was still alive Sybella wouldn't have looked twice at him.

She was that kind of woman.

Clearly her husband hadn't left her with much money either, given she was leasing the cottage.

He frowned. He could at least stop her payments. If they were seeing one another she could hardly be paying him rent.

Were they seeing each other?

Not that Sybella would accept any handouts. But he hated the idea of her struggling.

Maybe he could sort out the bed. Start with something basic.

Something solid.

Not a bed he would be occupying. Just a bed.

And under no circumstances was he delivering it himself.

He checked the text.

Can I have a yes or no on whether you're closing west wing down? Syb.

After all that, not a romantic bone in that sentence's body.

He exhaled a snort of amusement. She wasn't pining for him at all. Practical, realistic Sybella.

He texted her back.

No, dushka.

No, dushka?

Sybella stood at her kitchen sink, scowling at the message on her phone.

It had been a week since Nik had stormed into her world and made love to her so thoroughly and tenderly he'd set the bar ridiculously high for any other intimate relationship she might have one day, far into the future, and left her with a broken bed and a bit of a bruised heart because *she really liked him*.

Then she'd sent a text.

She'd been sitting in front of an old film last night, sipping on a glass of red and nibbling some comfort chocolate, when she'd worked up the nerve to text him. Not *Why haven't you called?* but a perfectly reasonable professional enquiry. She'd sat there while Jimmy Stewart carried a tipsy Katharine Hepburn back to her room, trying not to envisage Nik reading her text and saying *Sybella, who?*

Then *No, dushka* had popped up on her screen. She'd held her breath, feeling he was suddenly in the room with her, waiting for more. Only there was no more.

It answered her question whether she could show a pre-booked school group through the Hall on Thursday, but left her completely in the dark as to whether he was even interested in seeing her again.

She shoved her phone in her back pocket and ran the tap, frowning as her kitchen sink began to fill with dirty water.

Only it wasn't coming from the tap, it was surging back up the drain.

That wasn't good.

Sybella removed her gloves and opened her laptop, which was sitting on the bench where she'd been doing a little Internet surfing earlier this morning. She'd put 'Nikolai Voronov' into the search engine and up had come a few images of him in a suit at various glamorous functions with equally glamorous women clinging to him, and even more of him in hi-vis gear on mine sites. He did know how to rock a hard hat.

Irritably she wiped the screen of Nik Voronov and tapped the more prosaic 'blocked kitchen sink' into the search engine. The reality of her life restored.

She began rifling through the bottom odds-and-ends drawer, pulling out the shiny spanner her father-in-law had given her for just these emergencies.

Why pay a plumber you couldn't afford when you had videos on the Internet?

Inserting herself under the sink, she focused on fitting the head of the spanner to the grip on the pipe joint.

No, she certainly wouldn't be using those numbers he'd programmed into her phone again.

Frankly she didn't need a man in her life. She was a confident, independent woman. Able to clear drains with just a spanner and a bucket.

She repositioned the bucket.

But she didn't have the upper-body strength to turn the wrench.

'Mummy! Mummy!' Fleur's high, sweet voice came floating into the kitchen.

Sybella adjusted her face into something approximating calm and stuck her head up over the bench.

'What is it, sweetheart?'

'Mummy, the giant is standing in our garden again.'

I wish.

'Is he really? What do you think he wants?'

'Come and see!' Fleur urged.

Another time Sybella would have indulged her and played the game, but the man on the screen had moved on to unclogging your bath in the next video, she still hadn't loosened the pipe grip, and she had to meet Catherine in forty minutes.

'It's very cold outside. I think you'd be warmer in your jeans.'

Fleur hitched up her skirt to reveal she was, indeed, wearing her jeans.

Sybella's tension dissolved into a big smile. 'Excellent fashion choice. Now, I need you to go upstairs and make up your backpack. Do you know what you're taking to Gran's?'

'Ebby.'

Ebby was her much sucked-upon cloth doll.

'We're making a dress for her and fixing her eyes.'

Bless Catherine. 'Pack your jumper—the green one. Do you remember which one that is?'

Fleur nodded confidently, which meant anything could end up in there.

'Off you go. I'll be up in a minute to help. Mummy needs to beat a pipe into submission.'

Sybella crawled forward, angling the wrench at a better angle. She could hear the guy on the online instructional video telling her that sometimes a simple plunger would do the job.

She knew where she wanted to stick that plunger...

'You'll break it,' said a deep voice, testosterone wrapped in velvet, that had Sybella's head snapping back and hitting the top of the sink cavity.

'Ouch!'

She crawled out, her heart pounding in an attempt to escape through her chest, and angled a look up...and up.

Oh, blast.

Fleur had been right. There *was* a giant. Only he'd migrated into her kitchen.

CHAPTER TEN

SYBELLA WAS HOLDING a spanner, dressed much as she had been when he'd come here the last time, casually but this time in jeans and a jumper.

But the spanner in her hand, the brown water in her sink, the harried expression on her face gave him the feeling he was seeing Sybella as she really was, those little duck legs she'd spoken about churning around.

He took in the mess and began shedding his jacket.

'What are you doing?'

He took the spanner out of her hand and tossed his jacket onto a chair. 'I'll fix this. You go fix yourself up.'

Sybella just stood there. Had she missed something? Some lost text where he explained why he'd made no contact for a week? Although the ground shifted under her there, because she could surely have texted him something better than a line about the Hall.

And she was so *glad* to see him.

Then she realised she was standing in front of him in an oversized jumper with the neck and head of a giraffe appliqued on its front.

Yes, she would fix herself up. Immediately.

Nik had retrieved the culprit in the pipe, a plastic figurine about an inch in diameter, had the water draining away and had put through a call to a cleaning service when he realised he wasn't alone.

He turned around. A small dark head was bobbing around the edge of the doorway.

'Hello,' he said.

The head vanished. He waited. Gradually it inched forward again and a pair of big violet-blue eyes in a sweet squarish little face presented itself. The winter-dark hair that had fallen around her face the last time he'd seen her was tied up in bunches.

She was cute as a button.

'Do you remember me?' he said, keeping absolutely still and feeling completely out of his depth. He had no problem facing down angry mining bosses but confronted with a little girl he discovered he had nothing. 'I'm Nik. I'm a friend of your mama's.'

She didn't vanish this time; instead she edged her way into the kitchen, shy as a mouse. She was dressed in a long green skirt that didn't look entirely legit and some sort of long-sleeved yellow top with an appliquéd picture of a horse on it. Apparently the fashion had caught on.

Nik was struck by how little she was, and also that he was a strange man in her house. He reached for something to say that wouldn't scare her.

She beat him to it. 'You're not a real giant, are you? Because you can fit in a house.'

This was said in a piping voice with a great deal more confidence than he'd expected from her entrance.

'No, I'm not a giant,' he said slowly, trying not to smile.

'Mummy said you were an angry giant and a north god.'

A north what?

'I wasn't really angry with your mama. I got some things wrong. I'm sorry if I upset her.'

She lifted and dropped her small shoulders. 'That's okay.'

Nik remembered what he had in his hand and held it out to her. 'I think this might belong to you.'

The little girl trotted forward and put up her hand to take it. Nik didn't have much experience with kids—in his circle of friends only one had offspring and it was still a baby. He was struck by how tiny her hand was, how perfect her grubby little chewed-down nails. Her eyes were full of curiosity and liveliness and if she was shy it was leaving her fast.

She studied the figurine with the same interest she'd given to him and now seemed to forget he was there.

Nik heard the truck pull up.

He headed for the front door, yanked it open. Excellent. Edbury village might be full of crackpots and run on its own Brigadoon-style timescale, but money talked in London and one of the city's premier furnishing companies had delivered.

Which was when Nik became aware of a rabbit loping past him and out into the garden.

Hadn't Sybella referred to them as house rabbits?

He managed to corral the other one, closing the front door behind him. It took off in a flash into the sitting room.

Which was when her little girl appeared, said dramatically, 'You've done it now,' and disappeared after the fleeing rabbit. Then he heard Sybella shouting from an upstairs window.

One of the famous trucks from Newman and Sons with its distinctive gold lettering was pulled up in front of her house.

Sybella watched on in astonishment as the two men flung open the back doors of the truck.

As the pieces of a bed frame and then a mattress appeared and were carried piece by piece up her garden path she threw open the window and stuck her head out.

'I think you've got the wrong house!' she called down to them.

When the men ignored her and kept coming she leaned further out.

'Excuse me, lady of the house up here! This isn't my delivery!'

'It's the replacement for your bed.'

Sybella jumped as Nik's deep voice was suddenly right behind her in her bedroom, narrowly missing knocking her head on the window frame.

The scene of their crime.

She clutched her hand towel to her chest like a maiden in a pulp novel, her shower-damp hair hanging over her shoulders, the rest of her encased in a thick bath sheet, anchored under one arm.

'Nik.' It came out with a load of longing she'd rather he didn't hear. She swallowed, revised her plan. The plan she was trying to formulate as he stood there looking more gorgeous than she even remembered. The best she could come up with was, 'I didn't invite you up here!'

'Bit late for that.' He was looking at the bed. 'We'll get that shifted. You might want to get dressed and come down and supervise Fleur. She's trying to catch those damn rabbits. I think I let one out.'

'Oh, Lord!' Sybella dropped the towel—the hand towel, not the bath sheet—and went to hurry past him but he caught her around the waist with those big hands of his.

'One more thing,' he said as she looked up in astonishment, her body instantly melting like an ice cream in the sun under his touch, and he bent his head and kissed her.

A brief but comprehensive exploration of her mouth and then he let her go.

Sybella stuttered for a moment on her feet, not sure whether to tell him off or ask him to do it again, but that was all taken out of her hands when she heard a high-pitched cry from Fleur and she was down those stairs in a flash. Vaguely she was aware Nik wasn't far behind her.

Fleur was standing in the hall, holding Dodge in her arms, his head pushed comfortingly under her chin as Sybella had taught her.

'Mummy, Daisy got out.' She extended an accusatory

finger at the man standing behind her mother. '*He* let her out. She'll be squashed!'

Nik deftly set Sybella aside with the timely utterance, 'Go and put some clothes on,' and strode down the hall, clearly a man with a purpose.

Sybella sent Fleur into the kitchen to put Dodge in his hutch, grabbed her raincoat, shoved her feet into her galoshes and ran outside, doubting Nik was going to have much luck. She passed the two men carrying a quilted bed end. They stared at her with her bath sheet clearly visible under the semi-transparent plastic. She looked at the bed end, a little baffled by what she was supposed to do. She didn't want Nik buying her a new bed! But at the same time she was currently sleeping on a mattress on the floor and she had a frightened female rabbit to corral.

Sure enough, Daisy had hopped into the compost, long brown ears quivering.

Good girl, thought Sybella, making sure the bath sheet was secure with one arm, scooping Daisy out with the other. At least one of the females around here had some sense.

She carried her back to the kitchen and made sure the hutch was firmly latched. She could hear thumping overhead, which meant someone was in her bedroom. Just what she needed. A man-free zone since they'd arrived here six years ago and now she had them coming down the drainpipe.

She shivered in her towel and plastic raincoat. She really needed to put some clothes on!

Fleur was jumping up and down excitedly in the doorway. 'They've taken away the old mattress, Mummy!'

Sybella tried to access her own hallway but there were three men and Nik and a new mattress wrapped in plastic.

Which was when Nik came up beside her, put a hand to her waist and angled her out of the way.

'Do you think you can get dressed?' he growled.

'I'd like to. I am aware the delivery men don't know where to look.'

'I think they know exactly where to look. Go and put some clothes on.'

'I would but they're in my bedroom! Nik, listen, I can't accept this.'

'Let me do this for you,' he said for her ears only in that quiet, sexy Russian drawl of his. 'I did break it.'

She found herself a little transfixed by the sound of his voice, the look in his eyes. For a single moment she forgot the fact there were strange men in her house, she was wearing a towel under a raincoat and she had to meet Catherine in twenty minutes…

'Sybella! What on earth?'

Then she remembered, Catherine was meeting them, and it had just got worse.

'My mother-in-law,' she bleated. Then more plaintively, 'I have to get all this cleaned up.'

'I've called a cleaning service,' Nik said, observing the well-groomed older lady standing on the doorstep at the end of the hall.

Sybella blinked. 'I'm sorry?'

'Cleaners are coming. Go and dry your hair, whatever it is you need to do. I'm taking you and your daughter to lunch.'

'What about Grandma?' asked Fleur, looking up at her mother for guidance.

Sybella put a hand to her own temple. 'Catherine's spending the day with us,' she said, looking a little harassed. He could see what was coming. *Maybe this isn't a good idea*.

Nik didn't hesitate at this mere stumbling block. 'Catherine too, then.'

CHAPTER ELEVEN

'I BELIEVE YOU were seen having sexual relations with my daughter-in-law up against a car at the Hall.'

Sybella had taken Fleur off to the facilities, or 'loo' as she called it, leaving him alone with the real Mrs Parminter in the low-beamed, snug confines of The Folly Inn, a pub in Edbury with Civil War origins, according to Sybella, and an impressive wine list that spoke of Edbury's prominence on the Cotswolds tourist trail.

Nik cleared his throat. 'That didn't happen.'

The older woman lifted her wine glass with a faint smile.

'I didn't think it did. Sybella is too tightly wrapped up in the memory of my son.'

Great. He really didn't want to hear about the sainted Simon, who'd given Sybella some ridiculous but deeply felt anxieties about her body and left her with a baby, although he guessed the guy couldn't be blamed for that— he hadn't known a truck was coming for him. But he had brought her to a village with so few career prospects she'd been forced to invade his home. Although, Nik was no longer exercised over that little tweak in fate given it had brought Sybella into his life.

'I wish to God it had though,' Catherine added and tipped back the rest of her wine.

Okay, she now had his full attention.

He waited. He figured the stylish older woman was leading up to something and his input wasn't really needed.

'Why don't you take her away somewhere? Marcus and I can look after Fleur for a week, and you seem rather smitten.'

Smitten? Not a word anyone had ever used about him. He usually got ruthless bastard or ice man.

However, Catherine Parminter had just earned her lunch. Taking Sybella away somewhere—alone—had begun to look like an impossible task from the moment he'd clapped eyes on Fleur in the kitchen, and up until this moment he hadn't fancied his chances separating mother from daughter.

He caught sight of Sybella leading Fleur across the room. Male heads were turning. She looked sensational in a green jersey dress made sexy by the simple act of cinching a fabric belt around her waist. Not that she appeared to be thinking about herself and how she presented; she was obviously too busy keeping an eye on her small daughter.

'I believe I will,' he said, not paying much attention to the smug look that now settled on Catherine Parminter's face.

He stood up as Sybella approached.

'Everything takes double the time,' she said with a smile, 'but we get there eventually.'

Fleur wasn't interested in taking her seat. Nik didn't know much about kids but even he could see she was over-excited by the day's events and actively resisting her mother's attempts to get her seated back at the table.

'I might take Fleur for a ramble along the river,' said Catherine, pushing back her chair noisily. 'Why don't you finish that bottle of Merlot, Syb?'

Sybella gave her mother-in-law a look of outright surprise but Catherine was already moving her granddaughter off and there was nothing else for Sybella to do but sit down.

Nik seated himself and picked up the bottle but she shook her head.

'I don't know what's got into Catherine. She doesn't usually like it when I drink.'

'She thinks it might loosen you up.'

'Sorry—what?'

Nik decided to just put it out there.

'She wants you to get laid.'

'What do you mean?' Then her eyes widened. 'No! She didn't?'

'Apparently you're missing out.'

'I'm not! I mean, that's not true.'

'Obviously,' he drawled complacently.

She flushed and looked away, clearly flustered.

'Although it has been seven days,' he added.

'Try six years,' she said, then her eyes flew to his in dismay; she was clearly aware she'd given far too much away.

Nik was a little unsettled by the rush of male primacy he experienced at this news. She hadn't let on once in those cold blue hours of the morning when he'd been keeping her warm in that creaky, too small double bed that he was the first since her husband.

'Carino!'

Nik had his attention ripped off Sybella at this crucial moment by the too familiar rasp of what was becoming a weight around his neck.

Sybella was so startled for a moment she couldn't get past the blaring thought: *She's even more gorgeous in the flesh.*

Marla Mendez, trailed by a small entourage of equally happy, shiny people, had just upped the charisma wattage between The Folly Inn's snug walls and the spotlight was on their table. Which Marla was suddenly all over.

'Nik, darling, I have travelled into the wilds of rural England to find you. I wanted to see for myself if it was true. You have a house in the English countryside. How utterly *Russian* of you!'

Sybella watched as Nik lounged back in his chair and regarded Marla with the same cool distance he'd shown her when they'd first met. Only there was no gentlemanly rising from his chair. Even when he'd thought she was an interloper he'd held the door for her. It didn't dim Marla's wattage by even a degree.

'I absolutely want to see it. Have you stocked it with a private zoo? Aloyshia has a zoo—it's hysterical.'

'No zoo, Marla.' Nik surveyed the group of people moving over to the bar. Sybella was watching them too, and also keeping her eye on Marla, who hadn't looked at her once. He knew he had to introduce them, but something was crouched in the back of his mind, growling, warning him not to let Marla and what she represented anywhere near his time with Sybella.

The noise level from the bar shifted up a notch. Sybella flinched as one of the crowd dropped a glass and there was some laughter.

'Try and keep the noise level down,' Nik advised. 'This isn't New York. It's a family pub in a small village.'

'How quaint.' Finally Marla's dark eyes dwelt on her for a moment and Sybella realised she might be coming under the 'quaint' umbrella. Well, that was one for the books. Marla Mendez saw her as a threat.

Nik looked unimpressed. 'Why don't your people call me when you get back to New York, Marla, and we'll set something up?'

'Oh, no, you will have dinner with me, Nikolai Voronov. This is non-negotiable. I need your advice. Besides, I want you to show me this house of yours.'

Nik said something sharply in Spanish. Marla responded and then made a gesture at her that Sybella was pretty sure went along the lines of, *Lose the local...come and play with me.*

Sybella didn't know what came over her. But Nik hadn't introduced them, Ms Mendez was being very rude and Nik not much better, and frankly she wasn't going to spend another second sitting here like a gooseberry. She plonked her glass out of the way, leaned across the table, took Nik's face between her hands and kissed him. For a moment as she leaned in she saw his eyes flicker with surprise but he sure as hell kissed her back.

Then she melted back into her seat, straightened her dress and angled up her chin at Marla.

'Nik can't have dinner with you,' she said firmly, and her voice didn't wobble a bit, 'because he's having dinner with me.'

'Marla Mendez,' Nik said, amusement lacing his voice, 'this is Sybella Parminter.'

Nik's belated introduction was hardly necessary. She had all of Marla's attention now. 'Sybella,' Marla said, those dark brown eyes acknowledging her at last. 'I am staying at Lark House. Do you know it?'

'I know of it. It's an estate several miles from here,' Sybella said, looking at Nik. 'The Eastmans own it.'

'Yes, Benedict and Emma,' said Marla. 'They are having a party. You can both come, yes?' Suddenly she was beaming at Sybella as if they were friends.

'No party,' said Nik decisively.

'I'd love to go to a party at Lark House.' Sybella found herself staring down a Famous Woman who didn't have thighs and feeling amazingly good about herself. Certainty was rolling through her and with that came confidence.

There was nothing between Nik and this woman, not even a speck of sexual tension, and Sybella felt oddly freed by it. She wasn't that twenty-two-year-old bride any more, feeling as if she didn't measure up. It was as if she'd cut the cord on the spectre of the other woman who had haunted her brief marriage. Only she suspected now that other woman had been the Sybella who was sitting here now, claiming what she wanted.

She'd never felt able to assert herself with Simon for

fear of losing the place he'd made for her here in Edbury when he'd brought her home as his wife.

Whatever was between her and Nik, it wasn't about this woman thrusting herself into the middle of their intimate conversation.

She and Nik didn't have a problem. They just had an interruption to their lunch.

Phones had appeared stuck up in the air all around the pub, angled to take pictures. Sybella guessed at least as a non-celebrity she'd probably be lopped out of any shots that appeared on the Internet.

'We will have such a good time!' Marla put her hands on her hips and swivelled to face Nik. 'I will let you out of dinner, but invite me down to your yacht in Nice this year for Cannes and I will forgive you.'

'There's always an open invitation.'

As Marla retreated to her table on the far side of the room people actually got up and followed her.

Nik leaned forward, the bored look on his face during Marla's performance replaced by real concern.

'*Prohshu prahshehnyah.* I apologise, Sybella. I didn't know she'd be here.'

'Clearly. She followed you, *darling*, all the way to the wilds of Gloucestershire.'

Nik scanned her face. 'She didn't bother you?'

'No, but she's chomping at the bit to bother you. Luckily you'll let her on your yacht. Even if it is only this big.' She inched her thumb and index finger apart to show him.

Nik was observing her as if she'd turned into some species of wild animal he'd never met with before but fascinated him.

'Do you really want to go to this party?' He was looking at her mouth and Sybella, already stirred up by that kiss and her little flag-raising exercise over this man, could feel her erogenous zones jumping up to meet him.

'The Eastmans own the most beautiful stately home in the county,' she insisted. 'Of course I want to go to that party.'

He leaned forward. 'What would you like to do after the party?'

Right now her thighs were liquid and her nipples tight and she knew exactly what she wanted to do after the party and she guessed he did too.

If she were free to do it she would have dragged him into the coat room and made love to him within earshot of the entire pub. Only, she wasn't free to follow her instincts. Her mother-in-law would be back at any moment with her five-year-old daughter and that kiss was the best she could do with what she had to hand.

Instead she asked, 'What on earth do the two of you have in common?'

'Marla came to me for business advice.' Nik's thick lashes had screened his eyes and he sat back, and Sybella got the feeling he wasn't telling her the entire truth.

'You mine for minerals. She models lingerie. It must have been an interesting conversation.'

He looked almost weary for a moment and Sybella shifted forward. 'What's wrong, Nik?'

'She has a son,' he said unexpectedly, 'a few years older than Fleur, and she pretty much stocks her entourage with her family.' He frowned as if this bothered him. 'I think the two of you would probably get on well—if you could put up with the theatrics.'

'And you can't?' But her feelings softened. Single motherhood wasn't easy—for anyone.

'It's business, Sybella. She wants to design what she models and she has a very savvy designer on her payroll who happens to be her sister. I'm the money. Full stop. I'm expecting to see a tidy profit from this transaction, which interests me much more than seeing Marla socially.'

Nik knew then if he told Sybella about the other woman's impromptu striptease ending with her in his lap, even if it was a week before he drove into Edbury, it wouldn't go down well. Not after the story she'd told him about her husband and another girl.

No, Marla needed to keep her clothes on and to stay at the end of a long boardroom table and Sybella could never know the truth of just what his plans were for this small business venture. To use it and close it.

Because she was looking at him with those clear, frank green-brown eyes, and he knew she wouldn't understand.

He touched his hands to hers.

'What are you thinking, *moya krasvitsa zhenschina*?'

'I imagine being your girlfriend would involve more of this kind of thing, with other contenders for the title.'

Nik stroked the length of her thumb with his. She dropped her gaze to their joined hands.

'There are no other contenders.' He spoke softly, his voice roughened by the crackle of sexual tension in the air.

Meaning she was the one? Sybella guessed she had just declared something when she kissed him in front of, not only Marla Mendez, but the rest of The Folly Inn.

'But I told you once before, I can be an eminently shallow man.' He had lowered his voice. 'Because you do know I'm thinking about that roller-coaster ride from your delicate throat down to your slender ankles, and the place that probably thrills me most is when it reaches the lush promise of your lovely, voluptuous bottom.'

Sybella expelled a hot little breath and wondered if that coat closet idea was completely bonkers.

He put his hand under her chin and lifted it so she had to look at him.

'I flew back from Montenegro to take you to lunch because try as I might I couldn't keep away.'

That awful week of not knowing was suddenly at the forefront of her mind. 'But why did you try?'

They both heard Fleur's voice on the perimeter of their table and Nik raised a brow to signify the reason.

Fleur?

Sybella was suddenly a little confused. He'd kept away because she had responsibilities? Because she had a child?

She tried to pull herself together and look cheerful and composed for her daughter, but her head was pounding with the idea Nik found Fleur a stumbling block to their relationship.

Not that it even was a relationship. At the moment it was all very up in the air.

She tried to focus on what her daughter was saying.

'Mummy, Grandma says after tomorrow the ice rink will be closed. You promised and we never got to go!'

Ice rink? Sybella gave an internal groan. She *had* promised. She was the world's worst mother. 'We'll go next year, poppet.'

Fleur's lower lip trembled.

'Where is this ice rink?' Nik's deep voice had both Parminter girls turning their heads to look at him in surprise.

'Belfort Castle opens a rink every year from November through January,' Sybella explained. 'We missed it last year too.' She turned back to her unhappy daughter. 'Mummy is so sorry, darling.'

'Where is this castle?'

Sybella blinked. 'Half an hour west.'

Why was Nik asking all these questions? Couldn't he see it only gave Fleur more of a platform to agonise over it? But then, he knew nothing about children. He clearly didn't want to know anything about her daughter.

'We can do this now,' he said.

Fleur's quivering lip disappeared under her gapped

front teeth. She gave a tremulous little squeal. 'Mummy, Mummy, please. *Pleeeease.*'

'If your mother's agreeable,' he added, and suddenly Sybella's own platform for agonising collapsed.

He was making an effort. For her daughter.

'I think that would be lovely.' She gazed at him, feeling a lot of stuff that she'd have to shelve for the moment.

'What would be lovely?' asked Catherine as she reached the table.

'Ice-skating, Grandma!' Fleur was looking up at Nik as if he might pull a rabbit out of a hat for her. Sybella was aware she was doing much the same.

'Wonderful.' Catherine sat down, drawing Fleur up onto her knee. 'Will any of this involve Fleur spending some time with Marcus and me tonight while you take Sybella to dinner?'

'Catherine—'

'*Da*, if you would,' Nik interrupted her smoothly. 'I'm taking Sybella to a party.'

CHAPTER TWELVE

THE RINK IN FRONT of Belfort Castle glowed with fairy lights as the afternoon dwindled.

Nik parked the SUV and waited for the girls to organise themselves.

On the drive Fleur, buckled up in the back in her child's seat, chattered nonstop about various skating adventures she'd had. From the sounds of it she was the local Edbury skating queen.

'Great, so she'll be okay on the ice?' Nik queried as they approached the boardwalk where they could sit down and put on their skates.

The ice rink was swarming with couples and family groups.

'Fleur's never been skating,' said Sybella with a small smile.

'Okay, then what was the story about winning the race and her friend tripping up and breaking her wrist?'

'Fleur likes to make things up and they usually involve her friend Xanthe breaking something.' Sybella stood up, getting her balance. 'She has an active imagination. I don't discourage it.'

Fleur was dancing up to them now, wanting her mother to put her skates on.

He circled Sybella and Fleur on the rink, keeping an eye on the other skaters as Fleur continually took spills. For the first time in his life he wasn't entirely sure of his role here, but when Fleur toppled for the umpteenth time he leaned in and scooped her up before her bottom hit the ice.

She looked up at him with those big violet eyes, solemn as a church hymnal at this unexpected development, but as he set her on her feet again she kept hold of his hands and let him glide her along the ice. Sybella glided along behind them, applauding Fleur's achievement at actually staying upright, and exchanged a smile with him.

It didn't take long for Fleur to begin to flag and it was time to take her off the ice. She greeted his suggestion they go in search of hot chocolate happily enough.

They were standing a few yards from where Fleur was lined up to hand over the money to the lady behind the counter when he said without thinking it through, 'Poor guy.'

Sybella was so busy going over what today had held and what it might mean, she was delayed in processing what Nik had said.

'Who?' She looked up at him, aware he'd slid his hand around her waist while she'd been watching Fleur. 'Nik?' She raised her eyes to his.

'Poor guy, your Simon, not getting to enjoy any of this.' He looked into her eyes as he said it and Sybella knew then he wasn't going to tiptoe around the memory of her husband.

Thank God.

'But that doesn't mean you and Fleur can't enjoy it,' he said, proving he understood a great deal more than she was probably comfortable with.

Unaccountably a flood of hot, messy tears hit the backs of Sybella's eyes and scalded her face before she could even think to blink them away, and then she was tucked up in his arms, her face, her whole body out of the elements and safe, warm, protected.

'If it were me,' he said in a deep voice, 'I would want this. I would want the two of you to have this. It's okay to move forward, Sybella.'

She nodded her head resolutely against his chest, relief

making her a little light-headed. Then she tilted up her chin. 'Why are you doing all of this with us?'

He shook his head at the inanity of the question. 'Because you've let me.' Then he fitted his mouth to hers and she felt it to her toes.

When she floated back up to take in air there was a stillness about Nik that warned her something wasn't right. He was looking over her shoulder.

Sybella turned around.

Fleur was looking up at them, clutching her change.

'What are you doing to my mummy?'

Later in the early evening, as she drove her daughter round to her grandparents, Sybella acknowledged Nik had handled her immediate descent into panic mode with considerable sangfroid, keeping his hand firmly around her waist and making Fleur see it was all right for him to show her mother affection.

It wasn't as if Fleur hadn't seen her grandparents being affectionate with one another, or Aunty Meg locked in a kiss with the odd boyfriend, all of which Fleur ignored with the lofty disregard of someone who was five and a half. But it was different when it was her mother.

Sybella understood. What surprised her was Nik had understood it better. He'd also handled it better. She'd underestimated him.

Fleur had picked up on what Nik had told her—*I want to kiss your mama because she's so nice*—and when she'd seen Sybella in her frock and heels tonight she'd confided, 'I think Nik will want to kiss you again, Mummy.'

Sybella couldn't help thinking about her marriage as she drove back home.

If she'd had that time over she might not have come back to Simon, and she certainly wouldn't have married him until she'd felt secure in their relationship. She'd been so young, and maybe that was partly why she'd stayed faithful to his memory, perhaps for too long.

Simon had never not been her friend, but Nik was something more. He was her lover.

Nik's SUV was parked outside her house when she pulled up.

As she walked towards him his eyes told her everything she wanted to hear.

He reached into his pocket and produced a bracelet that slithered through his hand.

'I thought this would look well on you.'

He draped it over her wrist. The stones were small white diamonds. Sybella gave a soft gasp.

'Nik, I can't accept this. Diamonds?'

But he was trying to work the delicate silver catch with his big, blunt fingers and there was something about his lack of response and the concentration of his expression and his complete inability to finish the job that made her heart melt. This man who ran an empire was defeated by a delicate catch on a woman's bracelet. God help her, she didn't want to give it back, not when he was being so genuine.

'Here,' she said, handing him her evening bag, 'let me fix it.'

She carefully gathered both ends between the fingertips of her right hand and slid the catch closed. Then she held up her arm to inspect its beautiful drape to the top of her forearm. It was exquisite.

'You like it?' He asked as if it mattered.

'It's beautiful. I don't know what to say, Nik. No one's ever given me such an expensive gift.' She made a face. 'I shouldn't have mentioned that, should I, the cost?'

'I want you to be yourself, Sybella, and I want you to wear it, if you will.'

She stroked her bracelet and wished she had the courage to stroke his face and kiss him and take him upstairs to her new bed, but her newfound confidence of this afternoon seemed to have deserted her. Instead she took a deep breath.

'Didn't Marla say something about a party?'

Lark House was lit up like Christmas. It was also the closest stately home to Edbury Hall.

The owners were apparently happy to entertain the elusive Russian oligarch who was their nearest neighbour on such short notice.

Sybella loved this house. It had all the charm Edbury Hall did not, but, while it was open to the public for functions, it didn't require the services of the Heritage Trust. It was very much a family home, even if that family consisted of two socialites and their grown-up children and was open to weddings and functions on weekends.

All the lights were on, an assortment of cars filled the drive and were planted in odd positions under the oaks, and there were fairy lights strewn along the paths that led to the back terrace, where the party-goers were a blur of colour behind glass.

It was a freezing night and Sybella huddled in her wool coat as Nik put his arm around her and propelled her up those steps.

She hadn't felt this excited or nervous in years, but as soon as she stepped into the warm conservatory the number of people gave her a welcome feeling of anonymity. She was just one of many women in gorgeous bits of nothing. If anything she felt a little overdressed in her backless, knee-length pink silk georgette frock. But she could feel Nik's hand resting lightly above her waist, against her bare skin, and she felt a renewed surge of confidence.

Everyone wanted to talk to them, and then Nik left her alone with their hostess, Emma Eastman, a former model who had married a celebrity agent and was one of the locals who arrived on weekends and whose food bills for her guests helped keep Edbury's local food producers very happy.

'How can it be that you're local and I've never met you?' Emma asked bluntly.

Sybella considered mentioning she'd actually applied to Lark House for work experience but decided the wise course was to smile and say, 'It does seem odd.'

'Of course, we're *delighted* to get Nik here. He's so elusive. When Marla said he'd agreed to come we were over the moon.' She leaned close and said sotto voce, 'I have to say, my husband's line of work means I'm always entertaining performers, TV personalities, big egos, but Marla Mendez takes the cake. She just rang Benedict and invited herself.' Emma suddenly pulled a face. 'Oh, heck, have I spoken out of school? Do you know Marla well?'

'I don't know her at all.'

'Ah.' Emma looked around in a covert fashion. 'Well, just a word to the wise—she's not very happy with you. I suspect she thought this weekend was going to play out somewhat differently. Otherwise I doubt we would have got her here.'

Sybella didn't have to ask what Marla imagined might be different.

'You make a fabulous couple,' said Emma, clearly wanting to hear all the details.

'I don't know if couple is the right word. We've only known one another a handful of days.'

Emma's face fell. 'So you don't think you would have any sway with Nik if Benedict and I were to ask him to sponsor our Wells for Africa project? It would mean so much having his name attached, and I think it would go over well, you know, socially if he was seen to be contributing.'

Sybella felt as if she'd suddenly waded out beyond her depth. Her parents-in-law existed on the edges of the county set in the area, but she'd never paid any attention to it. She didn't like snobs—she'd been raised by two. But Emma's entire manner, even if it was a little manufactured, had something engaging underneath it. She seemed like a genuinely nice woman.

'I'm sure he's open to charitable enterprises—you only have to ask him. He's not nearly as ferocious as his reputation.'

Emma beamed at her. 'As soon as we heard he was bringing a local girl with him we knew Edbury Hall must be in safe hands.'

At dinner Nik was monopolised, but again she didn't mind, although it was a little disconcerting when the man sitting beside her slipped his business card under her plate.

'If you could get this to Mr Voronov, and let him know Forester & Bean have represented most of the established families in the area for over a century.'

Sybella politely smiled and went on with her dinner.

Nik sat opposite her, fielding questions from their host about the ecological impact of mining. Nik rolled out a convincing line about his company's determination not to log where it wasn't necessary and his refusal to use chemicals underground. Any mine was a major habitat modification and Voroncor did their best to limit biodiversity issues. But he admitted freely once a mine had gone in, the site would never be the same again.

Some of the other guests were clearly dinner table ecological warriors—rather like herself—but Nik handled them well. He explained Voroncor had posted bonds with all their sites. Once mining ceased the clean-up would not stop until they had proved the reclaimed land was once more productive.

'So you're not just digging holes in the earth and ruining habitat,' she said to Nik as he pulled her out of her chair after dinner.

'I'd be a poor excuse for a human being if I did,' he said, taking her hand. 'Mining isn't for sissies, Sybella.'

'I don't think anyone here is going to mistake you for a sissy, Nik. Do you know everyone here wants a piece of you?'

He had his other hand around her waist now and was leading her into the ballroom.

She had so many questions, but mostly what she wanted to do was be in his arms, far away from all these people.

'I do know every man here is envious of me at this moment.'

He finally held her in his arms as they drifted onto the dance floor and Sybella rested her head against his shoulder.

Envious? Probably not. But right now her heart was wide open and banging like a barn door and she was just waiting for him to come on in.

Because she could have this. Nik didn't seem to be going anywhere and she'd spent the last week pretending to herself it didn't matter if he came back.

All the silly things she'd been telling herself. None of it was true.

'I never get to do this,' she said confidingly, 'put on a beautiful dress and be admired.' She shook her head against his shoulder. 'I don't know why I'm telling you that. You're a man. You wouldn't understand.'

He stroked an invisible strand of hair from the curve of her neck. 'You've denied yourself a great deal, I think,' he said.

'Not any more.' Emboldened, she put a hand to his chest. 'Are you going to make love to me?' She framed the question she'd been longing to ask him all night.

'Is that a question?' His breath brushed her ear tip.

'Just looking for a time line.' Her skin felt hot; her words sounded so bold and sure.

'You think I brought you here to take another look at your beautiful lingerie?'

Sybella's heart skipped a beat. 'I didn't think men noticed those sorts of things.'

'I notice everything about you.'

Sybella swore she could feel his hand at her lower back through the boning of her gown. Impossible, and yet...

'I want you now,' he said against her ear. 'Is that a problem?'

Sybella moved her smooth cheek against his rough jaw. 'No, not at all.'

'But possibly not at a party,' he observed.

Sybella, a little weak with longing, couldn't at this moment see exactly why.

'Surely there's a guest room somewhere?' Then she sighed, because she would never do something like that. 'Oh, Nik, it's a long drive home.'

'It's been a long week,' he said, his mouth warm against her ear. 'I think we can withstand another half-hour in a car.'

She looked into his eyes and saw everything a woman could possibly want to make her feel like the only female in his universe.

His arm came away from her waist but he held onto her other hand and wordlessly he began to lead her across the dance floor towards the exit.

People parted ways to allow them passage. There was nothing subtle about what they were doing, leaving early, and Sybella was thrilled.

An hour later Nik didn't want to move. Sybella was draped across him. She stroked his chest, nuzzled him.

'I missed this,' she said.

'Six years,' he murmured against her sweet-smelling hair. 'It's a long time.'

'No, you.' She raised her pleasure-dazed eyes to his. 'I missed this with you.'

Nik experienced a surge of something he couldn't control. It was a wave of feeling that had him holding onto her. She didn't seem inclined to let him go either.

Every time he touched her it was like a conflagration of the senses. Every time it felt like the best thing that had ever happened to him.

Why were they denying themselves?

Then he remembered a small person who would arrive home in the morning.

He sat up, banging the back of his head on the frame of the backseat of the SUV.

Sybella winced for him and tried to sit up, but she was hampered by the space. He chuckled and she dissolved into helpless giggles. They had got as far as the Linton Way Forest when Nik had pulled the car off the road and into this clearing. It was private, but they could hear any cars going past on the road.

Nik was certain from the outside they would be invisible; the steamed up windows helped with that. Sybella, still in her dress but wondrously dishevelled, her hair falling down and the hem of her dress so high it hinted at the shadowy mystery between her thighs, gazed up at him. He, with his shirt hanging open and his trousers unbuttoned, was trying to make sense of what this woman did to him. They hadn't even made it into Edbury.

He drove them to the cottage and carried her inside. Put her in the shower and then crowded her against the splash back until the water ran cold. Then he wrapped his bigger, warmer body around hers in the new bed.

'I've got a boat moored at a place I own off the coast

of South Africa,' he said. 'Come there with me for a few days, just you and me.'

Sybella looked at him with those clear hazel eyes. He waited for her to say, *No, I won't leave my daughter* but she surprised him with a simple, 'I'd like that.'

No hesitation, no questions. Instead she asked, 'Can we do it soon?'

'I'll make the arrangements.'

She rubbed her cheek against his arm. 'I've never travelled outside the United Kingdom. Does that make me parochial?'

'No, *dushka*, just busy.' His hand stroked her damp hair and she was whisked back to that evening last week when he'd dried her hair with a towel and she'd first begun to let down her guard with him. He'd also just acknowledged how hard she worked.

There was nothing sexier.

Deep inside her a feeling Sybella had never had before began to stir.

'It's good to take a break from real life, yes?' he said, his chest rumbling against her back.

'Yes,' she sighed. Only later would she wonder if this was only that for him, a break from real life? When it felt all too real to her. But she quieted that thought because, after all, it was only a long weekend away.

CHAPTER THIRTEEN

SYBELLA CAME DOWN the stairs into the galley of the boat, her long bare legs appearing first and then her body clad in a black bikini, a diaphanous shirt unbuttoned and billowing around her. With her hair pulled back in a ponytail she looked happy and carefree and about twenty.

Lust licked along his veins, but it was mingled with something more lasting, something that went along with seeing her so light-hearted, simply enjoying herself and it had a corresponding effect on his spirit. He felt satisfied. *Da*, satisfied. He had her at last.

'Nik, who is this woman?'

It was then he noticed the magazine she was carrying and wondered which old girlfriend she'd stumbled onto, but then he saw the photograph of the eighteenth-century villa on the lake and he knew.

As she came closer she held out the magazine. 'It's got a feature on a Galina Voronov, a Russian socialite with fashion connections and a very nice villa on the shores of Lake Geneva. All very lah-de-dah. She apparently tried to sue you but that failed. You rate two lines, by the way, neither of them informative. Is she a relative?'

Nik ignored the magazine in favour of sliding one hand over her hip as he brought her in against him, the other expertly turning over pancakes in the skillet.

'Who taught you to do that?' she asked, distracted by his unexpected dexterity in the kitchen.

'Baba, my grandmother. We made *blini* all the time. She made her own jam from her orchard and I would stuff myself on them.'

They had a twenty-person staff on the forty-metre yacht

and their meals were sublime, but for their last day of four blissful days together on the boat Nik had sent their staff ashore and they were completely on their own.

He was making her breakfast. It was bliss.

'I can imagine you as a boy, always getting into trouble because you wanted everything your own way.'

'I might have wanted it but Deda made sure I was kept in check,' he said, but he was smiling as he upended the crepes onto a plate with the rest.

'What about your brother? It can't have been easy for your grandmother with two boys.'

Nik's smile vanished. 'My brother wasn't there.'

'I don't understand.'

'Sasha was living with his mother.'

'They split the two of you up?'

Nik looked grim. 'No, my stepmother split us up. At Alex's funeral she took Sasha by the hand and put him in a car and they drove away and I didn't see him again for ten years.'

Sybella was effectively silenced by that image.

'My reputation rises and falls on those blinis,' Nik said, as if he hadn't just dropped a bombshell. 'Why don't you take them out and I'll bring the coffee? Leave the magazine.'

Sybella put the old magazine down on the bench and put a hand on Nik's arm but he gave her a firm smile that didn't reach his eyes. 'Off you go,' he said.

When he reappeared with a tray, coffees and some condiments she knew he wasn't going to say any more, and it was clear this was a painful subject for him, as well it should be. She didn't want to pry, but suddenly she knew this terrible thing about his boyhood.

'I'm so sorry that happened to you, Nik,' she said as he set the tray down. 'Your grandfather would talk about you as a boy, but not Sasha. I didn't make a connection.'

'Why should you?'

Nik settled down opposite her at the table, all masculine grace in shorts and an open shirt, the brown hair on his body glinting gold after four days in the hot sun. Sybella thought she would never get tired of looking at him.

He sighed, rubbing his unshaven jaw. 'Deda and Baba both tried every legal means possible to bring Sasha home but it was like hitting a brick wall. It took Galina going into rehab for Deda to get custody.'

'Galina? The woman in the magazine, who tried to sue you?'

'The same.'

'What was it you said about rehab?'

'Alcohol. She'd run out of money and options, and Sasha was fifteen and I imagine every time she looked at him she saw how much he hated her. So Sasha came home to my grandparents. He was already six feet tall and carrying a mountain of resentment on those kid shoulders of his.'

Sybella weirdly felt a little sorry for Galina Voronov. From what Nik had said she was clearly a troubled woman, but to have your child look at you and hate you?

'How did your grandparents cope?'

'They got him a psychologist and did everything they could, but it was a rough first year. I was just out of national service and doing a science degree, living at the campus. I came home weekends but he resented me from the start, and we argued a lot. I can't blame him. I got everything that by rights should have been his.'

'What does that mean?'

She had linked her hand with his across the table top, but now that hand closed over hers and he smoothed his broad thumb against the pulse point at her wrist. How that had happened Sybella wasn't sure. It was like when they were in bed and one minute he'd be letting her have her way and the next she was exactly where he wanted her and happy to be there.

Yes, Nik was telling her a painful personal story and she was thinking about how sexually dominant he was.

'Nik? What do you mean everything that by rights should have been his?'

'He is their grandson, I'm the ring-in.'

'Nik, that's a terrible thing to say. I know you don't believe that.'

'*Net*, but I suspect Sasha did.'

He must have seen the look on her face because he squeezed her hand. 'When he was sixteen I took him with me on a geological survey in the Urals. I put him to work helping me out and we started to interact as brothers for the first time in over a decade. He was with me when I first saw the abandoned Vizhny mine and talked about putting some shareholders together and buying it up. Sasha said he wanted in, so when I finally made a bid three years later he fronted up with his life savings. It was a risk, our relationship would have imploded at that point if something had gone wrong but it didn't and it's made both of us rich men.'

Sybella got up and came around and climbed onto his lap and pressed her cheek to his rough one.

'I'm so glad you told me this.'

'It's over now,' he said, appearing more interested in how affectionate she was being than seeking comfort. He was stroking the side of her breast so she was distracted when he added quietly, 'Almost over.'

'Almost over?' She drew back and looked into his eyes quizzically.

'*Nichevo.*' He shook his head and gave her a rueful smile, the fingers of his other hand engaging with the ties holding her bikini top together.

'Stop it.' She fidgeted and began to laugh. 'I told you,

I am not walking around topless on this yacht, Nikolai Voronov.'

By the time she'd restored her modesty and been kissed the blinis were cold and the coffee was tepid and Nik had effectively changed the subject.

It was only when she took some of the plates inside that she saw him binning the magazine.

'Can I ask what the legal matter was about with your stepmother?'

He shrugged. 'It's not a secret, *dushka*. Galina was the daughter of a high-ranking Kremlin *apparatchik*. He pulled strings. She got control of our father's archive of work, films, documentaries. She owned all the rights for twenty years and, if that wasn't bad enough, she effectively locked it away so nobody could see it. He's virtually forgotten now in my country.'

'That's wicked.'

Nik stretched his arms and gave his shoulders a roll, showing off that honed physique she already knew very well. But she also got the impression he was shucking off all the tension that had gathered as their conversation had progressed.

'That's my stepmother,' he observed dryly. 'She's a classic fairy tale villain.'

'Will you ever get it back?'

He scrutinised her through those thick lashes. 'You underestimate me, Sybella. I purchased it for several million US dollars two years ago. We settled out of court. It paid for that very nice villa on Lake Geneva you were admiring.'

Sybella shook her head at the figures involved but mostly the weight Nik must have carried all those years, wanting to restore his father's reputation and unable to do so.

It wasn't just the absence of his brother that had weighted him down but the loss of his father's legacy.

'At least she's out of your lives. Is she out of your lives?'

Nik consulted his watch. 'How about we take the tender to a cove near here and I'll show you some of the sights?'

Sybella was changing into shorts and a T-shirt when she realised Nik had once again very neatly sidestepped her question for the second time.

An afternoon spent ashore, climbing to a lookout with spectacular views of the coast, concluded with a swim at dusk near the boat.

The water was warm and Sybella's legs entangled around his, her hair falling in heavy ropes over her shoulders like the mermaid he'd discovered she was, her arms looped around his neck.

Talking about his brother and his stepmother this morning had brought the two sides of his life dangerously close together.

He didn't want to think about his plans for Galina and the money she'd extorted out of him when he was with Sybella. She made it seem unimportant, and, worse, mean and small. Like a spiteful act she wouldn't recognise him as being capable of.

She bobbed in the water in front of him, holding onto him like her own personal life buoy.

'So have you met him? Your real dad?' She was gazing into his eyes as if daring him to change the subject.

Trust Sybella to be worrying over this.

'I've got a name. I know where he is.'

'And?'

'Helsinki.'

'And?'

'I still haven't done anything about it. I don't know if I ever will. I mean, he has a family, a life. I'm busy.'

He could feel her stroking the back of his neck, treating

him like Fleur or one of those damned rabbits she kept. Only he found he didn't mind because it was Sybella.

'No, you're not. You're just like all of us, a little afraid of what might happen when we let down our guard with other people.'

'Is that what I am, *dushka*?' He tried not to sound too disparaging of her well-meant words.

'You know you are.' She smiled at him as if she knew all his cynical thoughts but didn't believe one of them.

The truth was it was getting harder and harder to hold onto that cynicism when he was around Sybella. Her lashes were wet and sticking around her eyes like a doll's. She was so beautiful it hurt. Did she know how strange it was for him, letting another person into his head like this?

'I've let my guard down with you,' he said, almost as a warning, although to her or to him he wasn't sure.

Her arms tightened around him and he could hear her breathing quicken, the almost ferocious way she hung onto him as if that was all she'd wanted to hear, and it answered a need in him he hadn't known until now existed.

'How lucky you are, to at least have known one dad, and now you have a chance with another,' she said urgently. 'Don't let that chance go by, Nik.'

She meant it, and coming from Sybella with her history it had a great deal of force.

He put his mouth close to her ear. 'How lucky your Simon was, to be first in your heart.'

Sybella's grip tightened. 'He's not first in my heart any more.'

They were flying home to Heathrow in his jet from Cape Town International Airport when Sybella, comfortable in a ridiculously luxurious seat, began to giggle.

Nik, standing over her with two glasses of bubbly, raised an eyebrow.

'What's so funny?'

She looked up, smiling at him. 'One day I'll be telling this story and no one will believe me.'

'What, is it the champagne? I thought you'd appreciate it before you were back in that storybook cottage of yours hiding spirits in the airing cupboard.'

'How do you know about that?'

'Your mother-in-law at the restaurant.'

Sybella rolled her eyes.

'So this is my last taste of luxury?' she queried lightly as she accepted her glass, because suddenly they were bang, smack in the middle of making decisions.

'No, although…' He crouched down in front of her. 'How about I ask you what your plans are for the future?'

'Hugging my daughter and not letting her go for a couple of days,' Sybella admitted honestly.

'I was thinking a little more along the lines of your plans for me.'

He started to smile but he was serious too and she could feel her heart thumping like Dodge's hind legs on the kitchen floor.

She thought of her kitchen at this moment, the menagerie of animals, of Fleur running riot and leading a pack of her little friends up and down the stairs like Napoleon orchestrating his Grande Armée, and tried to picture Nik amidst it all. She failed.

'You won't fit,' she blurted out.

'*Lyubov*, I think we've already tested that out.'

Sybella couldn't help it. She snorted. 'I mean in my kitchen,' she said softly, worryingly.

'I'll build you a bigger one.'

She had a vision of her cottage writ large, squashing all the others in the row and Nik with a big hammer.

As silly as it was, it was also true. He had a way of taking over.

She knew she should be happy; instead she was beginning to panic. It was crazy.

'We'll take it a day at a time,' he told her gravely. 'There's no schedule on this.'

She snorted again. With Nik there was always a schedule. He was the busiest man she knew and she had seen the way his grandfather had jockeyed for his attention.

God knew she wouldn't be here if old Mr Voronov hadn't been driven to desperate means to get his grandson down to Edbury…

Sybella had the odd thought she didn't ever want to be in that position.

Driven to desperate means to get Nik's attention.

She just hoped he could accept she came as a package, and she still wasn't at all sure if Nik understood that.

It had been incredible. The boat, the time together. But it wasn't real life.

'One day at a time, Sybella,' he said, leaning forward until she was drowning in his eyes and all of her worried thoughts were subsumed, and then he was kissing her and nothing else seemed to matter.

They had been home for more than four weeks and Nik had spent most of that time under her thatched roof, although he was officially living at the Hall.

It was a situation that delighted his grandfather and caused no end of gossip in the village.

But Sybella didn't mind the talk, especially as she put her head around the door and watched Nik reading to Fleur. Her daughter was leaning against him on the sofa and had her thumb tucked inside her mouth and was deep inside the Wild Wood. Nik's dark velvet voice lent an exotic charm to the story Sybella knew herself off by heart from listening to his grandfather.

These Voronov men had somehow colonised her daughter's life, and for the better. Nik had made an effort to be around and was currently running his empire with a small staff and a state-of-the-art computer system he had set up at the Hall. Some evenings he could be found pacing into the night across her living room as he argued in a mixture of Russian and English via video conference with various boardrooms around the world. If Fleur wandered in he would break off to help her with some puzzle she had or answer her questions. She was a good girl and knew not to interrupt when people were on the phone, but it gave Sybella enormous satisfaction Nik didn't view her comings and goings in her own home as an interruption to his work.

After dinner, when Fleur had been put to bed and the house locked up and Nik had done his usual round of phone calls and she'd gone over the invoicing for the refurbishment of the gatehouse, they bumped into each other in the bathroom.

Nik was shaving, and she just wanted to be with him as well as wash her face.

She shimmied in between him and the basin. He grinned and she wriggled her bottom teasingly as she wrung the warm face cloth to clean off the remains of her make-up.

'Can you ever see yourself getting married again?'

The question took her off guard.

'I haven't given it much thought,' she said truthfully.

She couldn't help noticing what a good pair they made in the mirror. Because she was tall most men looked her in the eye, but Nik's height and strong frame made her curvy body shape fit him, and she saw what he'd been showing her in bed: that they were a perfect physical match.

She preened a little.

'You didn't like being married?' He drew the razor along his jaw.

'If that's a question about Simon wrapped up with a

bow, I did like being married. I guess I felt safe for the first time in my life.'

Nik stilled and met her eyes in the glass. 'You didn't feel safe before that?'

'I felt alone,' she confessed. 'For so long it was just me, and then Simon picked me up and carted me off to his life in the village with his parents and his sister, and their neighbours and friends accepted me just because I was his wife. It was an amazing time for me. And then, a few months later, he had the accident.'

Nik wrapped an arm around her. He didn't mouth any pointless platitudes.

'Can I tell you something?' she asked.

He looked down into her eyes and Sybella knew she was about to take a jump into the unknown. She hadn't told anyone this.

'I cried for Simon, of course I did, but I remember at the funeral thinking, *I'll have to leave now. I'll have to leave the village.* And somehow that felt worse, that felt like the bigger loss.'

It was an enormous admission and Sybella waited to feel guilty, only she didn't.

'Makes sense. It sounds like when you married Simon, you married the life you needed.'

'Yes, I suppose I did.' She relaxed against him, relieved he understood.

'Of course, thanks to Fleur I never did have to leave Edbury.'

Nik towelled his freshly shaven face and switched out the light.

'When did you find out you were pregnant?'

He followed her across the hallway to her room. The house was quiet but for the usual creaks and groans of age. Fleur's door at the end of the hall was ajar and Sybella could see the red glow of her nightlight.

'The day after the funeral. Meg needed a tampon on the day, and it occurred to me I'd been carrying that little box around in my purse for several weeks. So I did a chemist test and then I went to my doctor and my life changed. Again.'

She climbed into her new bed and he stretched out beside her. 'That's the thing about life—it's constantly surprising you.'

He put out the light and pulled her into his arms.

'I guess the long and the short of it is I got married young because I was alone in the world, but I'm not alone any more. I have a daughter, I have in-laws, I have a whole village.'

'And you have me,' he said, and her body began to hum as he slid his hands over her bare skin and found all the places that made her squirm and gasp and sigh.

She woke some hours later, hot and disturbed after a dream. She couldn't remember the contents, but a kind of anxiousness was knotting her chest and presently she got out of bed and quietly crept downstairs. She took her coat off the coat-rack and, wrapped up in it, stepped out of the back door and into her garden. It was the place where she did her thinking.

Spring would be here soon but it was still bitterly cold at night and she'd only stuffed her feet into her old slippers.

The sky over the Indian ocean had been so high and far-reaching. Here at home the sky was hugger mugger with the low hills, but that sense of snugness and enclosure made her feel safe.

'What are you doing out here by yourself?'

Nik wore a pair of boxer shorts, but if he was cold he didn't show it. His physical similarity to one of those more-than-life-size male sculptures the Italians liked to make in the Renaissance was all too obvious.

'I couldn't sleep.'

He didn't ask her why she'd decided to come out into the vegetable patch.

'Do you want to be by yourself?' His deep voice was pitched low.

There was something about the way he was standing there, not coming any closer, that sent a shiver hightailing down Sybella's spine.

'No, I don't. I don't want to be by myself.'

Before she could move his arms were closing around her from behind and she was washed with the feeling of security and rightness the dream had upended. She'd already begun to take this feeling for granted with Nik.

It was so dangerous. He could hurt her and she didn't know if she'd get over it.

But, Mrs Muir be damned. She couldn't go through her life wondering what might have happened if she hadn't let him in. The idea of keeping her heart locked up and on a high shelf held no appeal.

Sybella knew she'd remember this when she was old and grey and had great-grandchildren who would never believe their granny had once given her heart to a Russian billionaire and sailed the Indian Ocean in his boat, a man who had the world at his fingertips but right now wanted only her, Sybella Frances Parminter, and her wide, womanly arse. All at once she began to giggle.

'What's so funny?'

She looked up, smiling at him. 'One day I'll be telling this story about you and me and standing in a vegetable patch and no one will believe me.'

'Come inside, then.' He scooped her up and carried her back into the house and up the creaking stairs and past Fleur's room with its night light and into the corner bedroom where she had moved in alone, almost six years ago after Simon had died, and spent the first night wide awake, tearless and terrified because of the enormity of facing life alone—that was until her baby had kicked.

Fleur had kicked hard. As if to remind her being alone was no longer her fate.

It was time to stop being afraid and to accept that maybe Nik was her fate too.

Nik looked at the clock. He needed to get up but Sybella was lying partially on top of him, her mermaid hair strewn across his chest.

He eyed the low ceiling above them. If he stood up and extended his hand he could flatten his palm on that ceiling. He frowned. Damn this place was small. Built for pygmies. They needed to move.

Which was when he flipped his gaze from ceiling to woman and he grinned. He knew then he could get used to this very quickly. How in the hell had she pulled him around this far in the span of several weeks?

Only Sybella didn't give him a clue, she continued to rest her angel face in the crook of his shoulder, as if he were more restful for her than a pillow. He shared the sentiment. She was warm and her lavish curves cushioned him perfectly. They complemented one another in more ways than one.

He traced the fine skin beneath the soft arc of her pale lashes and trailed his finger down to the curve of her slightly parted lips. She grew more beautiful to him every day and stirred strong feelings in him he didn't recognise.

Smitten didn't even begin to cover it.

He cared about what she thought of him, and at the moment he had a lot to hide.

It was almost ironic when his phone lit up several minutes later and he palmed it off the bedside table, not surprised to see it was from his assistant.

Pavel worked the mad hours he did.

It was a message about an explosion in the Urals mine.

He left Sybella to sleep because he was accustomed to handling things alone, and only remembered to call her when he was in-flight and she wasn't answering.

He sent a message.

Sybella read the message.

Real life intrudes, accident at mine, no loss of life, I'll ring tonight.

For the next two days she didn't hear from him and consequently found herself up at midnight, boiling tea, standing over the sink and wondering how her bed had got to feel so lonely when he'd been sharing it for only a brief time.

Which was when it occurred to her there would probably be some information about the mine accident on the Internet.

She fired up her laptop and sure enough the screen filled with various links connected to Nik's name, but at the top with an accompanying small image was an article from an infamous British tabloid. *Marla puts raunchy moves on Russian oligarch!*

Sybella just stood there. For a moment all she could think was, *Don't look...don't look.*

But she was clicking and scrolling and, like Bluebeard's wife, once seen, she couldn't forget it.

There was an image of Marla Mendez in tiny black barely there underwear, holding a bottle of champagne. Another of Marla pouring champagne over her breasts, her virtually bared breasts, because the bra was basically there as a frame for the main event. Marla climbing onto some guy's lap. The fourth image was recognisably of Nik, in profile, sitting on a chair with Marla astride him, looking, well, looking...

It was hard to get past all the naked female flesh and *her boyfriend*, but Nik didn't seem to be touching her in any way or engaging with her.

Sybella leaned onto the bench and rested her head in her hands, utterly thrown.

It must have happened before they met.

She had no right to be angry or hurt or reproach him with it.

But, oh.

Her kitchen was dark and quiet around her, disturbed only by the ticking of the clock and one of the rabbits making scraping noises in his litter tray.

Nik phoned her first thing in the morning when she was still groggy.

'Sybella, did you see the photos?'

She sat up, rubbing her eyes still swollen from all her crying. 'Yes, last night. How is it going? Are you making any progress?'

He ignored her question about the mine.

'We were in a boardroom, she took off her clothes and I told her to put them on again. I had no idea it was being filmed.'

Sybella fell forward and touched her forehead to the mattress. *Thank you, God.*

She pitched her voice at exactly the right tone, gentle and amused. 'Nik Voronov, are you explaining yourself to me?'

There was a pause. 'Sounds like it.'

'It's fine. I understand. I didn't think anything of it.'

There was a lingering silence.

'Nik, are you there?'

'You are one incredible woman.'

She bit her lip. She'd got this right.

'I try. Now tell me about what's been going on.'

They talked for twenty minutes, he promised he'd do

his best to be back tomorrow evening to take her to dinner and then he had to go. She stepped under the shower, and if she cried a bit it was because she hadn't slept much last night and she had to take a tour today of a couple of dozen eight-year-old children, and it was stressful, and she missed him. It had nothing to do with Nik having his face pressed into Marla Mendez's breasts.

CHAPTER FOURTEEN

*Marla Mendez in Sex Shocker with
Russian Ice Man!*

SYBELLA STOOD OUTSIDE the Edbury newsagents, her whole attention riveted to the tabloid newspaper front page pinned up alongside other legitimate papers reporting on local and international politics.

As far as she knew Nik was in the Urals, dealing with some labour-hire problems on site in the wake of the explosion and had been for the last three weeks. He'd phoned a couple of times, sent a few texts, one saying he should be back in the UK this weekend and another asking her to check something in person with Gordon about the roof on the Hall.

He hadn't mentioned anything about a *sex shocker*.

'I'm sorry, Sybella,' called Leanne Davis, coming outside. 'Doug insisted we put it up…we're required to display all the newspapers. It's not personal, sweetie.'

'No, no, of course not,' murmured Sybella, unable to rip her attention off the image. They appeared to be coming out of a nightclub, Nik in an open-necked shirt looking well…gorgeous, and Marla Mendez in her usual skin-tight handkerchief.

It didn't make sense, and Sybella had to resist the urge to buy the paper just to find out what it said.

Nik had specifically told her he had not seen Marla Mendez socially.

'It's not true,' she called after Leanne, but it was too late, she'd gone inside.

She found herself half an hour later in her car, parked

across from The Glue Box, the local arts and crafts supply shop that held art classes for under tens, furtively peering at the tiny screen on her phone as she read the tabloid article. It was the usual 'friend of a friend' who said they'd been close for months, that Nik had flown her from Miami, where she was currently working, to his Cape Town compound for a secret tryst. She shut it off in disgust.

Me, he had a secret tryst with me.

But the tabloids weren't interested in single mothers living in the Cotswolds and she could hardly take out a full-page ad in the local paper outing herself as the most recent guest on Nik Voronov's boat!

She had just about convinced herself, as she crossed the road and dodged up the steps of The Glue Box, that it wasn't important and she should rise above it when she was bailed up by two of the mothers, one of whom actually asked, 'Can we expect more stories to come out about your rich boyfriend and other lingerie models?'

Mortified, she somehow resisted grabbing Fleur and running. Sybella made herself speak to the art teacher and gather the information flyers amidst a gaggle of other mothers who she was sure were whispering about her. In the car Fleur showed off the picture she'd done.

'This is Jack and this is the Beanstalk, and this is Nik!'

Sybella studied the drawing, the tiny Jack, the scrawny beanstalk and Nik, taking up half the page and coloured golden as the sun, and she realised what she should have been focused on from the start. Having Nik with them, sleeping under their roof, Fleur saw Nik as an established part of her life.

Clearly a big, important golden part.

Sybella started the engine, gave Fleur a reassuring smile. 'Shall we put it on the fridge when we get home?'

'I want to give it to Nik,' Fleur said, fussing with her container of fruit pieces.

Sybella knew then this morning she'd just been embarrassed, now she had a problem.

Nik found her the next day on her hands and knees in the gatehouse with a handful of other volunteers cleaning up after the builders. There was a flutter of movement and a sudden lull in noise to alert her.

One of the women gave her a nudge and Sybella sat back on her haunches and looked around.

Nik stood in the open doorway, arms folded. King of all he surveys, Sybella thought, putting down her brush and pan and rising to her feet. Despite everything that had gone down in the last few days there was a happy girl inside her doing cartwheels because he was back.

He was back.

The problem was she kept seeing him coming out of that nightclub. How many nightclubs had he been to in the last week?

None, Sybella, because he's been on a mine site. You know that.

'*Dushka.*'

In a couple of strides he was lifting her as if she weighed nothing and then kissing her. In front of everyone.

Sybella pressed her face close to his shirt front as he lowered her until her feet touched the ground, embarrassed but also incredibly pleased.

'What are you doing here?' she asked.

'I could ask you the same thing.'

'The builders need to be supervised, Nik.'

'This is why I have hired professionals.'

'I know, but the committee want to help. We want to be involved.'

'Cleaning?'

'It's a start.'

He stroked her hair back out of her face. 'Who am I to come between you and a bit of builders' dust?'

For dinner Nik took her to a gorgeous little place in Middenwold she hadn't even known existed, a Tudor dwelling as intimate and charming as she could have wished. Sybella resisted raising the issue about the pictures and tried to enjoy her dinner and the atmosphere and Nik's company.

But something of her low mood must have shown through because they left early. He put an arm around her as he led her back to the car, but nothing would lift this feeling. All the pretending nothing was wrong meant something important had shifted between them.

Nik left her in the car while he went to check on one of the brake lights, which gave her time to check her phone. No messages, but she couldn't help almost compulsively looking at those images again.

The little screen filled with the logo of the same popular British online tabloid she'd seared her eyeballs with a few nights ago. Only this time as she looked at it something struck her she hadn't noticed before.

It looked like a lingerie ad.

Sybella was making faces at it when Nik yanked open his door and brought the night and the familiar scent of his faint cologne and him into the cabin of the SUV.

She breathed him in and it just hurt more.

'What's happened?'

'Nothing.' She held the screen of the phone to her chest, not wanting him to know how vulnerable he'd left her. She felt she had precious few defences remaining against him, she could at least keep this one.

'Sybella, you look like someone died.'

Her eyes flew to his and he cursed. 'Sorry, bad use of language. Is this about those photos?'

'I can't help it. People are sending them to me.' She

looked down. 'Do you remember when you told me you'd never been personally involved with Marla Mendez?'

'Sybella, nothing happened, she ambushed me. I told her to put her clothes back on and I wasn't interested.' He sounded tired, which perversely annoyed her more.

'I know all that, this isn't about me not believing you—but why did you lie to me?'

'This happened before we were together.'

He was right, of course. But, 'My friends, workmates, my family, the whole village are looking at this and I know what they're thinking.'

'Who cares what they think?'

'Not you, obviously.' It just slipped out and she stared at her hands in her lap.

'Sybella,' he said, at least sounding as if he cared, 'I don't like it any more than you do but it is what it is.'

'I don't even understand why you're investing in her company.' It was on the tip of her tongue to ask him to pull out, but she felt as if it was her old insecurities at work. A lot of people probably relied on this project going ahead.

She needed to woman up.

But she couldn't help adding, 'Is this what you like?'

'That's not what this is.'

Something in her kicked. 'I asked you a question,' she said softly.

Nik made one of those frustrated male sounds but he didn't answer her. He was smart enough to know when to keep his mouth shut.

She should have been smart enough to shut hers.

'I guess it's what most men like. Woman in next to nothing writhing around on your lap.' She made a wry face at the little screen before turning it off. 'But the champagne is kind of overkill. No woman I know wants to be thought tacky. Who's she trying to appeal to, women who can afford her lingerie or teenage boys?'

'I have no idea.'

'Well, you should probably get up to speed on that, seeing you're her major investor.'

Nik grunted, but she could feel him watching her as if he was gauging the right time to say something to her. Only Sybella didn't want to hear it. She was afraid to hear it. She just wanted to go home.

'I want you to forget those photos,' he said as he closed her bedroom door. 'Because I'm not a regular in the tabloid press, Sybella. I leave that to my brother.'

Sybella slipped off her shoes and lost about three inches in height. 'Well, that's one blessing, I guess.'

'Give it a week and they'll be onto something else.'

'I guess.'

She was feeling vulnerable, any woman would, but Nik didn't seem to see it that way. But why would he? He came across as the guy who either pulled the sexiest woman in the world or, in his words, turned her down. She was the girl who had to live in a small village where everyone was going to pity her.

'But how would you feel if that was me in my underwear with another man?'

He began to chuckle. 'You?'

A flash of white-hot shame went through her, immediately followed by a huge rush of anger at the unfairness of it all. Because, no, she would be humiliated to see images of herself like that, and only two men had seen her in her underwear. And he knew that. She'd trusted him in the intimacy of their relationship to let him know how special this was for her. And now he was laughing at her?

'That's an entirely improbable scenario,' he said.

'Why? Because I can't get another man?'

He frowned. 'No, because I don't date women who flash their assets for profit on the Internet.'

'Funny, the world now thinks you do.'

Nik sighed. 'If this is about issuing some kind of public statement, you know I can't do that, Sybella. I don't play that game.'

'Well, no,' she said awkwardly, because she agreed with him in principle, 'but what about me?' Her voice went small. 'I'm put in a very difficult position.'

She hated having to say it, hated more that he didn't say it first!

'It's just I have to live here, Nik, and now I'm poor Sybella who can't hold her man.'

'Do people still think that way? I suspect that's more in your head than what's actually going on.' He sounded exasperated.

'Oh.' It came out on a little puff of pain.

'I am sorry,' he said, coming over and drawing her to him, his hands resting possessively around her shoulders. As hard as his words were sometimes, when he touched her he communicated a kind of tender restraint that never failed to move her. 'But do you really care what a few locals are saying about you? If I paid attention to the number of people who cursed me out I'd be a pretty poor businessman.'

'I know, but—'

'No buts.' He began unpinning her hair. She released a shaky sigh and tried to relax and let him do this for her, because she knew her hair was her greatest claim to beauty and he did admire it, but try as she might she kept seeing Marla's dark tide of glossy designer hair swaying over her perfect, lace-framed behind moving away from the camera.

She ducked her head. 'I—I can do that. Just leave it, Nik.'

Nik let her go and she scooted over to her dressing table and sat down to put some space between them.

She didn't know how she was going to climb into that

bed with him, because she kept having flashes of those images behind her eyes and everything about her body felt lumpen and unfamiliar to her.

'Sybella, you know there's nothing in this, don't you?'

She shook her head. 'I trust you, I do, it's just you told me nothing intimate had happened between the two of you, and now the photos exist. Why didn't you just tell me then?'

'Because it was tacky. Because I didn't want you having an excuse to call time on us.'

Sybella opened her mouth to tell him she wouldn't have done that, but the truth was it was the sort of thing she might have reacted badly to. It was only now, after more than a couple of months together, falling asleep in his arms and waking up beside him in the morning, that she felt she truly knew something of him.

'Back then, Sybella, I was just the rich guy who made things happen, remember? You would have gone home and never answered my calls.'

She didn't respond because he was right.

'There won't be any more tacky stories, *dushka*. I've always been far more interested in the bottom line than dating models.'

'The bottom line being women's underwear,' she said, trying to be funny but failing. 'Is there that much money in it?'

'Not really. Frankly, I'm more interested in seeing it fail than succeed.'

'Sorry?'

She met his eyes in the mirror and discovered he was looking at her as if gauging something.

'You want it to fail?' she pressed.

He was silent.

'Nik?'

'One of the investors is Galina Voronov.'

'Oh.' The evil witch in Nik's story. The woman whose child hated her.

'When I told you she took everything, I didn't tell you I had a plan to get it back.'

Sybella suddenly felt as if she'd missed some important facet of this conversation.

'But you have your father's film archive now—you paid for it.'

'*Da*, but now she must pay.'

CHAPTER FIFTEEN

NIK HAD FOLDED his arms and, with his height and the breadth of his shoulders, for a moment Fleur's childish nonsense about a giant in their garden flared once more to life.

'Pay?' she echoed. 'How?'

Nik looked back at her. His eyes were narrowed, his mouth taut and he appeared almost wolfish in this light. 'For her sins, of which there are many.' Then he smiled, although it didn't reach his eyes, and unfolded his arms to put a reassuring hand on her shoulder. 'Don't look so worried, *dushka*, I only want the money.'

Sybella gently dislodged his hand. 'No, you don't. You've got more money than the Bank of England.'

'You know me too well.'

Only she was starting to feel she didn't.

She jerked the chair around. 'What's going on, Nik?'

'Galina has invested all her cash assets in another one of Marla's projects. It's how Marla found her way to me. I'm pulling out of Marla Mendez Lingerie and when that happens all Marla's debt is going to come crashing through like a tsunami and it will swallow up the warehouses Galina's money paid for and as Marla's silent partner she will be responsible for those specific debts too. She'll have to sell the villa on Lake Geneva and the money I gave her will be gone.'

'But what about Ms Mendez?'

'Marla will land on her feet, *dushka*, and I'm not doing anything to her that she hasn't already done to herself. I didn't build that debt.'

'She has a little boy, Nik. This is going to impact on him too.'

'As I said, I didn't build her debt.'

'No, but haven't you agreed to sponsor her—surely you entered into a contract?'

'With everything built in I need to withdraw if I feel compromised.'

Sybella's face must have shown what she was feeling because he said more gently, 'It's business, Sybella. It happens.'

'But—but what about her sister, the one you said is the creative behind the label?'

'She's a woman with real talent. I'll make sure she lands on her feet and is given a new opportunity.'

Sybella couldn't believe what she was hearing. 'Nik, you can't play God with innocent people's lives!'

He began unthreading his tie. 'Short-term pain, Sybella, for long-term satisfaction.'

'Other people's pain, your satisfaction.'

She saw the tension rise in his shoulders. 'None of this satisfies me, Sybella. The only thing that would is if Galina had never come into our lives, but I can't turn back the clock.'

'But you can turn back now. You can change this, Nik.' Sybella stumbled to her feet. 'If you do this thing it makes you as bad as her.'

'Spare me the drama, *dushka*.'

'It's not drama, it's people's lives. Marla has a son, her son has an aunty—you're going to bring all this down on them to retrieve money you don't even need.'

'And as I said, it's not about the money.'

'No, it's something worse,' said Sybella chokily. 'If you do this it changes you. Listen, Nik, that day I came to the Hall to give your grandfather back those letters I overheard the two of you talking. You were being so tender with him, and all my prejudices about you fell away. I thought you were that man, hard on the outside because you've had to be, but with a genuinely good heart and the capacity to love your family.' Her voice got stuck. 'You are that man. Don't let her take that away from you.'

'Who are you talking about?'

'Your stepmother. You're letting your hatred for her twist you into something you're not.'

'And you're being naive, Sybella.' He began yanking at his shirt buttons, and as they gave a couple popped and hit the floor but he ignored them, as if a tailored shirt was like a tissue in terms of loss, and Sybella began to feel entirely too queasy.

He must have sensed her distress because he stopped and turned around, his hands resting on his lean hips, shirt gaping, more beautiful than any Norse god and certainly as dangerous in his power and unpredictability.

She might as well have ripped the page out of a magazine and stuck it on her wall; he couldn't have looked more unreal and out of place.

He didn't belong here. He never had. She'd let the giant into the house and only now was she counting the consequences.

'I'm a businessman and I've done some ruthless things in my time to get where I am.'

Sybella could only shake her head. 'I don't feel like I even know you.'

'Yeah, well, maybe you don't,' he threw back at her, pulling off the rest of his shirt and grabbing a fresh one from his open piece of luggage he'd brought in earlier and obviously intended to live out of. Another reminder none of this was permanent.

'But I'm not wasting any more time arguing over this. You just stick to your storybook world, Sybella.' He speared an assessing look up under those thick brown lashes. 'It suits you. I like you in it. I don't want you in this world. It can be equivocal and dark and you can't handle it.'

Sybella realised he was getting dressed again and that could only mean he was leaving, and that was when she realised what had been niggling at her.

'Is that what happened with your grandfather?'

He just kept buttoning his shirt, head down, profile pure chiselled stone.

'It is, isn't it? He climbed into his own version of a storybook to find peace in his last years, to get away from your anger.'

'Don't even start this, Sybella—'

'You probably can't see it,' she said, fumbling to make sense of concepts she'd just got her first glimpse of, 'you've been living it for so long. Nik, has everything you've done been about getting back at your stepmother?'

'*Da*, I built a multibillion-pound empire to spite Galina. You found me out.'

'No, I think you built your business the same way Mr Voronov found a picture in a book and decided he wanted to live in it. To make you safe.'

Nik shook his head, as if she was being ridiculous. 'I don't fear monsters in the cupboard, Sybella.'

'No, because you've had one living in your head. Nik, can't you see? You'll never get rid of her if you don't let it go.'

'Rid of who?'

Sybella sank onto the bed. 'I blamed myself for years after my parents abandoned me. Because they were my parents, the only ones I knew. Then I met Simon and his wonderful family, and they showed me how the people who love you treat you, and that's when I was able to let my parents go.'

Nik's features softened at the mention of her parents; at least he was listening to her, although he didn't look particularly convinced.

'Your grandfather came to Edbury because he's grieving your grandmother and *you* facilitated that by buying him the Hall, and then when things started happening that you didn't authorise, that you couldn't control, you started making a loud noise and threatening people. You were scary when you came down, Nik. You made all of us uneasy.'

'I was protecting my grandfather.'

'Understood, but there was no threat. It was all you.'

'I seem to remember finding strangers outside my grandfather's home and the house open to the public.'

But Sybella refused to be sidetracked. 'Something you would have known about if you'd talked to your grandfather. Is that what I can look forward to? Are you going to put me in a house, fence me in with staff and make sure I'm snug between the covers of that storybook you think I want to live in?'

'Now you're being ridiculous.'

'Am I? What are you protecting me from? That thing your stepmother is still managing to twist you into? What you've just told me paints you as a cold, amoral man seeking vengeance.'

'*Da*, and that is what I am.'

His eyes were hard as slate. Harder than those diamonds he drilled for. Making her feel real fear for the first time. Because she couldn't be with this man. She didn't know who he was.

She tried one last time. 'You're acting as if you have absolute power over these people. If you ruin Marla Mendez's label, you'll be bringing down stress and hardship on a lot more people than Galina. All she loses is money that wasn't hers to begin with.'

Nik felt something hot shoot through the centre of his brain and in its wake he could feel all the doubts he'd had himself, and ruthlessly crushed one by one as he'd walked this path.

But it was a different thing crushing Sybella's words. He looked at her and remembered the first time he'd seen her in full light. He'd thought she was a Christmas Angel.

He didn't even celebrate Christmas last year.

Sybella lived in a different world where people observed all the family and community gatherings, embraced the tenets of 'what you do affects your neighbour' and because of that you strove to do the right thing.

He even understood, given her past, why these things mattered to her.

He couldn't convince her he was right, and a big part of him didn't want to.

He was starting to wonder why he was even here. He zipped up his holdall.

'The moment Marla's label tanks and she moves on, so do I,' he said flatly. 'I want to hear no more of this, Sybella. It's not your concern. It's business.'

She gave him a stricken look. 'Where are you going?'

'I get the impression you don't want me here tonight, and, after three weeks in a mining camp in the Urals, I've had enough of cold, hard beds.'

The next day, hollow-eyed from lack of sleep Sybella took two tour groups through the west wing of the Hall.

After lunch she went down to the gatehouse, where builders were putting in the new exit door and a ramp for the disabled to bring the tourist centre in line with fire and safety regulations. She chatted with a few of the volunteers, trying to soak up some of their excitement and then headed home in the late afternoon just as the skies opened up.

Nik's SUV was out front when she turned up her street and the initial rush of joy was subsumed by uncertainty. She found herself sitting in her little car with the early spring rain beating down on the roof, wondering if she was ever going to find the courage to go in.

It was a lousy day, in keeping with her mood.

Catherine came out onto the doorstep and waved to her. Blast.

'Darling, Nik's here,' she said as Sybella slid past her, dumping her bags and coat in the hall. 'How is it going at the Hall?'

'We're on schedule to open the visitors' centre at the end of the month.'

Sybella submitted to a hug, then Catherine stage-whispered in her ear, 'Nik's in the kitchen. Fleur's playing with building bricks upstairs with Xanthe Miller. The coast is clear.'

'For what?' Sybella blinked at her mother-in-law.

'I think he wants to ask you something.'

This was also said in an exaggerated stage whisper. Sybella often thought Catherine was wasted in the local theatre group. She needed a bigger stage.

A little part of her lit that wick of hope that nothing—not even abandonment at twelve—had managed to snuff out in Sybella: this hope was that she would find her old, familiar Nik waiting for her and last night had been nothing but a horrible dream.

Nik was sprawled on one of her chairs in the kitchen that somehow looked extra tiny with him on it. His shirt was open at the neck and although he was wearing suit trousers, which meant he had been up in London, he looked a little un-put-together, surprisingly unshaven, which was unlike him. He was thumbing his phone.

Hard at work. On what? More plans to ruin the lives of people he didn't even know.

Sybella tried to crush the condemnatory thought. She really didn't want to fight with him.

'*Dushka*, I've got something to show you.' He patted

his knee as if she were just going to sashay over there and plant her behind down.

Sybella pictured herself doing it, Nik sliding his arm around her waist and kissing her neck and both of them pretending she knew nothing bad about him and they were all going to be fine.

Instead she came closer but not close enough.

With a slightly raised brow in acknowledgement of her decision he shifted to his feet because even being a bastard he was always a gentleman.

He showed her the screen on his phone. 'What do you think?'

It was a photo display of rooms, luxurious, spacious living areas, lots of glass, and several bedrooms that Nik scrolled through at top speed, barely giving her time to see it even if she were interested.

'Why are you looking at real estate?'

'It's an apartment in Petersburg I'm looking at purchasing.'

'Oh. It's very nice.' She wanted to tell him about the visitors' centre and she waited for him to ask.

'Purchasing for us,' he clarified. 'You and me and Fleur.'

Sybella literally rocked back on her heels.

'Why?'

'I want you to move to St Petersburg with me. We'll have no more talk about business. This will be our new start.'

Sybella just stared at him.

'Nik, I can't leave Edbury village. This is Fleur's home. This is my home.'

'It's not as if you won't be coming back—both of us have family here.'

'But I have a job here now too. I mean, the visitors' centre is due to open.' She stumbled over telling him because she'd been so excited and now it had just been rendered less important by Nik's out-of-the-blue decision.

'Great,' he said.

'There's a lot to do, but you've seen the plans. I think it's going to revitalise the village.'

'I'm sure it will.'

'The Heritage Trust have put me up for a local achievement award,' she blurted out, wondering why she needed to tell him that now.

'You've put a lot of work in.'

He was saying all the right things but he was watching her as if waiting for her spiel to be over so he could get back to what mattered. To him and his plans.

'The place will be up and running soon and I'm sure there are plenty of volunteers to take over. Hell, I'll employ people.' He gave her an intense look. 'I want you and Fleur in Pitter with me.'

'Nik, we belong here. My family, my friends, Edbury Hall is here and there won't be any volunteers unless I'm around to organise them.'

Nik was shaking his head. 'It's a job, Sybella. You can be replaced.' And with those few words he broke her heart.

Because as he dismissed her ambitions and small but significant achievement with a few tossed-aside words and voiced her worst fear, she could be replaced, the enchantment fell away and Sybella saw she'd been seeing what she wanted to see, not what was there.

A ruthless, ambitious man who got what he wanted when he wanted it.

'I worked hard to make a life here after Simon's death,' she said, finding it difficult to take a proper breath. 'I want to see Edbury Hall flourish and—and I want Fleur to grow up here, and I'm not coming to St Petersburg with you.'

'Then how does this even begin to work? You've seen

how my schedule's been. It's just not practical, Sybella.'
He sounded so cold and hard and certain.

'No, probably not, and above all let's be practical.' She
couldn't keep the bitterness out of her voice.

Nik shifted on his feet. His size no longer intimidated
her, but she could see he was pressing his advantage as a
big, tough guy who always got his own way.

'Sybella,' he said with finality, 'I have thousands of people who rely on me keeping my business interests turning
over. My working life is in Europe.'

If he hadn't told her about his plans for Marla Mendez's
label, Sybella knew she wouldn't be fighting him so hard
at this point.

If she didn't have Fleur to consider she probably would
have given in. Gone with him. Hoped they could build
something together.

But she knew now what he was capable of, and she
wasn't just planning a future for herself with him, she had
her daughter to think of.

'No one is asking you to change any of that. But you
have to give something, Nik. That's what a relationship
is. Give and take.'

At last that hard shell cracked and she saw some of the
old feeling in him.

'Give? I gave Deda a house to live in when he asked for
it. I have allowed you and on your behalf that lunatic historical society to keep the west wing of the Hall open to
the public against my better judgement. I saw this damn
apartment in St Petersburg and I thought of you. Of us.
What don't I give you?'

'Well, you could start by showing some interest in
something that matters to me,' she said quietly.

He gave her a long, hard look. 'This is what matters to
you—a tourist centre at the Hall?'

'What the Hall means to the people who live here, and

future generations. It's not about me, Nik, it's about living in a community and being a part of something bigger than you.'

He laughed derisively. 'When I came down here in January, I was convinced you had an agenda, that you were advancing some little cause of your own, and here we are, a few months down the track, and it turns out I was right.'

The unfairness of it barrelled into her.

'What cause? To keep the history of my village front and centre, so Edbury has something to be proud of? At least I'm doing this for good reasons, unlike you who thinks he can play God with other people's lives!'

'I knew we'd get back to this eventually.'

'Because it really doesn't matter to you, does it?' She broke down, tears filling her eyes. 'Ruin some strangers financially, shunt Fleur and me halfway across the world from everyone we love so you're not inconvenienced.'

'This isn't about my convenience, Sybella, it's you holding on tight to that dead husband of yours,' he shocked her by saying. 'Only think about how long it's taken you to get this far. Think about how hard you had to work to get it. Take it from me, your precious Simon wasn't thinking about you when he set up practice in a town where the only outlet for your career ambitions is some old pile you don't even have much interest in.'

'How dare you? What exactly are you accusing Simon of?'

He gave her a long hard look and she found herself reliving every tender, sweet moment between them. How she'd come to believe he saw something special in her as she did in him.

'Nothing,' he said tightly, shoving his phone into his back pocket. 'Forget it, Sybella. I wish you well with your activities in the Hall. You've fought hard for it.'

With that he walked out of her life, latching the garden gate behind him.

Her environs shrank back down to normal size and everything went back to being as if he'd never been there. Only a part of Sybella understood there would be no getting over him as she had her parents, and Simon. Because she'd found her true self with Nik, the real Sybella—strong, passionate and brave—who had been there all along, only she would have to be a little braver because she was once more on her own.

CHAPTER SIXTEEN

NIK STOOD ON the perimeter of the mine that had been the foundation of his fortune.

It was so vast and for once he didn't see the wealth it represented, the mastery over nature, the supplier of thousands of jobs. He saw it as what it would be for generations, even if he closed it now. A scar on the land. A reminder of all the destruction Sybella stood in opposition to.

She wanted to restore things, to use over what already existed, to make good on the past by bringing it into the present.

All he did was butcher and destroy the things that had hurt him. Lashing out like the nine-year-old boy he had once been, who had lost everything and wanted somebody to pay.

Anybody.

His stepmother was a convenient monster to slay.

Nik kicked a clod of earth near his boot and watched it spatter a few feet in front of him.

It had been three days since he flew out of the UK.

But not a moment passed when he didn't have the oddest feeling, as if something were screwing down in his chest. He woke in the night, chilled, furious with himself.

Every email his assistant passed on about the Mendez show in Milan next week had him visualising Sybella, the look of sheer devastation in her eyes.

He shouldn't have said what he had about her husband, even if it was true.

She thought he was trying to play God, when really all he was doing was trying to mend what was broken. Although ever since he'd told her his plans that broken thing hadn't seemed all that important. What had taken primacy was trying to fix things with Sybella.

He'd come up with the apartment on the spur of the moment. The look on her face. The way she'd pulled away from him. Her refusal to consider leaving the village. It had all coalesced to push him out, and all he'd heard was, *I came here with Simon. I stay here with Simon. You're not fit to wipe his boots.*

But if he was honest she hadn't said any of that. She'd been over the moon about the visitors' centre in Sybella fashion—quietly pleased, and then a little defiant at his complete lack of response.

No wonder she'd lost it with him.

Did he want her to fit into his life instead of making the adjustments to fit into hers?

He knew what a good, healthy relationship looked like. It was the one Deda and Baba had. It was exactly what Deda had been trying to get through his thick skull when he'd arrived down here in January.

'I've found you a girl.'

When had he started thinking he didn't deserve that? What was it Sybella had said? *'You're letting the hatred twist you into something you're not.'*

But deep down he'd always believed that he was that thing. He'd been fighting with this weapon inside him that told him he wasn't a Voronov, he could do whatever it took to play the world and people like his stepmother at their own game. Only that weapon was currently at his own throat and it probably always had been.

The day he'd left Edbury his brother had rung him. He was in the chapel in the west wing at the Hall and he'd been so frustrated after his argument with Sybella he almost hadn't picked up.

'Nice shot of you and Marla Mendez. Deda is furious.'

'Deda's the least of my worries.'

Nik had looked around the high vaulted ceiling of the chapel where apparently he'd agreed tourists could pay their *kopeck* for the privilege and gawp at the stained glass and the slabs on the ground under his feet, where he'd been told sixteenth-century inhabitants of the Hall were buried.

'He emailed me a photo, you and this woman you're seeing.'

'Sybella.'

'*Da.* You were carrying this cute little kid on your shoulders.'

'Fleur. Hang on, Deda emailed you?'

'Yeah, your Sybella got him up to speed on that. Great tits, by the way.'

Hitting his brother hadn't been going to promote family unity. Besides, he'd been a continent away. 'I'll pretend you didn't say that.'

'So you love her?' Sasha had asked.

Nik hadn't even had to think about it. 'Yeah, I do. I do love her.'

There was a pause. 'Are you going to marry her?'

'She's not very happy with me at the moment.'

'Whatever you've done, man, if she loves you she'll forgive you.'

But Nik knew one thing now as he stood on the perimeter of the road that spiralled down into the dark heart of the Voroncor seam: he had to forgive someone else first.

He needed to make a call and take a flight out to Helsinki tonight.

'What's happening, love? Has business called him away again?' asked Catherine, hovering over her as Sybella dragged out her wellies and Fleur's from the cupboard under the stairs.

It had been a week since Nik had stormed out of her

house. A week of pretending, and Sybella was running out of evasions to satisfy her eagle-eyed mother-in-law.

'I don't know.'

They'd been at the May Day celebrations since dawn and Sybella had brought Fleur home for a nap because it was a long day with fireworks tonight.

Fleur appeared at the top of the stairs.

'Ready to go, darling?'

'You're going for a walk?' Catherine demanded peevishly. 'What if Nik calls? Make sure you take your phone.'

'He's not going to call, Catherine.'

'I'll stay here in case he calls.'

Sybella handed Fleur her boots and then took her mother-in-law's face between her hands. 'Go home, Catherine. I love you to bits but please stop interfering in my love life.'

'I have to,' grumbled Catherine. 'Meg won't let me near hers.'

'I want Gran to come,' said Fleur grumpily, picking up on the adults' mood.

Sybella sagged but Catherine must have seen something in her face and, instead of arguing, she helped Fleur with her boots.

'I will see you tonight, pumpkin, at the fireworks.'

Sybella started feeling awful about her behaviour before she even herded Fleur out of the house. By the time she and Fleur were trudging across the field to the high wold she felt wretched. Catherine was the closest person she had to a mother and the older woman's anxiety over Nik's sudden departure a week earlier and determination to bring them together was only motivated by a desire to see her happy.

'Look, Mummy, pretty!' Fleur had a handful of yellow flowers she'd pulled out of the ground.

'That's called oxlip,' Sybella instructed with a smile, and leant down so Fleur could tuck a piece behind her ear.

As she straightened up she noticed properly for the first time that winter had completely melted away and the countryside was fragrant with wildflowers showing themselves among the new grass.

The village below them gleamed with the local mellow gold stonework that was peculiar to the region and the May sunshine hit the church spire.

From here she could see all the windy yellow roads with their stone walls cutting through the countryside below them and the odd car wending its way.

It wasn't a bad place to be miserable. And maybe Mrs Muir was right: there were all kinds of ways to be happy, and she would have to find a way by herself.

He wasn't coming back. And one day it wouldn't hurt this much.

Then she noticed a dark head bobbing up over the next rise directly before the valley dropped down into the village.

It was Meg.

She was running—well, hobbling, really—and as she closed the space between them Sybella saw why. She was wearing stockings and high heels, which looked odd enough as she picked and wove her way around cow pats and muddy spots. She was also carting something under her arm.

'What are you doing with a laptop up here?'

Meg was panting. Apparently cross-fit classes in a gym did nothing for your ability to run an obstacle course up a Cotswold hill.

She handed the laptop over and Sybella obligingly took it as her sister-in-law bent with her hands on her knees and huffed and puffed to get her breath back.

'You. Will. Thank. Me.' She sucked in a few more breaths and then made a gesture at the laptop. 'Fire it up. I've got something to show you.'

'You know the Internet connection is bad enough in the village. I don't know if we'll get it up here.'

'I broke speed laws to get here. Just open the blinking laptop!'

Sybella settled herself down in the grass and did as she was bid.

Meg had taken off her fancy shoes and was gingerly examining the soles, now sadly scuffed and damp.

'They're on the desktop,' Meg said.

Sybella clicked and the screen filled with two faces, one of them so familiar her throat closed over.

Nik and Marla.

'Why are you showing me these?'

'That was taken at last night's opening of Mendez's fashion label in Milan.'

'It went ahead?'

'That's not the question I expected. Why wouldn't it?'

Sybella noted the space between Nik and Marla was filled by a young boy with a shock of dark hair and soulful brown eyes, perhaps around eight or nine. It must be her son.

She could feel her sister-in-law watching her face with barely constrained glee, and then she forgot all about Meg and her entire attention was welded to Nik, and although she couldn't understand the Italian voice-over, she got a lot out of just watching the camera glide over him as he sat up front with Marla, her son, and all the other VIPs while bored-looking coat hangers strutted down the runway. Only…not all those girls were coat hangers. Several distinctly rounded, curvy girls swept the stage in just enough lace and satin to keep them decent. They looked *amazing*.

Marla Mendez's perfect face filled the frame and she said in English, 'I wanted the girls to fill out my sexier designs. I remember the day I had this exciting idea. I met up with Nik Voronov's fiancée, Sybella Parminter, and I,

Marla, looked at her and saw all the shape I wanted for my line. She is gorgeous. She is an oil painting. She has the boobs and the hips and the thighs. The definition of womanhood.'

Fiancée? Sybella felt Meg nudge her.

'So I have the nymphs, the dryads and the Venuses to embrace all body shapes. We women are many things and I want my line to reflect that.'

'How about off-the-rack pricing?' commented Meg.

Then Nik was answering questions.

He was definitely out of his comfort zone with women's lingerie, but then, given his brother was apparently the main driver of the market, he thought he might as well invest.

This brought laughter and more questions.

Then with a faint smile he said, 'No, I have no interest in living in Milan. I am taking up residency in the UK to be with the woman I love. If she'll have me.'

Sybella was vaguely aware Meg's phone was ringing but she couldn't take her eyes off the screen.

'It's Mum,' said Meg. 'She wants to talk to you.'

Sybella continued to gaze at the screen.

There was a volley of high-pitched squawking from the phone. Meg jumped. 'He's rung! Nik rang your phone. Mum says you have to ring him. She says it's no time to play coy. He's shown his hand.'

'I'm not ringing him.'

'She's not ringing him, Mum. Why *aren't* you ringing him? That's from both of us, by the way.'

Sybella had put down the lid of the laptop and was looking up into the sky. There it was, the definite thwack, thwack, thwack. 'Because he's already here.'

Nik saw the forest first and then the church steeple and finally the village spread out on the cleft of the wold.

His attention wasn't on Edbury Hall itself, but the grounds where tents and bunting had been erected. One of the lawns was covered in cars. Several weeks ago it would have been unimaginable. He'd have closed the lot down.

As the chopper flew over the village he could see the maypole on the green, no longer the solitary needle without a thread he'd seen it as when he'd driven into Edbury for the first time, but festooned with ribbons and encircled by dozens of little girls in white dresses, running happily, and not so happily as one or two took tumbles, and their parents and families and neighbours and school friends cheered them on.

He saw St Mary's Church with its glinting spire and the graveyard running up behind it with the tumble of stone markers, large and small. He saw the mass of forest where he and Sybella had first walked together and he'd fallen so completely under her spell it was astonishing he'd been able to walk without stumbling over his feet.

Then he saw her, out on the hill just as Catherine had told him when he'd rung Sybella's phone. Two small figures, but even at this distance he knew which one was Sybella.

'Take it over to the west,' he told his pilot, Max, and as the chopper came in closer the woman next to her began to jump up and down, waving her arms.

Nik was unstrapped and climbing out, the blades still rotating when he saw her coming towards him.

He didn't know where her friend had gone; he didn't care.

As he strode towards her he could see all the anxiety on her face and it tore strips from his chest.

'You didn't do it,' she said.

He came as close as he dared without touching her.

She was wearing a pretty floral dress and her hair was plaited but there were flowers threaded through it, probably for May Day, and she looked like a pagan goddess of spring in her wellington boots.

'I didn't do it.' He shoved his hands into the pockets of his jacket because it was hard to be this close to her and not touch her.

'Why not?' she asked softly, those hazel eyes as anxious as the first time he'd seen her, when he'd mistaken her for an intruder and been trying to scare her.

'I worked it all out. I kept thinking about what you said, about it twisting me, about how I use money and privilege as a weapon…'

She lowered her head but she didn't argue with him.

'You were right, I've known it for a long time, and I kept justifying it because I was angry.'

'She did a terrible thing, Nik.'

'She did, but that's old anger. Frankly, Sybella, I think I stopped expending all that energy on her when I bought back the archive. I did that for my father, by the way. It was my duty by him and then it was done.'

She shook her head. 'Then who were you angry with?'

'Deda, for taking me in when he didn't have to, and Sasha for holding it against me. But it was all me—neither of them felt that way.' His grey eyes searched her face for understanding. 'And that's when I knew I'd decided to be angry with you.'

'With me?'

'I didn't think you loved me.'

The words sounded like paupers, emptying their sacks to show the rich people how little they had. Nik, who had seemed to have everything—money, power, all the confidence in the world—was opening up his heart to her.

She realised right then and there he saw her as the rich one. The one with the love to give and bestow. Just as she had once seen Simon. But she didn't want to be that person with Nik. Because it was absolutely clear to her now that he loved her, had been trying to tell her for a long time how much he loved her, and she had been deaf.

'Do you remember what you said about being angry with Simon, for the accident, something that couldn't possibly be his fault?' He spoke slowly, as if he might stumble over the difficult words.

'Yes.'

'I know you loved him, Sybella, from the bottom of your heart, because that's who you are. What I worked out since I drove away from your house was why you were angry with me.'

'Because I love you, you silly billy,' she said, as if this were obvious.

He smiled then. That slow breaking dawn of a smile, and that he used it so rarely made her think it was only for her. And she knew now that it was.

'Where have you been?'

'I went to Helsinki and met my biological father.'

Of all the things he'd say she hadn't expected that.

'He's a geologist,' Nik added.

'Of course he is.' Sybella was smiling so broadly her face hurt as she stepped right up to him.

Nik fisted his hands because the urge to touch her was almost impossibly strong but he needed to tell her the whole story first. 'He shook my hand, Sybella, and he didn't ask his billionaire son for a kopeck. That's the kind of man he is.'

'He is your dad, then,' she said softly, 'because if the positions were reversed wouldn't you do the same?' She reached up to smooth back his hair in a gesture he'd seen her use with Fleur. It stopped the breath in his body. 'He must be so proud of you, all you've accomplished.'

'I don't know about that. He was interested in you. Do you mind that I talked about you?'

'It depends what you said.'

'I asked for his advice. I told him I was in love with

this beautiful, brilliant Englishwoman and she had a sweet little girl and she was surrounded by all these people who love her, and I'd stuffed up.'

'You're in love with me?'

Nik swallowed down hard. He wanted more than anything to take her in his arms, especially when she sounded so uncertain, but he had to get through this first. He had to give her that certainty they'd once held between them back.

'He told me thirty-five years ago he'd been in love with my mother but he could see that she loved my father more, and he let her go. He told me if he'd known about me it would have been different, he would have made a different choice. And I thought about that, Sybella. I thought about all the variables in our lives. What if your Simon was still here? What if Deda hadn't found that picture in *Country Life*? And I realised the only element in all of this that I could control was me. I had choices. If I went ahead and punished Galina I would lose you. Because you can't love the man who would do something like that, because of the woman you are, and that's the woman I love. That's the man I want to be for you.'

Sybella wasn't sure how it happened, but she was in his arms and it felt like coming home. Her whole life with its good and its bad had been leading up to this moment.

More than anything she knew now this was what the fates had had in store for her.

All the bad things that could happen to a person had rained down on her and then Fleur was born and her life had taken on new meaning, until this moment when it all made perfect sense.

Embodied in this one, extraordinary man. Who was hers.

'Oh, Nik, I've been so lonely without you,' she confessed in a fractured voice as the tears came. 'I don't care where we live. As long as we're with you it doesn't matter.'

'*Net*, it does matter.' His big hands smoothed over her back possessively. 'I want you and Fleur to be with me and I'll do whatever it takes to make that happen.'

She began to cry in earnest and he held her tighter. For once she was happy to give way to his natural dominance.

'I was so proud of you for going ahead with the show, for not withdrawing the funding.'

He framed her face, wiping away her tears with his thumbs. 'On that front I thought I'd have a lot of explaining to do.'

'No, Meg did that.' She sniffed happily, gulping on all the heady emotion surging through her. 'She explained everything, bless her.' Sybella pressed her temple to his bent one. 'I'm just so happy you're here.'

He dropped down on both knees in front of her and she heard Meg give a very un-Meg-like gasp of excitement some distance away.

'Sybella Frances Parminter, will you marry me?'

Sybella's face lit up with a smile she felt from her toes to her fingertips. 'Yes, of course I will.'

Then she fell to her knees in front of him and wrapped her arms around his neck and kissed him.

'That's my yes,' she said against his mouth, 'in case it wasn't clear.'

Then she kissed him again, and Nik wrapped her up in his arms and breathed freely for the first time since he'd driven out of Edbury.

He had her; he was home.

The four of them made their way down the hill towards the carnival atmosphere of the village.

Fleur on Nik's broad shoulders, Sybella holding his hand, Meg picking her way through the field in her heels.

Sybella's heart was overflowing with all of her blessings.

Later in the afternoon when family had been told, impromptu champagne had been drunk, her father-in-law Marcus had taken a walk with Nik from which they'd returned somewhat late, having ended at the pub, only then did Nik propose they go up to the Hall.

It was nearing the four o'clock raffle of celebratory hampers and Nik borrowed a megaphone from the guy who was going to call the prize. He walked out onto the lawn and people started to naturally gravitate towards him.

Sybella took Fleur's hand and his arm came around her.

'For those of you who don't know me, I'm Nikolai Aleksandrovich Voronov. I'm caretaker of this house.'

Sybella beamed at her daughter.

'Edbury Hall is forthwith reopened to the public—not just the west wing, but the entire estate.'

His voice carried over the assembled heads of the small crowd and a small cheer went up, interspersed with plenty of 'it's about time'.

'I'll be taking up residence in Edbury but let me put your minds at rest. I will not be turning the Hall into a compound and setting dogs on trespassers.'

Some of the children laughed but Sybella noted the arrested look on Fleur's face at the mention of a dog. She'd have to head that one off when things were a little more normal and she wasn't feeling so loved up. She looked up at her Norse god and didn't think that would be any time soon.

'And just so it's clear,' Nik said, grinning down at her, 'Sybella and I are getting married.'

At the end of the summer the bells of St Mary's pealed as the happy couple emerged into the glorious sunshine.

Sybella, in an off-the-shoulder gauze and white satin gown, her bridal veil set back on her head, and Nik, in a grey morning suit, came first, and then Fleur and her friend Xanthe swinging their baskets of rose petals, the families and friends of both bride and groom spilling out of the church behind them.

The bride had invited Marla Mendez to the wedding, as long as she brought her young son.

Twelve months along almost to the day Leonid Nikolaievich Voronov came into the world in the beautiful local stone house on the wold Nik had moved them into after the wedding.

Leo was christened in the Russian Orthodox Church in London in the presence of his Russian great-grandfather and his English grandparents, but not his parents as custom dictated. He was again christened in the village of Edbury at St Mary's and was carried in the arms of his proud older sister.

There was high tea at the Hall and the whole village attended.

Old Mr Voronov toasted his great-grandson and announced the Hall was being gifted to the National Trust and he was going to live in the new house on the wold with his grandson and his wife. The house was big enough to fit them all and small enough no one would be lonely.

Afterwards Sybella, holding her new baby to her breast, sat on the terrace in the summer sun, watching Fleur tumbling on the lawn with her friends and the absolutely ridiculously large sheepdog Nik had insisted on buying her when they'd first got married. A year down the track it was growing as big as a pony.

'What are you thinking, *moya lyuba*?' Nik's dark voice ran through her senses like dark chocolate and honey, all the things she'd craved while she was pregnant. He hunkered down beside them, stroking the fine pale quiff of hair that was all Leo currently had on his small head.

'How fortunate we are. How fortunate I am.'

'It was fate,' said Nik, a true Russian.

And Sybella was disposed to believe him.

'Although one thing still haunts me,' he mused.

She angled a curious look at him.

'What if Sasha had been the brother who came down that weekend?'

'I can't say I haven't given it some thought,' she said lightly, rubbing a finger consideringly over his lower lip.

'What did you come up with?' he growled, snapping playfully at her finger.

'Sasha's so friendly, he never would have thrown me down in the snow and shaken me like a rattle and sent me on my way.'

'Did I do all those things?' Nik's eyes kindled with hers. 'Shameful. You can never tell our son.'

'I will. I will tell him, when he's old enough to find the right girl, just so he'll know what to do.'

'He's a Voronov. He doesn't need advice about finding the right girl. It's in our blood. He'll know when the time comes.'

So spoke her alpha male. Sybella smiled indulgently.

'When did you know?' she asked.

'I believe it happened when I took off your ski mask, Rapunzel, and I looked into your eyes, but I definitely knew when I kissed you.'

'Like this?' She stroked his jaw with the backs of her fingers and Nik lost his train of thought, moving his mouth over hers once more, careful not to dislodge their small son, who was fiercely guarding his nourishment.

'Exactly like that, *moya lyubov*.'

She looked into Nik's grey eyes and wondered at the idea she'd ever found them chilly. She cocked her head to one side.

'Did I ever tell you? When we first met I thought you were a bear…'

* * * * *

MILLS & BOON

Coming soon

BOUND TO THE SICILIAN'S BED
Sharon Kendrick

Rocco was going to kiss her and after everything she'd just said, Nicole knew she needed to stop him. But suddenly she found herself governed by a much deeper need than preserving her sanity, or her pride. A need and a hunger which swept over her with the speed of a bush fire. As Rocco's shadowed face lowered towards her she found past and present fusing, so that for a disconcerting moment she forgot everything except the urgent hunger in her body. Because hadn't her Sicilian husband always been able to do this—to captivate her with the lightest touch and to tantalise her with that smouldering look of promise? And hadn't there been many nights since they'd separated when she'd woken up, still half fuddled with sleep, and found herself yearning for the taste of his lips on hers just one more time? And now she had it.

One more time.

She opened her mouth—though afterwards she would try to convince herself she'd been intending to resist him— but Rocco used the opportunity to fasten his mouth over hers in the most perfects of fits. And Nicole felt instantly helpless—caught up in the powerful snare of a sexual mastery which wiped out everything else. She gave a gasp of pleasure because it had been so long since she had done this.

Since they'd been apart Nicole had felt like a living statue—as if she were made from marble—as if the flesh and blood part of her were some kind of half-forgotten dream. Slowly but surely she had withdrawn from the sensual side of her nature, until she'd convinced herself she was dead and unfeeling inside. But here came Rocco to wake her dormant sexuality with nothing more than a single kiss. It was like some stupid fairy story. It was scary and powerful. She didn't *want* to want him, and yet . . .

She wanted him.

Her lips opened wider as his tongue slid inside her mouth—eagerly granting him that intimacy as if preparing the way for another. She began to shiver as his hands started to explore her—rediscovering her body with an impatient hunger, as if it were the first time he'd ever touched her.

'Nicole,' he said unevenly and she'd never heard him say her name like that before.

Her arms were locked behind his neck as again he circled his hips in unmistakable invitation and, somewhere in the back of her mind, Nicole could hear the small voice of reason imploring her to take control of the situation. It was urging her to pull back from him and call a halt to what they were doing. But once again she ignored it. Against the powerful tide of passion, that little voice was drowned out and she allowed pleasure to shimmer over her skin.

Continue reading
BOUND TO THE SICILIAN'S BED
Sharon Kendrick

Available next month
www.millsandboon.co.uk

LET'S TALK
Romance

For exclusive extracts, competitions
and special offers, find us online:

- 📘 facebook.com/millsandboon
- 📷 @millsandboonuk
- 🐦 @millsandboon

Or get in touch on 0844 844 1351*

For all the latest titles coming soon, visit
millsandboon.co.uk/nextmonth